Seducing
Adam

Seducing Adam

TARA MANNING

POOLBEG

Published 2001
Poolbeg Press Ltd.
123 Baldoyle Industrial Estate
Dublin 13, Ireland
Email: poolbeg@poolbeg.com
www.poolbeg.com

13 5 7 9 10 8 6 4 2

A catalogue record for this book is available from the British Library.

ISBN 1 84223 047 6

Typeset by Patricia Hope in Palatino 10/13.5
Printed and bound by
Omnia Books Ltd, Glasgow

Acknowledgements

Well, writing this book has been a long and winding road but now that I've finally reached journey's end there are a number of people whom I would like to thank for their patience, encouragement and faith in me. My parents, Col. Gerard Manning and my mother Emily, naturally enough head the list. So here's to you, Mam and Dad, for all your love, care and continuing support over the years and to you, Mam, for passing on both your ability to spin a good yarn and for your off-the-wall sense of humour which undoubtedly engendered my love affair with words and writing! Thanks also to my brothers and sisters, Gerard, Niall, Mark, Angela and Sharon, all of whom, in one way or another, influenced me *en route*, more especially Angela for her good sense and marathon phone-calls and Mark who is himself a creative soul and who knows only too well the force that drives me. Special thanks to my best friend Susan Cummins, a friend indeed through thick and thin, loyal, funny, patient, confidante and keeper of secrets never to be told. I love you Mrs! Thanks also to May Walsh, Mayo woman, friend and rock of good sense for putting up with me droning on and on day after day on our lunchtime walks by the Thames. Thanks, May for your faith, encouragement and optimism. The drinks are on me! Thanks also to Marga Cory for remaining a true friend despite my recent neglect of her as, tunnel-visioned, I slaved over a hot word processor. Danke, Marga!

Grateful thanks are also due to all at Poolbeg. In particular I would like to thank my editor, Gaye Shortland, for her ability to pinpoint exactly where I've gone OTT and drag me back down to earth, and for the words of encouragement especially in the early days when the spirit was willing but the inspiration occasionally went AWOL.

Last but definitely not least, I would like to thank my two beautiful sons, Tarek and Emmet, for having complete and utter faith in their mother's abilities. Bless you both, my darlings, and may the scales never fall from your eyes.

Seducing Adam is dedicated to Tarek and Emmet,
my very own reasons to be cheerful!

Chapter One

"Don't get mad. Get even!" Thoughtfully Jenny picked up the remote control and switched off the TV, the words of some other cheated-upon woman ringing in her ears. Don't get mad. Get even! Hardly a new concept but one not without merit. An oldie, but goody! But *how* to get even? Rush upstairs and decimate his shirtsleeves perhaps? Like that Cockney woman who had appeared on *Kilroy* recently.

"'E said it was only 'armless fun," she'd screeched, tipping what appeared to be a pile of rags all over the studio floor. "Now 'is shirts are armless too!"

The audience had erupted and Jenny, poor fool, secure at least back then in the knowledge that Adam would never cheat on her, had joined in with gusto.

"Good on you, girl!" she'd roared at the television, clapping like a seal and stomping both feet into the living-room carpet. "Serves him right!"

Not to be outdone, another woman had then taken

the floor. She, it transpired, had sewn a wet and very smelly kipper into the lining of her ex-boyfriend's curtains. Eventually as the smell got worse and worse and unable to trace the source, he and his paramour had been forced to move house. The real sting in the tale came from the fact that they had taken the curtains with them. Oh, the audience had relished that one too and had settled back in their seats in happy expectation of more dirt-dishing. Nor were they disappointed. The kipper's successor thoroughly cleaned the toilet with her husband's toothbrush, chuckling in silent glee as she watched him brush his teeth that night. Another had sprinkled her boyfriend's carpet with cress seeds, lovingly watering them every day so that when eventually he returned from holiday, there was enough cress on his living-room floor to fill all the egg-and-cress sandwiches in England.

When it came to revenge therefore, Jenny had quite a large armoury of ideas at her disposal. The problem was, though, that five minutes later standing in front of Adam's wardrobe, scissors at the ready, she found she did not want revenge. What she wanted, quite simply, was to have her husband back.

"I don't want revenge," she bawled to her friend later that evening, automatically holding out her wine glass for a top-up. "I just want Adam back." Mounty (Diana Mountford really, but Mounty to all her friends on account of always getting her man) shrugged.

"So what's the problem?"

"What's the problem? What's the problem?" Jenny, a

bit put out by what she perceived to a be somewhat cavalier attitude on the part of the other woman, raised her voice. "My husband is seeing another woman, twenty years younger I shouldn't wonder and with gravity-defying boobs straight out of Cape Canaveral. That's what the problem is, dammit!" Ruefully she glanced down at her own enormous mammaries, uncomfortably aware that there were smaller shelves in Do It All's. Impossible to believe now that, at one time, *she* too had been an *aficionado* of the 'pencil test'. Oh, yes! Many's the time she'd stood, parallel pencil to hand, ready to put *Cosmo's* theory of gravity through its paces. If, when placed beneath the boob, the pencil fell straight to the floor without any attempt by the said boob to grab it, you could, according to the magazine, sleep sound in the knowledge that your chest, unlike the swallows, had not yet started to migrate south. If, on the other hand, your boobs reached out and latched on so that you had play 'hunt the pencil' through folds of skin, then it was time to dispense with the solicitor, banker or whatever and start dating a plastic surgeon.

Alas, the times they were a-changing and, nowadays, like an elephant in Sri Lanka Jenny could carry not only whole logs beneath her breasts, but whole forests if necessary. Lately, even the simple act of buying a bra had become a minefield. Only yesterday, she had stood in the lingerie section of Marks & Sparks, bewildered by the wide choice available. Correction! Available to everyone else! Cross Your Hearts, lift 'em ups and push 'em outs, Wonderbras, tiny triangular bras, presumably for ladies with perfectly, proportioned, geometrical breasts. Here a scrap of lace! There a scrap of satin! And once, a peculiar article, a miracle of engineering, two half-moons reinforced with dainty underwiring. A balconette! Hopefully Jenny had looked around for the veranda-reinforced-with-a-forklift-truck version but presumably even miracles of engineering had their limits. Eventually though, spurred on by sheer doggedness and the fact that the bra she was currently wearing had somehow managed to work its way up around her neck and was trying to throttle the life out of her, she *had* hit pay dirt. A cross between a straitjacket and the Millennium Dome, it was large and white, very large and very white, and she clutched at it as a drowning man will clutch at straws. As Sod's law would have it though, another drowning woman had clutched at the same straw at the same time and, consequently, after an awful ripping, screeching noise, the kind of noise you imagine the *Titanic* must have made when she hit the iceberg, both had been left in possession of a solitary, white cup. A very large, very white, very solitary, cotton cup! To add insult to injury, as she'd slunk from the store, Jenny had seen two of the sales assistants clowning about with the cups pulled down around their heads like babies' bonnets. Which is why she was now sitting in Mounty's front room, bra-less beneath her sweatshirt and, with what appeared to be Ally McBeal's baby ensconced on each knee.

"Well, you *have* rather let yourself go recently," Mounty pointed out, reflecting something of Jenny's own thoughts but causing the bristles to rise on her neck none the less. It was one thing to criticise yourself, quite another for your supposed best friend to get in on the act. "No, hear me out." She held up a restraining hand before Jenny could muster a counter-attack. "I'm not siding with Adam. Heaven forbid! You know how I feel about him." Her nose wrinkled with distaste and Jenny, despite herself, grinned. Adam and Mounty had never got on. It had been a case of insults at first sight. She had called him a 'self-important, toffee-nosed git suffering from delusions of competence' whilst, as far as he was concerned, she was 'an East End slapper with tripe for brains'. Things had rapidly developed into a 'never the twain shall meet' situation and Jenny, who loved them both, had quickly learned the art of compartmentalisation. "What I'm trying to say," Mounty expounded, "is that men, and I use the term loosely here, are visual creatures. Women, as we know, being superior beings like to check out the ingredients in a packet. God knows how many hours of our lives we spend blocking up supermarket aisles squinting sideways and every which way at calorific values, fat grams, additives and so on and so forth." She waved an expressive hand, the cigarette between her fingers smokily illustrating her point. "Men, on the other hand, providing they like the colour, shape and size of a packet, simply place it in their basket and hotfoot it to the checkout." She took a long, appreciative sip of her wine. "And let's face it, my dear. Your packet is looking a wee bit past its sell-by-date these days."

"Well, kids and marriage tend to do that to you," Jenny snapped, immediately on the defensive, and playing the you've-never-been-married-nor-ever-had-any-kids-so-don't-know-how-wearing-it-is card, but Mounty wasn't biting.

"Ah, yes. Let's see!" Meditatively she tapped her chin, fingernails not too long, perfectly manicured, in keeping with the well-groomed, never-a-hair-out-of-place (and how the bloody hell did she do it?) rest of her. "David is how old now? Twelve? And Adam, to give him his due, provides for you so well that, unlike most of us poor mortals, you don't have to go outside your door to earn a crust. Added to all this, Mrs Mopalot or whatever her name is comes in every day to do the cleaning and cooking." She took another deep drink of her wine, sloshing it round and round inside her mouth letting the words sink in, then leaning slightly forward in her seat engaged Jenny in full-on eye-to-eye contact. "Tell me, Jenny, *what* exactly is it you do all day that you find so wearing?"

Jenny flushed, easy tears springing to her eyes. Cross words with Mounty was a new experience, one she didn't like, one that made her feel vulnerable like a kid in a playground whose best friend has dumped her for somebody else. Somebody with a better skipping-rope, somebody who doesn't have processed cheese sandwiches every day, somebody who'd give her their last Rollo.

6

"I thought you were supposed to be my friend." She almost cringed at the 'little girl lost' sound of her voice, especially when the other woman rose, came over and shook her gently by the shoulders.

"Jenny, Jenny, Jenny." Her voice was an appeal. "I *am* your friend: friend enough to tell you that you've lost the plot lately and now, because of that, you're losing your husband. But you *can* do something about it, you know. It's never too late! Just get up off your backside and get your act together!"

Pushing her away, Jenny jumped to her feet. "No," she said, shaking her head in furious denial. "You're no friend of mine, Diana Mountford! Friends don't kick you when you're down. Friends encourage and support. *Real* friends, that is!"

"And *real* friends tell the truth, even when it hurts." Mounty, her voice steady, firm in her conviction, followed her to the door. "Go on! Run home, Jenny. Turn on *Kilroy* or *Oprah* or *Jerry Springer*. Lose yourself in whatever chat show happens to be on. Keep living your life at second-hand. Do whatever it takes to avoid reality, only don't be surprised that your husband *prefers* reality, the reality of a woman who doesn't spend all day in front of the box gorging on crisps and chocolate." She raised her voice a little as Jenny lumbered clumsily off towards the sanctuary of her car, the flash BMW Adam had bought her on her last birthday. "And while we're on the subject, Jenny, have you ever stopped to wonder why David never takes *his* friends home lately. Could it be he's ashamed of his mother, do you think? Ashamed of what his mother has become?"

"Screw you!" Jenny fumbled with the ignition, tears streaming down her face. "Hell will freeze over before ever I'll ask for *your* help again. I must have been *mad* to think you cared. I should have my bloody head examined!" Stepping on the accelerator she screeched off down the drive, doubly bereft now that not only, according to Diana, had she lost the plot, but she had lost Diana as well. Diana, her best friend since forever! Since she *was* that little girl whose mate had deserted her in the playground, and Diana had come to her rescue. And guess what! She'd had cheese sandwiches every day too! Neither had ever been lucky enough to have had a packet of Rollos but, if they'd had, she was sure they would have given each other the last one! Jenny sniffed loudly. At least she *had* been sure until tonight! And troubles, unlike brassière cups, never coming singly, it looked as though she was about to lose Adam too. Adam, the only man she had ever loved; the only man she could ever imagine loving!

As Jenny's car disappeared into the distance, Mounty, closing the front door, turned to the man who'd materialised in the hallway behind her.

"You don't think you were too hard on her?" he asked, a guilty frown playing between his eyes.

"No, Adam!" Her voice was icy. "I do not!"

* * *

Jenny closed the front door behind her, sliding down its length, miserably letting herself fall on the floor, the tears undammed still flowing down her face. The house was dark, silent as the grave. David was sleeping over at a friend's house, ostensibly because Simon had a *wicked* new computer game but now, in the light of Mounty's words, Jenny wondered if it wasn't because he wanted to get away from her. Because he was ashamed of her!

Adam presumably was out wining and dining his lover. Where? Surely not in Spend a Penne, the little Italian bistro in the precinct. The thought horrified her. That was *their* place, hers and Adam's, where they had always celebrated high days and holidays and where Gianni, to all intents and purposes a jolly, fat, Italian waiter – only Jenny knew for a fact he hailed from Deptford – exuded *bonhomie* and garlic in equal proportions. Was he, even now, bonhommying Adam's new love while she, Jenny, sat bawling her eyes out, back to back with the front door and with the letter-basket digging cruelly into her head. Childishly wiping her nose on her sleeve, she masochistically drummed up imaginary visions of the other woman in Adam's life. *She*, of course, would be called something exotic, like Sabrina or Farrah and it wouldn't take a mathematical genius to work out that her mother had called her after one of *Charlie's Angels*, and since that show had aired in the late 70s, early 80s, you'd automatically know that she was only a twenty-something nymphet, with the smell of Johnson's baby powder only just masked by her Eau So Expensive! As it happened, Jenny had been a fan of *Charlie's Angels* herself, and many's the pre-disco night had found her torturing her hair with a blowdrier, desperately trying to achieve that flicked-back, blonde-maned Farrah Fawcett look. Farrah Forcing it, as it were! Occasionally she even fancied she'd been quite successful till some smart alec would ask if she was going up for Crufts, or loudly demand to know who let the afghan hound loose!

Farrah or Sabrina, Farina for short, assuming she was not a Kim Basinger type, would, of course, have a head full of glossy pre-Raphaelite curls *à la* Sarah Brightman, or, *à la* Zoë Ball, one of those short 'n' sassy geometrical cuts that would emphasise her naturally high cheekbones.

On and on Jenny worried, miserably gnawing at the hangnail of imagination, hurting herself like hell, but quite unable to stop.

Compared with the nymphet Farina, what must Adam see when he saw her? The Phantom of the Opera, that's what, and on a bad-mask-day too! A plump – okay, while she was flaying the skin from her back and rubbing salt in the wounds – a morbidly-obese-on-the-Richter-Scale individual, tilting towards forty and with hurricanes forecast. Small wonder then if he preferred the company of the fragrant Farina to that of his dull, old wife who was even now trying to decapitate herself on the post basket and wiping snot on her sweatshirt sleeve.

She could just imagine them in Spend A Penne, hands intimately linked, across the little corner table, *their* table, hers and Adam's, with the red and white gingham tablecloth, and the green Chianti bottle, a monument to the drippings of a hundred wax candles. *She,* of course, the new love, being fluent in three types of linguini would need no guidance with the menu. And much to poor old Gianni's mortification, she would also be discovered to be fluent in Italian and, with a superior, tinkling little laugh, would embarrass the poor old sod to death, when she discovered his own fluency stopped short at *pronto* and *putana!*

A food connoisseur, naturally, she would put Egon Ronay in the halfpenny place when it came to nouvelle cuisine and being the proud possessor of a 'nose', she would effortlessly be able to tell her Chablis from her Châteauneuf du Pape, from fifty paces and through a heavy cold. Adam, naturally enough, would marvel that he had ever seen anything in the unsophisticated, bazooka-bosomed Jenny, whose idea of culinary adventure was to choose the liver pâté over the prawn cocktail.

Dimly, against a background of sobs, Jenny registered the bells of nearby St Nicholas', tolling the hour. Ten o'clock and on Sky the *Jerry Springer Show, Uncut* was about to start. Under normal circumstances, Jenny would be ensconced in front of the telly by now, a big mug of coffee by her side, a bowl of crisps or popcorn within easy reach. Take one. Take two. Action!

11

And then she'd be away, instantly transported, courtesy of modern technology, into the lives of the participants, no matter how far removed those lives were from her own. Hillbillies, evangelists, Klan members. Non-partisan, Jenny immersed herself in them all.

"Ah'm a-sleepin with mah furrst kuhsin so y'all kin mahnd yer own darned business." The moral majority in the audience booing and hissing and Jenny, right alongside, holding up her palm as if to ward the TV off, joining in with the chat-show speak learned on *Springer* and other American chat shows of its ilk.

"Don't even go there!" she'd warn. "Don't even go there."

Thanks to the same shows, she was a walking oracle when it came to incest, weird religious cults, anorexia and its cousin bulimia. Ask her anything about spousal abuse, teenage goths, infidelity, the Ku Klux Klan, strippers who 'danced' whilst pregnant, obesity, and the inadvisability of taking Prozac on a schizophrenic stomach, and she could tell you. But Mounty was right! It was all knowledge gained second-hand because somewhere along the line she had relinquished reality in favour of a safe quick-fix of someone else's more 'adventurous' life. Someone she would never know, much less care about except, perhaps, for the brief period of time they occupied her TV set, and the majority of whom, let's face it, she would never in a million years *want* to know. And all the time the two she should have cared about, Adam and David, had been quietly living their own lives, helplessly watching her, wife and mother, turn into a slob who disappeared further and further into La La Land, unconcernedly leaving them to fend for themselves.

Sitting on a cold, stone floor hurt, Jenny found, as did the post basket, as did all this introspection. With difficulty she heaved herself back up along the length of the door and went to sit on the bottom of the stairs instead, still not bothering to turn the light on. Turning her attention to David, the gavel came down and Jenny judged herself guilty of neglect. Racking her brains she tried to remember the last time she had put herself out for him. When for instance had she last given him a birthday party, shunned Sainsbury's in favour of baking a cake for him herself? So what if they'd never been any great shakes despite her slavish following of Delia's 'Take one egg'. So what if, invariably, they'd sunk in the middle, or turned out lopsided? She had taken the time and that's what counted. They had been baked with love, and with the aid of a bit of chocolate scaffolding here, a garish mosaic of Smarties there, the end result had always been presentable enough to be wolfed down by both David and his friends. Speaking of his friends. Where *were* Nathan, Paul and Mike these days, the little boys from nursery school, whose childish voices had filled her sunny kitchen with their laughter, and who had gone on to befriend him all through junior school, all through the hectic days of *Teenage Mutant Hero Turtles*?

"I'm Leonardo!"

"I'm Donatello! Let's kill Shredder! C'mon, Michelangelo!" Headscarves purloined from her dressing-table drawer, makeshift bandannas.

All through the days of *Power Rangers!*

The same voices, different identities.

"I'm Red Ranger! He's the best!"

"And I'm Green Ranger. Let's morph!"

Jenny drew a long, ragged breath. When had he stopped morphing? Who were his friends now that the days of Playstations and *Gladiators* were here? When had he stopped speaking to her? And when, oh when, had she stopped listening?

And Adam? Her beloved husband. When had *he* stopped bringing his colleagues home to meet her?

"Darling, this is Pete. Pete, from Acquisitions. I'm sure you've heard me mention him." And she, unsophisticated in the pasta stakes maybe, and without the benefit of a 'nose' or Pre-Raphaelite curls, making all the right moves on the home-front nonetheless.

"Pete. But, of course! Do sit down. Can I fetch you a drink?" Adam, in the background, nodding appreciatively, showing his appreciation later in the privacy of the marital bed. And the next morning, even more appreciation in the form of roses, long-stemmed damasks delivered to her doorstep, each bloom punctuated with a frond of baby's breath and a card carefully pinned to the cellophane wrapper:

'To my beautiful wife. Eternally yours. Adam.'

Now, he slept in the spare room because her snores

disturbed him and it was a case of Barbra Streisand and "You don't bring me flowers any more".

It was also a case of 'you don't bring me anywhere any more'. When, for instance, had the company do become staff only? And, could it possibly have coincided with when her little black dress had become a large black marquee and she had had to trade in her high heels for basket-weave flatties, on account of her fat ankles boiling over the sides? Then again, the do *was* usually held on a Friday night, jackpot night as far as Jenny was concerned, when *Oprah, Sally Jessey Raphael, Rolonda* and *Jerry Springer* were back to back on Sky all night. In fact, now that she thought about it, she distinctly remembered, a couple of years ago, inventing a headache, and then settling down in front of the telly as Adam, Armanied to the gills and smelling divinely of Paco Rabanne, had gone off to the do on his own.

"You're sure you won't come?" He'd stood in the doorway, a small frown playing between his eyes, brushing an anxious hand through the wave of black hair over his forehead. "I don't like to think of you here on your own."

"Ah, I'll be fine. You go and enjoy yourself." It amazed her now to think of how cavalier she'd been, how dismissive, how confident of his love. It had never even occurred to her that he might be fair game for some other woman, one who didn't invent headaches, one who would have made Cinderella's slipper look like a barge, so dainty would her feet and ankles be.

"I'm a mess," she told herself aloud. "Not to put too fine a point on it, I'm a sheer unadulterated, pathetic mess!" Then, with a sigh, she pulled herself upright with the help of the bannister and went off to do what all messes do when they want to cheer themselves up: she went off to look at someone who was an even bigger mess than herself. As it was double-bill night, she reckoned there was still time to catch the second *Jerry Springer Show* of the evening and, as it happened, her timing couldn't have been more perfect as the title of the show was just flashing across the screen.

"HONEY YOU'RE A SLOB!" it screamed in green, neon letters. "SO, HAUL ASS OUTTA HERE!" Apt, thought Jenny, reaching for a packet of salt 'n' vinegar potato crisps and adjusting the volume to compensate for the noise of her crunching. Very apt indeed!

Chapter Two

"I'm sorry, Mrs Singh." Jenny pressed a handful of notes into the diminutive Indian woman's hand. "I'm sure you'll find something else very quickly and I'll give you a good reference of course." Mrs Singh took the money but made no effort to pass through the door Jenny was holding open for her.

"But why? Are my workings not good enough any more?"

Jenny rolled her head from side to side, unconsciously aping the Asian woman's movements.

"No, your workings – work – is fine. It's just that I've decided to do the housework myself, from now on."

"But why?" Mrs Singh persisted. "Is it because I'm after locking the pussy cat in the washing machine, yesterday?" She switched from rolling her head to nodding instead. "1t was bloody accident, you know, and I'm after finding him before I'm doing the hot wash."

Jenny sighed. This was harder than she'd expected.

"No, Mrs Singh! It's got nothing to do with the cat. It's just . . . it's just, my husband doesn't bring me flowers any more!" There, it was out, and boy did she feel stupid. Mrs Singh raised her eyebrows.

"Flowers? What you wanting with flowers? Flowers is nasty things. Flowers are dropping their pedals all over the floor. Flowers are pain in the ass!"

"Well, it's not just the flowers," Jenny admitted. "My husband is seeing another woman."

"So?" Mrs Singh shrugged, the shoulders of her sari almost reaching to her ears.

Astounded, Jenny stepped back a pace. Was nobody sympathetic to her plight? She tried again. "Mrs Singh, *my* husband is seeing *another* woman!"

"So!" She shrugged again. "Maybe he fancy a leetle Vindaloo. Somtheeng 'ot and spicy. When she give him the run, he come back to you." Jenny began to feel quite dizzy as earnestly the woman went into a series of rolls and shrugs. "Often I am praying that my own Ahmed, the beeg bastard, will peese off and leave me to my own. Ganesh, oh wondrous one, I am praying in the temple, please to make Ahmed, the beeg bastard, peese off. But . . ." she grinned lopsidedly, displaying teeth like broken bits of pilau rice, "nobody want the beeg bastard so maybe I kill him one day."

"Yes, well," Jenny began, sorry for Mrs Singh's marital problems but sorrier still for her own, "there you have it anyway. I've decided to do all my own housework and cooking from now on."

18

"Okay! Okay." The other woman, mercifully without either a shrug or a roll, suddenly capitulated. "I am not deaf. I am after being hearing you the first time. But I think you are beeg cow and I am being very glad your husband has found nice, young girl, more preety than you."

"How do you know she's prettier?" Jenny yelled after the Indian woman who seemed suddenly to have recollected a pressing engagement and who was haring off down the drive, her sari streaming out behind her like a red shout. "How do you know she's younger? Have you seen her? Maybe you've cooked for them, you old bat? Bhaji on the bed! Here in *my* house." Even as she made the accusation, she knew it was unlikely because, quite simply, apart from an hour or two a couple of times a week, when the empty cupboards forced her to go shopping, she rarely left the house. Still she was on a roll and in no mood to curry favour. "It's no wonder you were happy to turn a blind eye to Adam's little poppadums. What did you get? Ten quid more in your wage packet!"

"Peese off, big cow!" Mrs Singh squinted over her shoulder, burning up the tarmac in her haste to be away. "Peese off, big, ugly cow!"

Don't hold back, Jenny thought sarcastically, going back inside and slamming the door. Say what you mean! Mournfully she switched on the television in the kitchen to keep her company. Funny, she had always thought Mrs Singh liked her. Then again, she'd always

19

thought Mounty did too. As for Adam, funny how she'd thought he loved her. Funny how wrong you could be. Grabbing the Mr Muscle, she prepared to mount an assault on the north face of the Eiger of congealed curry that years of Mrs Singh's cooking had left on the cooker.

"But you were my best friend! I trusted you more than anyone else in the world. We've known each other forever, for God's sake!"

Brought up short, Mr Muscle instantly abandoned, Jenny rocked back on her heels searching for the source of the tearful voice coming out of the TV screen in the corner. *"How could you sleep with my husband?"*

"Yes. How could you sleep with her husband, Tammy Lee?" Oprah, righteous, shaking her head at the enormity of the betrayal. *"Isn't there supposed to be a sacred bond between best friends?"*

Absent-mindedly, Jenny rose, flicked the switch on the kettle, and pulled out a chair.

"Well, she a bitch too! She ain't all that!" The accused, accusing, with *attitude!* *"I got it goin on, gurrrl!"*

Warding off the television, Jenny, palm up, went straight into chat-show mode.

"Don't even go there," she warned. "Don't even go there! Y'all don't want to go down that road." At least, she reflected, as the closing credits of *Oprah* gave way to the opening titles of *Vanessa*, Adam had the decency – if by the widest stretch of the imagination you could call adultery decent – to go off with a complete stranger. If he had teamed up with Mounty she would have gone completely off her rocker. Now, she could only thank God that her prayers to make the two of them friends had fallen on deaf ears otherwise the words 'straw' and 'camel's back' would have sprung most alarmingly to mind.

Picking up a chocolate digestive, Jenny dipped it in her coffee, all thoughts of the cooker very far away as she settled back to watch *Vanessa*.

"BIG IS BEAUTIFUL. OR IS IT?" The topic for today, and Vanessa beaming, the studio audience clapping, catcalling encouragement as a three-piece suite, mother and two daughters, desperate for humiliation, waddled onto the set.

"Oi've got big genes," the settee announced, cheerfully oblivious to the laughter her comment had produced. *"Oi can't help me size, me. We're all fat in moi fambly!"*

Vanessa, coaxingly, unusually Twiggyesque in comparison to her guests, forcing confidences. *"But you do like your chips, Mo. Don't you?"*

Mo, nodding furiously, eager for pillorying. *"Ooh. Aahr loikes me chips all right, me."* Seeking confirmation from one of the armchairs. *"I do loike me chips, me. Don't oi, Sal?"*

"Aahr. Er do. Er loikes 'er chips all right, 'er do. Ain't nothing wrong with that!"

"Ain't nothing wrong with that!" This echo from the matching armchair. *"Us all loikes us chips, even our Polly."*

Polly! Cue and cut to an eight-year-old over-stuffed footstool emerging from behind the scenes.

21

Vanessa, maternal, coaxing again. *"Come on out, Polly!"* Bending down, conspiratorially, *"You like your chips too, Polly. Don't you?"*

Polly, less amenable to pillorying, sticking her middle finger up and jabbing it first at Vanessa, and then, at the audience. *"Sit on it!"* she said. *"Sit on it and spin!"*

"SPIN!" Jenny jumped up, reminded now that she had given Mrs Singh her marching orders, that there were a hundred and one things to be done around the house, including the washing, assuming she could figure out which dial did what! Almost one o'clock and David would be walking up the drive at any minute, stomach concave with the kind of hunger that only attacks twelve-year-old boys. Determinedly Jenny stuck her chest out. Whilst she might be no Mrs Singh, she could still rustle up a sandwich, couldn't she? How difficult could putting a couple of slices of ham between a couple of slices of bread *be*, for Heaven's sake! And you couldn't go wrong with ham, could you? Everyone liked ham!

"What's that?" Some ten minutes later her son gingerly lifted a corner of bread and peered suspiciously beneath it.

"Ham, of course! What does it look like? Scabby-legged horse?"

David ignored the joke, his eyebrows climbing in direct proportion to the lengthening of his jaw. "Ham?"

"Yes, ham!" Jenny snapped, annoyed at the way he was scrutinising it as if it was going to jump out and

22

bite him at any minute. "You know, like from pigs. Big pink things covered in muck that run around the farm going *oink, oink, oink!*"

"*Pigs!*"

She suspected he would have said 'Martians' in exactly the same disbelieving way. "Yes, pigs, David. Have you got a problem with pigs? Pigs *non grata*, perhaps?"

"Mum," David's voice was quiet, resigned, unsurprised apparently at his mother's little piggadilloes, "I'm a vegetarian."

"A vegetarian!" Now Jenny's eyebrows rose in direct proportion to her chin hitting the floor. "Since when?"

"Since I gave up eating meat." David was sarcastic. "Since I developed a social conscience, in fact."

Fancy that! Jenny gazed at her son in awe. He had developed a social conscience when, presumably, he hadn't even developed pubic hair yet!

"But what about McDonald's?" she asked, her mind drifting back to the days of Happy Meals and cheap toys in plastic bags so secure you needed two pounds of Semtex and a detonator to open them.

"I was a child then!" David was contemptuous, dismissive of his younger, more ignorant self: the self who'd thought Greenpeace were what was served along with your Sunday roast, the self that Jenny had bounced on her lap and who didn't frighten her like the closed-faced young stranger sitting at her kitchen table did.

"I'm sorry!" she said, aware that somewhere along the line she had failed him. David smiled and instantly her baby was back, evident in the dimple dancing in and out of his right cheek. Adam's dimple!

"That's all right, Mum. I wasn't very hungry anyway."

"Oh, I don't mean the sandwich, though I'm sorry about that too." Sitting opposite him, Jenny reached across and lifted one of his hands, absent-mindedly noticing that his nails were clean and not bitten to the quick the way hers had been at the same age. "I mean about everything. Like not noticing you were a vegetarian. Like not baking you a birthday cake. Like getting rid of Mrs Singh who I'm sure *knew* you were a vegetarian and who, presumably, made you delicious, vegetable samosas and baked you a birthday cake flavoured with rose water." Without pausing for breath she continued, "I'm sorry because I'm fat and because I make you ashamed and because you have to sleep over at friends' houses, and because you're too embarrassed to bring them here. And I'm sorry because I don't have a social conscience and because until last year I thought Ozone Layer was a champion hen."

Abruptly David held up his free hand, cutting her off. "Don't even go there, Mum!"

Stunned, Jenny realised that *Jerry Springer* must have rubbed off on him too. She had a lot to answer for, it seemed, though to be fair she hadn't realised *he'd* been watching it, would have banned him if she had!

"I'm not ashamed or embarrassed *and* I only became

24

a vegetarian this morning. As for Mrs Singh, I'm glad you got rid of her because she was always trying to persuade me to bump off her husband, Ahmed the big bastard!"

"But you're only twelve!" And have no pubic hair! Jenny was horrified at the thought!

David nodded. "I know. I told her that but she said there was plenty of time because, although she'd begged Ganesh in the temple, Ahmed the big bastard wasn't going anywhere."

Jenny shuddered. "I'm glad I got rid of her, now," she said, "even if she did leave a lasting impression." Ruefully her glance went to the mountain of curry on the cooker where the Mr Muscle had not even managed to secure a handhold.

Rising from the table, David rescued his blazer from the back of the chair, and attempted to force his arms into two sleeves that were turned inside out. "Mum," he asked, "can Simon stay over at the weekend? He's promised to bring *Master of Carnage*, you know the latest Playstation game, with him."

"Of course he can, darling," she said, waving him out the door and following with maternal eyes as he disappeared off back to school. "Sit on it, Diana Mountford," she said aloud, frightening a sparrow out of a nearby hedgerow. Her son was *not* ashamed of her! "Sit on it and spin!" Jenny felt suddenly, unaccountably happy. And then, she remembered Adam!

Did David know about Farina, she wondered,

dismissing the thought straight away. No, Adam might be lower than a snake's belly but not so low as to involve his son in his extra-marital affairs. And neither would she. If there was one thing she had learned from *Sally Jessey-Oprah-Rivera* it was that you must never use your children as a weapon. No need when you had plenty of other weapons to hand. Weapons like wet kippers, and scissors, and in, Mrs Singh's case, twelve-year-old pre-pubescent hitmen!

Sighing, Jenny began to clear the table dimly registering Celia Straw-legs, the fitness guru, performing her workout on television.

"Remember, girls," her voice was cosy, totally at odds with the lycra-clad, Amazonian body – 100% pure, in-your-face muscle, "a moment on the lips, a lifetime on the hips! Say it with me," she commanded, "all together now!"

"A moment on the lips . . ." intoned Jenny obediently, picking up David's rejected sandwich and sinking her teeth into it, " . . . followed up with chips!"

"Well done," said Celia Straw-legs. "Very well done, indeed!"

Chapter Three

"Jenny, are you eating something?" Mounty demanded.

"Yes," Jenny grinned into the receiver, "a large helping of humble pie!" Tucking the slimmers' chewing-gum out of the way, the smacking of which Mounty had detected, Jenny prepared to swallow the humble pie, whole if need be. "Look, you were right!" she said. "I *have* lost the plot recently but I need help to get it back. Your help!" Affecting a little-girl voice, she lisped down the telephone. "Will you help me, Mounty. Uh? Please! Pretty please! Uh? Uh? Uh?"

Mounty laughed. "Idiot! Of course I will. I'm only glad you're seeing a bit of sense at last."

"So where do you start?" Jenny asked as if she were a point on the M3, round which Mounty had to negotiate.

"With the gym!" Mounty was decisive. "We're going to enrol you at my gym and watch the pounds melt away."

"Suits me!" Jenny said, eager to start now that she

had surrendered herself into Mounty's care. "Move over, Celia Straw-legs. Let a real babe show you how it's done!"

A couple of days later, standing in Goldman's Gym Jenny shook her head in amazement.

"Gosh, you were right! I never knew losing weight could be this easy. Look, my bank account has already lost £500 in less than two minutes."

"Okay. Okay," Mounty admitted. "So it's not cheap but then the good things in life rarely are. Besides, you get a consultation with a personal trainer and regular follow-ups. So come on. Stop moaning and let's get shopping." She eyed Jenny's sweatsuit with distaste. "Hmm. Something more motivational, I think, and some new trainers."

"Lead on, Geronimo!" Jenny quipped, content to follow her into the bowels of hell if necessary but slightly relieved when she stopped short at Fitz U, the sportswear 'Shop of the Stars'.

"Try these." Optimistically Mounty held out a pair of leggings, extra large with a 75% lycra content and something long and thin that looked like Adam's black tie or the inside of a bicycle wheel.

"What's this?" Jenny held it up to the light, stretching it this way and that and earning superior sniffs from the sales assistant who was hovering at elbow-distance.

"A thong."

"A thong! A thong? For me?" Flicking it like a catapult Jenny roared, creasing up with laughter at the thought. "Look,' she explained kindly to Mounty who, to give her her due, was looking a little shamefaced, "if I was to put that on me, it would disappear up my butt and be lost forever."

"Quite," the sales assistant snapped, trying hard to keep her professional cool whilst relieving Jenny of the garment and doing her best to stretch it back into shape. "Now if madam would care to look at the Leisure Suits, I'm sure we can find something a little more . . . hmm . . . suitable."

Jenny shrugged. "Makes sense," she said, diving on a huge violet number that must have been designed with the Purple People Eater in mind. "Now this is more like it. Have you got it in a twenty? Good!"

"What do you say we get a coffee?" she asked when, tracksuit paid for and packed in a trendy Fitz U carrier bag, they emerged from the shop. "And a big slice of carrot cake. Only joking!" She giggled, seeing the look of horror on Mounty's face.

Mounty shrugged apologetically. "No can do, I'm afraid. I'm meeting someone for lunch and I'm running late as it is."

"A man?" Jenny queried, knowing Mounty had finished with her boyfriend lately. "A new man?"

"A man," Mounty confirmed smilingly but giving nothing else away.

Jenny knew better than to press her. When there was anything to know, Mounty would tell her, but not before then. "Okay." She kept her voice light. "Enjoy your lunch. I'll just carry on and get the trainers . . . and some carrot cake." She mumbled the last bit under her breath.

"Get the expensive ones," Mounty instructed. "Adidas or Reeboks, something like that. They're not cheap but they really are better, more impact-absorbing."

"Well, they'll have no shortage of impact to absorb," Jenny laughed, waving a casual hand and setting off in the opposite direction. She hoped Mounty's new man was better than the last who'd not only been full of himself, but full if *it* too! Strange how she had no difficulty in attracting men but just couldn't seem to find the right one to settle down with. Still, better luck this time, Jenny mused, her attention being immediately diverted as she passed an electrical shop in the window of which was a display of televisions.

"MAH HUSBAND DON'T LOVE ME NO MORE". The *Jerry Springer Show*. Green and pink neon titles. "SO AHM GONNA GIT ME SOME NEW LOVIN'."

"I'm interested in this television," Jenny said, stepping inside and beckoning over a sales assistant. "Would you mind turning the volume up?"

"Certainly, madam." The young man, sensing some easy commission, obliged. "It comes in 23, 26, and 28 inch screen with quadraphonic surround sound, nicam digital stereo and graphic equalisers as standard . . ."

"Sssh!" Jenny snarled, unimpressed with the sales patter. "I can't hear a bloody word!"

Around the corner in T42, Mounty ordered an espresso and turkey salad on pumpernickel bread. Hold the mayo!

"I feel awful, Adam. *Really* low! She *is* my best friend, after all."

"I know! I'm not exactly heartless myself." He frowned, which was all he seemed to do these days.

"She'd never forgive us, you know."

"Well, we're only doing it because we care and she *did* rather bring it on herself." Adam attempted a justification. "But seriously, Mounty, I can't tell you how grateful I am for all your help."

Mounty gave a careless shrug. "Someone had to do something. I mean she was *really* losing it." She looked a bit anxious. "Still, let's hope it all works out."

"Oh, it will." Adam assured her. "It's got to!"

"I wish I had your confidence. I really do!"

"Trust me . . ." he tried the old joke. "I'm a doctor."

"You're not though." Mounty made a little moue. "You're a merchant banker and we all know what that's Cockney rhyming slang for, don't we?"

"Bitch!" The insult was affectionate.

"Balls, said the Queen!" shot back Mounty. "If I had, I'd be King!"

"More coffee?"

"Yes, please." Mounty was fervent. "Straight in the vein if possible!" Adam grinned, wondering how he could ever have thought her an East End slapper with tripe for brains.

"One espresso, coming right up!"

* * *

31

"So, madam?" The sales assistant prompted some thirty minutes later when the chat show had come to an end. "Does madam wish to buy this set or is there another she might be interested in perhaps?"

"What?" Jenny shook her head indignantly. "Buy a set that shows such filthy programmes. I don't think so! *I'm going to get me some loving, indeed!* Hmmph! The very idea!"

"But . . . but . . . but . . ." The assistant attempted to stammer something about sets and channels being two separate issues but Jenny, trainers once more on her mind, completely blanked him.

"Cow!" he roared after her but only in his mind because *his* supervisor was watching. "Big, fat, ugly cow. Big, fat, miserable, ugly cow!" Satisfied with his choice of adjectives, he thought them over again and again, imbuing them with more and more feeling, till eventually they became like some sort of mantra etched on his brain that brought a glint of madness to his eye whenever a fat woman came into the shop.

"I want a pair of Adiboks." Jenny told the shoe-shop assistant in her best don't-try-and-fob-me-off-with-any-old-cheap-rubbish-just-because-I'm-fat voice.

The assistant choked, hastily converting a giggle into a cough. "Adiboks? I'm afraid we only stock Adidas or Reeboks."

Wearily, Jenny sank onto the nearest chair. "Look! I've been in every damn shoe shop in London and nobody stocks Adiboks. Just give me a pair of

32

Something trainers in size 8, broad-fitting and impact-absorbing, and let me be done with it."

"Certainly, madam." Shoulders shaking from suppressed laughter the assistant disappeared into a back room where the twin for the pink and white trainer that fitted Jenny's bill was kept. "I won't keep you a minute."

"Take your time." Jenny, easing her bunions out of her basket-weave flatties, sighed with relief. If only she could close her eyes and 'blink' herself home like the woman in *Bewitched* or was that Jeanie in *I Dream of Jeanie?* One of them, she remembered, twitched her nose, and one folded her arms and blinked. It didn't much matter anyway, because twitching or blinking, *she* had to face the tube trains, no doubt finding herself, as usual, with her face jammed into somebody's armpit: somebody who didn't 'act on Impulse' or on any other deodorant for that matter.

"Would you like to try them on?" The sales girl was back all too soon.

"That won't be necessary," Jenny said crisply, handing over her credit card. The truth was that she would sooner go to the electric chair than provide entertainment by trying to force her fat feet into the concoction of white and pink leather the assistant was placing in a box, and which reminded her of built-up, orthopaedic shoes. "I always buy my trainers two sizes too big." Contradict me if you dare, you little skinny-malink, her eyes said. I could do the pencil test once too, you know!

"Most people do, madam!" The assistant nodded

her head. "Only sensible to allow for the thickness of the sports socks."

Hoist on her own petard, Jenny blushed. "In that case you'd better see if you've any size 10s in stock."

"Yes, madam. Certainly, madam," This time failing dismally to suppress her giggles the girl hurried off, no doubt to give vent to a full-throated roar in the seclusion of the stockroom.

"Sod this for a game of cowboys!" Jenny muttered snatching back her credit card, thrusting her feet back into her flatties, and doing a quick bunk out the door. "I'm not playing!"

* * *

"I'm not sure you should have given Mrs Singh the Big E." With a clatter, Adam dropped the lid of an empty saucepan under which he'd been peering hopefully. "There's never anything to eat in this house any more."

Without replying, Jenny dropped her packages on the floor and bending over gave him the benefit of her size 20 bottom, sighing in satisfaction as her feet, eased free of their confines, oozed out like two red jellyfish across the floor.

"Honestly, my stomach thinks my throat is cut!" he continued.

Pity it isn't, Jenny thought viciously, beginning to unpack her shopping and lay it out on the work surface. Thank God for oven-ready meals! They made life a whole lot easier.

"Dinner'll be on the table in half an hour," she told him, struggling to unwrap a frozen pizza and showing remarkable restraint in refraining from frisbeeing it at his ear. 'Why don't you piss off down to Spend A Penne and take your schoolgirl Lolita with you,' is what she really wanted to say, her masochistic streak coming into play once more. 'Tell me now, Adam, just out of curiosity, you understand. Do you share a single strand of spaghetti with her, the way you did with me, her at one end, you at the other, the strand getting shorter and shorter till your lips meet in the middle and instead of spaghetti you're suddenly sharing bolognese kisses? And Gianni is standing there, all indulgent, his belly bulging out beneath his waiter's apron like a giant umbilical hernia.

"*Mamma mia,*" he says. "*Mamma mia.*" And suddenly the intimacy is broken and you're both laughing like drains as if Gianni saying *Mamma mia* is the funniest thing in the world. But your eyes promise more intimacy, much more intimacy, intimacy of the long-stemmed, damask roses kind. You don't give me flowers anymore. BECAUSE YOU'RE TOO DAMN BUSY GIVING THEM TO HER INSTEAD!' Of course she *didn't* say any of that. What she said was: "I got you the meat-feast with extra pepperoni, thick crust and with a cheesy rim."

"*Aah!*" Like one of the Bisto kids, Adam's nose went up in the air, nostrils dilating in anticipation like what's-his-name from the *Carry On* films. Huh! She'd bet anything he didn't do that when the fragrant one was around. No way! He'd be too busy holding in his stomach and trying to make his nose look aquiline.

"Anyway," she slammed the pizza in the oven, "I had to get rid of Mrs Singh. She was trying to turn David into a twelve-year-old hitman." Adam's eyebrows rose – twin, black arches of perfection. He really *was* very handsome, Jenny thought. Tall, dark and handsome. The only thing he was lacking really was the black charger. He did, however, have a black Merc, which, in today's climate, was a pretty acceptable substitute.

"Not Ahmed, the big bastard? She tried to persuade me to bump him off too but I didn't think for a minute she was serious."

Jenny busied herself with the makings of a green salad. "Maybe she wasn't," she admitted. "I'd decided to get rid of her in any case because I wanted to take over the housekeeping again. What?" she snapped, seeing that Adam was looking at her quizzically. "You don't think I'm capable, is that it?" Ruthlessly she drowned, then disembowelled a lettuce. "Let me remind you that when you were just a lowly bank clerk, not only did I do all the housework and cooking but managed to hold down a full-time job as well."

Adam shrugged, stepping back a pace as Jenny emphasised her point by waving the knife around, Bobbett-style. "But that was ages ago, before David was born. Things are different now."

Jenny glared, absent-mindedly grabbing a tomato

and hacking it to death. "Do you think, Adam, that because I'm not a nine-to-fiver, I'm living in the Dark Ages or something? I'm quite aware that time has moved on. God knows, I only have to look in the mirror to see that. But I'm not completely brain-dead. I've still got all my marbles, thank you very much!"

"That's not what I meant." Her husband shuffled uncomfortably. "I'm just worried that after all this time you might find it a little difficult to get back in the swing of things."

Jenny was sarcastic. "I'm not planning to do the cha-cha, Adam, simply to take charge of my household again. Have you any objections?"

Her blue eyes challenged him, sparks that had been dormant too long, suddenly igniting her whole face so that he was reminded of the Jenny he'd met at a disco back in the seventies. A callow youth, he'd been nervous of the willowy blonde with the bad Farrah Fawcett hairdo, nervous of the way she walked and talked and shimmered on the dance floor, a magnet to every red-blooded male. And he had been no exception. Acne notwithstanding, he had left his Courage on the bar and, after several false starts, had eventually hit first base.

"Would you like to dance?" he'd asked, standing back against the wall and talking out the side of his mouth so that, if she knocked him back, it wouldn't be so obvious to anyone looking on and in need of a good laugh. What he'd meant to say was: "I think you're beautiful, the most beautiful girl in the world and I'm madly in love with you." Actually he *had* said it, many times in fact, lying on his bed post-disco with Deep Purple thumping away in the background. But when it came to the crunch, what did he say? Would you like to dance? Full marks for originality! Nevertheless, she *had* danced with him and before the night was out he was holding her close and leaning his acned chin on her head, and the rest, as they say, was history.

"No!" he said now in answer to her question. "No objections at all."

"Good!" Grabbing a bottle of Newman's vinaigrette, Jenny liberally dashed it over the salad. "Not that it would make any difference if you had. I'm back, Adam!" Her eyes challenged him again. "Back on Planet Earth. One hundred per cent physically *and* mentally. Back! Like the Terminator and certain things are going to terminate round here. Savvy?" Plucking a spring onion from the salad bowl she slowly transferred it to her mouth and for a moment he was reminded not of the Terminator, but of a cigar-chewing Clint Eastwood.

"What things?" he asked innocently, watching her decapitate the spring onion with her sharp white teeth.

"Things!" she said knowingly and with emphasis. "Just *things!*"

Chapter Four

A few days later down at the gym, Jenny snorted disdainfully, nudging Mounty sharply in the ribs.

"Just my luck! There was I all keyed up expecting Adonis in a g-string, and what do I get? Adenoids in a leotard!"

A unitard, actually," Mounty corrected her.

Jenny nodded violently, so violently in fact that the Nike sweatband, *de rigueur* according to Mounty, slipped down her forehead and spread itself across her eyes like a designer blindfold, temporarily blinding her. "Right! A retard in a unitard."

"Oh, be fair, Jenny! Denzil's not so bad."

Jenny's eyebrows rose or would have if she hadn't been so busy hoiking the wretched sweatband back up across her forehead. "*Denzil!* I might have known he'd be called something like that. Only someone called *Denzil* would have the cheek to call a bone fide valued customer 'lard-ass'!"

Mounty giggled. "He *did* not!"

Jenny shrugged. "He might as well have." Ruefully she twisted her mouth up in a passable imitation of Gym Instructor's high, adenoidal vocals. "Tut, tut, tut! Madam's body-fat ratio is somewhat on the excessive side. Yes, indeedy. Seventy-five per cent and climbing. High in cholesterol, low in polyunsaturates, I shouldn't wonder."

"I can't believe I'm not butter!" Jenny had muttered, stepping off the fat monitor, a contraption which looked like your common or bathroom weighing scales, but deadlier by far on account of the bleep factor.

It was with some trepidation, shoes and socks dutifully removed, that she had stepped up on it in the first place and waited. And waited! And kept on waiting! Five minutes later and still waiting she took matters into her own hands and complained vociferously to the Instructor.

"It's not bloody working. It bleeped after a few seconds when *she* stood up on it." The *she* referred to was a blonde-haired, cropped-topped, lycra-shorted, stick-insect currently engaged in pedalling furiously on a stationary bike. Next stop Tour de France!

"*She*," Denzil had pointed out cruelly, "is a lot thinner than you. A stick of rock, as it were, to your Nelson's Column! A sausage to your salami!"

It was at that point that Jenny decided he must be gay. All that phallic symbolism! A gay, adenoidal retard in a unitard! Illustratively pointing a well-manicured, black finger to where her feet, two slabs of dough waiting to prove, rested on the monitor, he traced an imaginary line all the way up to the top of her head.

"The signal has to work its way up through all the layers of fat first and then, mission accomplished, hey presto, we get a 'bleep' and a printout. Like so!" With a little jump he sprang from one foot to the other, bending at the waist, leg extended outward, and scooped up the ticket of paper oozing out the back of the machine. A ballerina!

"Seventy-five percent fat! God, can you believe it!" said Jenny now.

Mounty was bracing. "Don't worry. You'll soon shift it!" Her eyes veered to where the stick-insect had relinquished the bicycle in favour of something, all silver weights and black straps, that resembled a medieval torture rack or a fetishist's wet dream. "If she can do it, so can you!"

"No!" Jenny's eyes grew round with disbelief, hypnotically round, as she followed the undulations of the lycra-shorted bottom. Left cheek up! Right cheek down! Up, down! Up down! "You mean, she . . .?"

"Well no, actually." Mounty came clean. "But you *can* do it. I *know* you can."

Dryly, Jenny disengaged her friend from her arm upon which, in her fervour, Mounty had been swinging causing the loose skin underneath to waft back and forth like the flaps on the wing of a plane. "Your faith in me is truly touching! Now, if you don't mind let's put some of your faith into practice."

"Right!" Mounty was suddenly all business. "What would you like to try first?"

"How about that thing?" Gingerly, Jenny pointed to an electronically operated treadmill. "That looks easy enough!" And so it was until a surfeit of confidence caused her to increase the pace to the point where she suddenly found herself experiencing life as Road Runner. And worse still, Road Runner running up a fifty per cent gradient. As her legs turned into a blur of purple mixed with something white, her trainers she guessed, it dawned on Jenny that it was really no surprise Oprah Winfrey had managed to lose all that weight at the gym. If she, herself, managed to last another five minutes, she would emerge as only half the woman, not least because fright alone would have turned her into a shadow of her former self. Only *seconds* later, as she found herself being steadily, inevitably dragged backwards towards the edge, it became apparent that she had as much chance hanging over a cliff by a daisy petal, as she had of remaining upright on the bloody treadmill for another five minutes. In the circumstances there was only one thing left to do. Scream! Very loudly. Which she did!

"Help! Help! Somebody stop it!" Jenny yelled as her own life *and* Road Runner's flashed before her eyes. "It's out of control! I'm gonna die, David will be left motherless and Adam, the two-timing son of a bitch, is gonna marry Farina!"

Too late! When it came to a battle of wills the

treadmill won every time and another moment witnessed Jenny, a human cannonball, catapult backwards faster than the speed of light, her unscheduled flight abruptly terminating in a headlock beneath the sweaty and very hairy armpit of a bodybuilder.

"Th-thanks." Gasping shakily, she cautiously extracted and patted her skull in an effort to determine if her brain was still intact. "Y-you saved my life, or at least your armpit did!"

"Who the fuck is Adam? Who the fuck is Farina?" Brushing her thanks aside. the bodybuilder, a dead ringer for Mike Tyson, trapped her up against the pec deck as his eyes, wild from steroid abuse, begged her to give him an excuse, *any* excuse to go and beat the crap out of the unknown pair.

"Ah, they're no one, just someone!" Cryptic though Jenny's reply was, the bodybuilder seemed to make sense of it.

"Well, that's all right so. But you let me know if you want them sorted. Right?" Menacingly slamming one closed fist into his palm, the Tyson clone eyeballed her. "Right?"

"Oh, yeah, sure, right!" Like a nodding dog in the back of a 60s Cortina, Jenny nodded furiously, her crimson face horribly at odds with her purple tracksuit.

"And another thing."

"Yes?" Jenny hoped the stiff smile on her face had reached placatory on the smileometer." There's a stop button on the treadmill. S-T-O-P spells stop. Right?"

The bodybuilder looked absurdly pleased, probably at his ability to spell something correctly .

"Right." The smile had gone past placatory. The dial had moved to ingratiating. Jenny could feel it sidling up her cheekbones, the corners of her eyes coming down to meet it.

"Use it!"

"Oh, I will," Jenny promised, sincerity and gratitude oozing from every pore. "Oh definitely, I will."

"Honestly, Jenny, what are you like?" Mounty said crossly, appearing suddenly at her elbow. "I can't leave you for five minutes without you getting into mischief."

"Not exactly getting into him . . ." Jenny giggled, *compos mentis* once more, now that the bodybuilder had moved off to gaze neanderthally at himself in the wall-to-wall, floor-to-ceiling mirrors, and utter testosterone-filled, grunting noises. "More like giving him head – my head under his arm!"

Mounty sniggered. "Is that why there's a pubic hair on your lip?"

"Oh yuck! Another one who doesn't act on Impulse!" Repulsed, Jenny set about removing the offending item, her fingers making delicate pincher-like forays across her mouth. "Maybe I should just leave it there and give Adam something to think about other than Farina."

"Farina?"

"Adam's girlfriend!" She linked her arm though

Mounty's and they headed for the showers. "You know the type. All Estée Lauder, big hair, and knickers like bunting on a maypole. Triangular and flying free!"

Incredulous, Mounty pulled her arm free, spinning Jenny round to look at her. "What? You mean you've seen her?"

Jenny shook her head. "Nah!" She tapped her head. "Only up here, but it doesn't take a psychiatrist to figure that one out."

"Oh really?" Unaware of the strange note that had suddenly entered the other woman's tone, Jenny jerked her head knowingly.

"Oh come on, Mounty! Oldest story in the book. Middle-aged man seeks fountain of youthful woman for restoration of faltering ego and even more faltering erection. Only big-haired, big-chested, teeny-weeny-knickered applicants need apply!"

"So you think we're past it at our age, do you?" Beside her, Mounty had begun the delicate operation of peeling her dampened Speedo leotard from her body, a procedure that required total concentration if reams of skin were not also to be removed.

"Does a butt fart backwards?" Jenny hooted crudely. "Let me put it like this. We're so far over the hill that if we underwent regression therapy, the hypnotist would point it out as a landmark in another life."

"Speak for yourself!" Insulted, Mounty stooped down, pulled her legs free and viciously kicked the inoffensive garment underneath the changing-room bench. "I'm damned if I'm past anything. If anything, I'm better than I was when I was in my twenties."

"A better liar anyway!" Jenny jibed then shrieked as Mounty smacked her across the bare back with a wet towel. "It was a joke! Honest! You're not past it! *I'm* the one who's past it. You're gorgeous! You are. Really!"

"Say it again!" Mounty commanded, lassooing the towel around in the air.

"You're gorgeous" Jenny giggled, diving into the nearest shower cubicle and slamming the door behind her. "A gorgeous big liar who's over the hill!"

Chapter Five

"I told you it would never work. His eyes are too close set *and* he has a dimple in his chin. Look at all those film stars with dimples in their chins. Womanisers and sex addicts, all of them!"

Wryly, Jenny regarded her mother, wondering for the umpteenth time why she couldn't be like any other self-respecting, pension-collecting, twin-set-wearing, sixty-five-year-old. Oh no, just her luck to get saddled with Gloria whose idea of conservative dressing was to cover her slave-bangle tattoo with a studded, leather armband and exchange her thigh-high, puss-in-boots boots for six-inch, ankle, patent-leather models. She had always been the same, way-out even when way-out was the norm, the forerunner of Cher, a biker babe long before biker babes were invented. Even if her Harley was actually a Lambretta! By all accounts, Jenny's father had fallen in love with her mother's thighs before ever his eyes graduated, first to her cleavage, and then to her face. It was a work of art, he said, the way she steered the motorbike. Never mind the handlebars, the thighs had it! A nudge of the right and it went left. A nudge of the left and it went right. And she had ridden him for years in exactly the same way, steering him this way and that till one fateful evening his eyes had lit upon *Xena, Warrior Princess* or rather upon her thighs and the excitement had proved too much for a man of his age.

"The poor old bugger," her mother had remarked sadly whilst frantically engaged in trying to wrest her stiletto from the mud piled up beside the open grave. "Cut down to thighs, at last!" Now though, her mind was engaged upon other things, although the stilettos remained the same.

"Personally, I blame his mother. I mean, what did she think she was doing calling him after a philanderer anyway? The poor sod didn't stand a chance what with his close-set eyes, dimpled chin and a name loaded with womanising characteristics. Stands to reason he's going to turn into a first-class, adulterous bastard!"

"There's nothing wrong with his name! Besides his biblical namesake wasn't an adulterer. I mean Adam wasn't married and it wasn't exactly like Paradise was inundated with women anyway, was it? There was only one, Eve! And if God hadn't meant there to be any hanky-panky, what did he think he was doing filling them up with sex hormones in the first place?" Despite her spirited defence of the first man ever, Jenny could, nonetheless, feel herself bristling beneath her mother's disdain, metamorphosing once more into a tubby schoolgirl, with an acned chin and navy gym knickers. "And neither is *my* Adam a first-class adulterous bastard. Just having an affair, that's all!"

Her mother's eyebrows, plucked and drawn in *à la* Garbo, climbed up to rub shoulders with her black roots.

"Just an affair? So tell me, Jenny, if you're so *sangfroid* about the whole matter why have you landed up in my living-room climbing out of your panties with rage!"

"I am not climbing out of my panties! And that's a terrible expression for a woman of your age to be using. Why can't you be like other people's mothers? Why can't you have chintz curtains and potter around pruning roses and mixing up herbal remedies like normal mothers do? Why can't you have bridge parties and say civilised things like 'My dear, that's simply divine' and 'Yes, Vicar, I'd be delighted to arrange the harvest loaves next week?'"

Gloria yawned loudly and reaching out a hand, the nails of which were fully two inches long and adorned with miniature pictures of the Kama Sutra, possessed herself of a generous glass of whisky.

"I wondered when we were going to get on to that old chestnut. I wondered how long it would be before you started blaming me for everything that's wrong with your life." Dryly she mimicked her daughter's voice. "Why can't you be like normal mothers? Normal mothers don't wear leather. Normal mothers don't swear. Normal mothers don't have L O V E and H A T E tattooed on their knuckles. Normal mothers bake, sew, dust and fart in tune." Uncrossing her rubber-clad legs she leaned forward a little, unmindful of the whisky slopping over onto the carpet turning a tiny pile of cigarette ash already resting there into the Black Sea. "I'll tell you what, Jennifer. You're so far up your own backside looking for normal that it's abnormal. Have the courage to be yourself; be what's *normal* for you. Shit or get off the pot! Maybe if you weren't so busy turning yourself into a fat, insignificant clone of everyone else, Adam wouldn't need to go in search of pastures new!" With difficulty she heaved herself up from the leather settee which, with the tenacity of a dirty old man, was endeavouring to cling on to her rubber-coated backside. "Now if you don't mind I've got to walk Rover."

Resignedly, Jenny too rose to her feet. "I didn't know you had a new dog . . ." she began, then broke off as the door opened to admit a long-haired, twenty-something, biker-type youth around the neck of whom reposed a rather large, studded dog-collar.

"Good boy, Rover!" her mother cooed, as possessing himself of a leather lead he got down on all fours and presented it to her in his mouth. "Dud Wover wanna go walkies? Dud he? Dud he?"

"Oh, Christ!" Jenny groaned as the daft bugger began play-snapping at her mother's ankles and turning circles on the carpet. "Why can't you be normal?"

"Remember what I said." her mother called warningly as her indignant daughter disappeared through the doorway. "Close-set eyes, dimpled chin and an adulterer's name! All the trademarks of a first-class, philandering bastard! Just like Adam!"

"Remember my father!" Jenny spat back. "As I recall, you gave him a dog's life too!"

Stung by the allegation which, even as she made it, Jenny knew to be untrue, her mother brandished the lead in her direction.

"Attack, Rover!" she roared. "Go get her, boy!"

"Aw, shit!" Jenny yelled, taking to her heels and lumbering clumsily off up the street as the human Rottweiler, snapping and snarling, canonballed after her. "Aw, shit!"

Back home she made a mental note to remove the wire letter-basket from behind the door before she was left with a permanent dent in her skull. As a child, 'under the stairs' had been the place of choice for tears and melodramatic fantasies, in which all those who 'done her wrong' would be sorry. In vivid detail and technicolor imagination she had followed *them* following *her* to the grave. Arrayed in black, and dabbing their eyes with delicate white scraps of hankies, they would each and every one admit their part in the unhappiness which had led to her taking her young life. Often and anon she had indulged in comforting visions of herself in her coffin, looking serene and beautiful, despite having hung herself from an electricity pylon/thrown herself under the Gatwick Express/cut her own throat or disembowelled herself with an apple-corer.

"Such a pity!" she'd imagined them saying. "The world is a poorer place today and did you ever see a corpse that reminded you more of the young Grace Kelly?"

Thanks to Adam, a hoarder of the first order, 'under the stairs' in this house had become synonymous with the Krypton Factor obstacle course: a no-man's-land of broken sports equipment, prototype hoovers and fishing gear inherited from his late father which Adam never used and, now that he had hooked the mermaid Farina, was never likely to use. Not unless they made waders with six-inch heels and fish that smelled of Chanel No. 5, Jenny thought spitefully.

In any case, in this house *'behind the front door'* despite the post-basket, was Jenny's new substitute and she was particularly careful to let herself slide down the length of it the way broken-hearted heroines in Mills & Boons did.

"Jemima slid down the back of the front door, her heart beating like a trapped bird. How could Eric have treated her so?"

How could Adam have treated her so? Jenny thought assuming the M&B position. And her mother? How could she have set Rover on her like that? Well, they would be sorry, both of them. When she was lying there cold and dead with one perfect teardrop on her cheek, they would be sorry. Adam would rest his dark head, greying distinguishedly at the temples naturally, in his hands, and moan out his regret at her passing.

"I didn't deserve her," he'd say. "She was the perfect wife and mother. Okay so she was a bit plump and had a penchant for garlic, but she was worth her weight in gold nonetheless. Gravity-defying boobs aren't everything," he'd sniff. "Neither is a 'nose'! Neither is a nubile, compliant nymphet with legs as long as the M1 and a great line in fellatio."

And, from her mother, dressed down for the occasion, as a mark of respect, in PVC ankle boots. "I called her my little emperor, you know, on account of the Caesarean they performed to bring her into this world. Okay, so I went up a size in leathers and my nipples got to shake hands with my knees but, hey, she was worth it. I just don't know what I'd do if I didn't have Rover here to comfort me!"

But, what of David? Abruptly Jenny sat up, flinching as she impaled herself once more on the edge of the post-basket. What kind of oration would he give her, standing by the graveside in the black Nike tracksuit she'd bought on his last birthday, which had cost her an arm and a leg and which he'd detested because all his mates had started wearing Kappa?

"Mum was *wicked!*" Maybe, or: "Mum was just Mum. She bought me a Playstation which is pretty cool but I was hoping she'd buy me the latest Dreamcast machine only she can't now because she's dead so maybe Dad's new girlfriend will buy it for me instead. Pleeeeease,

Farina! Pleeeeese! You're much prettier than Mum ever was. Honestly. *And* you cook better too. *And* you make Dad happier!"

Abruptly Jenny pulled herself to her feet. There was no way she was going to die and let that woman get her clutches into David. Nothing, not even the prospects of looking like a young film star, albeit a dead one, was worth the luscious Farina gaining favour with her son, infiltrating *her* home and family, chucking out her chintz, and feng shui-ing all over the place with her husband. Besides, after weeks of back-breaking work-outs at the flab-lab she could almost get her jeans up over her knees now. Only when she could pull them all the way up *and* close the button without cutting off her air supply would she be ready to shuffle off her mortal coil. So, by her reckoning, she had a lot of living to do yet.

"I've got a lot of living to do yet!" she told the hall mirror as she passed by on her way to the fridge in search of something yummy to raise her blood-sugar levels.

"Not from where I'm standing, mate!" the mirror retorted causing her to stop in her tracks and peer more closely at the reflection glowering back at her. "See how many companies would sell *you* life assurance, you big, fat slob," it jibed. "None without a full CT scan and an ECG first, anyway!"

Jenny bridled at her reflection, which disturbingly seemed to have taken on all the characteristics of a sumo wrestler. Puffy cheeks, currant eyes, manic leer. All that was missing was the bald head. Instead, curiously enough, it seemed to have an old English sheepdog atop its skull, a wild, shaggy canine oddly reminiscent of a bad perm with piebald tendencies.

"Huh, you can talk!" she told it scornfully. "Who nominated *you* Miss World. The last time I saw hair like that Toyah Wilcox was in the charts! Way down at the bottom!"

"Oh, yeah?" The reflection screwed up its nose. "Well, the last time I saw fat like that it was on top of the EU beef mountain!"

Jenny began to enjoy herself. Obviously this was going to be a no-holds-barred contest. A real slanging match!

"Oh yeah? Well, *you're* so ugly you'd make an onion cry!"

"Is that a fact?" The reflection appeared unfazed. "Well, every time *you* bend over you cause a solar eclipse." Top that, it seemed to say, as frantically she racked her brains for an even more cutting retort.

"Oh, yeah?" she began, satisfied that she had found one, then broke off abruptly as David's puzzled voice drifted down from the upstairs landing.

"Who are you talking to, Mum?"

"Talking? I wasn't talking. I was humming!" Unconvincingly, she frowned up at him.

"You were talking," David insisted, "to yourself, in the mirror."

Jenny blushed. "Oh, *that* talking. Well, it wasn't exactly talking, more like practising."

Disbelievingly David curled his lip, a real pre-teen stoking-up-a-surplus-of-hormones curl, that put her in mind of the young Adam, who, come to think of it, she had first met when he wasn't all that much older than his son was now. "Practising?"

"Yes, practising! For amateur dramatics." Truth to tell, Jenny was more than a little shocked by the ease with which the lies tripped so glibly off her tongue. "We're doing *The Pirates of Penzance* and I'm the pirate!"

"Yo, ho ho and a bottle of rum!" David sneered taking the stairs two steps at a time and landing with a thud at the bottom. "Come off it, Mum. Can't you come up with a better excuse than that? Since when have you ever been interested in amateur dramatics?" He grinned. "Besides, senility is nothing to be ashamed of. It comes to us all if we live long enough!"

"Oh, is that a fact, Dr Know-all?" his mother retorted making a dive for the umbrella stand and wresting a rather vicious-looking walking-stick out of its clutches. "Well, any more cheek from you and I guarantee that *you*, for one, can mark it off your wish list. Now go out and play with an oncoming bus while I go and put the dinner on."

Hands raised in an attitude of mock surrender, David headed for the front door. "All right, all right, demented woman, I'm outta here. By the way, Dad phoned. He said he's working late and you're not to worry about dinner cos he'll grab something later."

"I bet he will!" Bitterly Jenny watched the door slam

behind her only offspring as he headed off for yet another sleepover with Simon, his mate of the month. "I bet he'll grab everything he can get his hands on, the miserable, lecherous git! No fear of him going hungry, not when he's feasting on the pleasures of forbidden fruit." Miserably, Jenny turned back to her reflection in the mirror. "Talking about grabbing, I guess it's just you and me for dinner then." She sighed. "How does steak and onions grab *you*, followed up with a big tub of Ben & Jerry's triple chocolate fudge with marshmallow pieces?"

"Now you're making sense!" her reflection approved, accepting the flag of peace. "Race you to the fridge!"

Later on, nursing a large spoon and with the promised Ben & Jerry's on her lap, Jenny found that, for once, she couldn't get interested in *Springer*. Instead her eyes strayed almost constantly to the ornately decorated cuckoo clock above the television. Vulgar in the extreme, she only kept it for reasons of sentimentality because Adam had bought it for her while they were on honeymoon in Vienna.

"Because I'm cuckoo over you," he'd said. "And like the birdy in the clock, I want to shout about it, every hour on the hour." Time, however, like the hands on the clock, had moved round in circles and now he thought *she* was the one who was cuckoo, only cuckoo in a straitjacket kind of way. She could just imagine him on the subject to Farina.

"My wife," he'd say, strain apparent in every twitch

57

of his manly cheek, "doesn't understand me. Not her fault, poor thing. Gone a bit cuckoo, don't you know. Runs in the family. Mother as nutty as a fruitcake! Father, a leg-man. What can you do?" And Farina, lisping, her own long, fuzz-free leg draped provocatively round his waist. "Poor darling. Such a lot you've been through. Let me kiss you all better."

With a Herculean effort Jenny wrenched her attention back to the TV where a black woman, wearing Medusa's head, was intent on beating her rival in love to death in front of an audience of millions.

But it was no use. Like a moth drawn to a flame Jenny's eyes rose once more of their own volition and settled on the clock where the big hand was on twelve and the little hand was on two. And Adam expected her to believe he was working late! Oh, she didn't doubt for one moment that he was on the job all right, only not the job for which he collected his salary and paid his taxes.

"Let me at her," Medusa pleaded, wrestling Jerry's security man to the floor. *"She a ho. She stole mah mayn!"*

"Yeah!" Jenny empathised, caught at last despite herself and shadow-boxing with her spoon. "Let her at her and then give *me* a go!"

Chapter Six

She'd missed all the warning signs, of course. Ridiculous really when you considered the fact that they were everywhere. Ridiculous and ironic when you considered how often she had filled in the questionnaires in *Cosmo* and *Marie-Claire*. Just for fun, you understand, at least back then. Questionnaires with headings like 'How to spot if your man is a lying, cheating bastard', or 'The Ten Cardinal Signs of Infidelity'. Mind you, the titles might have varied considerably, but the content was more or less the same.

1. *Is your man working later and later in the evening?* – Yes, above and beyond the call of duty.
2. *Has he changed his brand of aftershave?* – You betcha! Out with Paco Rabanne! Long live something unpronounceable by Jean Paul Gaultier or, the Frog in a Frock, as Adam used so scathingly to refer to him. Pre-Farina, naturally!
3. *Has his taste in music changed?* – Yes! Yes! Yes! His

treasured Deep Purple LPs have been relegated to 'under the stairs'. The Bee Gees, far from *stayin alive* were dead as the proverbial doornail and, if there was 'a wonderful noise coming up from the street', it wasn't on account of Neil Diamond but R Kelly's 'I Believe I Can Fly' blaring out of his Merc as he left for work. Well, Jenny thought sarcastically, if Adam believed he could fly, she wouldn't be long about clipping his wings for him.

4. *Has your man taken to using youth slang, words like 'wicked' and 'facety' and 'respect', words he would normally tell his teenage children off for using?*

Does Nixon tell porkies? Only yesterday he'd said his pizza was 'cool' and when she had offered to put it back in the oven he'd said no, what he actually meant was that it was 'bad'. Then, when she's said she would take it back to the supermarket and complain, he'd said she was 'sad'.

Wearily, Jenny switched off the TV and headed for the bathroom where her reflection, for once, stayed mercifully quiet. Fat, but quiet! It had, she noted, as she disrobed in front of the mirror, pendulous breasts. This was not a surprise, so the shock factor was not quite so great as it might have been had she been under any illusions that she was Kate Moss. It was, nonetheless, rather depressing, especially when you took into account the fact that, in some countries, pendulous breasts were actually considered to be an asset. Objects of desire. Symbols of fertility. It was a well-known fact, for instance, that in parts of Africa, the more pendulous the breasts, the more desirable the woman. Jenny had her own theory on that one. The more pendulous the breasts the more they pendulumed back and forwards, the more the men's eyes followed them, ergo the more mesmerised they became, till hey, you could tell them shit was chocolate and they'd swallow it whole!

Farina had pert breasts. Pert! That was a word they always used in novels to describe something that was young and hence, by association, good! She had pert breasts, they wrote, or a pert nose or her bottom was pert! And if they weren't referring to pert parts of her anatomy they had her saying or doing 'pert' things. As in:*"No!" she said pertly, with a pert jerk of her pert chin. "You are impertinent, Sir. How can I accept your hand, when you are already betrothed to another?" So saying, she wrinkled up her pert nose and deperted!*

There was nothing pert about Jenny, not unless the comparison was actually by way of Perth which, by all accounts, was a sizeable place.

God knows, her stomach had enough stretch marks, bumps and contours to rival any ordnance survey map whether in Australia or anywhere else but at least there was a space between her thighs now where before there had been only eczema.

"One small step for mankind . . ." Jenny's reflection gave the victory salute, "one large step for Jenny Wrenny."

"Yuch!" Jenny retorted, catching sight of the nest of hair

beneath its armpit. At least it explained where the Amazonian rainforests were disappearing to. There were probably whole tribes of primitive people indigenous to her armpit. In fact, it wouldn't surprise her if David Bellamy were to emerge any moment, scything his way through the undergrowth and going, 'Oi, say, wha 'ave we go' eeah, an 'airy Mammoth, as oi live 'n breathe!'

"Ah, well!"Jenny sighed, reaching for Adam's Gillette Sensor 'for the closest shave possible'. To paraphrase that old song of the sixties there was a 'time to be born, a time to live and a time to de-fuzz'. Snoring apart, it was no wonder her husband chose to sleep in the spare room. After all, it would take one hell of a man to try and seduce a Yeti much less be seduced by one. And that, Jenny realised in a rare moment of clarity, was exactly what *she* was going to have to do if she was to win her husband back. Physically, she had already made a start by enrolling at the gym. Mentally, she had almost, if not quite, weaned herself off chat shows. Spiritually, she sang Handel's *Messiah* when hoovering the living-room carpet. Emotionally though, she was still bereft and would be, she reasoned, until such time as she could figure out a way of seducing Adam.

Despite it being half-past three in the morning, Jenny dropped the razor like a red-hot poker and ambled off to call Mounty.

"Mounty!" she hollered excitedly, as a sleepy voice on the other end picked up the receiver. "I know what I've got to do!"

"For Christ's sake, Jenny," Mounty protested. "It's bloody three-thirty am. Can't you do whatever it is you have to do in the morning?"

Eager for feedback, Jenny was dismissive. "Three-thirty schmirty! Listen, you cranky old bat, you! I'm going to seduce Adam."

"What?" Wide awake now, Mounty shot up in the bed as Jenny, on the other end of the phone line, plucked a stray hair from her nipple, hoping in a detached part of her mind that fifty more wouldn't queue in its place.

"That's right. *9½ Weeks* stuff! Mickey O'Rourke and Kim Basinger. Ice-cubes and blindfolds. The whole shebang! So what do you say?"

"What do I say?" Mounty echoed, her sleepy eyes travelling admiringly over the naked torso of the dark-haired man sleeping beside her. "I say do your worst, kiddo! I really mean that and may the best woman win!"

"Thanks, best friend, I will!" Confidently, Jenny replaced the receiver and toddled off to do battle with her reflection once more before turning in for the night, or what was left of it. "Mirror, mirror on the wall," she grinned, "who is the fairest of them all? Speak now," she goaded, "or forever hold your peace."

The mirror, aware of its fragile status, had no problem with lying. "You are." it told her. "And, by the way, did anyone ever tell you you look a bit like the young Grace Kelly?"

Chapter Seven

"You've got to get back to the way you were when he first met you. Before you became part of a couple. Before you turned into his wife. Before you became Junior's mother. Before you submerged your own personality in him, in the house, in the baby. I mean, what was it about you that attracted him in the first place? What made him single you out from all the other women in the world and go, hey, this is the woman for me? This is my helpmeet, my soul mate! Hers is the womb in which I will plant my seed and multiply! I mean, honey, like you've got to reclaim yourself."

On *Oprah*, the 'relationship counsellor', a red-haired woman, bearing the unlikely name of Charm Skule together with a very severe facelift, stopped making inverted commas with her fingers every time she made a point, sat back and waited for the obedient sound of applause and pennies dropping.

For Jenny, furiously pedalling away on a stationary exercise bike in front of the TV, the penny dropped too.

The woman was right. If she, herself, could suddenly be transported back in time and find herself standing beside the Jenny as she was when Adam first met her, would she find anything in common with the Jenny of today? Very little, she surmised, her legs going round like pistons in an effort to encourage the fanwheel at the front of the bike to activate itself and drench her with blasts of cool, clear air. For starters, the Jenny of the 70s was half her age, a perfect 10, with a proclivity for ABBA, blue eyeshadow, and peep-toe sandals with plastic butterflies. 70s Jenny drank Pernod and blackcurrant, cried over *Love Story*, lusted after John Travolta and Donny Osmond and had a laugh like pebbles rattling around in a tin can. 70s Jenny tossed her blonde hair and, at the drop of a hat, took off to Spain with Mounty and the gang, drank cocktails on the playa, did the hokey cokey, turned all around and came back lissome and tanned to her job as a legal secretary. Actually, that was a lie. Never in her whole life had Jenny managed to get a tan which, in retrospect, given today's preponderance of melanomas amongst the general population, was probably a good thing. It hadn't seemed like that at the time though, as her complexion took its cue from the local fish restaurants, turning first prawn pink, then poached salmon, working up to a boiled lobster and culminating in red mullet, the catch of the day. In despair she had turned to 'tan without sun' tablets and instant tans that turned her such a vibrant shade of orange that her mother had rushed her to the Hospital for Tropical Diseases, convinced she had contracted some fatal foreign disease.

Of course, modern Jenny could now look back and laugh in an affectionate sort of way at her younger, more innocent self. But that was the 'self' Adam had fallen in love with. Feisty, independent, fiery but, most of all, fun. 70s Jenny! Strangely enough, now that she thought about it, the youthful Jenny, just like David, had had a social conscience too. In fact, at the tender age of thirteen, she had sneaked off to an anti-American protest march in the centre of London, bearing a placard which had taken her three nights to make and of which she was inordinately proud. Unfortunately, before ever she got there, it had become trapped between the doors of a tube train, so she ended up having to shout her slogan instead: *"Yanks scram from Vietnam! Go home, you bums, go home!"*

Jenny grinned as she remembered how she'd given it her all and how, as a reward, a hippy type, a true refugee from soap and water, had initiated her into the joys of smoking dope, on the steps of the National Gallery. That was when she had seen her first Lowry, though not in the gallery itself. It was just that after a few drags, the people walking in Trafalgar Square metamorphosed before her very eyes into the matchstick men and matchstick cats and dogs subjects of his paintings. Hours later she was still seeing them: matchstalk men playing hide-and-seek in her mashed potato, matchstick cats walking upside down on the ceiling, clog-wearing matchstick spiders crawling all over her bed. That had been the unwitting Jenny's first and last foray into the seedy world of drug-taking.

Still pedalling furiously, Jenny picked up the towel lying across the handlebars and mopped the perspiration from her brow. The American woman was talking again. She did make a lot of sense, it had to be said, even if that Kelly green satin outfit she was wearing made her look like a reject from a St Patrick's Day parade.

"Have you lost your spirit, hon?" Once more she resorted to digital punctuation. *"Have you lost your essence?"* The victim on the end of this inquisition looked like she had lost consciousness never mind anything else but Jenny, at least, was enthralled. *"You see you've got to reach down inside yourself. You've got to find you again. You've gotta get back to the you you were before ever you looked into his eyes and said 'I do'."* Intimately she leaned forward, patted the coma victim on the knee. *"Do you think you can do that, hon? Do you think you can reclaim yourself? Your soul? Your spirit? Your essence? You!"*

"Aaamen!" This from *Oprah*, the word being picked up like a ball and bounced along the sound waves of the audience.

"Amen!"

"Hallelujah!"

"Thank you, Jesus!"

68

At the very back someone got carried away and started speaking in tongues.

"Because, if you can," the counsellor nodded beatifically, appearing to have been suddenly elevated to the position of preacher-woman, *"I promise you, hon, you will get your man back. You will wrest him from the arms of the temptress. You will make him forego the apple in the Garden of Eden. And why? Because you, hon, will be the apple in his eye. The butt in his bed! The pip in his zip!"*

"Amen!" said Jenny as the closing credits rolled across the screen making a conscious decision to reclaim herself. "Amen! Glory be!"

"Oh, come on, Jenny! You know chat shows are off the menu!" Mounty protested when excitedly Jenny tried to tell her about the counsellor on *Oprah*.

Holding up her hands in surrender, Jenny nodded. "I know, I know. Still it's not that easy, going cold turkey. Besides, I worked out a system of payment. For every chat show I watch, I have to exercise all through it. For example if I watch *Oprah*, I do thirty minutes on the bike. If it's *Springer*, then it's down on the floor, stretches and crunches. *Jenny Jones* is weights-with-two-baked-beans-cans time and so on and so forth. And look!" Demonstratively Jenny tugged at the waist of her tracksuit. "It's really working. Soon I'm going to have to trade in the PPE for something smaller and, before you know it, one day I'll be going, going, going for a thong!"

Mounty sighed. "Well, I suppose if you must you

must and admittedly you have lost weight. Still I'm not sure that all this American psychobabble does anyone any good. I mean, do we really need advice from a country where the President can be impeached for improper use of a cigar? After all he was only Havana good time!"

Jenny giggled. "Oh well. Some you Lewinsky, some you lose! But seriously, Mounty, this woman made perfect sense. I mean, when Adam first met me, I was bright-eyed and bushy-tailed. I used to make him laugh . . ."

"And now," her friend interrupted callously, "you're bleary-eyed and bushy-haired and you make *me* laugh!"

"Oh, be serious, Mounty!" Jenny aimed a swipe across the table, almost upsetting a cup of coffee. "I mean, somewhere along the line I've lost my essence. Do you know what I mean?"

The other woman shook her head. "Nope, but maybe the waitress does. Excuse me." She beckoned over a passing waitress. "My friend's lost her essence. Did anyone hand it in?"

Blushing, Jenny waved the puzzled woman away. "It's not funny, you know. I knew who I was back then. I was Jenny the Raver, Jenny the Secure, Jennifer Juniper!" Miserably she stirred her coffee, black, no sugar, hold the calories. "Now I'm just Jenny the Raving, Jenny the Obscure and Jennifer Whoniper! Is it any wonder Adam's taken to tailing tottie!"

Unimpressed, Mounty took a dainty bite of fat-free muffin. Well, 98% fat-free anyway which is as good as it gets. "Oh, stop wallowing, Jenny. Besides, it's still just speculation on your part. When all's said and done, the poor man could be white as the driven snow. If he *is* pointing Percy, it's probably only at the porcelain. After all, a man's gotta do what a man's gotta do."

"No way, I'm not buying that! I've filled in enough 'Is your man a dirty, stinking, lying, cheating son of a bitch?' quizzes to know that he's playing away from home." Glaring absent-mindedly, Jenny caught the eye of a passer-by, who had stopped outside to read the menu, causing him to quickly rethink his options and take his hunger elsewhere "What I don't know is, who with? Mounty?" Jenny broke off as her companion suddenly turned a virulent purple and took to shooting crumbs across the table with the velocity of a Tommie gun. "Mounty, are you all right?"

Dabbing at her streaming eyes with a serviette, the other woman rose hurriedly from the table. "Jusht shwalloed shometing the wrong way. Musht jusht get some air."

"Okay. Right, you go ahead. I'll get the bill!" Jenny nodded, valiantly resisting the urge to thump her between the shoulder blades.

"Is your friend all right?" Swiping Jenny's Visa through the credit-check machine, the waitress followed Mounty's exit with a concerned eye. "Such a lovely lady. Comes in here regular with her man-friend, she does. Fine thing he is too. Tall, dark and handsome." Jerking her shoulder towards the kitchen behind her, she winked hugely. "As I said to Marilyn, back there – a man like that can warm his calluses on my corns, any time!"

Jenny grinned, signed the chit, emptied her spare change into the saucer by the till bearing the cheeky message, 'To earn is human. To tip is divine!' and hurried after Mounty.

"T42," she sang when she caught up with her, "and Two for Tea, me and you and you and he . . ."

Mounty raised a puzzled eyebrow as Jenny leered wickedly, tapping her nose like an East End barrow boy.

"What on earth are you going on about now?"

Casually Jenny linked her arm. "Oh, I know all about you, Diana Mountford. You and your fancy man! Tea and crumpets in T42." She licked her lips. "'Tall, dark and handsome', the waitress said. Mmm, sounds just my type. So when do I get to meet him? Mounty? Mounty? Are you all right, Mounty?"

Mounty, once more the archetypal damson in distress, choked, gasped, clutched at a passing litter bin and draped herself across it. "Jusht something stuck in my throat. Be all right in a minute."

Jenny whistled teasingly. "God! If just mentioning the man has you gasping and panting and molesting litter bins, what on earth must you be like over hot, buttered crumpets? I'll tell you what though," she laughed giving in to the urge and thumping her friend hollowly on the back, "when you've finished, can I have him? That is, if there's anything left."

Chapter Eight

"Now, now girls!" The yoga instructor clapped her hands. "I said we'll try a half-lotus, not a half-nelson. Lady in the purple tracksuit, please take special note!"

"Bet you're sorry you came now." The woman to Jenny's left shot her a sympathetic look whilst trying to align the heel of her foot with the bridge of her nose. "That Cynthia Shawe-Legg can be a right snotty cow."

"Tell me about it!" Jenny puffed, wondering how on earth anyone could have the gall to call yoga relaxing. "Besides, I'm only here to reclaim myself and rediscover my essence."

"Inner Child!" the woman offered, then seeing the other's puzzled frown, "I'm here to discover mine. That little girl who was short-changed all those years ago! That little girl whose tears I suppressed. Well, I'm here to find her, to give her validation. She's going to *walk, walk in the light!*" The woman turned an earnest, sweaty face towards Jenny. "Confronting your emotional baggage, that's what it's all about! Until you do, it gets in the way of present relationships. That's why my husband took off with that Sasha bitch!"

Sasha! Why was it the 'other woman' was never called Irene or Anne or Joan, ordinary names? Had their mothers got some sort of in-built maternal antennae that warned them that one day their Pamper-wrapped bundle was going to turn into a *femme fatale* who would make a career out of stealing other women's husbands and thus, they'd better give them fitting mistress-type names? Sasha! Chloe! Minette! Farina! Exotic mistresses! Neurotic wives!

At the top of the room, Cynthia Straw-Legs, as Jenny called her, was demonstrating 'the snake'. "I want you to lie flat on the floor, girls. Not on your back, Purple! On your stomach. That's right, flat as you can. Make like your belly-buttons are nailed to the floor and slither. Good and again. Slither. Now you're getting the hang of it. Nice big sliding movements. So good for the pelvic bone!"

"I bet she's a mistress," Jenny hissed as her classmate slithered past in search of her Inner Child. "Stands to reason with a name like Cynthiaaah!"

The woman shook her head. "Nah. She's a lezzer. A bull-dyke!"

"You're joking!" Jenny's chin hit the floor.

"Gospel truth! Hard to tell these days, isn't it?"

Jenny giggled. "You said it! I'd never have guessed in a million years. I mean she's got a ribcage, lycra and big hair, all the raw material of a mistress."

The woman sniffed, giving a half-hearted slide as she caught Cynthia's eye on her. "You too, eh?"

Jenny flushed. "What do you mean?"

"Husband run off with a bimbo?" She waved a dismissive hand, quickly tacking it down by her side as the instructor shot her a venomous look. "Oh, it's nothing to be ashamed of. Practically all the women here tonight are in the same boat; all of us looking for our Inner Child, lost essences, fragile self-esteem, seeking some form of enlightenment and fulfilment that we fondly hope will have hubby racing back to us and divesting himself of his Y-fronts before he's even halfway up the garden path. All except that woman over there! She's looking for a lost contact lens!"

"God, are we that transparent?" Jenny groaned.

The woman laughed. "No. It's just that we watch too much *Oprah!* And worse still, we believe her!"

"Right!" The yoga instructor uncoiled her long body and once more clapped her hands for attention. "Enough of the serpent! Let's glory now in a Tree of Life. Purple! Raise your right foot, please! Not like that! Higher! Now, position it on the inside of the left thigh."

"I bet that's what she said last night!" Jenny's companion winked suggestively.

Jenny sniggered, managing to stay upright for only a moment before her Tree of Life slowly toppled in an undignified heap to the floor.

"Ouch," she groaned, "I think I broke a branch!"

"Timbers away," chuckled her companion following

suit, then freezing as the slinky fit-as-a-butcher's-dog body of Cynthia Straw-Legs loomed over them both, arm raised, index finger pointing like the angel with the flaming sword evicting Adam and Eve from the Garden of Eden.

"Ladies, ladies, ladies! I'm not at all sure you have the desired qualities we look for in all our yoga devotees. Under the circumstances, Purple, you might think about pursuing another route to self-fulfillment. Likewise, your companion!"

Giving her tracksuit bottoms a superficial brush down, the other woman rose slowly, deliberately to her feet, showing solidarity with Jenny in the linking of her arm.

"Huh! We were just going anyway. But tell me, love, before we go. Is that your real face or did the wind change suddenly?"

"Ooh, you are awful," Jenny stuttered as, laughing like drains, the pair of them practically fell out onto the pavement. "But I like it!"

* * *

"Why *haven't* I confronted Adam?" Jenny's voice rose. "*Why* haven't I confronted Adam?"

"Yes?" encouraged her mother, who had dropped in unexpectedly, just as Jenny, freshly showered after her abortive yoga session emerged from the bathroom, her cosy old, candlewick dressinggown wrapped protectively around her. "Why haven't you?"

Jenny shrugged, pouring a large measure of whisky into two tumblers, one of which she slid across the coffee table towards her mother. "I don't know. Maybe you could tell me, seeing as how you seem to think you know everything."

"Not everything." Gloria remained calm in the face of her daughter's childish outburst. "But I have been on this earth a lot longer than you, so longevity alone qualifies me to know more than you, at least on certain subjects."

"But not on this one!" Mutinously tossing back her drink, Jenny reached for the decanter and poured herself a second measure.

"You're scared," her mother accused. "That's why you're intent on playing the ostrich! You think if you confront him, it'll bring matters to a crux, that he'll leave you and it'll be red sails in the sunset with this other woman. By turning a blind eye you're fooling yourself into believing that half a loaf is better than no bread at all."

"Well, isn't it?" Jenny flushed angrily. "If you were starving, wouldn't you think half a loaf was better than nothing?"

Her mother nodded grimly. "Maybe so. But we're not talking bread, Jenny. We're talking your *husband*. You know, the man who promised to love and cherish you, for richer or poorer, in sickness and in health, till death you do part, amen!"

"Do you think I don't know that? But I just can't take

the risk of him leaving me. And not just me, David too!"

Casually, her mother crossed one suede-covered leg over the other. The look today was Billy the Kid. There were fringes down both sides of her trousers and her boots, knee-high, could best be described as palamino. All that was missing was the horse, although she *had* left Rover outside, tethered to the garden fence. "But what if he doesn't leave you? What if all this infidelity is only in your mind? What if you're making yourself as miserable as sin over nothing?"

"No!" Jenny was adamant. "He's changed, Mother. Nowadays it's all designer stubble, baseball caps turned backwards, for God's sake, and he's even taken to saying 'yo'!"

"Yo?"

"That's right. As in. Yo, there David, gimme five!"

"Sounds like he's turning into a middle-age cliché. You know, male menopause and all that. Falling testosterone levels. Failing hair follicles."

Miserably Jenny twined her wedding ring round and round her finger. "I don't think so, although that might go some way towards explaining his behaviour if it were the case. But no, I'm a big girl now and the facts speak for themselves. Adam, bless his cotton socks, is playing footsie with some floozie, in some posh hotel's jacuzzi! And that's that!"

"And you're just going to stay shtum, washing his boxers, and skivvying after him. For what? In the hopes that one day the scales will miraculously fall from

Prince Charming's eyes and he'll suddenly realise his Cinderella has been there all along, hidden beneath a pile of dirty laundry and a mountain of pots and pans?"

"Now you're being facetious!" Jumping up from the settee, Jenny strode over to the window, through which Rover could be seen attempting to cock a leg against the fence-post, much to the amusement of the neighbourhood children. "I *am* going to stay shtum, though, at least for the moment. I'm not going to issue any ultimatums that might drive him into taking hasty actions we might both regret. Me, most of all!" Lifting her chin, she turned back to face her mother. "I'm going to win him back, Mother. I'm going to make him see that the Jenny he fell in love with and the Jenny of today are one and the same person. I'm going to slim down, shape up, broaden my mind and my interests and make him see me again. Not just as the woman he lives with, but as the woman he lives for!"

"Nice speech, Jenny." Her mother too, rose to her feet. "There's only one thing wrong with it as far as I can see."

"Which is?"

"You seem to be prepared to do all the changing. What about Adam? If you're right and he really is cheating, doesn't he need to change too?"

Jenny shook her head. "No! It's all my fault. You yourself said that I was busy turning myself into a fat, insignificant clone of everybody else. I've been giving matters a lot of thought and Mounty is right, I got complacent. My package is way out of date! My can is dented. I'm in the bargain bin, half-price with a torn label! I fell into the trap a lot of girls do when they get married. I got lazy. I thought I didn't have to try any more, that Adam would love me, come rain or come shine." Earnestly Jenny paused, hand raised to unlatch the door for her mother. "And it's not just that I let my figure go forth and multiply, spreading itself into the four quarters of the earth, it's that I stopped setting challenges for myself as well. I forgot that the brain needs exercise too. Use it or lose it. Isn't that what they say? No, it's my fault if Adam grew bored with me. I'm just not in his league any more."

"Oh, throw yourself on his funeral pyre, why don't you?" Gloria's voice was dry. "Listen, Jenny, I agree that you need to take yourself in hand, but for *your* sake. But let's have less of the *mea culpa* and woe is me breast-beating. To be boring about it, two wrongs don't make a right."

"I know that, and I hate what he's doing but I love him, Mother, and I want him back." Stepping back, in order to allow her mother past, Jenny set her lips. "Correction! I'll get him back!"

"Down, boy!" The older woman remonstrated mildly as Rover, who had taken to whimpering and scraping pitifully at the door, threw himself, upon her appearance, into a mad frenzy of delight, chasing a non-existent tail round and round and uttering excited little yelps. Untethering his leash from the fence, she turned once more to face her daughter. "You know, Jenny, there's a lot of truth in the old saying 'Be careful what you wish for or you might just get it'! Maybe it's something you should think about."

Jenny shook her head. "I don't need to think about it but, while we're on the subject, maybe you should think about doing us all a favour and having Rover neutered or castrated or whatever it is they do to male dogs."

"What?" Her mother feigned shock. "It certainly wouldn't be doing me a favour but you know you might just have put your finger on something, though not literally. I mean, maybe you should give some consideration to having Adam's bits bobbed. Remember you can't play the lottery without a full set of balls!"

"It's a thought!" Jenny admitted, watching through slitted eyes as the black Merc, Adam at the wheel, hove into view. "Watch this space."

Chapter Nine

"Jenny, have you seen my white shirt anywhere?" Exasperated, Adam rummaged deeper and deeper in a basket of unironed laundry, spewing garments left, right and centre in search of the missing article.

"The Van Heusen. The one with the pleated front and the double cuffs?"

Adam nodded, surfacing for air. "Yes. Where is it?"

Jenny jerked her chin. "It's in the basket."

"It's *not* in the basket." Deliberately, Adam enunciated each word, slowly, clearly as though he were talking to an imbecile or an alien who couldn't be expected to be up to speed on the English language.

"It *is* in the basket!" Irritatingly, Jenny widened her eyes, drawing out the words. "Only it's pink now!"

"Pink!"

Jenny nodded."Yes, you know. Pink, pink to make the boys wink!"

Adam groaned, melodramatically clapping his

hands over his eyes. "But I was going to wear it tonight!"

"You still can, only now, instead of white, it'll be pink!" Jenny grinned. "Just think how nice it'll be, to be – in the pink!"

"It's not funny. You know tonight's a big night for me."

Jenny shook her head. "No, Adam. Actually, I really know very little about you these days. How would I when I rarely see you? And when I do see you it's 'What's for dinner?' and 'Where's my shirt?' Anyone would think I was your mother, instead of your wife!"

Having located his newly dyed shirt, Adam bestowed upon it a brief glance of despair, before tossing it back on the pile. "*You* rarely see *me?* What about you! If you're not gallivanting off to the gym these days, you're tying yourself up in knots at yoga and, as if all that wasn't enough, you've only gone and enrolled for IT classes. God knows what David must think! Talk about a latchkey kid!"

"Well, if that isn't the pot calling the kettle black-arse!" Angrily, Jenny turned away from the cooker where she'd been adding a tin of kidney beans to the chilli con carne, Adam's favourite, bubbling away on the cooker. Not that he was going to be there to eat it! *Seemingly* he had more important fish to fry elsewhere. "I thought you would have been pleased that I was getting out more. Sampling life on the outside, as it were. I know David certainly is and as for your latchkey allegations, stick them on your needles and knit them!

My having a life of my own can only improve David's. Of what benefit is it to him to have a mother who's only half-alive?" Furiously she tapped the bottom of the tin with a dessertspoon, releasing the last few beans clinging stickily to the bottom. "No, Adam! Don't make David an excuse for your ulterior motives. It might suit you to have me going around like a zombie, but leave David out of it."

Sulkily, her husband began picking up odd garments he had dropped on the floor, tossing them in a careless heap back into the basket. "I don't know what's got into you these days."

Jenny could have told him what had got into her. It would have been so easy. All she had to do was open her mouth and let her tongue run away with her.

"Yo!" she could have said. "Don't play me for a fool, Ad baby! I know all about your bit of skirt. Do you think I don't read *Cosmo*? Do you think I haven't twigged all your little euphemisms for nookie as in 'doing overtime', on a 'rush job" (ha, ha), 'installing a new system' (goes in as a hard disk, comes out floppy), and the one that really makes me laugh, albeit cynically, 'something urgent's come up'." She knew well what had come up. She also knew that only when it went down would he bother coming home, if at all.

"Nothing's gotten into me," she said mildly, determined, as she'd told her mother, to stay shtum. "Why don't you wear your Pierre Cardin? It's hanging up in your wardrobe."

Ungraciously, Adam headed for the stairs. "I suppose I'll have to. By the way, don't wait up. It looks as though it might be a long evening."

"So what's new!" Jenny hissed sarcastically, as his footsteps sounded on the landing above. "Tell me something I don't already know!"

It wasn't fair, she thought, half an hour later peeking from behind the living-room curtains, as Adam, black-tied and resplendent in Pierre Cardin, gave his teeth a perfunctory inspection in the rear-view mirror and, satisfied that no green vegetation was stuck between them, roared off up the drive. Begowned by Versace, becoiffed by Nicky Clarke, bewaving like the Queen, *she*, Jenny, should be sitting there beside him, her feminine fragility the perfect foil to his dark masculinity. Instead, like an abandoned dog at Battersea, she was left with her nose pressed up against the window, all soulful-eyed whilst her beloved master took off with some other bitch, leaving her bone alone.

Ha! She could just see the pair of them arriving at the do and Buffy Mansfield, the MD, trotting out to bury his nose in the fair Farina's cleavage, his hand with the chipolata fingers reaching round to pinch her buttocks. Her pert buttocks!

"What ho, Adam old chap!" he'd bluster, his usual disjointed sentences falling over themselves in their haste to get past his dentures. "Somewhat of a dark horse eh? Where've you been stabling her then, this little filly of yours? Sweet little goer on the rough I'd say. Pleasure to break her in? And the old mare? Out to pasture, what? Proper order! Proper order!"

Just who did he think he was calling a mare, the old bastard? *She* wasn't fit for the knacker's yard yet. Not by a long chalk! Disgruntled, Jenny turned away from the window to see to the chilli, which had taken to hissing and spitting and lobbing kidney beans at the wall in an effort to attract her attention. He could cup Farina's buttocks, and impale his nose on the underwiring of her Wonderbra till the cows came home, for all the good it would do. According to his wife the last erection Buffy had seen was the Eiffel Tower in Paris and the sight had given him such an inferiority complex that nowadays about the only thing he could erect was a sad smile of remembrance.

"Can I have some of that chilli, Mum?" Startled out of her contemplations, Jenny reduced the heat beneath the saucepan and turned to where David, half in, half out of his jacket had come in the door.

"I thought you were a vegetarian?"

David shrugged, finally pulling himself free and tossing the jacket in a careless heap over the back of a kitchen chair. "I was until I learned about animal husbandry."

"I see," Jenny said, the tone of her voice making it perfectly clear that she saw nothing of the sort.

Going to the fridge, David poked around inside of it, extracted a can of coke and pulling the ring out, flopped on to the nearest chair. "You see, Mum," he explained kindly, "people farm animals, yes?"

Jenny nodded. She could follow that much, without *too* much trouble anyway.

"But *why* do people farm animals?"

Jenny hazarded a guess. "To eat?"

One-handed, David applauded against the kitchen table. "Exactly! Someone give that woman a medal."

"I'm sorry, David. That still doesn't explain why this morning you were vegetarian and this evening you're not. I mean, for heaven's sake, only at breakfast you were reading the cornflake box to ensure no animals were hurt, killed or maimed in the production. I mean, give me a clue here. Help me out. What's turned the herbivore into a pelt-clad, carnivorous, caveman high on the scent of newly killed blood?"

"Omnivorous," her son corrected her. "From now on, I'm a vegetarian meat-eater. And it's all down to animal husbandry, as I've said earlier. You see, Mum, if everybody decided not to eat meat, there would be no need to farm animals and the likelihood is that, with nobody interested in breeding and feeding them, eventually they would die out altogether like the dodo bird and the sabretoothed tiger and T-Rex."

"T-Rex? Wasn't he a pop singer?" Jenny asked. "Didn't he sing *Ride a White Swan* and meet a sticky end in a purple mini?"

David groaned, theatrically banging his head back and forth against the table. "Tyrannosauras rex, Mum. The dinosaur, you know?"

"No, I don't know, David. Contrary to what you

might think, the dinosaurs had died out long before I made my appearance on this earth. Now hang up your jacket and go lay the table, there's a good boy!"

"Mothers!" David snorted, grabbing up his unfortunate jacket and skewering it on the coat-stand in the corridor. "You can't live with them and you can't live without them."

"Sons!" his mother called after him. "The greatest misnomer of all!"

"You can talk!" David snorted, going over to the fashionably distressed Welsh dresser and taking down a couple of fake willow pattern dinner plates. "What about women? Break it up and what do you get. Wo men! As in, women bring woe to men!"

"Do you know, I think it's probably a very good thing you're no longer vegetarian." Carefully Jenny ladled a large dollop of chilli con carne onto his plate. 'Considering you're turning into a right little male chauvinist pig!"

"But you love me anyway," David chuckled, attacking his dinner with gusto. "Which is why you're going to give me a big piece of tart for dessert."

Jenny shook her head. "I would, only I don't think there's any left. You know how partial your father is to a nice bit of tart."

"Talking of Dad, are you two getting divorced, Mum?"

Startled, Jenny dropped her spoon on the floor, sending bits of minced meat flying every which way like jumping fleas in a circus. "Whatever makes you ask that?"

David shrugged. "It's just that you're never together any more."

"What do you mean? We're always together," Jenny blustered.

"No, you're not." David shook his head, calmly continuing to masticate his food. "Dad's always working late and you're always down at the flab-lab or out at psychic fairs or something. You never *do* anything together. Except row!"

Oh God! Jenny could feel the food turning to sawdust in her mouth. Where was Oprah now when she needed her? What was she supposed to say that wouldn't give him some terrible personality defect or complex or whatever in years to come? What could she say that, several years down the line, wouldn't have him carving up people willy-nilly and all because his mother did his head in at an impressionable age! Manson blamed his mother, didn't he, *and* the Boston Strangler? Elbow deep in female intestines, Jack the Ripper probably blamed his too, if the truth be known. Frantically, Jenny racked her brains, hoping against hope that David wouldn't notice the panic in her eyes that had them standing out on stalks like a Looney Tunes cartoon character. She knew all the trite, pat phrases by heart, of course. She had even rehearsed them in anticipation of this moment rearing its ugly head, never for a second believing that it actually would.

"This is not about you, darling. Mummy and Daddy just can't live with each other any more. It's nothing you've done. We both love you still."

But somehow, now that the moment *had*, in fact, arrived, they just didn't sound right.

"I don't know, David," she said putting her cards on the table despite her best intentions but not wanting to insult him by skirting round the issue. "I don't want a divorce. I love your father but he just doesn't seem to see me any more. He's moved on in life, left me behind."

"You think he's got someone else, don't you? That's why you talk to yourself in the mirror. That's why you're trying to turn yourself into Pamela Anderson, isn't it? You think if you can wear tight jeans and do clever things like surf the Net, that he'll love you again – that he'll think you're a big cheese."

Miserably, Jenny pushed away her plate of half-eaten food. "Is it such a bad thing to want to be a big cheese?"

Slowly David, laid down his fork, his finger stealing up to flick a bit of mince from between his teeth. "You're daft, Mum. Dad loves you. He's always looking at you when he thinks you're not watching."

"Is he?" Jenny felt a glimmer of hope as she gazed into the earnest eyes of her twelve-year-old son. "Really?" David nodded, squinting his eyes and putting his head on one side.

"Yeah, like this!"

"Oh!" Jenny felt the small hope flutter and die. She knew that look. It was Adam's considering look, the one he wore when he couldn't figure something out, usually a problem that had him stumped. He wore it when doing complicated crosswords in *The Times* and when filling in his end-of-year tax returns. So now she knew exactly what Adam thought of her. She was a problem, one for which he didn't yet have the solution. But when he found it, like yesterday's cryptic clue, Jenny knew she was history! "I'll tell you what." Valiantly she pinned a bright smile on her face for David's benefit. "I think there's some Ben & Jerry's in the freezer. You fetch the ice cream. I'll fetch the spoons and I just might, just might mind you, let you stay up to watch *Night of the Raving Dead Zombie Killers.*"

"Safe!" David yelled excitedly. "I love you, Mum. You're the best mother in the whole wide world."

"Am I, son?" Jenny smiled at the accolade, her eyes bright with unshed tears. She could remember a time when, according to Adam, she was also the 'best wife in the world' as well as the 'best lover'. Still one out of three wasn't bad although to quote from the words of an up-till-now, long-forgotten teacher, scrawled across her report card. "Jenny is not stupid but she *could try harder!*"

"That teacher was right!" she told her reflection in the stainless-steel sink, sloshing Fairy round the greasy plates. "I'm not stupid! I'm going to try real hard. I swear I am. You'll see! The change in me is going to be so miraculous I'll make the Virgin Mary look like a slapper by comparison."

"Yeah, yeah, yeah," the reflection gurgled, wearing its I've-heard-it-all-before-and-don't-believe-a-blind-word-of-it look beneath the sudsy water, "blow it out your ass, Momma!"

Chapter Ten

"Don't look at me like I'm an erosion on your cervix," Jenny thought as the recruitment consultant leaned back behind her look-at-how-important-I-am, kidney-shaped desk and, not so much smiled at, as sneered at her.

"So what exactly did you have in mind Mrs – eh . . . um . . .?"

"Treigh. Pronounced 'Tree!" Jenny supplied, wanting to shout that it was emblazoned all over the CV upon which the other was beating an insulting piss-off-and-stop-wasting-my-precious-time-you-peri-menopausal-calcium-deprived-candidate-for-a-dowager's-hump tattoo with her long, acrylic talons.

"Ah yes . . . Mrs Treigh!" Delicately arched eyebrows climbed a fraction, encouraging her, Jenny supposed, to spill her guts all over the Aubusson autumnal-coloured carpet.

"I thought MD would be nice," Jenny quipped.

"Failing that, something in the Stock Exchange, futures broker maybe. offshore oil magnate? Something power-suited, anyway. Girl about townish. Kick-ass heels by Dolce & Gabbana. Leather briefcase by Gucci. Watch by Philippe Patek, lapis-lazuli face with diamond hour pips. Ah, heck I don't know. You tell me!" What she really wanted to say was, "Laugh! Go on, I dare you. Just for the heck of it. Just to see if your 'face by Elizabeth Arden' really is crack-proof as well as smudgeproof, waterproof and proof that behind your 'near-as-nude- foundation' lurks a heart as sunny and gay as Elton John's underwear drawer."

Cautiously, as though it were one of those 'mission-impossible' tape-recorder type things that would self-destruct in thirty seconds or less, the human waxwork slid the CV back across the desk.

"I'm not sure that we can help, Mrs Treigh." *Your mission, should you wish to accept it, is to shove this CV as far as possible up the further reaches of your nethermost regions and never to darken this door again.* "I'm afraid Richard Branson filled our last entrepreneurial type position only this morning, although I'm sure Sainsbury's would welcome you with open arms. They're crying out for shelf-stackers at the moment and, who knows, a woman of your calibre might even make check-out girl in a year or two." Coolly delivering her barb through lips as pursed as a chicken's anus, Rosalind Peabody, for such was the cow's name according to the neat stack of business cards piled up on one side of the desk, sent deliberately bored-to-tears eyes over Jenny's shoulder to where the next candidate awaited, a more promising-looking specimen altogether, not a day over twenty-five and possessed of a professional, brown, Pantene-girl bob.

Angrily Jenny jumped to her feet and, hands gripping either side of the desk, leaned menacingly over where closer inspection revealed that the 'face by Elizabeth Arden,' whatever else it was, was definitely not shockproof.

"Now look here, Miss Vinegar Tits, *I* have my finger on the pulse." Her breath was hot, garlic-scented, a vampire's nightmare. "I am a woman of the nineties, a child of technology. Okay, so I may be . . . er . . . um . . . over thirty and have borne a child but I can assure you I didn't lose my IQ along with the afterbirth. My brain, I'll have you know, is *virgo intacto*."

"What? Never been used?"

Jenny narrowed her eyes. The sarcastic bitch recovered quickly. She had to give her that. Leaning further across, Jenny treated her to the full panoramic tour of her mercury fillings.

"No! Oh pan-sticked one! My cerebral hymen has been breached since long before you were an escapee from your father's condom. I was simply employing a metaphor. You know, an allegory?"

"I have an allegory to peanuts." The brown-bob, who up till now had been quietly chewing on the corner of her Moroccan, leather-bound CV, couldn't help interjecting, thus destroying the recruitment consultant's optimism with one fell swoop. "The merest hint of a peanut in the room and I'm history!" In an atmosphere of frosty unity the other two women studiously ignored her, intent as they were upon cutting each other down to size.

"I'm sorry, Mrs Treigh." The RC, the least contrite of any woman Jenny had ever known, shook her French-pleated, blonde head. "You can't blame me if society is ageist. What can I tell you? Employers today don't want women whose breasts have put Newton's theory of gravity through its paces over and over and over again. What they want is pert, alert, forward-thinking, upwardly mobile Barbie dolls and open-plan offices designated as HRT-free zones!"

Pert! There it was, that word again! The Farina factor. Rosalind Fresian-face had it in spades. So did the brown-bob with the life-threatening allegory. Everything about them spelt pert. Jenny could just imagine Michael the Archangel, or whoever was in charge of making up the prenatal blueprint for the Farinas of this world, doing a three witches of Macbeth on it, slaving over a hot cauldron and lobbing in big handfuls of characteristics like they were going out of fashion:

"A pinch of pertness to get on other women's wicks. No, better make it a handful. Pert breasts, better make that a couple of handfuls. Here, Gabriel, give's a hand with that sex appeal. Better make that a bushel and, to finish, a shit-load of adulterous tendencies just to put the cat amongst the pigeons."

Brushing all thoughts of malicious archangels aside, Jenny resumed her attack.

"You're talking through your sphincter muscle! Age and experience must count for something. Otherwise it would be swastika rule all over again."

Eva Braun across the desk looked like she thought this idea might have a certain appeal about it. "I'm really very sorry, Mrs Treigh, but there's nothing I can do for you. Have you ever considered voluntary work. Oxfam? Age Concern?"

Jenny gritted her teeth. "I suppose that's your idea of wit, is it? A cast-off working with cast-offs and not even getting paid buttons?"

The neo-Nazi tittered. "What about alternative comedy, then? Jo Brand, eat your heart out! You've certainly got the . . . er . . . personality for it! And the hair!"

"Aw, sod off!" Jenny swore, losing interest suddenly, grabbing up the despised CV and heading for the door. Briefly she stopped off at the brown bob. "I shouldn't bother sticking round here, if I were you. Not if you're as allergic to nuts as you say you are!"

"Oh, I am!" Uncomprehendingly, the un-bright Pantene-girl widened her eyes. "I carry a hypodermic with me at all times."

"Really! Well, if you're short of somewhere to stick it, I have a good suggestion." Behind her, the recruitment consultant examined her reflection in the glow of her computer terminal, her lips registering a cupid's bow of satisfaction at what she found there.

"Remember, Mrs Treigh," she said sweetly, "there's always Sainsburys!"

* * *

"I swear I'm really depressed. I mean I never thought finding work would be this hard. Don't get me wrong. I didn't just expect to breeze into a job but there must be something radically wrong with me when I can't even get past the agency stage." Thoroughly disheartened, Jenny scrutinised the bottom of her glass beneath its sediment of red wine.

Signalling to the young waiter for a fresh bottle and ignoring the look on his face that said more clearly than any words that he wished he could pour it into the cups of her Wonderbra and mop it all up with his tongue, Mounty patted her friend on the hand in a 'there, there' kind of fashion.

"There's nothing wrong with you. These things just take time, that's all."

"Time is what I haven't got. Adam is slipping away from me, even as we speak. Every moment brings him one step closer to the tantalising tentacles of the fair Farina and one step further away from me. Unless I can turn myself into a go-getting, vamp-cum-tramp-cum-executive ass-kicking career woman in record time, Adam's the petitioner in divorce proceedings, and David's just another kid from a broken home."

Mounty sighed, relieved the waiter of the bottle, and refilled both glasses. "Look, Jenny, I know this isn't what you want to hear but sometimes things happen for the best. It might not always seem like that at the time, but ultimately they can work out far better than you would have believed possible. Sometimes, in order for a tree to continue to grow and thrive, you have to lop off the dead wood. If you don't, the rotten bits can drain the life from the good bits and the whole lot can become diseased, with no good coming of it for anyone. It's kind of like taking one step back to go two forwards."

A querulous note entered Jenny's voice. "What the bloody hell are you on about, Mounty? Have you been at the garden manuals again? Been sniffing the old slug repellent, have you? Here am I giving you the lowdown on my broken heart and what do I get, a flaming workshop on Dutch elm disease!"

"Don't be childish!" Mounty sent a quelling eye to where the waiter had begun to do something suspect with his hands beneath counter level. "All I'm saying is that sometimes what seems to be a disaster of epic proportions can turn out to be a blessing in disguise."

"So Adam's two-timing with some two-titted titbit is a blessing in disguise, is it?"

"You know very well that's not what I'm saying." Crossly Mounty confronted her friend. "But you do have to take some responsibility too, you know. It takes two to make a marriage . . ."

"And only one to break it," Jenny interrupted. "Look, you've already had your kicks on Route 66,

Mounty. We've been through the entire bit about me being past my sell-by date and being chat-show fixated, and I've done something about that. Hell, Denzil, his fat-monitor and I have become bosom buddies down at the flab-lab. Look beneath the surface and my pecs are flexed. My adductors structured. I've abandoned the comfort of my Sloggies for the torture of a catapult masquerading as knickers. I can do a Kate Bush on it now on the treadmill as in 'running up that hill'. Plus it's been weeks since I OD'd on *Springer*. In the words of British Rail, I'm getting there. Don't you think Adam should get up off his tracks and come halfway to meet me?"

Mounty shrugged. "Maybe."

"Oh, maybe! Only maybe! Well, thanks for your support. Don't bother voting for me in the next election, will you?"

"Life isn't always so simplistic, Jenny. One and one doesn't always equal two. Sometimes it just equals two ones."

"Is that cryptic shit supposed to mean something?" Growing more angry by the minute, Jenny dipped a finger in her wine glass, unhygienically stirring it around and around in a fashion that had the waiter hovering worriedly nearby, armed with a J-cloth.

Mounty nodded. "Yes. Yes, it does mean something. It means that a couple, although together, can be separate and apart. Two individuals as opposed to two *together*."

"So what are you trying to say exactly: that Adam and I are finished and I should just get over it – that the roof over our heads is all we share?"

"Well, aren't you? Isn't it?" Maddeningly Mounty adopted what Jenny always referred to as her 'set' face, where her chin came up and not a muscle moved. It was a stance she invariably adopted when nothing could convince her that she was wrong. Jenny had to try though.

"We have David in common, don't forget, and a long catalogue of shared history. I knew him in the days of acne and premature ejaculation – those hazy, lazy days of Deep Purple, kipper ties and boogie nights. I knew him when his dreams were young. She can never have that!"

"Acne and premature ejaculation! Would she want it?" Mounty's eyebrows took a turn for the cynical. "Anyway, history is in the past and that's where it should be left. Dreams change. People change. Sometimes one person changes more than another and the one who won't or can't change gets left behind. That's life!"

"Is it indeed, Esther Rantzen? Does that happen just with husbands and wives or would you say friendship is prone to the same malaise?"

The other woman shrugged. "I'm just saying is all! There's no need to take offence."

"There's every need," Jenny corrected her. "You're supposed to be my best friend yet here you are playing devil's advocate on behalf of some tramp who thinks cellulite is a pocket-sized mobile phone!"

"You're probably way off-beam, anyway. Can't you credit Adam with some taste? He's not the kind of man that can be gulled into falling for nothing more than a pretty face and a well-stuffed sweater."

This time Jenny signalled the waiter over who responded with less alacrity and not an ounce of lust.

"Well, thank you for that profound insight into my husband and pardon me, but didn't you used to be the person who was always at his throat? Weren't you the one who said and I quote 'Adam Treigh is so full of pretensions he makes Princess Michael look like Mother Theresa of Calcutta?'"

Mounty shifted uncomfortably on her barstool. "Okay. So I admit it. I hold my hand up. But that was before."

"Before what?"

Skilfully, Mounty evaded her question. "Lord, is that the time? I should have been somewhere else, like yesterday!"

"I thought we were going to make a night of it." Jenny accused.

"And so we will, another time," Mounty promised, shoving her share of the bill into Jenny's hand. "Only right now, as they say, time and tide wait for no man and my man waits for no woman."

"Huh, suit yourself," Jenny muttered, wanting childishly to remind her of the vow they had made years before in the playground at Hill Grove. A disgusting ritual in which there had been a palmed exchange of bubble-gum-flavoured spit, the seal of their sacred and binding promise never to let a man take precedence over their friendship. And up till now they never had. Mounty had it bad, obviously. Cupid must have let her have the whole quiverful. On close inspection of her conscience, Jenny found she was happy for her. Really she was! Nonetheless it hurt that she was being so secretive about this particular conquest. Time was when they couldn't wait to parade Tom or Paul or Clint before the other, phoning without fail later on to see if the jury verdict was in.

"Well, whadya think? Isn't he brill? Isn't he a dead ringer for John Travolta?"

"He's got spots!"

"Yeah, but only on his forehead. Besides he's got a long tongue."

"What's that got to do with it?"

"Well, it means we can kiss from a distance so I don't have to get too near."

Shrieks of laughter. Jenny and Mounty. Mounty and Jenny. The terrible twosome as they'd liked to term themselves although, truth to tell, their escapades had been pretty mild. Both might have been a bit more daring had Mounty not had a stepfather like Vlad the Impaler, and had Jenny not lived in fear of her mother being summonsed by the headmistress and turning up in a leopard-skin micro-mini, fishnet tights and no knickers.

"Uh?" Jenny brought her attention back to where

the waiter was leaning so far over the bar he was in danger of doing a headstand onto the concrete floor. "Did you say something?" Panting in garlic-scented English, his eyes superglued to Mounty's jean-clad bottom (no VPL of course) as it wiggled out the door, the waiter nodded furiously

"Yes, I am saying *I* would wait for your friend!" Dramatically he kissed his fingers to the air. "She *all* woman, your friend. Juicy like plum and ripe for dee plucking."

"Careful how you say that!" Dryly, Jenny downed the last of the wine. "In any case, you'd have a long wait, mate! Mounty doesn't go in for toy boys much. No! Her tastes run more to the urbane, sophisticated, city-slicker type, possessors of corporate shares, bank accounts with Coutts, and Brooks Brothers shirts. In fact, if I didn't know better, I'd say my own old man would be right up her alley. Figuratively speaking, of course!"

"Ah." Absent-mindedly mopping up the spills from Jenny's wine, a dreamy look draped itself across the waiter's Latin features. "What I would give to be strolling up 'err alley."

"Well, if you've got a big ship, that should be no problem to you."

"Eh?"

"You know." Jenny giggled, more than a little drunk. *"The big ship sails through the alley alley oh . . ."*

"Eh?" The waiter repeated dazed and confused, his

English vocabulary, already a strictly limited edition, disappearing faster than a vegetarian at a cannibals' convention. "Eh?"

"Otherwise," Jenny made a sad attempt at hiccuping behind her hand, "piss off and paddle your own canoe. Or, better still, find yourself a Farina and look out for the yield sign at the entrance to *her* alley!"

Gallantly the Italian connection made an attempt at understanding. "You is leetle beet peesed, yes? You is out of tiny mind?"

Shakily Jenny climbed down from the barstool. "Yes, Mussolini. I am well and truly scuttered, as my Irish grandmother used to say! I am also on the verge of forty, a sufferer of stress incontinence and a candidate for HRT, that magic cure for old age, cleverly conjured up from pregnant mares' urine by men in white coats. In other words," Jenny gave vent to a sudden burst of unmelodious song drunkenly recalled from a school production of *The Pirates of Penzance*, "*I am the very model of a modern Major General.*"

Alarmed, the waiter reached for the telephone. "De men in white coats? Sound like a bloody good idea to me."

Holding up her hand, Jenny reeled towards the door. "Jusht remember, Muss. I was that pirate but Adam's the one getting the yo ho ho!"

Chapter Eleven

"So where's your friend these days?"

Stepping with alacrity off the fat-monitor, Jenny shrugged. "It's a love thing," she told Denzil, the gay, adenoidal retard-in-a-unitard denizen of Goldman's Gym with whom, now that her fear of his fat-monitor had diminished, she was on quite sociable terms.

"As opposed to a loyalty thing?"

"No, it's not like that! It's kind of natural to send your friends to the back of the queue when you're first getting to know somebody new. Well, somebody special, anyway."

The gym instructor sniffed, whether from disdain or an excess of pollen, Jenny had no idea. Then again, like the ropes that had replaced the veins in his upper arms, it *could* just be another side effect of the old anabolics, she supposed.

"Very understanding of you, I'm sure, but I doubt if I'd be quite so wrapped about with good will to all men if it happened to me, though."

No, more like wrapped around with good willy to all men, Jenny thought sarcastically. "Look, it's not like that," she insisted. "Mounty and I have been friends for yonks. We chose our first bras together, for goodness sake, swopped tips on inserting Tampax, de-blackheaded the back of each other's necks with a sharp pin. Those things count for something, you know."

"Methinks the lady doth protest too much!"

"Oh Lord!" Jenny sought patience from the Artexed ceiling. There were few things in life that incensed her more than someone going all Shakespearean on her, unless it was someone going all Freudian instead. "How many times do I have to tell you, I don't mind? I'm happy for Mounty. I'll dance at her wedding, wear a big hat, sing 'Ave Maria' standing upside-down on my head, turn a blind eye to her Uncle Stan pinching my ass. Anything! Anything at all, to prove how absolutely, enormously chuffed I am for her."

"Assuming she asks you to her wedding!"

Shamelessly, Jenny inserted a finger beneath the rim of her leotard, tugging it down over the edge of her buttock and encountering resistance all the way. The fourteen had been a mistake. Why on earth she had to choose it was anyone's guess when, in the cold light of day, she knew well she was a sixteen, a generous sixteen. Last year she would have killed to be a sixteen and now that she was, there she was already gawking at the grass in the fourteen field and rabid to get at it. Little by little, she had to remind herself, time and time again. She had already gone down four dress sizes. Nowadays, she was the proud possessor of a waist, (oh all right then, if you want to be picky about it, two slight indentations above her hipbones), could bend down without her stomach taking up residence on her lap, and the eczema beneath her boobs had been relegated into the annals of itchy memory.

"Oh, that's enough! You're just trying to stir the pot, Denzil. Just be careful it doesn't boil over and scald the nuts off you."

The gym instructor sniffed again, and put the mystery at an end by reaching into his pocket and pulling out a Vick inhaler. Neither anabolics nor hay fever. Just a stuffy nose!

"Hmmph! Suit yourself. If you won't be told you won't be told but, just remember, there's none so blind as those who will not see!"

Jenny giggled. "Oh, dear! Your clichés are showing. I'd never have taken you for that type of boy!"

"Yes, well I'd never have taken you for stupid but, well, there you have it!"

"I'm not stupid," Jenny began then broke off as Denzil grabbed her.

"Look, can you not see she's jealous of you? She could never look like you in a thousand years. *She* wants what you have!"

Restraining an urge to burst into hysterical giggles, Jenny calmly detached his hand from her arm. "You poor, deluded fool! Mounty could never look like me in a thousand years because, unlike me, she's a gorgeous, size ten, razor-cheek-boned, go-getting, executive babe with breasts like upturned wineglasses!"

"With or without the stems?" Denzil was at his cynical best again.

Determinedly, Jenny ignored him. "And men just fall at her size four high-arched pedicured feet! Narrow-fitting."

In rapid succession, Denzil sighed and snorted, seeking inspiration himself, but scorning the ceiling in favour of the muscle-bound, taut backside of a body-builder working the mountain-climber. "You just don't get it, do you! Sure, your friend is pretty. Pretty thin. Pretty tall. Pretty pretty. Pretty average! You, on the other hand are beautiful, a work of art, a Reubens on legs. Not only do you have bone structure you have infrastructure. *You* are a diva, a drag queen's idol." He shrugged, a gesture that brought his shoulders up around his ears so that for a moment Jenny was reminded of Quasimodo. The bells! The bells! "If I weren't a dyed-in-the-wool pillow-biter and proud of it, given the choice, in another life I'd come back as you!"

"Reubens. Reubens." Jenny mused, hardly listening to the rest of his flowery oration. "Aren't they the ones who sang *Sugar Baby Love?* Or was that the Rubettes?"

"Rubettes," Denzil confirmed. "Wore daft white berets, though the lead singer was a real babe. Lips like a bicycle tyre! Reubens was an artist."

110

"Ah, yes. Italian geezer." Jenny nodded as a distant memory of Sr Gonzaga bleating on about the Renaissance painters stirred faintly in the darkest recesses of her mind. "Painted big women, didn't he? Legs like hocks and butt-cheeks like the Hindenburgh. Hey! That supposed to be a compliment, is it?"

Denzil held his hands up. "Ouch! Don't shoot. Besides, lots of people like beef on the bone."

"Sarky git!" Jenny couldn't help but grin. "Look, I want to be a spare rib, honed and toned. I want to look in the mirror and say hi to my skeleton! I want to play 'When the Saints' on my ribcage with a wooden spoon. That's what I want, what I really really want! Thin power!"

"Well, don't go overboard. Health is wealth, remember. Honed and toned I can go along with. Them bones, Them bones, Them dry bones, I can do without. Besides, to get back to your girlfriend, she's thin isn't she, but is she happy?"

"Ecstatic, I'd say." Jenny nodded vehemently.

"So why is she not married yet? I mean she's no spring chicken, is she? I'd say she's knocking on for forty if she's a day."

Jenny ignored the reference to forty. It brought her out in spots and made her come over all-unnecessary. "Listen, marriage isn't the be-all and the end-all. Mounty's a career girl. She's had her fair share of marriage proposals, just never found the right man, that's all."

"Unlike you."

"That's right, but I was lucky. I met Adam when he was just a young pup and his eyes weren't fully opened and, as love is blind, he married me anyway!"

"Don't knock yourself," Denzil cautioned. "There's plenty round who"ll be happy to do that for you. Including your friend!"

Jenny groaned. "Oh, here we go again. What has Mounty ever done to harm you? Stolen your favourite leotard? Robbed your boyfriend? What?"

"Nothing!" Denzil confirmed. "But then again it's not me she's out to harm. It's you!"

"Just full of the joys, aren't you, Denzil?" Wearily Jenny waved him away, before heading in the direction of a treadmill. "Now if you don't mind, I'm paying a whacking great subscription for the use of this place and I have promises to keep."

"Promises to who?"

"To myself," Jenny told him, deftly keying in weight, speed, distance and goal and confidently stepping up her pace as the machine got to work. "To myself."

And I have promises to keep too, Denzil thought watching her legs whizz round like pistons. A promise forced out of him by her friend when he had accidentally bumped into her, last week, slaving over a hot husband in the men's changing rooms. Jenny's hot husband! Adam Treigh, one of Denzil's pupils from the fencing class he taught on Sundays.

"Because, if you open your big mouth and say anything," Mounty had threatened him, mock-sweet, illustratively carving one of her long nails across the width of his throat, "Adam will say you propositioned him in the shower room. Quite unprofessional, don't you think? A sackable offence, surely!" And because, being a fudge-packer in a still predominantly homophobic world, the cards were already stacked against him, Denzil had promised to stay shtum. But that didn't mean he had to like it. Neither did it mean he couldn't throw out broad hints but, Jenny, sweet fat thing, had cloth ears when it came to her friend.

"Size ten," he heard her mutter as the sweat beaded on her brow and dripped onto the end of her nose. "Size ten. Size ten. Size ten. Size ten."

Jenny had found a new mantra!

Chapter Twelve

"You really ought to get out more, you know. See a bit of the world. Eat from the table of life's colourful hors d'oeuvres."

"What, like go for a Chinese, you mean? Begin at the very Bejining."

"You know very well it's not. Still, if you insist on playing thick as a plank, I'll say no more. Far be it from me to interfere in your life."

"Yes, indeed, why break the habit of a lifetime? Why send shock waves around a world already suffering from drought, disease, famine and war, with the odd bit of old pestilence chucked in for good measure."

Jenny's mother bridled beneath the sarcasm in her daughter's voice. "Are you saying I wasn't a good mother?"

Does a bear crap in the woods? Jenny thought, forbearing from voicing the thought but reluctant, nonetheless, to let her mother off the hook completely.

"Well, you must admit you were never exactly the hands-on maternal type. For God's sake, when other mothers were throwing up their hands in horror at Lance, or Donna or Samantha raiding the drinks cupboard, you were pouring doubles down my throat and letting me stay up to watch *Psycho* and *Nosferatu*.

"So?" Gloria frowned. "I never believed in treating children like morons. Children are just mini-adults and should be treated as such. I hold my hands up. I never subscribed to the goo-goo, gaa-gaa-ing school of child-rearing. For Heaven's sake, what does that accomplish except to add insult to injury by turning an already social inept into an inarticulate social inept? Babies aren't my bag. What can I tell you? As far as I'm concerned they represent all the worst traits in human nature. Number one, they're smelly with control over neither bladder nor bowel. Two, in less than a week they're already accomplished projectile vomiters and, in less than a fortnight, bang, your home goes from Homes and Gardens to puke city. Three, they're loud and disruptive, belching, farting and bawling to beat the band. Four . . ."

"Okay, okay!" Jenny held up her hand to stem the flow as one by one, on her fingers, her mother enumerated the faults of the world's infant population. "I get the message. Mary Poppins you ain't! Still a bit of jam roly-poly might have been nice now and again."

"Jam roly-poly. Bed at seven o'clock, even on long, hot summer evenings. Scrub your neck and wash behind your ears. Pull your socks up. Mind you don't dirty your clothes! Pah! You should be grateful to me for raising you the way I did: for not forcing convention down your neck; for not interfering in your life but leaving you free to be yourself; for allowing you to break free from humanity's herd!"

"Yes," Jenny nodded vehemently, "but that was part of the problem. I was seen, never herd. More often than not I was on the outside looking in. When the little clique, the 'in crowd' at school, were swopping make-up tips, cures for acne and the finer points of French kissing, there was I, wandering lonely as a cloud, Cathy's ghost scraping at the window of Wuthering Heights desperate to come into the warmth. Only I never got an invite. If it wasn't for Mounty I would have cut my throat with a false finger-nail!"

"Ah yes, Diana Mountford! The goddess, Diana. Diana the hunter. Beaus and arrows! I wonder who's kissing her now?"

Resolutely, Jenny laid down the iron with which she had been pressing one of Adam's shirts. It was the pink, originally white, number which he had reluctantly conceded might do a turn some day, if he was reduced to penury and sleeping on a park bench with drop-outs and winos.

"You never liked her, did you? I never understood why. I mean she was always polite whenever she met you, wasn't she? She watched her p's and q's and never put a foot wrong. No matter how hard you tried you simply couldn't find fault with her."

"Exactly!" Her mother scowled as the iron gave a little hiss of impatience. "And that's what I don't like about her. She's too good to be true. She never lets her guard down, never lets her slip show, never lets her humanity show. So what's her angle?" Crossly, Jenny picked up the iron again and went full steam ahead at a pair of David's bastard-to-iron but height-of-fashion army combat trousers.

"Oh, you've been watching too many episodes of *NYPD Blue.* Mounty doesn't have an angle. She just happens to be an exceptionally nice person. Unfortunately the tabloid mentalities of this country find it very difficult to accept that such people can, occasionally, exist."

"So where is she now, in your hour of need, as it were? As I recall you've already left two messages on her answer machine this evening. If she was any kind of a friend she'd hotfoot it here, armed to the gills with a bottle or two of the hard stuff, a box of Thornton's handmade truffles, a crate of man-sized tissues and a shoulder ready for the wetting of all wettings."

Jenny sniffed. "She's not my keeper, you know. She *does* have a life of her own, a house, a job and a new man. She can't provide me with round-the-clock surveillance. Besides she *has* been very good to me. It's down to her that I joined the gym and started to take stock of my life. And, only last week, we met up at Plonkers to try out the new Beaujolais. So, you see, she *is* a good friend and when I'm down and troubled, she'll come running. So why can't people just get off her case and go get a life for themselves?"

Infuriatingly her mother grinned like a cat that got the cream. "Which brings us round full circle. *You* need to get a life for yourself. *You* need to get out more instead of immersing yourself in self-imposed purdah. Adam's not nailing *himself* to the cross, is he? Oh no! According to you he's doing the horizontal lambada, the pelvic pogo, the chick-on-a-stick routine, all over London and with wild and frequent abandon. So, why don't you post David off to one of his friends for the night, dust off your glad rags and come clubbing with Rover and me? At the very worst you might enjoy yourself."

"I don't know." Dubiously, Jenny unplugged the iron. "It's years since I've been clubbing. Besides, from what I hear, those places are chock-full of fourteen-year-olds, all long legs, painted-on lycra, skin eruptions and out of their heads on E."

Helpfully, Jenny's mother dismantled the ironing-board, swearing as she almost kneecapped herself in the process.

"Not this place. It's what you call select. A club for like-minded adults, not a pustule or trainer bra in sight. So what do you say? Come on, live dangerously. Otherwise you'll always be on the outside looking in." That final phrase did it!

"Okay, but I know I'll regret this."

"What's to regret?" Gloria shrugged, holding both

hands out palms up, in a distinctly Francophilian gesture although, to Jenny's knowledge, she had never been within a spit of France in her life. "You can either stay here inhaling the starch from Adam's shirts and getting high on old memories, or, you can trip the light fantastic with Rover and me and make some new ones of your own."

Slowly, Jenny moved to the phone to make arrangements for David to sleep over with his friend.

"All right, I'm convinced. Pick me up at half-past eight. That should give me just enough time to get to work with the Polyfilla and find something that fits me."

"Right! Rover'll be delighted."

"Will he?" Jenny looked doubtful again. "Well, if he is, it'll probably only be because he's relieved not to be the only one who's bloody barking mad!"

* * *

"Tell me I'm dreaming, Mother. Tell me it's a nightmare and I'm going to wake up any second and laugh at the vagaries of the human mind. Tell me anything, only don't tell me this is what I think it is?"

"Oh, shush. Don't go getting all chastity-belted on me. Surely the name should have given you a hint or are you really that naive, Jenny?"

Panic-stricken, Jenny turned back towards the tail-lights of the black taxi receding into the darkness of the road ahead, desperate to whistle it back, knowing even as her fingers reached her mouth that it was already too late. "I thought you said 'Jane's', not 'Chaynes'. I thought you said a nightclub, not a torture chamber. I had no idea you were going to take me to a fetish club."

Dryly, her mother rattled the handcuffs swinging loosely from her wrist. "So where did you think we were going, to the Savoy? Don't you think black patent shorts, bondage masks and nose-rings might be a little excessive for that establishment? A little, 'not quite the dress code we expect from our clientele, Madam!'? Now stop acting like a virgin on the hysterical and come inside. My buns are freezing in this get-up."

"I can't." Mutinously, Jenny stuck out her chin, unaware that her bottom lip was trembling like Vesuvius on the brink of an explosion. "Adam would be disgusted. You know how much he hates what he calls weirdos. He'd go mental if he thought his own wife was mixing with them."

"Adam Treigh is a racist, bigoted, homophobic creep of a slime-ball. Slime oozes from the man's pores. He is completely devoid of morals and standards except the double standards by which he lives his life. Did I ever tell you how it broke my heart when you married him?"

Jenny nodded. "Well, I knew you hadn't signed up to his fan club. From what I recall you would have preferred me to marry that Hell's Angel from Wapping, the one with the Viking helmet and flashy chromified motor-bike."

"Ah yes, the Harley Davidson." Jenny's mother

looked positively orgasmic at the recollection. "He could have saddled me up any time! But not you, of course. You couldn't wait to sign your heart away to a self-important pen pusher with plums in his mouth and a briefcase full of infidelities."

"That's a lie!" Crossly Jenny shrugged off Rover's paw which, by stealth, had been trying to inveigle her up the steps and into the cave-like interior of Chaynes. "Adam has never strayed before. He's a good father *and* a good husband. Farina's just a phase. She won't last. I'll win him back. See if I don't!"

"Well, not by perishing the brass monkeys off yourself out here, you won't. Look, come inside, just for a bit. Actually you don't have to have a bit, if you don't want. It's all consensual, between consenting adults. You don't *have* to do anything you don't want to. You can just sit and have a drink. You can even brood if it makes you feel better but for pity's sake get a move on before *rigor mortis* sets in and my buttocks shatter into a thousand pieces."

"Oh, all right!" Ungraciously, Jenny allowed herself to be led up the steps and into the club proper where the amount of slapping leather in progress would have put a whole troupe of line-dancers to shame.

"Lie down and make a Y!"

"What?" Jenny almost jumped out of her skin as some jerk in a g-string, his head wreathed in a leather mask with a zip for a mouth sidled up to her and treated her to what was obviously his killer chat-up line.

"There's a reserved sign for you in my bed," he tried again. His second-best chat-up line?

"Oh yeah?" Jenny snapped, patently unimpressed by either. "Well, there's a reserved urn for you in the crematorium, mate. So sling your hook or I'll sling my fist." Behind his zip, the mask slobbered and Jenny groaned as the realisation dawned on her that the freak was into domination and right now he was seeing her in the guise of Queen Dominatrix. "Look," she tried to reason with him as he fell to the ground and began kicking himself in the naked ribs with her foot. "I'm not into this shit, honest. I'm only along for the ride. Actually," she caught herself, "I'm not along for the ride, any ride. It's all a mistake, really. I thought this place was called Jane's, you see, not Chaynes. I hate chains. They're heavy and they make a noise. I hate leather too. The smell makes me sick. It reminds me of horses. I hate horses. I hate anything equine, in fact. Do you believe me when I tell you Mr Ed used to bring me out in a rash? Poison Ivy, the doctor said. But it wasn't. It was Mr Ed. Ah, what the heck!" Jenny broke off as her bumblings appeared to be having no effect whatsoever. "Have this one on me." Wresting her foot free of his grasp, she drew it back then let him have it full force, right between the legs. The agony and the ecstasy! Enough force in that one kick to provide him with wanking material for a year!

"A goddess," Jenny heard him mutter as she walked away in search of her mother, leaving him writhing in torment on the wooden floor, "a veritable goddess."

"A goddess!" Isn't that what her mother had called Mounty, albeit sarcastically. Caustically, Jenny glanced around the dim interior of the nightclub, her eyes veering away then coming back to focus in astonishment on the wire cage suspended from the ceiling in which a woman, naked but for the seven-tongued whip she was wielding, was bumping and grinding to the rhythm of *Wild Thing*. Not just any woman though! Her mother! Huh! Jenny thought dispiritedly, heading for the door and willing to take a gamble on encountering Jack The Ripper mark 2 in the seedy streets outside, rather than spend another moment in this den of iniquity. Thank God Adam was only ever into the straight stuff. Funny business, as he called it, made him sick. Confront him with a pair of crotchless knickers and you'd be scraping him up off the ground for a week. As for Mounty, you could bet your life she never had to demean herself by kicking masochists in the g-string. No way. With Mounty it would be all champagne, satin sheets and Julio Inglesias crooning away, à *Latino*, in the background – 'When I fall in love'.

* * *

She would have been very surprised, not to say gobsmacked, to know that not a million miles away, Mounty, basqued and suspendered to within an inch of her life, was at that very moment teetering in six-inch stilettos up along the naked, supine, acquiescent spine of Jenny's own husband.

"I hope Jenny doesn't see the marks." Giggling, Mounty reached the base of his neck, turned about and began the precarious journey back to where his white hairy arse could be seen rising up from the bedclothes like the dome of St Paul's Cathedral.

"Separate bedrooms!" His voice was muffled, his face submerged in the sheets.

"Oh yes. I forgot. Because she snores!"

With an effort Adam raised his chin just enough to allow his mouth freedom of speech. "Not any more, she doesn't. As it happens, since she started losing the weight, she's becoming much more fanciable again. In fact, one of these nights I might even force myself to give her a shag. Aw shit!" Adam shot up suddenly, his hand reaching around to cradle his left buttock where a rather nasty weal was making itself apparent. "What did you do that for? That hurt!"

Brazenly, Mounty rested her high-heel on the summit of his backside. "It was meant to," she said and her eyes, as she gazed at his naked hide, were as cold as the Arctic.

Chapter Thirteen

"I don't know what you did to Marcel last night, but he's never been off the blower since."

"Marcel?"

"You remember, studded g-string, zip for a mouth, executioner's mask?"

"Oh, Zippy! The sick git from last night!"

"The very one. What *did* you do to him, by the way?"

Jenny giggled. "Kicked him in the testimonials. Hard!"

"Well, now he wants yours." Her mother coughed, choked, spluttered a bit and coughed again. At the other end of the phone Jenny waited patiently. It had taken a lot of money and energetic carousing to put that cough there and, as always, after a hard night's drinking and smoking it was determined to give good value.

"What do you mean?" Jenny asked eventually, knowing by the lengthening silence between the hacking, that the lungs were gradually returning to normal.

"Just what I said. He wants your testimonials. Something about a job."

Idly, as she reflected on this piece of information, Jenny stuck out her tongue at her reflection in the mirror above the telephone table, noting as she did so, that it was covered in a film of something white and furry, interspersed with the odd lurid, green streak.

"What kind of a job? Spanish inquisitor? Hangman? Pol Pot? What? Actually, the way I feel this morning I wouldn't need much persuading to batter the living daylights out of him. Or you, come to that, or that insult to the canine world you insist on dragging round with you. I mean a fetish club, for God's sake! Whatever possessed you?"

Her mother groaned, an indication that not only her lungs, but also her head was in a less than robust condition.

"Oh, never mind the recriminations. Save them for when the drums stop banging. Now do you want the job or not? Percy says it's a once-in-a-lifetime opportunity and you'd be a fool not to take it. Especially at your age. Jobs aren't like buses, you know. Once you hit the 40 terminus there's a long wait for the next one to come along and a great, big queue in front of you!"

Jenny leaned a little closer to the mirror the better to examine her tongue. Did old age turn not only your hair white but also your tongue?

"Thanks for the vote of confidence," she said, only it sounded like 'anchs or eh ot a onfideens' as she extended the organ all the way to the root in a desperate effort to detect any early signs of dementia that might be lurking. "Anyway," she retrieved it, tucked it back behind her teeth, "I thought you said his name was Marcel? Mum?" Puzzled, Jenny looked into the earpiece which, seemingly of its own volition, had suddenly entered into a faithful rendition of one of Simon and Garfunkel's most famous ballads. "Mum? Are you still there?" Nothing! Just the *Sound of Silence* and Jenny banging and shaking the receiver, peering alternately into both ends, in the hopes that by vandalising the apparatus, communications could be re-established. This, in fact, was a tactic with which she was very familiar having had occasion to use it frequently around the house. Take the toaster, for instance. Two bangs with a closed fist and it popped better than Pamela Anderson's shirt-buttons! One kick, two bangs on the door of the washing machine and hey presto, it was good vibrations all round. As for the TV remote control, pitching it against the wall worked well, she found, both for its performance and her stress levels. Actually it was doubtful if any item, domestic or technological, in Jenny's household had escaped the *treatment* at some time or another and, as a short, embarrassed grunt hissed reluctantly from the handset, her faith in the crash, bang, wallop school of DIY appeared, once more, to be entirely justified. Curiouser and curiouser, thought Jenny, as the grunt receded purposefully back up along the telephone line again, leaving only silence and the odd burst of static.

"M-o-t-h-e-rrrr?" Starting as an alto, Jenny drew out the word, gradually running up along the scale before emerging triumphantly at the end as a fully-fledged boy soprano, complete with a bad case of undescended testicles. "Mother! What's going on? What are you not telling me?"

"It's Rover." Gradually the disembodied voice returned. Faint at first but working up to a Devil-take-the-hindermost volume before too long.

"Rover? What on earth has that aspiring crotch-sniffer got to do with anything?"

Jenny sensed an embarrassment about the older woman, an unusual, almost palpable discomfiture that oozed out along the telecommunications highway and into her ear like a menopausal hot flush.

"Well . . . Percy is *his* name." And then, in a rush to get the worst over and done with! "Percival Throgmorton Cuthbertson the Third, actually."

"Never! You're pulling my leg!" Jenny giggled hysterically, something she tried to avoid as a rule, having discovered it acted as a trigger for her stress incontinence and usually led to a mad rush to the loo or a wet gusset. Sometimes both! "Percival Throgmorton Cuthbertson the Turd! The dog turd! Don't you just love it? Don't you just want to set it to music and boogie on down. I'm not surprised he changed it. I mean, anything's got to be better than that!"

Embarrassment gave way to resignation. "Oh, go

on, laugh! Get it out of your system. Yours is precisely the kind of reaction poor Rover has had to put up with all his life."

Jenny, like her mother, much given to Euro gestures, shrugged, a deep Gallic shrug that brought her shoulders almost parallel with her ears. "So, when he decided to change it, why didn't he choose a normal name then? Tom or Dick or Harry! Why Rover? Surely that's jumping out of the frying pan into the fire? I mean, you don't hear other people going around calling themselves Spot and Brandy and Bouncer?"

"It's an abdication thing."

"As in Edward and Mrs S? Don't tell me he's minor royalty. An exile from some far-flung, exotic land! A prince among men! A pedigree amongst mutts!"

"No. He's a media mogul, actually. And very stressful it is too which is why, in his private life, he likes to abdicate all responsibility and transmogrify himself into a dog."

"And say, if by accident he trans-moggierified himself, would he turn into a cat?"

"You see!" Her mother sounded aggrieved. "I knew you'd take the mick. I knew you wouldn't understand, not in a million years. And then they talk about the generation gap . . ."

"Actually, I do understand." Jenny made heroic efforts to stop her lips from twitching and to suppress the laughter in her voice. "I've seen something similar on that satellite sex show, *Jerk-Off*, only the freaks on that wanted to regress to being babies again complete with bibs, giant terry-cloth nappies and litre bottles of milk. Worse still, they filled their nappies and not just with number ones! I swear you wouldn't believe it. Solicitors! Politicians! Stockbrokers! Sitting round sucking their thumbs and shoving Smarties up their nostrils like their noses were safety deposit boxes. All desperate, apparently, to escape the stresses and strains of Execuland by reverting to the halcyon days of loose bowels and nipples on tap." Despite her most valiant efforts a giggle escaped her. "At least Rover only cocks his leg!"

"But you don't approve?"

"What do *you* think? A grown man acting like Lassie? But then again, when have you ever needed my approval?"

"God!" Beneath the hangover from hell, her mother's patience was wearing thin. "You never miss an opportunity to snipe, do you? Now, do you think you can put your childhood grievances, both real and imagined, aside for just one moment and let me tell you about the job which, after all, is why I called you in the first place, despite the Queen's Fusiliers using my brain for target practice."

"Ah yes, Marcel. The stud in a hood! The header in leather!"

"Head of In Kamera, actually, the production company that makes quite a few of those docu-drama and chat-show type programmes you like so much. Including *Martyna*."

132

"No!" Jenny almost dropped the phone. "But that's my absolute favourite. Well, next to *Springer*, that is. Martyna Michaels walks on water! Did you see that show she did with that all-lesbian chapter of Hells Angels from Slough? Dykes on bikes? God it was brilliant!"

"Never watch it!" her mother confessed, preferring *Kilroy*, though she'd gone off him a bit since he'd banished the bouffant and flattened his fringe *à la* George Clooney which was all right if, like the latter, you were the rugged type. Unfortunately, Kilroy was of the smoother-than-an-Immac'd-leg type, and the effect, far from being sexy, was more like a melted ice-cream cone dripping all down his forehead. "Still, if you play your cards right, you might well find yourself rubbing shoulders with her."

Jenny could hardly believe her luck. "All right, I'm sold! Now what rock does this Marcel live under and what do I have to do to pass the interview?"

This time it was her mother's turn to giggle. "You passed it last night. In fact, you could say it was a bit of a walkover. He's expecting you this afternoon at two o'clock. Just make sure you wear your highest heels and, just for insurance purposes, your forbidding face; the one you always wear around me should be more than adequate. He likes the school-marm type, I believe. Stern nannies! That kind of lark! Nursery puddings and weekly enemas. Typical English public school product!"

"With enemas like that who needs friends!" Jenny joked, thrilled beyond measure at the prospect of working in such an exalted atmosphere. Breathing the same air as Martyna Michaels! Walking the same corridors! Possibly even making her coffee. And maybe, just maybe getting to see her in action. Shelf-stacker in Sainsbury's! Sit and spin, Rosalind-bovine-features, Jenny thought, hanging patiently on the line as her mother gave way to another bout of arguing with her lungs. Stuff your poxy losers' jobs! *I'm* going into TV! *I'm* going to be a luvvie! Get thee behind me, Emma Thompson!

"What you need," she told her mother as gradually the choking died away to just five beats between splutters, "is the hair of the dog that bit you. And I don't mean Rover!"

"What I need," her mother corrected her, "is a complete reincarnation, starting like in the next five minutes. And I don't give a toss who I come back as, so long as they've a teetotaller's head and are twenty years younger! Now, it's been nice and all that but –"

"Okay. I'll phone you later: let you know how I got on. And Mum, thanks!"

"De nada! Now go kick some ass!"

"I will!" Jenny promised fervently, replacing the handset and going in search of her Roland Cartier, black-patent, court shoes, the ones with the four-inch, spike heels and nose cone like Apollo 13. Absent-mindedly turning on the radio, she plunged into her giant pine wardrobe, frenziedly swatting coats and dresses aside in an effort to locate the plastic refuse sack in which she kept clothes and shoes that *'might do a turn someday'* or that *'I might fit into when I lose another four stone'* or purely for reasons of sentimentality as in *'Adam always loved me in this outfit and I was wearing it the night David was conceived and can't bear to throw it away, even if polyester catsuits are no longer in vogue'.*

"And now for a complete change of mood," the disembodied DJ's voice announced, as a flurry of cool, blue tones spilled out across the bedroom and into the back of the wardrobe where, sandwiched between a pair of crimplene hot-pants left over from when she was just thirteen and a victim of her mother's dress sense, and a rainbow-coloured ra-ra skirt left over from the eighties, when she was a victim of her own, Jenny struck gold. "Have you guessed it yet?" Professionally smooth, the DJ teased his audience. "That's right, it's Ol Blue Eyes' daughter, Nancy Sinatra, with 'These-Boots-Are-Made-For-Waaalking'."

"Or kicking!' Jenny giggled aloud as dishevelled but triumphant she emerged, stilettos in hand.

Chapter Fourteen

"I thought you'd be happy for me. Hell! In my more optimistic moments, I hoped, maybe even a little bit proud. But, oh no! Perish the thought! Instead you stand there gawping at me like I've got 666 tattooed on my scalp. I'm surprised you haven't thought to grab a crucifix and back slowly away from me in case I sink my teeth in your neck!"

Very much Lord of the Manor, Adam stretched his hands high up above his head, barely managing to stifle a yawn as Jenny, disappointment evident in every line of her body, launched into a furious attack.

"Oh, hark at the drama queen! Talking nonsense as usual! What do you expect me to do? Get down on my knees and salaam you because you've managed to get yourself a job. I mean it's hardly what you call respectable, is it? Hardly the stuff Chancellors of the Exchequer or Madam Speakers are made of, is it? And *you* expect me to be proud! Of what, for goodness sake? My wife, working for perverts? Chief bottle-washer and gopher to the nation's degenerates? Never mind that you don't bloody need a job since poor sod Bonzo here works his rear end off to make sure you and David don't go short of anything."

Except love! Jenny thought in the face of her husband's scorn, fighting to keep back the wretched tears that were threatening to spill over and reduce her to a mere caricature, that well-known creature, the helpless female. Tears of frustration! Tears of rage! How dare Adam burst her bubble. Talk about cloud nine! Leaving the offices of In Kamera this afternoon she'd practically been orbiting the Mir space station so thrilled was she that, for the first time in years, someone had seen her as a person in her own right, and not just as Adam's wife or David's mother or Mounty's friend. Someone had seen her, not as an appendage to anyone else, but as someone who had a valuable contribution to make, as herself, as Jennifer Lorelei Treigh, née Thompson. Okay, so that someone had been Marcel and fair enough his interview techniques *had* been somewhat unorthodox in that he'd conducted the whole process whilst lying flat on his back and talking to her left ankle. And so what if he'd already had a sneak preview of her credentials last night and was only going through the motions. Mule kicks aside, she still had what it took! He'd read her CV, hadn't he, breaking off to comment favourably on the new IT qualifications she had recently gained at evening classes, as well as her 'life experience' which he pointed out was of more value than any amount of certificates in blue, wooden frames could ever be. After all, he'd assured her ankle earnestly, everyone knew housewives and mothers had to wear several hats at once: accountant's, manager's, entertainment officer's, diplomat's, butcher's, baker's and candlestick maker's, to name but a few. And it wasn't as if you could get that kind of experience out of a textbook!

Much to her surprise, Jenny found that she liked him. Bereft of his mask he had a round, rather cherubic face, the kind you either wanted to pat or smack hard. His body matched his face in that it too was rotund, his limbs no more than a collection of squat cocktail sausages that jerked spasmodically now and again as if being tossed about in a deep fat fryer.

And then came the icing on the cake! Martyna Michaels had walked in and she, Jenny, had been introduced by Marcel as 'my new PA'. And the great chat-show goddess had unbent and smiled and shaken Jenny's hand, welcoming her on board in exactly the same rich, syrupy voice she used to extract skeletons from her guests' closets. On board! Office-speak! Such a long time since she'd been surrounded by any of that and now with the advances in technology, she looked forward to learning practically a whole new and exciting vocabulary. A kind of Freemasons' code in the office. A secret handshake or twitch of the eye. If you weren't in the know you were scuppered. Hive down.

Touch base. Downsize. Database. Networking. The system's crashed. And that old chestnut, which like all true classics remained in vogue even now as it did when quills were considered high-tech gadgetry: it's in the post!

Jenny couldn't wait to be fluent in office-speak, couldn't wait to be part of the inner sanctum, networking up a storm, crashing whatever needed crashing, touching base left, right and centre, and downsizing with like-minded colleagues. Colleagues! She liked the sound of that and said as much to Marcel, who took advantage of her excitement by giving a quick, surreptitious lick to her shoe. That lapse aside though, it had to be said he really had behaved with the utmost propriety and Jenny, as a gesture of goodwill and having first obtained his solemn and binding oath that from now on he would leave his fetish at home, favoured him with one last, powerful kick in the goolies.

"So you work your butt off to bring home the bacon." Jenny's chin came up. "I'm not denying that and I'm grateful. Don't I show my gratitude in a million ways? Don't I clean, cook and play happy families? But I'm not fulfilled, Adam. Waging warfare with a toilet duck on the world's germ populace doesn't cut it for me. And try as I might, I just can't seem to work myself up into a state of bliss over the whiter-than-snow whiteness of my smalls or the oriental ambience of the latest air freshener."

"Oh Lord," Adam rolled his eyes. "Have mercy,

Jenny. Don't go trotting out the Germaine-Greer-speak. Not again! Not yet, anyway. Not, until after we've eaten. An army marches on its stomach remember, and I might be more inclined to liberate you from the kitchen sink after you do what any good, obedient wife should do and feed me."

Jenny shot him a freeze-the-balls-off-you look. At times like this she couldn't fathom what she'd ever seen in him. Well, she could, but the picture was a bit out of focus. "That's right, Adam, turn it into a joke. Well, I'm telling you I *need* more! I'm not one-dimensional, you know, a cardboard cut-out. *I* am a Rubik's cube, a complicated puzzle. Along with the physical, there are mental, emotional and spiritual aspects to my being none of which, be under no illusions, are remotely enhanced by trailing death-trap trolleys round supermarkets or scoring over OAPs on zimmer frames by bagging the last cut-price chicken! If you want to know the truth, my chakras are out of alignment. I need balance and harmony. Yin and yang. T'ai and chi!"

"Tom and Jerry! Laurel and Hardy!" Adam was sarcastic. He didn't even have to speak for Jenny to know that. Rather it was apparent in the sardonic lift of his right eyebrow. "You need to see a psychiatrist! A shrink. A skull detective! You're off your rocker. Out of your tree. Doolally!"

Palm up, Jenny halted the traffic. "Enough already! I can only cope with one insult at a time. Nonetheless, the signal has gotten through loud and clear! Correct

141

me if I'm wrong but it would appear that your faith in my faculties is somewhat impaired; that you wouldn't trust me within seven miles of a blank cheque; that you suspect a cardigan, close-fitting and with very long sleeves might be in order."

"The thought *had* crossed my mind!" Amazing! Even whilst defecating on her from a great height, Adam was extraordinarily handsome. A cross between Pierce Brosnan and Pierce Brosnan, there was nothing she wanted more than to carry him off to a remote cave somewhere and ravish the boxers off him. First of all, though, she wanted to beat him till he cried, then beat him some more. Dryly it occurred to her to wonder whether Marcel had been right about her after all, whether that night in Chaynes he had sensed something dark, violent and sadistic in her persona which up till now, like a nun's knickers, had remained hidden from general view. Still, for every negative there is a positive and, looking on the bright side, at least she wouldn't starve if Adam upped with his human trampoline and did a runner; not when she could stick a card up in the local telephone box:

"New on the beat!
A real little belter!
Will whack you with her rhythm stick!
    Takes Amex, Switch and Delta!"

Of course if Adam thought he was fooling her with all his old palaver he was sadly mistaken. No way, José! *She* had his number. It was all to do with conscience.

Oprah *et al* had taught her that; all those programmes on which the cheater had rubbished the cheated in an effort to justify putting his hands in someone else's sweetie jar.

"Iffn you wuz takin cahir ov biznizz ah wooden hev tah gow gittin it offa her! She blows mah whistle fer me. Real lahd. Don't yah, Arleen!"

"Luk at yew. Yew'r all so darned ugly. Ah seen purdier waarthawgs on mah grandaddy's faarhm! Thet's fer shuah!"

"You're dumping on me," Jenny accused. "Why? Afraid you're going to have to get your finger out and do something around here? Spend some time with your son? Run him to his football club? Take him bowling and to Quasar? Spread yourself a little more thinly? Iron the odd shirt maybe? Shelve some of that unlimited overtime you put in most evenings? Spend a little Q-U-A-L-I-T-Y time with your *family?*" Got him! Was that a fleeting expression of guilt on his otherwise flawless, film icon's face? A recognition that there was at least a grain of truth in her accusations? Was it hell!

"Bollocks! I just don't understand what you think you're going to accomplish by going out to work. Especially as you dispensed with Mrs Singh specifically so as to take – and I quote – control of your household again."

"And so I have taken control. Who do you think washed the clothes you're wearing? Who do you think roasted the beef which, even now, your digestive juices are in the process of de-enzyming? Who shot Cock-Robin?" Purposefully Jenny rose from her chair, walked round and placed her hands on the back, leaning slightly forward – Ken Livingstone about to call for an all-out strike. "Read my lips, Adam! I *need* more! Repeat. *I* need more! Savvy?"

Unable to come up with any concrete argument, Adam, like a rat in a trap, beat a hasty retreat into that age-old bastion aka male chauvinism. "Typical bloody woman! Never know your own minds from one minute to the next. First you want to stay home and play 'Hi honey, I'm home', the next you want to be Shirley Conran. Talk about moving the goalposts. Is it any wonder us men end up as raving alcoholics, workaholics or worse!"

Shagaholics? Jenny thought, regressing, yellow-bellied coward into her usual craven, chicken-hearted state before finding her voice. Why, oh why couldn't she just come out with it! Come in, Number Fifteen, your time is up. *I know what you did last summer!* Yeah! And last month! Last week! And possibly last night, come to that! Cue the creepy music, *du dum, du dum,* rising to a crashing crescendo! Adam Treigh you are hereby charged that on nights a, b, c and on to infinity you did unlawfully have carnal knowledge with a woman not your wife. How do you plead? Guilty or not guilty? And, before I pronounce sentence, tell me was it worth it? Torture me with every gory little detail. Leave no duvet unturned! Tell me about her crater-free, soft, satin skin. Tell me how she smells of male fantasies and deep, exciting uncharted waters. Tell me what her pet name is for you, and yours for her! Petal? Dimples? Mush-mush? Remember how you played pinball on my cellulite? What do you play with her? Pass the Penis? Hide the Sheet? Musical bares? Don't hold back now. Heap ashes on my head! What do your colleagues think, apart from old Buffy who slobbers over anything female so long as it's got a pulse – present company excepted, of course, old mares not being any good for a ride!

"Adam and Farina make such a lovely couple!" Is that what they say? *"So well suited, don'tcha know. An improvement on the last one? I'll say! This one has ankles!"*

Adam Treigh, I hereby sentence you to . . . to what? Death? No way! She couldn't live without him. Exile? Ditto! To what, then? To righting the wrong! To making amends! To . . . seduction!

"Why are you looking at me like that?"

Reluctantly, Jenny let go of her daydream, turning a puzzled face to where Adam was regarding her with an expression plainly bordering on fear. "Like what?"

"Like I'm the fly and you're the spider!"

Jenny grinned, delighted by the analogy. "And where in this equation, one wonders, is Miss Muffet? On her tuffet, do you suppose?"

"What?" There was no doubt about it. Adam *was* afraid. There were little blobs of sweat beading his brow and one, bolder than the others, rolling steadily down his aspiring-to-be-aquiline nose.

Jenny grinned again, the Cheshire cat! Now you see

me! Now you don't! *"And along came a spider."*
Maddeningly she reached out, wriggled her fingers at
him. *"And sat down beside her. And frightened Miss Muffet
away!* Shall *I* frighten Miss Muffet away, Adam? Buffet
her tuffet? No more curds and whey-hey-hey!"

"What *are* you – nuts?"

"Possibly. In which case, being of unsound mind, I
could quite easily get away with murder. So, look out
little Miss Muffet. Ready or not. Here I co-me!"

Jenny shrugged, feeling a Jack Nicholson manic-
type leer taking possession of her features.

"Huh! I've had enough of this! I'm going out!"
Somewhat unsteadily, Adam headed for the door while
his wife pretending unconcern went straight from *The
Shining* into her *Nightmare on Elm Street* routine, the one
that in the not-so-distant past used to have David
shrieking in mock terror and hurling himself into the
protective circle of his father's arms. 'Help, Dad!
Freddy Krueger's after me! Old Pizza-face!'

"One – two," Jenny crooned in a sing-song voice as,
ramrod-backed, Adam made his bid for freedom,
"Jenny's coming for you – three, four – better lock your
door!"

Chapter Fifteen

"Let's face it, I'm just not cut out for this seduction lark any more than a eunuch is cut out for a willy-warmer. Never mind soft words, sonatas and suspenders, I want to *kill* the bastard. I want to grind his face into the muck left by seven thousand rhinos fed exclusively on a diet of All-Bran. I want to dismember him, slowly, limb from limb, joint by joint, muscle by muscle. I want to volunteer him for the electric chair and volunteer myself to pull the switch. I want – I want . . . Aw, shit! I don't know what I want!"

"God, you've got it bad, haven't you?" Opposite Jenny, Poppy, she of the lost Inner Child and fellow ejectee from Cynthia Straw-legs, ill-fated yoga class, nodded comfortably and with a kind of grim satisfaction. "What did he do to you to get you so hot under the collar? Good at the old bed-aerobics, was he? Is that why you're so desperate to get him back? Did he make your toes curl? Did he get into all those nooks and crannies? Did he go bump in the night?"

"Well, yes and no," Jenny admitted. "But that's not why I want him back, dammit. I want him back because, sad cow that I am, I love the creep!"

"Hence the seduction campaign!"

"Hardly a campaign." Ruefully, Jenny passed the last chocolate éclair over to her companion who had been making lust to it with her eyes for the past ten minutes. Funny that! Once she would have wrestled her for it, got down on the floor and fought dirty. Nails, hair-yanking, biting. The works! Now it didn't cost her a thought. "The problem is my big mouth. *A soft word turneth away wrath.* Isn't that what it says in the Bible? And so I psyche myself up. Tonight, I tell myself, I'm going to be soft, gentle, feminine, one of those 1950s houswifey types in a gingham pinny, all pin curls, bow-lips and a Colgate ring of confidence. Hard day at the office, dear? Never mind. Here you go, pipe, slippers, martini, shaken not stirred. All this plus a willing domestic slave to pander to your every unreasonable demand! What's that? You lost a million quid of the bank's money today? Never mind, dear, they're lucky to have you! Lick! Lick! You're thinking of buying yourself a bachelor pad right in the heart of Soho? Soho what! You deserve it, you hunter, gatherer, provider you! No! Really! Never mind my heart, lung and liver transplant. You need the money more than I do. A bachelor pad sounds great. Just what the doctor ordered!"

"And all this debasing yourself, does it work?"

"Does it buggery! The truth is I never actually get

round to that side of things. You see, despite my best intentions, whenever I open my mouth, tidal waves of bile rush out and Adam turneth full-circle on his heels and goes straight into his *Escape from Alcatraz* routine."

"Well, why have virago when you can have Viagra, I suppose?" Dryly, Poppy wiped a grain of sugar from her top lip with the tip of her finger and popped it in her mouth.

"Exactly! Oh, God, Poppy, tell me what to do."

"Pulleeese! Talk about the blind leading the blind. What do I know about men? Any man I've ever had has upped and left like a hot snot as soon as he got the combination to my combinations. What you need is a good book."

"Been there, read that. Even had a cup of tea!" Jenny sighed. "But it's just not the same, Poppy."

The other woman held up her hand indicating that Jenny wait for a moment whilst she finished masticating the chocolate éclair she'd shovelled into her mouth practically whole.

"Don't be daft. If I'd meant as a substitute I'd have recommended a vibrator. No, I meant one of those self-help, guide-book thingies the Yanks go in for." And, as Jenny looked blank. "Oh come on, you must know, the literary version of those chat shows you're so hung up on? *Penis Envy – Much Ado About Nothing; Lose the Fat Forever – Get a Divorce; Be Chased, Not Chaste!*"

"I'm not sure if any of those would help." Doubtfully, Jenny mopped up a stray blob of cream with the tip of her finger, absent-mindedly copying Poppy's actions, and transferred it to her tongue.

"No? Well, you might find one on seduction. It's worth a try, isn't it?"

"Anything's worth a try," Jenny admitted. "I'd even give one of those medieval scold's bridles a go if it would curb my tongue long enough to get me past first base with Adam; just long enough to have him notice me as a woman again: a warm flesh-and-blood desirable creature capable both of receiving and giving orgasmic pleasure. Especially receiving! In multiples!"

Poppy sighed, looked reflective. "Ah. Those were the days. Days of wine and ooohses! Still, sentiment aside, there's a lot to be said for not lying in a wet patch all night. Actually, I'd trade all the orgasms in the world if only I could find and liberate my Inner Child."

"No luck? Not in the church, then?" The church to which Jenny was referring was actually the local spiritualist meeting place where, upon ducking in out of the rain one evening, she had re-encountered Poppy who was busy laying claim to every spirit the medium was calling forth in the vain hopes that it might be her Inner Child travelling incognito.

"I have a Zulu warrior up here on the stage with me. A proud and fearsome hunter straight out of darkest Africa! Can anyone claim him? Come on now. Don't be shy. He must belong to someone. Three feathers on his head and few more strategically placed about his person! Does anyone recognise the E-Fit?" Jenny had hardly been able to believe her eyes as Poppy, her short-lived yoga companion, had shot up out of a chair a few rows away and begun waving furiously.

"Me! He belongs to me!"

The medium did a good impression of Doubting Thomas. "I don't think so, Missus. I can't see the likeness, myself. If anything, I think he's more likely to belong to this black gentleman over here! Does he ring a bell, sir, this fine specimen out of Africa, seven foot tall and with a new-killed leopard slung over his shoulder?"

"Ain't nobody ringin me bloody bell!" With an indignant flick of his dreadlocks the Rastafarian she'd singled out sent a smack-fuelled glare to where the spirit was supposedly standing. "We don't got no Zulus in Brixton, man! Send de blood clot back where he come from. Me waitin for Bob Marley!"

"See?" Poppy was triumphant. "He doesn't want him. Why can't I have him?"

Mellow, the Rasta shrugged. "Hey, no woman, no cry! You want him? Me cool, man!"

"Well, he's gone now anyway. Someone's Aunty Dora has edged him out of the way. A forceful woman, Aunty Dora, with a good swing in handbags and a degree in nagging. Can anyone place Aunty Dora? Come on now, what am I bid?"

"Me! She belongs to me!" Poppy, again!

And so it had gone on with various spirits apparently trotting out of the distinctly dodgy ectoplasm surrounding the medium (dry ice, Jenny suspected, chemically altered to the colour of runny green snot) and Poppy cheerfully claiming kinship with one and all till Bob Marley put in an appearance and the Rastafarian, taking no chances, forcefully evicted her. Never having been a fan of reggae Jenny had followed, helped her out of the gutter, soothed her ruffled feathers and borne her off for a large G&T, ice and a slice.

Now they met on a regular basis, principally, if Jenny were honest enough to admit it, because there was quite a large gap in her social calendar now that Mounty was dating/fornicating/hibernating with her new love interest and apart from the occasional, somewhat stilted phone conversation, communication levels were at an all-time low.

"We're a right pair, aren't we?" Ruefully, Jenny examined the bottom of her near-empty coffee cup as if seeking answers from the dregs. "What with me trying to seduce my own husband and your Inner Child running amok somewhere. Where will it all end, I ask you!"

"Well, you know what they say. When you've hit rock bottom there's only one way left to go and that's straight back up!"

"Hey, you're not wrong. Actually you're dead right. Why didn't I think of that? Where did all my positivity go? God, I feel like I've really let Oprah down. Talk about a wet please-walk-all-over-me blanket! Well, no more Mr Vice Guy! Adam's had his nose in the trough for far too long. Time he got his oats elsewhere, like from me!"

With a grin and an unladylike burp, Poppy eased her stomach away from the table. "Atta girl, Boadicea! Get in charge! Hop into your winged chariot, grab the reins and go get that sucker!"

"Yeah!" Fuelled by Poppy's fervency, Jenny leapt to her feet. "Just watch this space. That man is going to be so got they'll have to invent a new word for it. But first . . ."

"But first . . .?" Poppy prompted.

"I'm gonna get me one of those books you were on about and if reading the damn thing doesn't do any good I can always throw it at him."

"Yeah. Throw the book at him!" Poppy nodded. "Give him chapter and verse. After all, good sex is like a good book. The beginning should grab you, the middle should hold you and the ending should be nothing if not explosive."

"But what about Farina?" As usual the little imp that was negativity couldn't help but put in an appearance on Jenny's shoulder.

"Huh!" Poppy was dismissive. "She's just a short story. Over and done with in just a few pages whilst you – you are an epic!"

"Which one? *War and Peace? Gone With the Wind?*"

"I can't think about that now. I'll think about it tomorrow!" Poppy joked, borrowing from Scarlett O'Hara's famous last words. "In the meantime, how about an éclair for the road?"

Jenny shook her head. "No thanks. Better strike while the iron is hot and the bookshop is still open."

"Okey-dokey! Call me."

"I will," Jenny promised but it was doubtful as to whether Poppy even heard her, riveted as her attention suddenly was on the large Black Forest gateau a waitress was bringing through from the kitchen. "Of Kirsch I will. Cherry oh!"

Chapter Sixteen

"I want to die! Oh God, I want to die so badly I can taste it! I want the ground to open up and swallow me. I want to embrace the Grim Reaper, lie down by his scythe. I want my name to be erased forever and for all time from the annals of living memory."

"Do you indeed?" Jenny's mother yawned widely, patting her fingers against her mouth as though uttering a Red Indian war cry. "Look, Jenny, if you were as dramatic in the marital bed as you are on my living-room carpet, I'm sure Adam would never have had the energy to go out putting it about in the first place!"

"Drama!" Jenny practically spat, flouncing over to the sideboard where her mother kept a liberal supply of spirits and reaching for the brandy decanter. "Trying to be dramatic in the marital bed, well okay table, is what's got me into this mess and I swear I want to *dieeee!*"

Sighing, Gloria threw her eyes up to Heaven and resigned herself to a long evening of daughterly hysteria. "Pass me a drink, a large one, and start at the beginning. What's all this about beds and tables?" Doing as she was told, Jenny, glass in hand, flopped into an untidy heap on the floor opposite, her eyes coming into direct line with a particularly knotted, varicose vein running the length of her mother's leg and disappearing beneath the hemline of her patchwork, leather mini-skirt.

"It was Poppy's idea, actually. Or at least the book was!"

"Ah yes, Poppy. The lost Inner Child woman?"

Jenny sniffed, nodded. "Yep. The little blighter's still on the loose too! Anyway Poppy suggested I get one of those self-help books . . ."

"I have a few myself actually. *How to Treat your Man like a Dog; K9? Don't Whine; Give the Dog a Bone.*"

"Yeah, that kind of thing." Jenny interrupted hastily, fearful that her mother would go off at a very long tangent and that all roads would, eventually, lead to Rover. "Only I got one on seduction. *80 Ways Around the World – To Seduce your Lover!*" Jenny took a long swallow of her drink, desperately trying to control the trembling of her voice. "And it was a good read, funny too. From China: Go to Wok – Make him sweet, not sour. From Ireland: In a stew? Get your Shamrocks off! From Germany: Things gone from bad to Wurst? Stick your nose in his lederhosen!"

Her mother giggled! "So which country did you opt for?"

"Japan, for my sins!"

"Ah let me guess. *If you knew Sushi like I know Sushi . . .*"

Jenny shook her head. "No, it was all about turning yourself into a living table. Apparently rich, Japanese business-men types go to these restaurants where all the waitresses lie round starkers with bits of sushi, sake, teriyaki and God knows what else balanced on their bodies and when the men have finished eating, the table is their afters as it were."

"And you thought turning yourself into a piece of Sheraton sounded like a good idea?"

"Oh Lordy! I know it sounds moronic but desperate measures and all that!" Her chin came up, a weak attempt at bravado. "It was different, anyway. Not your usual run-of-the-mill blindfolds and feather dusters stuff."

"No argument there! So, cut to the chase. What happened? Did Adam lose his appetite at the sight of a piece of lettuce covering your groin? Did he turn into an iceberg, make his excuses and leaf? What?"

"Worse!" Before she could continue Jenny felt the need for another, reassuring, false-courage-giving gulp of brandy. "He – he brought a colleague home!"

"What!"

"You heard me!" her daughter nodded furiously. "For the first time in yonks the bastard decided to bring a colleague home for dinner."

"And *you* were the dinner! Oh, Jenny!" Unable to

help herself her mother burst out laughing and to Jenny's surprise she found an answering urge in herself.

"That's right! Picture the scene! David's safely out of the way at his mate's house. I spend a good hour whipping up all sorts of goodies that won't melt, slide off or scald my sensitive bits; another hour bathing, waxing, perfuming the body beautiful. And, as if all that wasn't enough, then I have to work out the logistics of getting me onto the carpet in a pose both sexy and alluring; balancing the damn food on my spare tyre and, the piece de resistance, skewer an olive onto each nipple without dislodging the pimiento stuffing."

Gloria spluttered. "Oh God. I only wish I'd been a fly on the wall. What did Adam say?"

"He said 'Darling, I hope you don't mind but I've brought Jim, here, home for dinner . . .'"

"And?"

"I don't know. All I do know is that I jumped up like a scalded cat, turned my arse to the pair of them, high-tailed it up the stairs and locked myself into the bathroom for the next twenty-four hours. I'd still be there, in fact, only David came home desperate for a pee and madder than hell that he'd missed the 'food-fight' in the living-room."

"Oh, Jenny! There's more of me in you than you'll admit to."

"Maybe!" Jenny gasped, wiping eyes that were

streaming now. "But *I* wouldn't be caught dead wearing that mini!"

"So what happens now? Is there a plan B?"

"No!" She shook her head. "No plan B! But I still haven't given up on plan A, though I know the memory of me with my butt covered in black-bean sauce will live with him for a very long time. Still, they say time is a great healer and – well maybe one day –"

"They also say time to call it a day and time to know when you're beaten. Don't you think that time might be now? For your sanity's sake? For the sake of all our sanity?"

"Not a chance!" Jenny mutinied. "I married him for better or worse and he made the same vows. Time to remind him of his!" Using an armchair for leverage, Jenny pulled herself up from the carpet, flicking her fingers over the knees of her jeans. Yes, jeans! Not barrage-ballooned tracksuit bottoms or shapeless, polyester pants with a permanent crease down the front and elasticated or drawstring waists. Proper denim-blue, bona fide 501s! Okay! Okay! So it took five minutes to do the buttons up but, hey, they *did* up and that's what counts! *And* they were a fourteen! "Besides, as I've said a hundred and one times before, I love him!"

"Well, he couldn't love *you*, not if he's off mowing some other woman's lawn and, come to think of it, *have* you managed to pluck up the courage to ask him outright yet?"

"No, but I've thrown out broad hints so I'm sure he knows I know!"

"But you're sure he's firing on all cylinders with someone else?"

"As far as I know! He hasn't been putting his tiger in my tank, and that's for sure!"

"So, that's all you're worth, is it?" Slowly, deliberately, Jenny's mother lit up a cigarette, her eyes all the while holding those of her daughter, retina to retina, in a kind of visual headlock. "A womanising bastard with close-set eyes, a dimple in his chin and a member with no allegiance to any specific club! Did I bring you up with so little self-esteem? So little self-respect?"

"No, you brought me up like vomit!" Jenny shot back, not because it had any real bearing but, because she'd heard some comedian say it and had sworn to use it herself at the first opportunity. Guessing as much, Gloria ignored the witticism.

"Take a good look at yourself, Jenny! You've come a long way and in just a few, short months. All credit to you! All right, so your evening of sex and sake got the chopsticks but, look at it this way; not so long ago you wouldn't let your own shadow see you naked much less stretch out like a human buffet. If you're confident enough to do that, you're confident enough to offload that slimeball you married. I swear, that man puts the rat in prat!"

"I wish you wouldn't talk about him like that! He's *still* my husband *and* your grandson's father!"

"More's the pity! Because he's fallen down on both counts! Badly!" Climbing on her well-worn soapbox Gloria continued berating the absent Adam despite the ever-growing, mulish look on her daughter's face. "Even a squirrel would have been a better husband to you and a better father for David. At least squirrels mate for life and hoard their nuts instead of spreading them about willy-nilly. *And* they provide for their young!"

"That's not fair. Adam *does* provide for us."

"Materially, yes," Her mother conceded. "But now that you're working you can do that for yourself. What about emotionally? Physically? What about just being there for you, giving you the odd hug when PMT strikes or just because you're you and he feels like it. You know, the little things, the touches, the kisses, the pillow-talks, the empathy that makes a relationship between two people special! What about all that, Jenny? Eh? Is that not important?"

"Of course it's important!" Jenny bit her lip. "We *had* all that in the past. Why do you think I'm trying so hard to get him back?"

"Exactly!" Her mother threw up her hands. "I rest my case. As I said before *you're* the one making all the running. It takes two to tango but he'd rather be quick-stepping the other way. Get a life, Jenny! Get rid of Adam!"

"Never!" Rebelliously, Jenny picked up, shrugged herself into her jacket. Denim to match her jeans! "Why should I let *her* win?"

"Win? Don't be silly! Nobody ever wins by backing a loser. If he'll cheat on you, he'll cheat on her. Leopards don't change their spots. Once a cheetah, always a cheetah!"

"You're wrong! You'll see."

"I'll toast to that." Dramatically, Gloria held out her brandy glass. "Here's to Clearasil for leopards!"

"Cheers!" Jenny took her cue, but her own glass was already drained on the sideboard.

Chapter Seventeen

If the Mounty won't come to Mohammed, Mohammed must go to the Mounty. Or at least that had been the plan but seemingly nobody had been home when, armed with a bottle of Beaujolais, Jenny had rolled up and knocked smartly on the door.

"Come on. Come on. Bring out your dead! Open up, you old slapper, you!" But the door had remained firmly closed against her, the blinds on the windows (Mounty loathed nets with a passion) fully lowered like eyes that are hiding a secret. Puzzled, Jenny had walked round back to investigate the garage only to find Mounty's fire-engine-red Ferarri, pulling power on wheels as she dubbed it, still there, crouched in the semi-darkness, its lights mimicking the windows of the house, fully retracted and giving nothing away.

"She's gone away, love. Italy, I think. Not that I hold with the place myself! Too many Eyetalians for my liking!"

Startled, Jenny emerged to find a woman she took to be Mounty's neighbour making her way towards her.

"Oh right! Thank you. She must have forgotten to mention it."

"Ah!" The woman tapped her nose, sidling up to the fence dividing her garden from Mounty's and leaning her chest, the hanging gardens of Berlei 50 DD, over it. "That's love for you. Everything else goes clean out of your mind. Not that I blame her, mind you. A hunk like him doesn't come free with every packet of cornflakes. If he were mine, I'd nail him to the bed and only let him up again when the vicar had done his duty. And, only then, with one of those tracking device things they use on prisoners, strapped around his ankle."

"Really?" Jenny regarded the woman with interest. From what she was saying it looked like Mounty had hit the jackpot. No wonder she was keeping a low profile these days; probably had the vicar on a retainer if the truth were told. "That special, is he?" Casually, Jenny tried to elicit more information from the nosey neighbour who, like all professional gossips, was only too eager to spill the beans.

"Special? I'll say. This one is real fairy-tale stuff. You know, the tall, dark, handsome prince the fairground Tarot reader tells you is just around the corner; only, when he does round it, lo and behold, he's usually turned into Plug, the fat, ugly dwarf from the Big Top who makes a living by pouring paint down the inside of his trouser-leg and farting the Last Post through a bugle?"

Jenny grinned, her imagination caught by the breathless description.

"Only this prince stayed a prince!" said the woman.

"Wow! I don't suppose you know his name, by any chance?"

Mrs Nosey-N shook her head. "No. Plays her cards real close to her chest, that one. Only, I'd put money on it he's a married man."

Coldly Jenny raised her eyebrows but the woman mistook the gesture as a sign of encouragement. "Oh? What makes you say that."

The other woman roared. "Well, it's the jungle noises coming from the bedroom, isn't it? Married-man-let-loose noises, that's what they are. Talk about the call of the wild! I swear I don't get a wink of sleep even though there's a good step between her house and mine. Lucky cow!" With the equivalent of a nose-tapping glance, she tugged at Jenny's sleeve. "Mind you, even if you never heard a sound, you'd know anyway by the way he sneaks in behind her, looking over his shoulder constantly like *Crimewatch's* Most Wanted."

Jenny bristled. "Look, I've known Diana Mountford a long time and let me assure you there's no way she'd entertain a married man even for one second, at least not in the way you mean." Tugging her sleeve free, she stepped away from the fence. "So I'll thank you to keep your slanderous remarks to yourself."

The neighbour squinted. "Oh, touched a raw nerve, have I? Your own husband wouldn't happen to be playing an away game, would he?"

"No!" Jenny snapped. "No, he wouldn't! Now, if

you don't mind, I've got better things to do with my time than to stand here listening to a pack of scurrilous lies."

"Hmmph! Suit yourself. It's no skin off my nose, I'm sure."

Squinting her own eyes, Jenny stepped forwards threateningly. "Any more of that kind of talk and there'll be plenty of skin off your nose, believe me."

* * *

"I wouldn't mind if you and Dad got divorced." As usual, David had chosen a time when he had his mouth full to have a heart-to-heart. He swallowed convulsively. "I mean, it would mean I'd have two of everything, wouldn't it? Two homes. Two bikes. Two Playstations."

"Two mothers?" Jenny could feel her heart dropping right down into her shoes, the spike-heeled Roland Cartier numbers she had taken to wearing to work and had forgotten to kick off in favour of her flatties.

"Don't be silly, Mum. Even if Dad does marry again *she'll* only be my stepmother. Nobody can take your place! Really, you must learn to value yourself more."

Despite her anxiety Jenny grinned. "Who's been watching *Oprah*?"

"*Sally Jessey-Raphael*, actually! But seriously, Mum, there's no point in you moping all over the place. Dad's not moping, is he? No way! He's off in – where is he?"

"Tuscany."

"Yeah, Tuscany! Setting up deals and things for the bank. You can't wheel and deal if you're moping, can you?"

"No, I don't suppose you can. Do you want some more pasta?"

David nodded."Yes, please. This bolognese is cool, man. I'll bet Dad's new wife can't cook for nuts!"

"Dad's new wife?" Jenny frowned. "Dad doesn't *have* a new wife, David. Dad has an *old* wife. Me!"

David nodded, sloppily sucking a sauce-covered strand of spaghetti into his mouth. "I know. I mean *when*."

"When! Well, you've changed your tune, haven't you?" Jenny found herself rapidly going off the mound of pasta on her own plate. "Weren't you the one who was telling me not to be stupid, that Dad was always watching me when I wasn't looking?"

"I know." Casually reaching for the glass of milk by his plate he took a long swallow, wiping the resulting white moustache away from his lips with the back of his hand. "But that was before."

"Before?"

"Before I saw them together."

Shakily Jenny pushed her own plate away, dimly aware that the food she'd already eaten had somehow transformed itself into a piece of solid lead in her stomach. "You saw them together? When?"

David shrugged. "Oh. A while ago!"

"And you didn't think it worth mentioning, is that it? Didn't think I'd be interested, eh?"

167

"I had to think about it. Besides, I knew you'd be upset."

"Upset!" Jenny banged on the table. "You bet your life I'm upset. What did the trollop look like, anyway?" Jenny hated herself for asking but, heck, she was only human.

"I couldn't get a good look. They were too far away. Dad was holding the car door open for her. But she did have red hair!"

The bitch! Red hair but I'll bet her pubes don't match! Jenny thought viciously, rapidly reviewing her mental picture of Farina. "Maybe that was his secretary?"

"No!" David was merciless in his certainty. "*She's* got blond hair, big boobs and looks like what's-her-name that does those car adverts. Claudia thingy. You know the one? Dad gave me a fiver not to tell you about her when I bumped into them once on my way home from scouts. He said he acted on the 'need to know principle' and you didn't need to know! He said you'd only get hold of the wrong end of the stick and go upsetting yourself unnecessarily."

"Oh, he did, did he?" The dirty, rotten, scum-sucking, serial adulterer! "And what did he bribe you with this time?"

"Nothing! He didn't see me. Too busy playing Sir Walter Raleigh."

Well, I'll pull his bloody cloak out from under him! Viciously, Jenny stabbed her fork into the mountain of pasta on her plate, twirling it round and round, a physical manifestation of the whirlwind of confusion within her. "And does he know what the butler saw?"

David shook his head. "No. I kinda felt a bit funny about it but I'm all right now cos I know *you'll* find somebody new too. Because you're not fat any more, are you, Mum! *And* you *do* things now. I mean you don't vegetate like you used to. I *was* a bit worried when I thought Dad might go off and leave you on your own because you might not be able to cope but, you *can* cope. Can't you, Mum?"

"Well, thanks a bundle, David. Talk about backhand compliments! But yes, I expect I'll cope. I don't suppose I've got much choice. Besides your Dad is bound to see sense sooner or later and come home with his tail between his legs."

David rose and carried his plate, licked clean, over to the sink. "Shame! I could have done with another Playstation. Honest, Mum! When it comes to computer games, I'm the main man!"

Ah, the games people play! Jenny mused sadly, watching him switch his attention to the freezer section of the refrigerator in which reposed his favourite brand of ice lolly. Everyone was playing games; her mother and Rover playing at animalympics; her boss playing at masochism; Poppy playing at soul-searching; Mounty playing, period; Adam playing away. As for herself, well she was just playing dumb! Or maybe plain dumb! Still, games usually presupposed an element of competition – therefore there were winners and losers.

With a supreme effort she pulled herself together. David's news had certainly been a shock to the system. No doubt about that! Still, as they said in show business, the show's not over till the fat lady wins! But *I'm* not in show business. Gloomily, Jenny peered at her reflection as she made her way up the stairs later that evening.

"Well, you are in a way." For a change its response was encouraging. "On the fringes as it were. Hanging on Martyna Michael's coat-tails. So here's another old showbiz saying for you. Go break a leg! To be specific, go break Farina's leg!"

Tenderly, Jenny picked up a duster and polished away a smear on her reflection's nose "You know, if I tried really hard I might get to like you!"

"Yeah?" Inevitably the mirror reverted to sarcastic type. "Well, if I tried really hard *I* might get to relish being the spitting image of a cow's backside!"

"Moo!" Jenny stuck her tongue out and continued on her way. *"Moo! Moo! Moo!"*

Chapter Eighteen

"I don't get it! I mean I just don't get it!" Casually, Martyna Michaels perched atop her desk, her miles-long 15-denier-clad legs elegantly punctuated at the feet by a pair of high-heeled Italian sandals that frequently had Marcel positively frothing at the mouth. "I mean what will it take to make you come right out and tackle him. Do you really need to witness it with your own eyes; catch them in *flagrante delicto*, as it were?"

"Flagrante Delicto?" Jenny furrowed her brow. "Isn't that one of those off-the-beaten-track places featured on *Wish You Were Here* recently? Sandwiched between the arse-hole of Morocco and Tunisia? A real coup for Judith Chalmers, if I remember rightly, and the very next week, there was a real coup when General Shish Kebab and Colonel Marijuana from nearby Tentville turned up and started shooting the djellabas off each other."

Plainly unimpressed with Jenny's feeble distraction techniques, the chat-show hostess brought a shapely hand up before her nose, scrutinising the silk-wrapped talons for tell-tale signs of regrowth around the cuticle. "Cut the crap, Jenny. I mean it! For goodness sake, how many horses' mouths do you need to hear it from and don't go giving me all that balls about loving him. *Nobody*, not even the most self-abasing, characterless, devoid-of-all-self-esteem, mono-celled micro-organism could love someone who treats them the way Adam treats you."

"Marcel could!"

"Agreed! But then, Marcel is the exception that proves the rule and if you think you're wriggling off the hook that easy, think again! It's D Day, Jenny. Decision day. Time to perform or get off the potty. You do not love Adam! Adam is a habit, a bad habit like picking your nose or farting in a crowded lift and exiting on the next floor. Now repeat after me. I hate habits! Nuns wear habits! I hate nuns!"

After the intensity of the lead-up, Jenny couldn't help but giggle. "You're mad!"

"No way!" Deliberately the other woman shook her head, her mane of dark hair, now that she was off the air, liberated from its habitual French pleat. "You're the one who's mad; mad to stay with a man who thinks so little of you that he thinks he's shagging for Britain and trains all year round; mad not to see that you're worth more; mad to try and hang on to something that simply isn't there."

"Mad for it!" Marcel added, coming into the room

and honing in on Martyna's high heels like a Klingon on the Starship Enterprise. "Just one lick, please." Dropping to his knees he sniffed the air around her feet as resignedly the chat-show hostess slipped off one of her shoes, extended a foot and chucked him under the chin with her silky toes.

"We were just talking about the devoted Adam."

"Oh God! Not again!" Marcel rose morosely to his feet. "You don't half run on, Jenny. I swear I hate that man! Just the sound of his name sends me insane."

Miffed and not a little hurt, Jenny began busying herself tidying coffee cups onto a psychedelic, plastic tray preparatory to bringing them through to the kitchenette for washing. PA, she had quickly learned, whilst sounding delightfully impressive, was no more than an upmarket label for a gopher whose duties ranged wildly anywhere between booking champagne parties aboard Concorde one minute, to sourcing the latest range of fetish headwear for Marcel the next. So much for databases and networking! As for downsizing, the only downsizing going on around here was Marcel and Martyna cutting *her* down to size!

"I'm not that bad, am I?"

"Worse!" The pair were unanimous in their condemnation. Quickly, Martyna drained the dregs of her coffee before, none too graciously, Jenny whisked the cup away.

"Honestly, Jenny! The man's name is never off your lips!"

"I think you must be confusing him with chocolate!" Odd that, Jenny thought, as the pair chuckled at her remark; odd how she still felt obliged to make 'fat jokes' at her own expense even though her jeans size told her she was no longer fat. Maybe there was something in Martyna's theory, after all. Maybe she *was* that self-abasing, characterless, devoid-of-all-self-esteem, mono-celled micro-organism and that's why she felt compelled to put herself down. The thought hurt!

"I'm hurt!" Jenny told them, grabbing an errant teaspoon that looked like it had gone seven rounds with Uri Geller and jamming it into a mug. "I'm really hurt!" This was good! That German counsellor on *Sally-Jessey* liberally advised people to share their feelings.

"Open up to the vorld and the vorld vill open up to you. Tell the vorld your business and make it the vorld's business. Share your feelings vith the vorld, vy don't you? Go on! Gif it a dry!"

"I'm really, really hurt!" Jenny tried again as the 'vorld', at least in the office, turned a deaf ear and began chuntering on about ratings, nepotism and rats at the BBC. "I'm hurt so badly I'm bleeding all over the carpet!"

"You'll be bleeding pissing off down the dole queue if you don't wash those cups and get back here *tout de suite* with your pencil and notepad." Flashing a grin, Marcel took any harm out of the words. "Then you'll hurt twice as badly! And whilst you're faffing about

174

with the Fairy, see if you can't come up with an idea for a decent show. I swear, good ideas are about as rare as a sighting of Michael Jackson without a scalpel hanging out of his nose. But please," he held up a restraining hand, "nothing beginning with the 'A' word."

"What!" Astonished, Jenny rocked back on her heels. "Do you mean it? I mean, you'd really consider my ideas?"

"Why not?" Languidly, Martyna Michaels slid off the desk, retrieving her miniskirt en route from somewhere around her crotch area and smoothing it down to its full six inches. "There's only so many *'I was kidnapped by a little, green man with a big, anal probe'* and *'My husband's run off with my neighbour's pot-bellied pig and now they're expecting the sound of little trotters'* shows you can do! In Kamera is now at the begging-bowl stage. Any contributions will, I assure you, be gratefully received. Right, Marcel?"

"Right! So long as they don't begin with . . ."

"I know, I know," Jenny interrupted. "The dreaded 'A' word. Don't worry, from now on my alphabet begins with 'B'. And I *have* some ideas as it happens. I just didn't mention them before in case you thought I was being presumptuous, what with me being the new kid on the block around here and you TV types being so sensitive."

"Cobblers!" Marcel sniffed. "Martyna wouldn't know sensitivity if it jumped up and bit her in the *derrière*, which is what makes her so good at what she does. As for *moi*, I like to think of myself more as the artistic type though, admittedly, there are parts of my anatomy which could, in all fairness, be described as sensitive. Want a look?"

"Pass!" Jenny grinned. "I have a delicate stomach, cups to wash, invoices to pay and a rep coming up from Leatherhead with the latest samples in fetish wear."

"Leatherhead?" Marcel looked pleased. "How appropriate!"

"Yes, well don't get carried away. For once, it's not for you but for the guests on Martyna's show next week. You remember, the one about mammy's boys with a penchant for rock chicks?"

"Ah, yes! *'Sonny, she's a slapper. Leather go!'*"

"Right!"

"That's not tomorrow, then?"

"Uh huh! Tomorrow's is *'I'm no atheist. I just don't believe in Goth'*."

"God, who comes up with those titles? Honestly, they're becoming more Springeresque than the man himself."

"You did," Jenny and Martyna accused simultaneously.

"Of course I did. What a genius I am! Remind me to give myself a rise. Speaking of rises, you won't mind me sitting in on that meeting with the sales rep, Jenny, will you?

"Not at all. Just be careful not to rubber me up the wrong way for the rest of the morning, that's all."

"Ho ho! Hah hah! Funny girl. Rubber you up.

That's a good one. Maybe, as well as coming up with some ideas, you should have a bash at writing some of the titles. What do you think, Martyna?"

"Why not? They can't be any worse than yours. I mean who can forget your 'in extremely bad taste' *pièce de résistance* on Prince Charles recently."

"Prince Charles. Throne alone! Actually, I was quite proud of that. I'm just looking forward to the day when I can pen a title for Di's successor. What about 'Throne out!' No? Well then, what do you reckon to 'They shoot horses, don't they?'"

"Tacky!" Jenny anchored the tea tray firmly against one hip, endeavouring vainly with her free hand to open the door. "Definitely tacky. Now, do you think you could drag yourself away from your creative muse long enough to hold this door open for me? Thank you!"

Out in the kitchen, alone with her thoughts, Jenny wondered why she no longer felt quite as exhilarated about being asked to take a more active role in Martyna's show; why it was the gloss seemed suddenly to have worn off the day. It was Marcel's remark, of course.

"They shoot horses, don't they?"

Horses! Mares! Old mares, to be specific. Fit only, if they were lucky, to be put out to pasture. Failing that, a bullet in the brain maybe, or an undignified end in a tin of genetically modified cat-food. When surveyed, seven out of ten cat owners said their cats preferred Old Woman cat food.

"I'm not an old woman," Jenny shouted, grabbing a mug and viciously submerging it beneath the water as though it might suddenly discover itself the possessor of both a voice and an argumentative nature and refute her statement out of hand. "I'm not an old mare. I have nothing in common with Camilla P-B except, maybe, that her fella is Royalty and mine only thinks he is! 'They shoot horses, don't they?' Well, not if the horse has a kick like a mule and knows where to land it!"

"Jenny?" Puzzled, Martyna Michaels' voice followed her into the kitchen. "Are you all right? I thought I heard shouting!"

"I'm fine!" Jenny called back, surprised to find that she meant it. "Absolutely kicking!"

Chapter Nineteen

"God, I feel awful. So disloyal! I mean I don't want you to get the wrong impression of Mounty. I mean, she's wonderful really . . ."

"But . . .?"

"But she's changed. Since this new Lothario arrived on the scene, she's just not been the same."

Mournfully, Poppy swallowed the last crumbs of a cream doughnut. "Shit! I hate women like that. One minute they're all over you like zits on a teenager, the next they're blanking you like your nose is peeling and you're ringing a bell. And why? Because . . . eureka! They've found a man! A *man*, no less! All hail and bow to the great God, Penile Two-Balls!"

"No!" Vehemently, Jenny shook her head. "Mounty's never been that type. If anything her philosophy has always been hump 'em and dump 'em. She never put any man before her friends."

"Until now!"

"Exactly. He's no good for her, Poppy, not that I've

met him or anything. I just sense it. And that's another thing. Why hasn't she let me meet him? I've met them all before – the long and the short and the tall. Well, any she's dated for more than a few weeks, anyway. But for some unknown reason, this latest bloke seems to be strictly off-limits."

Poppy shrugged and widened her eyes dramatically. "Could be she's hiding a deep, dark secret."

"I must admit the thought *had* occurred to me. Like what though?" Intently Jenny leaned across the table, narrowly avoiding dunking her elbow in a puddle of spilt coffee.

"Like, maybe he's a well-known personality/film star/politician/football player; someone who wants to guard their privacy; someone who doesn't want to wake up one morning and read about their latest sexual exploits in the Sunday tabloids. You know, like banner headlines, three inches high? *'Hung like King Kong. He Gorill'd me about my Fantasies,* says X's latest conquest, *then Sent me Ape in Bed.'* Absent-mindedly, Poppy doodled her index finger in the pool of coffee and drew a matchstick man on the table. "Then again, could be the oldest story in the book. He's married and she's sworn under penalty of no more illicit nookie, magnums of champagne and silk drawers from Janet Reger to keep her gob shut."

"Nah. Not Mounty! She's got far too much self-respect ever to settle for being someone's bit on the side. Besides, she's always said how she despised women who hurt other women."

"Yeah?" Poppy added horns and a tail to her matchstick man. "Well, circumstances alter cases."

"Could be," Jenny mused, thinking how Mounty's nosey neighbour had said something along the same lines. "But I sincerely doubt it. I'll tell you what I do know though, and that's that she's hardly spoken to me over the last few months and on the very few occasions when I *did* actually manage to persuade her to meet me, she was like a cat on a hot tin roof. Talk about BO. I was positive I must be reeking like a two-month-old corpse." Aggrieved, Jenny rubbed out Poppy's doodle and embarked on one of her own. "*And*, as if that wasn't enough, she only goes and pisses off to Italy recently without breathing a blind word and yours truly only finds out because Mrs Nosey-Neighbour next door can't wait to puke it up."

"Fishy! Definitely fishy! Still, my money's on the married man theory. Maybe it's someone you know and because she said all that stuff about sisterly solidarity, she's ashamed of looking like a hypocrite in front of you. You know, the modern-day equivalent of Emmeline Pankhurst selling the suffragettes down river."

"I shouldn't think so. Since David was born, my social circle has shrunk to pinhead proportions. Apart from a couple of Adam's colleagues, fat bores all of 'em, Mr McCloskey who comes in once a week to do the garden – eighty if he's a day with a bad case of Alzheimer's – Denzil and Marcel, one gay, the other a perv, I don't really know any other men." Jenny grinned. "Oh, apart from Adam and *they* cordially hate each other's guts!"

Poppy looked thoughtful. "Aha! Love and hate! Opposing colours on the spectrum but closer on the emotional scale than one might suppose!"

"Don't even go there!" Jenny warned a sudden note of steel entering her voice. "Mounty might be behaving out of character but she's still my best friend. And as for Adam, he's much too busy laying all his love on the nubile Farina even so much as to glance at Mounty."

Poppy backed down immediately. "Fair enough. Just a thought! Stranger things and all that!"

"Yes. Well, not in this case. There's more likelihood of Adam hitching his wagon to my mother than to Mounty."

Yawning loudly, Poppy, not bothering to hide her mouth with her hand, treated sundry diners and waiting staff to unspoiled views of her tonsillectomy. "Okay. Okay. Don't labour the point. Anyway, fancy a game of noughts and crosses?"

"Only if I can be noughts!"

"Oookay!" Dabbling in the spillage once more, Poppy expertly drew a small grid and quickly popped a grain of sugar in one corner. "Imagine that's an X." Following suit, Jenny placed a crumb in the centre, her eyes rising expectantly to Poppy in order to divine her strategy. Would she move right along the top of the grid, or down the side? Up or down? As schoolgirls, she and Mounty had often played noughts and crosses, giggling away at the back of the class. The pair of them, in cahoots! Two against the world! And Mounty, tongue concentratedly between her lips, had always come out on top, filling her box with a neat row of Xs. Funny how things didn't change much. When she left school she had gone on and on filling her box with a neat row of exes. Until now!"

"Bugger!" Jenny swore as Poppy popped a final X in a neat row of three and drew a watery line through it. "Not fair. I wasn't concentrating."

"No? Well, you know what happens to people who don't concentrate. They end up losers!"

"I know. You're preaching to the converted. After all, that's how I lost Adam. By not concentrating. On him! On our marriage! On David!"

"Oh oh! I feel a quick stage-left coming on." Leaping to her feet, Poppy almost overturned the table. "I can't help it." Shrugging she cast a quick look of apology at Jenny. "All that ashes on the head stuff and self-flagellating brings me out all peculiar!"

Jenny groaned, sticking out a detaining hand. "God, I'm sorry. I must be turning into a real bore."

"Well, I'll put it to you like this, you'd never be out of a job in Texas."

"Well, thanks a lot, Poppy. With friends like you, who needs . . ."

"Mounty?"

I do. Jenny thought sadly, with an airy wave, as they split up and headed off to their respective cars. I do!

* * *

Sometimes she thought he was going to come right out and tell her – sometimes, when he got that goldfish look on his face where his mouth opened and closed but nothing came out – not even a bubble. And she would steel herself in anticipation waiting for the finger on the button that would irrevocably change everything, for the bomb to drop, for the mushroom cloud to shoot up in the air – waiting for the fall-out! But seemingly, neither of them had the courage, Adam to tell, she to listen and the 'Jenny, I'm having an affair' she would hear in her mind would translate in real terms into 'Jenny, what's for dinner?' or 'Jenny, have you been using my brand new razor to shave your legs again?' And she would exhale her relief in a hurricane, glad not to have her hand forced before she was ready and set about preparing the dinner with gusto and categorically denying, till she was blue in the face, all knowledge of the two-inch hairs clogging up his razor.

Indeed, there was still the odd occasion when she was almost able to forget about it all, to convince herself that Paradise was open for business as usual and that she and Adam had tickets for the front row. Those were the increasingly rare nights on which he stayed home and, fed and watered, they all settled down to shout out the answers to *Who Wants To Be A Millionaire* or *Catchphrase*. Revelling in the commonplace role of wife and mother she would fuss about pouring them both a glass of wine, Coke for David of course, unnecessarily plumping up the cushions on the settee and just generally soaking up the sheer ordinariness of it all, the rightness of it all. Too often though, Adam's mobile would ring and he'd disappear upstairs to take the call in private, returning with a closed and shuttered look on his face once more, and going out 'to the pub' soon after. Maybe it was a case of wishful thinking but sometimes she imagined he looked almost as unhappy as she herself, hunted almost, and she wondered, given the chance, if he too wouldn't like to turn the clock back. But life, as her mother often said, wasn't like that. Actions had consequences and if Adam was reaping the consequences of his actions, then she and David were as well and he, at least, was having some fun in the process. Still, she couldn't help but see the 'ordinary' times as a bonus, a kind of island of tranquillity in otherwise shark-infested waters and wish that they were marooned there together, a kind of latter-day Robinson Crusoe and his Girl Friday.

Presumably it was this same wish that had formed the basis of the very strange dream she had one night and which, even now, she found difficult to believe didn't, in fact, happen. The prelude had been a hectic day at the studios, the kind of day where everything that can go wrong does. The mikes had been the first thing to go on the blink. Then the star guest due to appear on *Martyna* had got involved in a motorway pile-up and ended up having a starring role in the operating theatre of a nearby hospital instead. Marcel had been like a demon from hell on account of breaking the zip on his best leather hood and the make-up artist, a woman more beef per pound than a herd of Aberdeen Angus, had thrown an unholy fit when her suppliers had sent the wrong brand of foundation. And as if all that weren't enough to cope with, Jenny only had to go and shunt a police car on the way home. Small wonder then that when she finally got to bed that night she was completely and utterly exhausted, falling asleep almost immediately her head hit the pillow. There were no dark handsome strangers in her dream, no sandy beaches, no blue skies. Neither were there monsters chasing her or confused scary images of tumbling inexorably over a cliff with no one to hear her cries. No, quite simply she dreamt of Adam, standing by her bed, dimly registered his form fading in and out of her consciousness, his face bent over her, tender and loving like in the old days. Drowsily, she felt the light butterfly touch of his lips on hers, the velvet stroke of a finger gently smoothing back a lock of hair from her forehead, heard his voice, barely a whisper.

"I love you, Jenny. I've always loved you."

In the morning she'd looked for him. The dream had been vivid – so vivid she could still feel the heat of his lips on hers, feel the warmth of his love surrounding her, cherishing her, making her feel special. And she wanted it to have been real – so desperately wanted it to have been real that when got up and read the note he'd left behind she was physically sick.

Gone to Italy on a spot of business. Expect me when you see me! Adam.

Chapter Twenty

"Mum! Mum! Look what Dad got me from Italy." Proudly David modelled the Juventus football strip his father had brought him from Italy. "Wait till Simon gets a load of this. He'll be sick as a parrot!"

"Wow! Georgie Best eat your heart out!"

David looked puzzled. "Who's he?"

Jenny grinned. "Ah. Nobody you'd know. He was well before your time, and Beckham's, come to that. Anyway, you look..." She racked her brains for a suitable adjective, "wicked!"

Raising his right palm, David gave her a high-five. "Way to go, Mum! And Dad didn't forget *you* either. Wait here!" Dashing out of the kitchen he reappeared a moment later, something long and phallic-like clutched in his hand. "Here! Dad asked me to give you this; said he had to dash out on a bit of business."

Yeah, right! Jenny thought, but hid her feelings from David who was dancing impatiently from one foot to the other as she struggled to undo the wrapping.

"What is it?" His face fell. "Oh, the leaning tower of Pisa! That's nice, Mum!"

"Isn't it though?" Inanely, Jenny grinned, as though to be the proud possessor of a fifteen-inch, cream-plastic pepper-grinder was the culmination of all her greatest desires. And not just any old pepper-grinder what's more but one with such severe curvature of the spine that she reckoned if she were to go outside and throw it, it would return full circle like a homing pigeon or an Aborigine's boomerang.

"Do you like it, Mum? Really?"

Jenny dropped a light kiss on his anxious brow. "Really and truly!" She'd rather die than let him know that for a brief moment she'd hoped it might be one of those big, long bottles of Galliano, the contents of which form the basis of any good Harvey Wallbanger. God, did she ever learn! Once a dog in the manger, always a dog in the manger! Adam might not have been interested in banging her himself but he certainly wasn't going to let Harvey Wallbanger! You could bet your bottom dollar that when it came to his little bit of tit though, *she* hadn't been a last-minute thought in the Duty Free: a convenient way of disposing of his last few *lire*. Oh no! Not on your Nelly! Bitterly, Jenny conjured up a picture of Adam devouring a Margarita pizza on a piazza in Pisa, an intense frown of concentration on his face as he gave due care and consideration to the merits of Roman thongs, over ginormous bottles of Cerrutti.

For David's benefit, she gave the despised pepper-grinder pride of place on the Welsh dresser, then shooed him out the door to his mate Simon's house before turning her attention once more to the perfidy of mankind in general and Adam in particular. Bit of business, indeed! Farina, drenched in Cerrutti and looking forward to being thrown to the loins, was probably even now sliding up and down on his Marco Polo.

"Ah. There you are, the Italian stallion!" Jenny couldn't help taunting some time later when Adam, lithe, late and presumably laid, reappeared and made his way into the kitchen, his eyes straying hopefully in the direction of the cooker having discovered, no doubt, that man cannot live by love alone.

Running a weary hand across his brow, he flopped into the nearest chair. "Don't start."

"I've started, so I'll finish," Jenny quipped, rummaging about in the refrigerator and extracting a clove of garlic which she sniffed dubiously before consigning it to the rubbish. "Gone off, like a lot of things around here!"

Adam sighed. "Oh, here we go round the mulberry bush again. What's got into you lately, Jenny?"

"Not you and that's for sure!"

"And just what exactly do you mean by that!"

"Do you really want to know, Adam?" Jenny challenged him head on. "Do you really want to hear about how I'm feeling because, if you do, you'd better prepare yourself for a life stretch."

Adam rolled his eyes. "Why didn't I just stay in Italy

where the going was good and the wine plentiful instead of coming back here . . ."

"Where the going is rough and the whine is plentiful, instead?"

"Something like that, all right."

"Yeah? Well, why didn't you? David and I probably wouldn't even have noticed. I mean it's not like you spend any time here, is it? I sometimes wonder if you're not just a figment of my imagination. A mirage in the desert of suburbia."

Infuriatingly, Adam leaned back and stretched his long legs out to their fullest extent for all the world as though he were reclining on a beach in Brighton. All he needed was the handkerchief on his head, sandals and socks and the illusion would be complete.

"Exaggeration is an art form with you, isn't it? I mean if it was a degree subject you'd come out as a don."

Savagely, Jenny grabbed the leaning tower, ungently twisting the base so that a shower of black pepper cascaded into the frying pan below. "For someone straight out of Italy that's rich." She affected a husky Godfather-type voice. "How do you like your horse's head? Well done or in the bed?"

Despite himself, Adam laughed and once more Jenny found herself hating him for the way he made her love him.

Did Farina's heart turn over, she wondered, the way hers did when he laughed, and the little crow's feet gathered about his eyes and fanned out in an arc that suddenly made old age seem like a much more attractive proposition? Did she feel that sudden lurch in the pit of her stomach that made her feel like her uterus had prolapsed straight onto the floor? Did she have this insane desire to absorb him, inch by gorgeous inch, through her very pores, so that when he merged with her they became one being, a perfect unit of body, soul and mind? Or did she, in her youth and beauty and innocent lasciviousness take his homage entirely for granted? The triumph of beauty over age and experience! The triumph of the mistress over the wife!

"Jenny, are you all right?"

Shit! First he goes breaking her heart. Then he thinks nothing of breaking her train of thought! "Of course, and why wouldn't I be?" With a savage whack of her best Sabatier carving knife she lopped the pope's nose off a chicken and lobbed the bird whole in the pot.

Warily, Adam kept his eye on the knife, poised for flight at the first signs of any sudden movement. "Well, it's just that one moment you're going all Marlon Brando on me and, the next, you're frowning like the bank manager has called in your overdraft. Talk about mercurial. It's like I never know where I am with you, any more."

"Maybe that's because you're never *anywhere* with me. In fact the only time I'm aware of your presence these days is when you've got your gob wide open like a baby gannet waiting to be fed."

"That's not fair."

"Tell that to the judge!"

"What judge?" Drawing in his legs, Adam sat up straighter in the chair.

"The divorce judge!" Now what the hell had made her say that? It was like she had a death wish, a perverse urge to bring about the very thing she feared most. In another life she must have been a lemming.

"You're not serious!"

"Oh, you reckon, do you?" Shit! There she went again, shooting herself in the foot and putting it in her mouth. "Well, just watch this space!"

"You've got no grounds." Adam assumed an air of martyred patience, the manner he used, she suspected, when explaining to lesser, somewhat agitated mortals why their stocks and shares had failed to produce the handsome dividends he'd all but promised them heretofore. "Desertion? Unreasonable behaviour? You know . . . grounds! You can't just say I want a divorce and bingo it's granted."

And what about adultery? He'd left that out, she noticed.

"If that was the case every Tom, Dick and Harry would be doing it."

"Every Tom, Dick and Harry *is* doing it," Jenny deliberately misunderstood him.

Adam groaned."Oh, be serious, can't you?"

"I am being serious, Adam. Perfectly serious! You want grounds? I've got grounds. Acres of grounds.

Whole rolling vistas! A green belt developer's dream!"

"Like?"

"That's for me to know and for you to find out. In other words, my solicitor will be in touch with yours!"

"You *are* joking, right?"

"Yeah. Well, all right." Discretion being the better part of valour, Jenny thought it only prudent to backtrack a bit before she dug herself in too deep. "But I don't want you to be under any illusions that I'm content to let things meander along the way they have been. I've been turning a blind eye for so long now that people are beginning to call me Nelson."

Adam groaned. "God, you're really full of the brown stuff, Jenny. One day you'll say what you mean in plain English and we'll all die!"

"Perhaps not all!" Lifting the lid of a saucepan bubbling on the cooker, Jenny tossed in a handful of chopped herbs. "Perhaps only those with something to hide, eh Adam? Not that you, being pure as the lily, need be concerned. You, being white as the driven snow, I mean! You being –"

"Oh, sod this!" Adam leapt to his feet. "If I'd wanted a diatribe I'd have gone to the Tory conference at Blackpool. You can stuff your flamin' dinner. I'm off to Spend A Penne!"

"Yeah? Well, just remember to wash your hands," Jenny screamed as a moment later his disembodied head passed the kitchen window. "After all, *I* don't know where they've been!" Actually she could make a damn good guess where they'd been and the thought was enough to put her right off her dinner, so much so that seconds later found her relapsing for the first time in ages in front of the TV.

"Je-eh-ry! Je-he-ry!" Almost of its own volition Jenny's hand, in conjunction with those of the *Springer* audience, came up in a winding motion as the great man himself appeared and leered salaciously at the motley assortment of guests assembled on the stage.

"Ladies and gentlemen. *'You borrowed my man. Now it's payback time!'* Say a big hello to my first guest, Bordello from Ohio. Hi, Bordello! Welcome to the show! Now you've got something to say to your ex- boyfriend's new girlfriend, haven't you?"

"Sho hev, Jayree." Bordello, who had obviously been the inspiration behind Phase II of the US army's latest weaponry, wasted no time in striding over to her adversary and clocking her one around the head with a fist the size of a jet stealth fighter. "Hey Bitch! Speak to de hand, cos the face don't understand!"

"Wow!" Jenny thought, settling back with a family-size packet of buttered popcorn. "I wonder if she gives lessons!"

Chapter Twenty-one

"You want to be careful or you'll start suffering from yo-yo syndrome."

"And what's wrong with yo-yos, might I ask? David has one and pretty nifty he is with it too when it comes to doing tricks. Rocking the cradle. Round the world. Splitting the atom ..."

"Walking the dog?"

Jenny grinned. "No! He leaves that to my mother!"

Denzil, the gym instructor, used by now to Jenny's little eccentricities didn't even attempt to decipher that remark.

"Yes, well good for David but not so good for you. Do you realise your weight has yo-yo'ed up by a half stone? Carry on like this and before too long you'll be right back where you started and all your good work will have been for nothing."

Grimacing, Jenny stepped off the fat-monitor. "Okay. Point taken. You're right, of course. When it comes to fighting the flab, there can be no room for complacency. Besides, I've seen a dinky little black dress that would be just right for the firm's Christmas party and I'd kill to get into it."

"Yes. Well, fortunately, you don't have to do anything quite so drastic. Just cut back on the fat grams, step up on the exercise and before you know it you'll be shimmying in your little black number with the best of them."

Jenny turned a glowing face to the gym instructor. "I can't wait. Do you realise, Denzil, that it'll be the first time in God knows how long that I'll actually be *going* to a party? To be honest, I thought parties were a thing of the past for me, like acne, teenage crushes and position sixty-nine. I just hope Adam will be proud of me."

Denzil's eyebrows rose. "Adam? Is he going then?"

Jenny smiled shyly. "Actually. I haven't asked him yet. To be honest I'm a bit nervous. Well you know things haven't been too good between us lately?"

Denzil nodded. "You did mention it once or twice, all right." He wondered what she'd say if she knew exactly how much he *did* know about the situation. He wondered what she'd say if she knew he'd happened upon Adam and Mounty just the other night, groin to groin in Stringfellows and talking in tongues although, to be fair, Mounty seemed to be making most of the running and Adam had almost jumped out of his skin when he'd caught Denzil's eye upon them.

"Listen." His conscience clearly on the warpath, he'd followed Denzil out into the Gents. "It's not what it looks like. I'm trying to break it off with her but it isn't easy."

"Really?" Denzil just about resisted the urge to miss the urinal and pee all over his shoe. "Well, you've a strange way of showing it."

"Yes, really!" Adam ignored the jibe, jiggling about uncomfortably in his recently acquired Italian leather shoes as if he could sense what was in the other man's mind. "Oh, don't be so sanctimonious, man! Haven't you ever found yourself in a dodgy situation before?"

Denzil re-zipped his flies, flushed the handle. "Of course I've been in dodgy situations. Show me the man who hasn't but *I'm* a free agent. I don't have a wife and child and, thanks to my sexual leanings never will have, as you and your lady-friend have no doubt already twigged."

Adam stuck out a detaining hand as Denzil made to storm off. "Wait! About that business in the gym. Listen, I'm really sorry! You must think I'm a right shit but, really, I'd never pull a stunt like that. Neither would Mounty. It's just that she panicked. If ever you lose your job it won't be on account of us. I promise."

"Jesus!" Denzil pushed past him. "That's big of you. Maybe I should go down on bended knee or, on second thoughts, maybe not. Who knows, you might think I'm coming on to you and that would really be playing into your hands, wouldn't it?"

"I'm *not* homophobic," Adam insisted. "And, if you'll let me, I'm trying to apologise."

Striding over to the door, Denzil yanked at the

handle, paused and turned back. "Well, you can stick your apology where the sun don't shine because, quite frankly, I don't give a flying fuck what you or that tramp you hang around with thinks of me. Still, while you're in apologetic mood why don't you try levelling an apology or two in the direction of your wife and child?"

Adam shrugged, a good attempt at indifference, but there was a hopelessness about his eyes not entirely lost on the other man. "Listen, what can I tell you? None of this was meant to happen. Sometimes I feel like that old guy, Rip Van Winkle, who fell asleep under a tree for a thousand years and when he woke up everything had changed. Irrevocably!"

"Fairytales!"Denzil almost spat. "Wake up to yourself, Treigh, and get a grip. Millions of people, including me, would give their eye-teeth to have half of what you just chucked away. But the loss is yours. Don't think that Jenny will be on the shelf for long. She won't. They're already queuing up for her."

"Are they?" A flash of something remarkably like pain flashed across Adam's face.

Denzil took pleasure in rubbing salt in. "Oh, come on. Surely you don't expect her to sit at home sewing her shroud and reading her Bible, do you? Jenny is a very desirable woman. Even I can see that and if I wasn't as bent as a paperclip I'd be round there serenading her myself."

"I know she's desirable." Adam flushed. "I don't need you to tell me that. She's my *wife*, for God's sake!"

"Interesting!" Denzil quirked an eyebrow. "From

where I'm standing it looks like you've completely forgotten."

A short while later, still sickened on Jenny's behalf, he'd left the club and that despite a taut-buttocked youth in a sailor outfit giving him the glad eye.

Strange, up till now he'd never had a problem with his homosexuality but somehow Jenny brought out the protective hetero-caveman instinct in him. Briefly he flirted with the idea that he might be bi. What was that his mate who swung both ways said? Oh yeah. "Don't knock it till you've bi'ed it!"

Now he regarded Jenny worriedly. "Look, Jen, I don't want to rain on your parade, but what if Adam won't go to the Christmas do?"

"Well then. In that case I'll take you. What would you say to a night of vino, vol-au-vents and very, very good company?"

"I'd say, why not, but only if I can wear my pink lurex tux."

Jenny grinned. "You can wear whatever you want. Let me tell you, amongst my colleagues, especially Marcel, nothing will look out of place."

"Right!" Businesslike, Denzil rubbed his hands together. "Well if you *do* want to fit into that dress I suggest you make a start. Look, Miss World over there has just vacated the treadmill. You'd better get in there quick before someone else grabs it. Actually, your friend spent ages on it earlier. No fear of *her* letting herself go."

"Mounty was here? When?"

"Oh, not so long ago. In fact I think she's probably still here. I'm sure I overheard her saying she was going for a swim."

Decisively, Jenny headed for the swimming pool. "Right! I'll be back shortly."

"But what about the treadmill? You know Saturday is our busiest day. You probably won't get a look in later."

"Well, do me a favour, Denz, and stick an out-of-order sign on it or something. I've just got to see if I can catch Mounty before she leaves."

I wish you would catch her! Denzil thought angrily, heading off to stick an out-of-order sign on the treadmill. The whole situation made him madder than hell. He was sick of the sight of that cow carrying on with Adam and poor Jenny running around like a headless chicken with no idea of what her best friend was getting up to. At least Adam had the grace to look uncomfortable whenever the two men bumped into each other and had given up coming to fencing class, which was just as well or Denzil might have been tempted to run him through with the rapier. Not so Mounty, however! He could see the certainty in her eyes that she had him over a barrel; that fearful for his job, he'd stay mum and Jenny would be none the wiser. Wrong! She had only to open the pages of the *Joys of Sex* guide to see that there was more than one way of being screwed as, no doubt, she would find out one of these days when the inevitable shit finally hit the fan. A great believer in the law of karma, Denzil consoled himself that one day Mounty would get her come-uppance – threefold.

Knowing her friend's affinity for anything containing bubbles, Jenny checked first in the jacuzzi and satisfied that Mounty was not one of the pair of lovers swallowing each other's faces in there, went to check out the swimming pool instead. Going to the edge she peered in, searching for Mounty's lissome, aerodynamic form which, unlike the threshing multitudes herself included, scarcely disturbed the surface of the water. Eventually she saw her, streaking up the fast lane, her hair, a titian cloud, spread out about her. Fondly Jenny watched her gliding from one end to the other till eventually, like Aphrodite, she rose gracefully from the water and headed for the showers.

"Jesus, Mounty," Jenny confronted her, as dechlorinated and smelling of something exotic, she emerged from the shower a few minutes later. "So well you might look guilty! Why didn't you tell me you were coming here this morning? We could have worked out together. I'm beginning to think it would be easier to get an audience with the Pope these days than to manage to have a decent chinwag with my best friend."

Caught off guard, and unlike her usual cool self, Mounty stammered a little. "Oh-er-em. Sorry, Jenny. I thought you might be busy what with your flash new job and everything. I mean us lesser mortals can't be seen to impinge on your time."

Outraged, Jenny took a step backwards. "What? What the hell are you on about, Mounty? I'm *never* too busy where my friends are concerned." The barb went deep, Jenny noticed with satisfaction, as a deepening flush enveloped the other woman's neck and face. "And what's all this crap about a flash job? My job isn't flash, Mounty. Far from it! I'm a glorified gopher, for Heaven's sake. Nothing more!"

Interesting, Mounty thought. To hear Adam talk, you'd think she was head of the BBC these days. It was all Jenny this and Jenny that and primitive, ill-judged, tail-feather-waving displays of male pride.

"Well, good for you, anyway!" Infusing a heartiness in her voice she was far from feeling, she sat down on a changing-room bench and rummaged about in her holdall. "I hope you weren't waiting too long by the pool?"

Jenny sat down beside her. "Nah. Not that long. I looked for you in the jacuzzi first but that was occupied by a couple of lovebirds swallowing each other's faces. For a moment I thought you'd struck lucky."

"Did you indeed?" Mounty pretended amusement, quickly pulling a towel over her wet hair so that her face was hidden from view. Really, she was going to have to put the screws on Adam. All this ducking and diving was driving her mad. Okay, so Jenny would go ballistic when she found out but love conquers all and one day she'd understand that neither Adam nor she had had any control over their feelings. It was nothing personal! It was just one of those things.

Teasingly, Jenny ruffled the towel against her wet hair. "Hurry up, and I'll buy you a coffee. That is, if you can spare the time for one."

Desperate to collect her thoughts, Mounty shooed

her away. "Sure, no problem. You go grab a table and I'll be right out. Then we can have a good gossip and catch up on each other's news." Even if it was an edited version on her part, she thought dryly, as Jenny hurried off to discomfit some diners by dint of standing beside their table and staring pointedly at their empty plates. Usually, after a couple of minutes, all but the most rhino-hided took the hint and departed.

"Ah, there you are." The proud possessor of a table for four, Jenny shoved a glass of V8 towards her. "I know how health-conscious you are. Personally I'm still a caffeine addict. Most of us are at In Kamera. Though cocaine comes a close second with some of them."

"Really?" Mounty evinced amazement though truth to tell she knew exactly how they felt. As a matter of fact she could do with a good snort of the white stuff herself especially as, without further ado, her lover's wife leaned forward and in a 'just between us' manner urged her to spit it all out.

"So come on. Give! What was Italy like?" With a salacious wink, Jenny rubbed fingers and thumb together. "Tell me all the gory details. Was he pristine in the Sistine? Or did he roama your catacombs?" Sitting back she took a sip of her drink. "Anyway, I must say you look great, Mounty. Really marvellous! Love in the eternal city clearly agrees with you."

"Thanks." Mounty could have returned the compliment. As a matter of fact she'd never seen Jenny look so radiant. Yes, that was the word for it! Radiant! Gone was the Lassie hairdo. In its place was a sleek, blonde, highlighted bob that curved gently in around her jaw-line, the sides cleverly accentuating those amazing cheekbones that had only recently been excavated from beneath the fat of ages. Apart from a lick of a mascara wand and perhaps a hint of tinted moisturiser she was also amazingly devoid of make-up. Even her beloved blue eyeshadow, a hangover from the 70s had gotten the bum's rush and now there was just an expanse of incredibly unlined eyelid-framing eyes that were not so much blue as oceanic. For the first time in her life Mounty felt herself playing Miss Havisham to Jenny's Estella – a role, she didn't relish one little bit. And the galling thing was that she, herself, had been instrumental in Jenny's transition from ugly duckling into fully-fledged swan. She might have thought twice about matters had she had a crystal ball at her disposal when Adam had come-a-calling with that irresistible hangdog look on his face. But alas, such had not been the case.

"Look, Mounty," He'd shuffled about on the doorstep like a man who had suddenly discovered his underpants to be the breeding ground for a hundred different species of fleas. "Can I come in for a moment? I badly need your help."

He badly needed *her* help! Jesus, that was a turn-up for the books. Mounty couldn't have been more surprised if George Clooney himself and the whole cast of *ER* had turned up on her doorstep and begged her to play doctors and nurses.

"I know you and I haven't always seen eye to eye but . . . it's about Jenny!"

It would be! Resignedly, Mounty had stepped back from the door. Fat chance of him calling for any other reason. It was strange though how, right from the word go, he'd always managed to make her feel inferior, almost as if she was going to spout jellied eels from every orifice and start dropping her aitches all over the place. Talk about Eliza Doolittle! Never mind that she could hold her own with a shit-load of toffee-nosed, high-powered directors at work, slamming agendas and deadlines beneath their noses with an aplomb bordering on the contemptuous. Invariably, for some unfathomable reason, when it came to Adam Treigh, she regressed in a flash onto the street corner of a past life where she found herself accosting passers-by with bits of lucky heather.

"Luverly lucky 'eather, Guvnor. Buoy sam fer yer loidy! Tuppence a sprig 'n cheap at 'alf the proice!"

"You'd better come in," she'd said and he had and spent two hours droning on and on about Jenny, how worried he was about her, how she was neglecting herself and how she only ever seemed to come to life when Jerry Springer was on TV and did Mounty think she could shake her up a little because, he knew, if she'd listen to anyone it would be to Mounty. Flattery will get you everywhere!

Come on, how could she resist? It was the equivalent of the USA asking Cuba for a handout. Besides which, Mounty, like most women, was possessed of an insane desire to be *needed* and so when Professor 'iggins had sent up an SOS it was inevitable that Eliza would break her vowels running to his aid. What's more, her motives had been pure – well, to begin with, anyway. After all, she and Jenny had been friends for years although she, at least, was realistic enough to realise that it was more because they had both been marginalised by their wealthier, more confident peers, rather than their being soul mates. And, as Mounty didn't want to spend every lunchtime eating processed cheese sandwiches alone, any more than Jenny did, what could be more natural than that they would form their own leper colony? A question of two odd socks joining forces to make a pair! And if they *had* gone on the odd junket abroad with the other girls, then it was only under sufferance and because, the bigger the booking, the bigger the discount. Once in Ibiza, or Benidorm or wherever, the chosen ones would do a flit, and Jenny and herself would be left once more to their devices, knocking back cheap sangria and fending off the Spanish flies of every Don, Juan and Pedro. Not, mind you, that she hadn't clicked a few castanets in her day, the Antonio Banderas school of Spaniard being very hard to resist, as well as find. Yet to hear Jenny talk you'd think they'd been voted the Miss Homecoming Queens of 1976 or something. You'd think the fact that they could count on one hand the number of party invitations either one of them had ever received would be enough to tell her something. But no, the penny never appeared to drop and to this very day, she wore the same rose-coloured spectacles and hankered after the good old days. How she had ever managed to land Adam was a mystery although, to be honest, he hadn't been any great shakes back in the early days which made his superior attitude doubly hard to bear. Still, time is a great healer and by the time Jenny had walked him up the aisle, Adam Treigh was a vision of true manliness. And as Sod's law would have it, at the same time as they had taken their vows, swearing to forsake all others, the scales had fallen from Mounty's eyes and she acknowledged, if only to herself, that she was in love with her best friend's husband. Not that she'd done anything about it. How could she? You'd want to be blind as well as deaf and dumb not to see that Adam and Jenny were two halves of the same coin and when David had come along, bingo, they were the perfect nuclear family! And so Mounty had made a life for herself, clawing her way up the career ladder, comfort-buying Ferraris and designer clothes, mating, dating and vainly waiting for someone else to touch her heart in the way that Adam did. Only no one ever had! So, let's face it, when it came to a chance to score brownie points with the man of her dreams, Mounty was going up for every badge on offer.

"Look, if you want Jenny to change, then you've got to provide her with sufficient motivation."

"Like what?" Intently Adam followed her movements as she'd poured a brandy into his glass, unnecessarily steadying his hand with her own, letting her fingers linger just that moment or two too long.

"Like make her jealous."

"How? Jenny doesn't have a jealous bone in her body."

"Oh, really?" Mounty shot him one of those arch oh-you-are-such-a-silly-billy-type smiles. "That's all you know. There isn't a woman alive who hasn't got a touch of the little green eyes of the little yellow god about her. And Jenny is no exception!"

"No?"

"No!" Mounty said firmly.

"So what do I do?"

"Well, you could make her think you're having an affair. That's always a good starting point."

Adam drained his glass, held it out for a top-up. "No. Jenny knows I'd never cheat on her?"

Mounty raised her eyebrows. "You'd never cheat on her! I suppose you've never even been tempted?"

"I'm not saying that," Adam admitted. "In fact I came very close once with a secretary who looked like Claudia thingy off the car advert . . ."

'But you stopped short of the dirty deed?"

"Yes!"

"Why?"

"Because I bumped into my son and it brought me to my senses, made me feel sordid, like a kerb-crawler at King's Cross. I even bought him off for God's sake – gave him five pounds not to tell his mother."

"And did he?"

'"I don't think so. At least she never said anything if

208

he did, but I still feel like a right shit about the whole thing."

Mounty tried a bit of delving into the male psyche. Let him off the hook and he'd be forever beholden. "There's no need. The fact remains that you *didn't* do anything and you know, not to put too fine a point on it, Jenny isn't entirely blameless." Placing one hand on her heart, Mounty held up her free hand, palm outwards. "Look, don't get me wrong. Jenny's my best friend and everything but even I can see she's not the same old Jenny. I mean you've moved on whilst she's stayed static. It must be very hard for you in front of your colleagues. Embarrassing."

"Not really." Surprisingly, Adam bridled. "I never went in for the trophy wife kind of thing. I love Jenny. I've always loved Jenny. I don't give a toss if she's not a nuclear scientist or a supermodel. As far as I'm concerned she'll always be ABBA's Dancing Queen. What I do give a toss about is the fact that she seems to be on another planet these days and neither David nor I can reach her."

Mentally Mounty kicked herself for wading in too hard. Softly, softly catchee monkey! "Well, of *course* you love her. But love is a two-way street and Jenny needs to be reminded of that. So, to my mind, one of the best ways of doing that is to rekindle her interest and, let me tell you, you'll rekindle it quick-smart if she thinks you're having it away with someone else."

"You really think that would work?"

"Piece of piss!" Mounty assured him airily. "Just

follow the old lipstick on the collar routine, work late on a regular basis, change your brand of aftershave and race for the phone every time it rings and before you know it she'll be jumping through hoops to get you back." Adam looked considering. Darkly handsome and considering. Pulse-racingly, dark, handsome and considering. Discreetly, Mounty laid two fingers across the inside of her wrist. Yep! Going like the clappers!

"I suppose it's worth a try, but you'll help me, Mounty, won't you? I mean, with all the finer details?"

"Trust me," Mounty grinned. "I'm pretty good on detail." And so she'd proved as, in a matter of days Jenny was round blubbing like a baby, totally oblivious to the fact that the object of her angst was earwigging at the door.

"You don't think you were too hard on her?" he'd asked when like a harpooned whale and bleeding from the heart Jenny'd lumbered off home in her car.

"No, Adam!" she'd said. "I do not. And just remember, if you can't stand the heat, stay out of the sauna. If you want Jenny back you've got to be prepared to see this through, all the way to the nth degree. There's no point in backing out at the first hurdle. A little bit of jealousy won't kill Jenny, you know. But it might very well cure her."

"You're right." Decisively, Adam followed her back into the living-room where Jenny's wine glass, still three-quarters full sat, a lipstick-rimmed reproach, on the coffee table. "Are you sure me stopping out all night is such a good idea, though? I mean she was pretty down in the mouth."

"Of course it's a good idea. Start as you mean to go on and what better way to make her think you've scored in an away game than by staying out all night?" Mounty grinned. "Besides which, the bed's already made up in the spare room and you wouldn't want me to have wasted all my energy now, would you?"

"I suppose not!" Adam returned the grin.

"Good!" Airily whisking away Jenny's glass, Mounty took another from the display cabinet. "Now, as it's still quite early, what would you say to a pizza, a video and a nightcap, in that order?"

"I'd say luvely jubbly," Adam laughed, as picking up the phone Mounty dialled the number of the local Pizza Hut.

"Deep pan, extra pepperoni and a cheesy rim okay with you?"

"Perfect! Just perfect!"

* * *

"Perfect! Just perfect!" Mounty answered in answer to Jenny's query about Italy. "I could have stayed forever."

"Ah, pillar talk amongst the ruins. So romantic! But I digress. Roman Holiday uncut please. X-rated version. Speak now or forever hold your Pisa!"

Mounty shrugged. "There's not a lot to tell. We went. We saw. We bonkered! If I'd known how interested you were I'd have taken a camcorder."

"If I *had* known I'd have made you take a camcorder," Jenny said pointedly.

"Yeah. I'm sorry about that, but it was really a last-minute kind of thing. It was a business trip really. I only went along at the last moment. Excess luggage really."

"Well, you could have sent a postcard. Still, I forgive you. Millions wouldn't! But seriously – when am I going to meet this paragon? I mean you're my best friend. It's my job to vet your boyfriends. Remember John Travolta!"

"Patience is a virtue," Mounty hedged. "All in good time."

"Yeah, but that's the point, Mounty." A little hesitant, Jenny tore the corner of a sachet of Canderel and emptied it into her coffee. "There never seems to be a good time. And not just to meet *him*. It's like I never see you any more. Hell, I miss you."

Evasively Mounty's eyes slid away, came to rest on a point somewhere over her Jenny's shoulder. "You've got the Inner Child woman."

"Poppy? Yeah, Poppy's great but she's not you. *You're* my best friend! You know more about me than anyone else. I *trust* you, Mounty. I don't want to lose you. I mean we're two sides of a coin, you and me. One for all and all for one etc. etc. I wasn't going to remind you but remember that vow we made at Hill Grove – you know, never to let any man come between us?"

Pushing her chair back Mounty, unable to take any more, rose suddenly to her feet, an ugly blush suffusing her face. "Look, just cut it out, Jenny! I just can't handle this right now. Can't you see you're crowding me?"

"What do you mean?" Shocked, Jenny followed suit. "I'm *not* crowding you. I've never crowded you. What's going on, Mounty?" Close to tears, she leaned across, laid a restraining hand on her friend's arm. "Did I do something to upset you? Please, Mounty, you've got to tell me."

Shrugging her off, Mounty rounded on her, her face contorted with such an array of emotions it was impossible to tell which was the more dominant. "Oh, for Christ's sake, Jenny, why do you have to make this so hard! Just piss off, why don't you? I'm *not* who you think I am." Mounty's voice rose, causing heads to turn, conversations to fall silent. "Do you hear me? I was *never* who you thought I was!"

"But Mounty . . ."

"But Mounty nothing! Just run along, Jenny." A sneer entered her voice. "Because you can run now, can't you? You're not a blob any more. The thing from the deep! You've found your legs. You don't need me to prop you up anymore. You've got cheekbones and ankles just like you've always wanted. Now fuck off, why don't you? Just fuck off and leave me alone."

Bewildered, Jenny ran after her as, the red-hot picture of fury, she headed for the exit.

"But why? At least tell me what I did. Surely you owe me that much! Mounty! Wait!" Jenny's voice broke as strong arms appeared from nowhere and held her back.

"Let her go, Jenny! She's not worth it!" Wrapping both arms around her, Denzil, materialising just in time, held her close until her struggles ceased and she buried her face in his shirtfront. Deliberately, his glance raked the curious bystanders. "Show's over, folks. You can all go back to minding your own business now. Come on, Jenny."

Sobbing, Jenny allowed him to lead her into the seclusion of a nearby staffroom.

"I just don't understand, Denzil." Helping herself to a handful of tissues from a box on a nearby coffee table, she blew her nose. "I mean, what did I do?"

"Nothing! You did nothing!" Gently, Denzil manoeuvred her into a chair.

"But I must have. Mounty wouldn't have gone off the deep end like that for no reason. I only wish she'd tell me what. I mean, how can I make things better when I don't even know what's wrong?"

Furiously Denzil drove his fist into his hand. "Listen. You've done nothing wrong. If anyone's done anything wrong, it's that cow and, to be brutally honest about it, you're far better off without her."

Oblivious to the war the man beside her was waging with his conscience, Jenny sniffed. Should he tell her what he knew, get the whole sordid shebang out into the open with one fell swoop? Or, given her present state of hysteria, wouldn't it be more prudent, kinder even to let sleeping bitches lie? At least for the moment. After all, Mounty and Adam were bound to betray

214

themselves sooner or later, a case of the murderer always returning to the scene of the crime. And, come to think of it, who was to say she wouldn't turn round and shoot the messenger? The bearer of bad tidings. Anyway, when you came right down to brass tacks, was it really his place to rattle the cage in the first place? He was, after all, just the gym instructor. The man with the calorie plan! Ultimately his involvement stopped at the gymnasium door. Except that it didn't. Not if he was being honest! Jenny was more than the personification of his pay cheque. She was a friend. For God's sake, he himself was the runner-up in the stakes to accompany her to her Christmas do, the first party she would be attending in her new and improved format. A major milestone in the life of any thirty-nine-pushing-forty-year-old woman! Mentally he tossed a coin. Friend, he told. Coward, he didn't. Best of three. The coward had it!

"Would you like me to phone someone to take you home?"

Jenny gulped, shook her head and dabbed furiously at her eyes. "No. Honestly. I'm all right now. I don't know what came over me. It's all my fault really, a case of me clod-hopping in where angels fear to tread. I'll phone Mounty later and apologise."

"Do what?" Incredulous, Denzil's eyebrows rose.

"Apologise," Jenny reiterated, helping herself to another tissue and unconsciously shredding it into confetti-sized pieces. "Well, look at it this way." Her voice was defensive. "I was quizzing her left, right and centre about her trip to Italy, couldn't leave it alone if the truth be known, although I could see that she didn't really want to discuss matters." Candidly her eyes sought his. "What if things didn't go according to plan, Denzil? What if she got the big E? What if Casanova blew her out?"

"And what if pigs could fly?" Dismissively, Denzil shook his head but Jenny was determined.

"No, hear me out! I mean, would *you* want someone rubbing salt in *your* wounds when all you wanted to do was slink away quietly and lick them?" Remorsefully, she shook her head. "Poor Mounty. I can't believe I was so insensitive."

"Poor Mounty, my arse in farcical!" Appalled, Denzil realised she'd gotten hold of completely the wrong end of the stick. If ever there was a time to put the record straight it was now, but the yellow streak on his back was a mile wide and before he knew it, Jenny was on her feet and heading for the door.

"Look, you've been great, Denzil, really supportive, but this one's my call and I've got to sort it out. I'll catch you later, yeah?"

"Yeah, sure! Whatever blows your skirt up!" The age of chivalry was truly dead he thought sadly, as Jenny, still a damsel in distress, plunged blindly into the wilderness in solo search of the nasty she-dragon. But alas, such were the trials and tribulations of life and Denzil, however guilty he might feel, was realistic enough to realise that a limp dick was no substitute for a trusty sword.

Chapter Twenty-two

"Getting off your face is not going to solve anything."

"No?" Balefully, Jenny regarded her mother over the lip of a whisky bottle.

"No! Now stop hogging the bottle and pass it over this way."

"Shan't!" Childishly Jenny hugged it to herself. "Shan't. Shan't. Shan't!"

The older woman rolled her eyes. "Jesus Christ! What did I do to deserve you? Murder someone in a past life? Try to blow up the Houses of Parliament? What?"

Jenny hicked, belatedly remembering to cover her mouth with her hand. "Thass not very nice. You're supposed to be my mother. Full of maternal instinct and wise advice."

"Yeah! Yeah! Yeah! Play it again, Sam." Forcibly wresting the bottle from her, Gloria poured herself a generous glass. "You know full well the only Dr Spock

217

I ever went in for was the one from *Star Trek*. It was the big ears that did it for me."

"Beam me up, Scottie!" Jenny hicked again and tumbled off the arm of the settee upon which she'd precariously perched herself.

"You see?" Jenny's mother addressed the third occupant of the room. "She's always been the same. No fight in her! I remember when she was six . . ."

"Oh, Lord! Don't start dredging up the sins of years past. I'm sure Poppy isn't at all interested in my infantile shortcomings."

"Yes, but the point is thing's haven't changed. Children grow into adults, mature and hopefully get a bit of sense but you – you're stuck in a time warp. Talk about Peter Pan!"

"Crap!" Jenny sobered up enough to bridle indignantly. "I don't know how you can say that. For God's sake, I got married, didn't I? Had a child? I've even got myself a job now. How much more grown up than that can you get? Honestly, I don't know how you have the brass nerve to accuse me of being stuck in a time warp? You're the one who's stuck in a time warp. I mean, look at you. Who do you think you are, Barbarella the OAP?"

"In essence!" Her mother nodded slowly, ignoring the jibe. "You haven't changed in essence. You still let people walk all over you. You're still grateful for the crumbs that fall from sundry and assorted tables. It's like you're saying, hey, I'm a football, come kick me!"

"Rubbish! I've *lost* my essence, just like Poppy's lost her Inner Child. That's exactly where the problem lies. That's why Adam took off with Farina. That's what I'm fighting so hard to get back. The essential Jenny! The Jenny my husband fell in love with and upon whose compliant body he fathered a child. The Jenny he wooed with long-stemmed, damask roses and with whom he boogied long into the night to the pulsating sounds of Status Quo and Thin Lizzy."

Wearily draining her glass, her mother rose and went to stand by the window through which Rover could be seen outside enthusiastically endeavouring to bury a giant bone without aid of a garden implement.

"Stop the world, I want to get off! But you're right, though. I am stuck in a time warp. You see, I keep having the same conversation with you, over and over again. It's like one of those terrible recurring nightmares. You know the minute you close your eyes that it's going to happen but, somehow, you're powerless to prevent it."

Jenny winked in Poppy's direction. "And then she wonders why I suffer from a bad case of dramatitis. Hereditary, I'd say, eh Poppy?"

Poppy shrugged uncomfortably, an innocent bystander caught in the line of cross-fire."She only wants what's best for you. We both do!"

"Well, in that case, you've both got to accept that *I* know what's best for me. Mounty is best for me. She always was."

"Was! Past tense. And that's where you should leave

her, firmly in the past! Come on, she bawls you out of it in public, refuses to take your calls. What does she need to do to get the message through to you that that particular umbilical cord is irrevocably severed? Hire a biplane to trail it in smoke across the sky? Flash it up on the World Cup scoreboard. What?"

Tentatively dipping a foot into stormy waters, Poppy showed her hand. "Your mother's right! For as long as I've known you, that woman has caused you nothing but angst. Maybe she *was* a good friend but something has changed that, at least from her point of view, and short of stretching her on a rack, you might have to accept that you'll never know exactly what!"

"Well, thank you, Poppy!" Gloria said. "Isn't that exactly what I've been trying to get through to her thick skull. But she won't buy it. To hear her, you'd think Mounty was Snow White and Little Red Riding-Hood all rolled into one, a kind of a fairytale character who can do no wrong."

Jenny glared. "It's called loyalty, Mother."

"Oh, yeah? And Prince Charles is called royalty, but that didn't stop him from doing the dirty!"

Hopefully, Poppy tried to introduce a measure of calm into proceedings. "Look! We know you're hurting, Jenny. We just don't want you to hurt even more."

Jenny set her lips. "Mounty's hurting. She *needs* me, even if she can't see it right now and I'm *not* going to give up on her."

Her mother sighed, turning back from the window.

"But *she's* given up on you! Isn't that what we're trying to tell you?"

"Maybe temporarily," Jenny conceded. "But, when she calls out my name, I'll come running to see her again." Poppy groaned. "Leave it out. Anyway, if you ask me, there's more to this than meets the eye. Monkey business, if you get my drift."

Jenny giggled. "Actually, you're not far wrong. According to her next-door neighbour there aren't half some jungle noises coming from Mounty's bedroom. She also reckons he's married, nasty old cow, something to do with him sneaking in and out and looking over his shoulder! As if!" Jenny giggled again, blissfully unaware of the significant looks passing between her mother and Poppy.

"When did you say she met him?" Casually, Poppy leaned over and helped herself to the rapidly dwindling whisky bottle.

"I didn't, but it's been a while now. In fact, if I recall correctly, it was shortly after hubby and I first started experiencing marital difficulties." Palm outward, she held a hand up. "In fact, I tell a lie. It was around the time when I first became *aware* that we were experiencing problems and Mounty pulled out all the stops to help. Unfortunately, when the boot was on the other foot and she needed my help, what did I do? Rub salt in the wounds, that's what. No wonder she's gone to earth."

"Foxes always go to earth!" Her mother's voice was dry. "Personally, I say, send in the hounds."

"Hear! Hear!" Poppy nodded agreement but Jenny narrowed her eyes.

"Honestly. If I'd known how well suited you two were, I'd have introduced you ages ago."

Gloria raised her eyebrows. "Yes. Well we're obviously more suited than you and Mounty. At least we think along the same lines." Again there was a deeper significance to the words and to the look that accompanied them that was entirely lost upon Jenny.

"Huh, that's not saying much. According to you, you're well suited to that mutt out there too." Mockingly, Jenny's glance went to the window where Rover had appeared, grimy-nosed and with his tongue hanging out. "Do you like dogs, Poppy? Because, Mum does! Don't you, Mum?"

"Actually, I do." Poppy refused to be baited. "For a long time I thought my neighbour's German shepherd might actually be my Inner Child. Something about the eyes, you see! Knowing! As if he'd lived many lifetimes. But then he took a chunk out my ass if you want to know, and I realised it was just plain viciousness and that he could reincarnate to infinity and beyond, but his destiny was always just to be a mutt! Speaking of which, what breed is Rover?"

Jenny's mother grinned."Oh, a spaniel. Most definitely a spaniel."

"Big ears," Jenny said dryly. "The Dr Spock of the canine world. What else?"

"Exactly." Her mother's voice was lustful. "You know what they say. Big ears, big –"

"I think it's time we were going." Shakily, Jenny rose to her feet. "Come on, Poppy, that is unless you want to witness an elderly woman, who should know better, make a complete spectacle of herself."

"Huh! Hell hath no fury like a daughter scorned!" Swinging her hips provocatively, Gloria sauntered over to the kitchen cupboards and extracted a large tin of Pedigree Chum, beef with marrow and bits of horse-flesh flavour.

"Yep. And there's no fool like an old fool. Don't bother to show us out. We can see you've got your hands full." Then, ushering Poppy out the door and dropping her voice. "Or will have, in about five minutes flat!"

Poppy giggled. "Do you think your mother could be my Inner Child?"

"Definitely not!" Hooking her arm through Poppy's, Jenny hauled her off in the direction of the nearest pub. "More like Genghis Khan's!"

"Set 'em up, landlord," she rapped, a short time later down the Dirty Dog as Poppy, ever on the alert, looked hopefully into his eyes for signs of a wayward offspring, finding, alas, only astigmatism and a sty in the corner of his left eyelid.

"G & T," she said forlornly. "And make it a double."

* * *

Not a million miles away, Adam and Mounty were making a double bed having first had the pleasure of tossing it and each other.

223

"I still don't know what possessed you to fly off the handle with her." Ham-fisted, Adam yanked half the duvet across the bed and stuffed it under the mattress. "It's made life damn difficult for me, I can tell you, having to watch her mooching around with a face as long as a a a wet week. As for poor David, he said he'd jump off the nearest cliff only she might beat him to it."

Scowling, Mounty tugged the duvet back. "I couldn't help it. The charade was just becoming too much for me. I mean she was so Pollyanna that day in the gym, beaming at me like a lighthouse beacon, quizzing me on Italy and never making the connection that you and I had been away at the same time! To the same country! I mean, go figure!"

Like a man with a mission, Adam ripped the duvet out of her hands. "Well, of course, she wasn't going to make the connection. As far as Jenny is concerned you and I are anathema to each other. How is she to know that *you* found the antidote."

"I found the antidote? What are you trying to say, Adam? That *I* made all the running. That *I* seduced *you* and therefore you can be absolved from any blame?"

Adam gave up all pretence at bed-making. "Well, you did in a way. I mean I only came to you for help with Jenny –"

"But I pounced on you, ravished you on the spot and frightened you so badly that you kept coming back for an action replay. Right?"

"Oh, all right. Not exactly. But I *was* vulnerable. My

wife had gone AWOL if not physically, then mentally. I was feeling neglected."

Furiously, Mounty smoothed the duvet and followed suit with a pillow.

"Listen, Adam, you're up to your dick in this business. Don't start trying to lay all the blame at my door."

"But you're supposed to be Jenny's friend."

"And you're supposed to be Jenny's husband!" Mounty glared. "Actually you're supposed to be *my* husband. Isn't that what you said the first night you came, if I recall correctly. 'Oooh, aaah, oooh! I should have married you, Mounty'. Isn't that what you said?"

"Maybe! But that was just the satisfied ramblings of a post-coital man."

Picking up a discarded shoe, Mounty chucked it at his head "Bastard! Is that all I am to you? An easy lay? A bit on the side? The interval in a movie before you go back to Jenny, the main feature?"

Embarrassed and a little helpless, Adam shrugged himself into his jacket, automatically patting his pockets to check for car keys and wallet before heading for the door.

"Look, Mounty, I'm not proud of any of this and I know it's hard but, like it or not, our race is run. It was good while it lasted but there's no getting away from the fact that I'm a married man. It should never have happened and it was never for keeps. You knew that! We were just a timely diversion to each other, weren't we?" The last was said more in hope than belief.

Quickly interspersing herself between him and the door, Mounty held out a hand, half-restraining, half-appeal. "Wait, Adam! Is that really what you think? Do you think that's all *I* saw you as? Some kind of diversion? A bit of slap and tickle with a best-before date?" Maddeningly, her eyes filled with tears. Maddeningly because she, Diana Mountford, was usually so in control. Not by dint of indulging in frequent and prolonged bouts of maidenly hysteria had *she* managed to accumulate notches on her bedpost and red Ferarris with personalised number plates. "Just what sort of monster do you think I am? Do you think I just hopped into bed with you willy-nilly without ever a thought for Jenny?"

Shuffling uncomfortably, Adam did a quick survey of his toecaps. "Look, just leave Jenny out of this."

"Leave Jenny out of this?" Honestly, Mounty would have laughed were it not for the fact that her heart was in the throes of some kind of seizure or other that called for the services of six paramedics and a defibrillator. "Don't be absurd. How *can* I leave her out of this when she *only* happens to be the central issue here?'

"Yes, well she *only* happens to be my wife." Adam's voice, as he tried to sidestep her, was heavy with irony and something else. Guilt maybe? Shame?

"Yes, and she only happens to be my best friend! Or *was* my best friend, past tense! Don't you think that causes me a pang or two? Knowing how I've deceived her? Knowing how she's been beating herself up over you? Lending her my shoulder and my ear, crying crocodile tears right alongside of her when all the time I was scheming and dreaming and counting the minutes between pokes from her bloke? Getting it on with you wasn't a decision I took lightly, you know. But, then again, this wasn't a relationship I took lightly." On a roll, Mounty nodded violently. "Oh so well you might raise your eyebrows, Adam, but, believe it or not, I was racked."

"And I was wrecked." Never a man comfortable with raw emotion, her erstwhile lover attempted to lighten the atmosphere. "And, in any case, get real, Mounty. This was never a *relationship* per se. Call a spade a spade. This was a fling. Enjoyable but, by its very nature, short and sweet. Time now for a reality check!"

Mounty bit her lip, eyes bright still with unshed tears. She hoped she could keep it that way. Didn't want to give him the satisfaction of seeing her break down and bawl like a kid who's just discovered the lead singer of Boy Clone has gotten himself hitched and consequently she'll never see her wedding pictures in *Hello* or hear him serenade her at Glastonbury!

"A reality check? Is that what they're calling it these days? In my day things were simpler. You were given the 'big E', shown the door, dumped, given the bum's rush. But, reality check? Well, well, you live and learn! I suppose that's another Americanism like getting 'kicked to the kerb'." Mounty challenged him. "You want to call a spade a spade, Adam? Then cut the bullshit! The reality is you're dumping me."

Trying discreetly to check his watch, Adam sighed deeply. "Look, can't we just be civilised about this? What we had was good, even great at times, but as the old saying goes, all good things must come to an end. I have responsibilities, a wife and child I've neglected for far too long. Like it or not, Mounty, our race is run. We've lapped the circuit. Gone for gold! Now, if we're clever, we can both come out as winners."

Scathingly Mounty's eyes dropped to crotch level. "Linford bleedin' Christie! Without the lunch-box."

"Oh, enough! You're being childish now. I must say I *am* surprised. I thought you were New Woman personified, the love-'em-and-leave-'em kind, the always-prepared-with-a-condom-in-her-handbag kind! The kind of woman who doesn't confuse sex with the four-letter 'L' word."

"In other words you thought I was a slapper. The kind of woman prepared to drop her drawers with the same frequency as her aitches. The kind of woman worthy of screwing but not of loving? The kind of woman you wouldn't take home to mother. Am I right?"

Adam shook his head."No! That's not what I meant, at all. Simply that, I thought you were the independent type. A bra-burner, a fully-evolved-from-the-mire-of dependency type woman."

"Yeah, yeah. A slapper, like I've already said."

Putting his hands on her shoulders, Adam tried gently to push her aside. "Look, all this to-ing and fro-ing is getting us nowhere. The fat lady's sung, the show's over and it's time to go home. I'm really sorry if I've hurt you, Mounty. It wasn't intentional, believe me. More like a case of different perceptions. We can still be friends though, can't we? I mean, when the dust settles. You'll always have a special place in my heart."

Stepping aside, Mounty motioned him to the door. "Oh Christ! Not that old chestnut! Oh look, just go, Adam, will you! Go if you have to but don't insult me."

Suddenly inadequate, Adam shrugged. "I'm sorry, Mounty. Really, I am."

"Yeah, whatever! Save it for your wife!"

Reminded, Adam came to a sudden halt. "Speaking of Jenny. You won't . . .?"

"Of course not. What would be the point now? Jenny is the innocent party in all this. We've already hurt her enough. Think of it as honour amongst thieves."

"Thanks. Well, I'd better go."

Her throat blocked, Mounty nodded and a moment later found her listening to the sound of his footsteps crunching across the gravel, the scrape of metal upon metal as he unlocked the car door and then the inevitable revving of the engine signalling his departure from her life. Elvis has now left the building!

"I hate you, Adam," she murmured, forehead resting wearily against the closed door, but sadly there *was* no hate in her voice, only humiliation and a profound sense of loss that, oddly enough, had as much to do with losing her best friend as her best friend's husband.

Strange how she had to go all round the houses before she discovered that she actually *did* love Jenny. All for one and one for all! What a joke! Poor Jenny, she hadn't realised she'd been flying solo on that one, not to mention harbouring a viper in her bosom. If only she could turn the clock back. Bollocks! If she *could* turn the clock back, Mounty was honest enough to admit, she wouldn't change a thing except perhaps Adam's hair trigger, which, despite Jenny's claims to the contrary, was still very much in evidence.

Chapter Twenty-three

"There's nothing for it. You're going to have to go on in her place."

"Me? Are *you* crazy? I wouldn't have a clue what to do assuming my shaky knees would allow me to stand up in the first place."

"Piddle! Of course you can. Nothing to it really *and* you're well qualified to host this particular show seeing as how you're caught bang, slap in the middle of a lurve triangle yourself."

Adamant, Jenny shook her head. "No! I won't do it. You can't make me."

Dramatically, Marcel made a pretence of banging his head against the wall. "You're right, of course. I can't make you. Still I thought you'd *want* to do it for Martyna's sake if not for mine, not to mention the terrific boost it would give to your, let's face it, less-than-glittering career."

Jenny sniffed. "Look, you can cut out the emotional

blackmail. It's hardly my fault if Martyna ate a dodgy prawn. Besides, aren't you supposed to be able to round up a substitute? After all, everybody knows things can go wrong on a live show. *Usually* people know well enough to have a contingency plan in place."

Marcel sighed. "I did but the stupid cow's gone and gotten herself caught up in the middle of a tailback on the A3."

"Well, what about you? Why can't *you* do it. Okay, so you're not Geraldo or Jerry Springer but I don't suppose the viewing public would take exception to having to look at your face for only thirty minutes or so."

"Ah but they would! Why do you think I like to wear my mask so often?" Urgently, Marcel gripped her shoulders. "At school people blessed themselves and crossed the road whenever I hove into view. And that was just the teachers. As for the parents, do you believe me when I tell you *they* used me to make recalcitrant toddlers behave. *'If you don't stop that crying, Jermayn, see that ugly monster over there with the bony knees and school uniform? Well, he's going to come and get you!'* So you see, you've got no choice; you've got to do it. People don't want the elephant man at nine o'clock in the morning. They want bubbly, glamorous blondes with short skirts and nipples straining through their well-cut, designer-labelled, silk shirts."

"I can't. I just can't."

Marcel scoffed. "Of course you can. I thought you

were all into *Oprah*, positivity and German counsellors with obscure degrees from non-existent American universities. You've got to be like the little engine and tell yourself you can."

Jenny scowled. "What little engine?"

Marcel shrugged. "Oh I don't know, some little bastard, Thomas Tank Engine or something. I mean does it really matter? The point is he had to go up a big mountain, thought he couldn't, told himself he could and *did!* It was all in the point of view, you see. He took a different perspective. Instead of saying 'I can't', he said 'I can' and so can you! Be like that little engine, Jenny. Say I *can!* Take a different perspective."

"I can't!" Jenny shook her head. "Bugger the little engine. He didn't have to appear live in front of ten million critical members of the public. No dice, Marcel! I'd sooner streak naked down the middle of Oxford Street on Christmas Eve with my arse decked out in fairy lights. You can paddle your own canoe on this one."

"Fair enough." Dejectedly Marcel slumped into the nearest chair. "No one can say I didn't try my damnedest to stop In Kamera from going under but with rats deserting the sinking ship left, right and centre I've no option but to scuttle what's left of her. You can call in and pick up your cards this afternoon."

"What?" Outrage draped itself across the Jenny's features. "You're giving me the sack? Why? Because I won't play the game; step into a breach for which I'm totally unqualified, not to mention unsuitable? That's not fair, Marcel! I'll go further. That's sodding totally out of order! Honestly! I thought better of you than that!"

Marcel held his hand up, waving it furiously like a swot in a classroom desperate to attract the teacher's attention. "Hold your horses! Figure of speech, Jenny! Besides I'm not just talking about you. We're all in the same boat. All scuppered! The fact is Martyna's talk show is In Kamera's flagship programme, as it were, and if we're unable to keep it afloat then there's nothing for it, I'm afraid, other than to give her a decent burial at sea. Personally, I blame Kilroy. Since he changed his hair back, the fickle are flocking back in droves, though I'd never say as much to Martyna."

Jenny wavered. "Just this morning, you say?" Marcel shot upright with the velocity of a condemned man suddenly receiving a last-minute stay of execution.

"Just this morning! I promise!"

"Well, okay," Jenny muttered, the words being dragged past her lips by seven huskies, a sleigh and a team of Eskimos. "Just today then. But I swear if you try and drop me in it tomorrow I'll personally castrate you with a pair of rusty pliers."

"Done!" Truth to tell, Marcel would have sold his soul to the devil, not to mention helping him to load it onto his handcart, if only to extricate himself from the mire of falling ratings. "Let's get you into make-up and wardrobe."

"Look at that." Jenny held out a trembling hand. "I haven't seen a shake like that since my bum was size twenty."

"Well, it's not size twenty any more." Determinedly, in case she should change her mind, Marcel quickly manoeuvred her out along the corridor and into make-up, keeping up a stream of small talk he hoped would inveigle her into forgetting the horror of her situation. "It's a peach of a bum, a veritable damson, rotund where it ought to be rotund, firm where it ought to be firm, yielding where . . ."

"Marcel." Jenny turned and shoved him out the door. "Shut up!"

* * *

"Lucky you're so petite." The wardrobe lady, herself built like Attila the Hun, rummaged in a gigantic wardrobe, emerging a moment later arms full of the designer suits that were Martyna Michaels' signature. "You'll have no problem slipping into one of these. Now, what do you say to the navy-blue Chanel number?"

"I'd sooner an invisible cloak but, if that's not an option, then I don't suppose it much matters what I wear. I doubt if Joan of Arc was too pushed about *her* couture when they set light to her *derrière*."

Attila sniffed. "Oh come now. It's not all that bad. Martyna does it every day."

"Martyna's trained for it. Been lobbing it to sundry

and assorted audiences since kindergarten." Jenny's voice was dry as The Hun helped her out of her 501s and into the Chanel outfit which in a detached, but vain, part of her mind Jenny had to admit suited her right down to the ground. Actually it ended some six inches above the knee, shorter than Jenny would normally dare wear but, conversely, was undoubtedly the longest garment to be found in Martyna's wardrobe. "Oh God! Everybody's going to see my trembling knees. Quick, go and tell Marcel I've changed my mind, that I've dropped dead of a heart attack, been abducted by aliens. Anything! I must have been absolutely mental to agree to this. Inform my solicitor, quick smart! Tell him I wasn't *compos mentis,* that I agreed under duress. Tell my mother. Actually don't tell my mother." Jenny buried her face in her hands. "Oh woe is me! What am I going to do?"

"You're going to stop the hysterics and get yourself into that chair so I can do your make-up or I'm going to have to smack you hard across the face. That's what you're going to do." One look at the wardrobe lady's meaty hands and Jenny was in no doubt that she meant every word. Suddenly deflated and meek as a lamb, she allowed herself to be plonked into a black leather chair reminiscent of something to be found in either a barber's shop or a dentist's surgery (chosen, no doubt, by Marcel with a view to dubious after-hours activities) and a moment later found her submerged beneath a layer of foundation so thick, Attila had to drill holes in her nostrils to allow her to breathe.

"Studio lights!" she explained perfunctorily. "Too little make-up and you'll look like something the cat dragged in from the nearest graveyard." True to her word, the foundation was followed up with several layers of eyeshadow, mascara, lipliner, lipstick and blusher till Jenny felt more like Coco the Clown than a glamorous chat-show hostess.

"Jenny, you look great!" Tentatively Marcel insinuated himself inch by inch back into the room. "Oprah Winfrey, eat your heart out!" Huffily, Jenny turned her head away only to have it yanked back a second later by The Hun who was intent on skewering her hair into a chic chignon.

"Blow it out your ass, Marcel."

Attempting reassurance in his best would-you-buy-a-used-car-from-this-man voice, Marcel, the picture of guilelessness, spread his hands.

"Look you'll be fine. Honestly! There's nothing to worry about. We'll just have quick run-through and hey presto, Bob's your uncle!"

Determinedly Jenny ignored him as Attila gave a final tweak to the hairdo and, well satisfied, hoisted her enormous bosom back up from where it had fallen down around her waist.

"There! You look cool, baby. A real work of artifice, even if I do say so myself. Now, go git those mothers!"

Approvingly, Marcel winked at the giantess's departing bulk. "That's the spirit! You've really surpassed yourself, Goldy girl!"

Immune to compliments, at least where Marcel was concerned, the woman shot him a filthy look from over her shoulder. "Don't I always, shrivel-dick?"

"Shrivel-dick?" Despite the drumming of a nervous bladder which was threatening to discharge its contents all over the floor, Jenny couldn't help but giggle as an enraged Marcel retaliated by sticking up his middle finger in the direction in which the wardrobe lady had disappeared.

"Purely conjecture, I assure you," he sniffed. "Nasty old German lezzie! Wouldn't know what a dick was even if she found it stuck up her –"

"What's that?" Jenny interrupted hastily, pointing to the peculiar-looking box-thing he was holding in his hand and unwilling to be a party to his lurid imagination.

"The mike." Successfully diverted, Marcel showed her how to position the earpiece, clipped the microphone onto her collar, then worked his way around to secure the pack discreetly under the back of her jacket. "Now look, don't worry. This kind of show more or less runs itself. All you have to do is listen carefully to the instructions I give you through the earpiece and everything will be hunky-dory."

"What about the autocue?" Jenny looked hopeful.

"No autocue," Marcel shot her down. "You can't script a live show except for the introduction and one or two little interludes. No, what you've got to do is hone in on one or two 'gobs', people so desperate for attention that they'll practically take over and do the whole show for you. Try and get one from each side of the fence in order to get the controversy nicely fuelled up. We usually pre-select them anyway. Remember now and again to remind them that swearing is a no-no." He winked. "*Not*, between you and me, that it does the show any harm. Just look at *Springer*, more bleeps than dialogue and his ratings are through the roof!" Fixing her with what he fondly imagined was a steely eye, he wagged an admonitory finger. "Remember though, you are strictly just a conduit for the opinions of the audience. No matter how much garbage is being spouted, or how much some obnoxious git gets up your pipe, I don't want you shoving in your oar and taking sides. You hear me?"

"As if!" Jenny was scornful. "When it'll be all I can do to open my mouth and squeak."

"Even so. I want you to make like you're a dentist. Your job is to extract all the rotten matter, get to the root of things, leave the patients bloody but still alive, emerging quite unscathed yourself from the ether-filled chamber of horrors, *and* reeking of roses, no less!"

Throwing her eyes skywards, Jenny implored the Heavens. "Marcel," she said, "you're full of bull!"

Complacently, Marcel briefly consulted his watch, rubbed his hands together. "Right, it's party time. Do or die! Into the breach! Get up off your knees, Jenny, You'll tear your Aristocs."

"Bugger off!" Jenny snarled. "Can't you see I'm praying for a miracle?"

239

None too gently Marcel hauled her to her feet. "Miracle bedamned! You're on the air in approximately ten seconds flat. Now get your ass in gear, pronto!"

"When this is over I'm gonna kill you," Jenny threatened, lips frothy with a mixture of fear and rage. "I'm gonna tear you limb from limb. I'm gonna sever your ears from your head and kick you unconscious."

Simpering, Marcel hauled her through the door and into the TV studio where the glare of a hundred spotlights hit her between the eyes with all the force of a ten-ton sledgehammer. "I bet you say that to all the boys."

Chapter Twenty-four

It was worse than she imagined! A million times worse! The warm-up man had not so much warmed up the audience as incinerated them and now, judging by the looks on their assorted, ugly faces they were baying for blood. Jenny's blood!

"Quick, intro first," Marcel hissed through her earpiece as frantically Jenny tried to locate the camera with the red light to which, apparently, she had to address herself. "Then head straight for the Barbie-doll, seated front-row, right-hand aisle seat. Goes by the name of Lynn-Lola 'n dubs herself a professional mistress. A real 'gob' if ever there was one. Jenny, girl, you've got it made!"

"Ladies and gentlemen." To Jenny's amazement, after an initial false start or two that made her sound like an old tractor revving up, her voice, when at last she found it, came out strong as a bell and crystal clear. "Today's show is entitled 'Wedding rings don't mean a thing!' I'm Jenny Treigh standing in for Martyna Michaels who, unfortunately, cannot be with us today due to an altercation with a plate of garlic prawns."

"Good girl!" Marcel hissed unnervingly in her ear as a desultory chuckle made its way around the audience. "Now go get the 'gob'!"

Obediently and on rubber legs from which the bones had been removed, Jenny not so much walked as boinged over to the chosen target.

"Ah, Lymphoma! Lymphoma from Essex. You, I understand, are a *'professional'* mistress. By that I take it you don't believe in the sanctity of marriage?"

"Lynn-Lola!" The Barbie, all black roots and hair extensions corrected her. "Yep! It's no holds barred, as far as I'm concerned." She widened her eyes. Blue eyeshadow, Jenny noticed and shuddered, remembering how, not so long ago, she herself was guilty of the same fashion *faux pas*. "I mean, it's not my fault if a wife can't keep her husband at home. I mean if *she* was taking care of his needs he wouldn't have to come running to girls like me."

"There's a name for women like you," came a voice from left of field.

"Excellent! Another 'gob'. You're up and running now, Jenny!" Marcel's voice crackled and spat in her eardrum as an older, more restrained version of Barbie stood up and shouted her contribution.

"Slag! That's the word!"

"Trollop!"

"Tart!"

"Whore!"

"Jezebel!"

The older woman's supporters consulted their collective mental thesaurus, lavishly adding to the adjectives hurtling like missiles towards young Barbie who had begun to bristle like a nubile hedgehog.

"Just because you lot are old bags," she spat. "I mean, who'd want to shag you lot, anyway?"

Jenny drew in her breath. "Please, Lymph . . . Lynn-Lola! Remember this is a daytime television show. No swearing, please." In her ear, Marcel chuckled complacently while, suitably chastened, the young woman adjusted her cleavage and pouted into the nearest camera which, did she but know it, wasn't switched on.

"Sorry. It's just that those old cows make me so mad. Why can't they realise they're past it? They've had their fun. Now why don't they just lie down and die?"

Suggestively licking her lips and dressed to kill in matching leopard-skin Wonderbra, hot pants, and thigh-high boots Jenny's mother would kill for, her mate jiggled her own boobs and endeavoured to seduce the same camera.

"Yeah! I mean, get real. What man in his right mind is going to fancy that – to this!" Fluttering her eyes, she pointed to the nearest, brittle-boned, long past humping-age octogenarian then back again to her own voluptuous figure.

"One with more than one brain cell, maybe!" There,

it was out and, guess what, Jenny didn't give a damn despite Marcel's sudden whinnying like a stricken stallion in her ear.

"Conduit, Jenny! You are just the conduit!"

"Excuse me?" Barbie's mate raised her eyebrows. Pencilled in, not real!

"Listen." Hands on hips, Jenny towered over her, the dragon looming over St George. "Women like you make me sick to the pit of my stomach, make me want to puke, make me want to spew, if you must know. Have you any idea what you do to families? Breaking innocent wives' hearts, breaking innocent children's hearts, tearing at the very rock of society, the cornerstone of civilisation, the foundation of humanity. The family!" Her breath was warm, foetid, which is what comes of breaking your diet and pigging out on vindaloo the night before. "We don't invite you into our lives but you're always waiting, aren't you, tentacles outstretched like a female tarantula, biding your time, waiting for that one moment of weakness, that tiff, that difference of opinion that will send our husbands scuttling out the door and straight into your drawers." Baring her teeth she brought her nose down inches from the Barbie clone's. "Where they're always assured of a warm welcome! Isn't that right?"

"Jenny," Marcel's voice seethed, more outraged squeak than appeal. "Stop the madness. Stop the vendetta. She's *not* Farina!"

Reminded, a glint of madness came into Jenny's eyes. Ah. Farina!

"Know Farina, do you? One of your set, is she?" Throwing up her arms she nodded vehemently. "Of course you know her. It follows. Bimbos go together like false eyelashes and false fingernails, helium tits and high heels, collagen and college degrees. No! Scrap that one! Anyway, you get the general drift." Jenny backed off a bit, addressed the audience as a whole. "Let me tell you a story, ladies and gentlemen, a new take on the three bears, if you will. You see there was Mummy Bear, Daddy Bear and little Baby Bear. They lived in a lovely house which was anything but bare. Daddy Bear was a merchant banker and Mummy Bear, apart from being his wife was, to use an American euphemism, a home maker. Baby Bear went to school and played on his Playstation though not at the same time. Daddy Bear drove a Merc and brought home lots of lovely money with which they bought lots of lovely porridge. The three bears were very happy; well, most of the time anyway. Let's face it, they had their ups and downs like anybody else but, all in all, they rubbed along tolerably well together." Pausing for a moment before continuing her hyperbole, Jenny savagely ripped out her earpiece through which Marcel could be heard hyperventilating like a warthog on heat. "Sadly an opportunist was waiting in the wings. Farina aka Goldilocks! Only she wasn't interested in porridge! No way José! *She* wanted the whole enchilada! The big cheese. The sugar daddy!" Jenny's voice wobbled. "And one night when the Mummy Bear was innocently watching *Jerry Springer* and the Baby Bear was having a sleepover with his mate of the month, Farina, the dirty rotten excuse for a creature of the female gender saw her chance, spirited the Daddy Bear away and hid him in her knickers." Pausing dramatically, she pointed an accusing finger, first at the pair of Barbie Clones in the front row, then one by one through the serried ranks of bimbos scattered throughout the audience, a sprinkling of peroxide in a midden of mouse. "And so, ladies and gentlemen, another stalwart family bit the dust, brought to its sorry knees by trollops like her, and her and her. Don't look for the fairytale ending to this story," she warned, "because there is none! Let's just say, when the Mummy Bear got there, the cupboard was bare."

"Cut! Cut! Cut!" Marcel yelled racing into the studio and forcibly wrestling Jenny to the ground as around them pandemonium broke out, Bags versus Slags, and fisticuffs rent the air, even as loud and uninhibited swearing turned it blue. "Jesus Christ! If you wanted to destroy us so badly, why didn't you just put a bomb in the studio. I trusted you, Jenny, but you've annihilated me."

Gasping, Jenny extricated her windpipe from under his left elbow.

"Oh I'm sorry, Marcel. I just couldn't help myself. That smug little bitch really got under my skin. I swear I really wanted to punch her lights out!"

Clumsily, Marcel pulled himself to his feet and Jenny along with him, fussily dusting a hand down his trouser legs.

"Oh, well, I suppose it was only a matter of time

anyway before In Kamera gave up the ghost. All you did really was to expedite matters and at least we went out with a bang."

And what a bang, Jenny thought, as all around them seats were upturned and smashed, together with sundry bones and noses, and bimbos divested themselves of their Wonderbras using them with deadly accuracy as catapults whilst, not to be outdone, the wrinkly brigade produced nail-files and illegal weaponry from about their persons, jabbing wildly at any youthful flesh that came their way.

"Bye bye, movers and shakers. Hello, butchers and bakers." Hastily ducking down, Marcel narrowly escaped being garrotted by the octogenarian who, for want of any other weapon, had removed her stockings and, due to failing eyesight, was now making wild grabs in the direction of anything spotted moving on the periphery of her vision. "Hello, ignominy and the world of dole queues and means-testing."

Half-hearted, Jenny attempted to console him. "There's nothing wrong with butchers and bakers. Some of them make a damn good living!"

"I know but *I* don't want to bake apple turnovers and carve up carcasses. *I* want to direct. Cameras, lights, action! That's *my* world, Jenny. But there's no way back, is there? All that's left me now is the life of a hod carrier or at a push a descent into the cheap and seedy world of porn. Speaking of which, how does *The Degeneration Game* sound to you? Catchy, isn't it?"

Jenny groaned as a new and horrific thought suddenly struck her. "Oh, Lord. Martyna'll have my guts for garters. Trust me to make a total hash of things. Little did she know when she ordered that plate of prawns that they'd cost her more than just a gippy tummy and six rolls of toilet paper."

Marcel shook his head. "Don't worry. Martyna'll be fine. ITV has been trying to poach her for years. It was only her loyalty that kept her with In Kamera for so long. Actually, you've done her a favour really. A big budget outfit like ITV can do far more for her than we ever could."

Jenny's lip trembled. "Still, I can't help but feel bad about things. I mean I shouldn't have gone off the deep end like that. If only I'd listened to you!"

Comfortingly, Marcel squeezed her arm. "Nobody ever listens to me and well, at least you were true to yourself which is more than most of us ever have the courage to be."

Jenny was rueful. "Hardly courage. More like stupidity. Anyway, I'm really sorry, Marcel."

"Don't beat yourself up about it. What's done is done and, like I said, it was really only a matter of time anyway. We'd all heard the death knell long before that particular show aired. Now, get yourself off home, if you like. To say you've had a traumatic morning would be an understatement."

Jenny nodded gratefully. "Thanks, Marcel. You're a gem! And yes, if you don't mind I will go away and cower in a dark corner somewhere. In fact, I might never come out again."

"Don't even think about it," Marcel warned. "I want you back at work tomorrow morning. I mean, okay, we've capsized and are taking in water by the *Titanic*-ful, but we're not sunk yet. Besides no one else can make coffee the way you do."

"Gee thanks. You've really boosted my self-esteem but, okay, if I haven't overdosed in the night you might just see me tomorrow. *A mañana* then!"

"Yep, *a mañana!*" Equilibrium almost restored, Marcel sketched a quick salute before turning about and re-entering the fray where the octogenarian, stocking stretched to the consistency of barbed wire, was waiting to pounce.

"Kilroy," she warbled as nylon met carotid, "this one's for you!"

* * *

On the train home Jenny, paranoid that the world and his wife were watching her and revelling in the complete moron she'd made of herself on the TV that morning, took refuge behind a tattered copy of *Ms London* some kind soul had had the foresight to leave behind.

'Ere, George, that's that strange woman off the telly, innit? Blimey she's even worse in the flesh. Wha evah possessed them to put that old trout on in place of Martyna Moichels? Still, it were a laugh though, eh? I thought oI'd piss meself, me oi did!"

Thank God none of her immediate family or friends were likely to have copped it. Dubious though she was about Kilroy's hairstyles, her mother remained true blue to the man himself and Poppy would only have been likely to watch if she'd thought there was the remotest chance of her Inner Child suddenly turning itself in on live TV. As for Mounty, after their little contretemps, Jenny had no idea what *she* was doing lately and Adam, pinstripe-suited, and Gucci-booted would, presumably, have been playing the great 'I Am' at work. As for David, safely at school, thank the Lord, he need never get wind of what a complete and utter ass his mother had made of herself that morning unless one of his friends' parents happened to catch the show and spill the beans. Emerging from the station she skulked all the way home, keeping close to the walls, eyes down avoiding any possibility of eye contact with another human being or of anyone being able to point the sneering finger of recognition. Letting herself in the front door, she immediately assumed the M&B position cursing herself, as usual, for her failure to remember to remove the post-basket which, never one to let an opportunity pass, immediately lunged for her fontanelle.

Christ! Tenderly, Jenny rubbed the sore spot. It was one thing after another. Why didn't she just face it? She wasn't cut from the cloth of greatness. She was just Mrs Average, a sow's ear destined to remain a sow's ear despite frenzied and prolonged attempts to turn herself into a silk purse. Oh, sure she had managed to shift a wheelbarrow of lard. Sure her underwear had gradually become less like a winding sheet and more like a string bean and sure, she now had the dubious honour of having bony ankles that jutted admirably out above her size fives, narrow-fitting. But really, in the grand scheme of things, did it really matter whether her knickers were a size ten or a twenty? The hell it did! Was the world a better, kinder, more forgiving place because her feet took up less acreage? The hell it was! So why didn't she just chuck the towel in and go get a load of *Jerry Springer* and a king-size bar of Whole Nut? The hell she would! Still nursing her sore head, Jenny rose to her feet. Actually, in retrospect, that wasn't such a bad idea. At least with Jerry she was on safe ground. *He* made no demands of her. *He* didn't give a fiddler's fart if she did nothing with her life other than watch chat shows till the cows came home and clock up calories. No! With Jerry what you saw was what you got. Sleaze and plenty of it! Just what the doctor ordered! What better way of taking your mind off your own troubles than to gloat at the misfortune of others? Unfortunately though, Jerry wasn't on for another couple of hours and she simply couldn't face *Oprah* and her panel of in-your-face psychotherapists. She'd gone far too far beyond the pale for any of them to be of any use. No! No one could help her now! She was a terminal case, a cancerous growth, a human tumour on a one-way ticket to oblivion.

"God, you're a right sad cow, you!"

"What?" Jenny's head came up to find itself directly in alignment with the hall mirror in which her reflection, panda-eyed with smudged mascara, was not so much reflecting as glaring.

"I mean, get a load of yourself. Talk about the wreck of the *Hesperus!* Why don't you just pop out to the nearest barn, get a big rope and go hang yourself!"

Wiping her nose on the sleeve of the Chanel loaned to her by 'wardrobe', Jenny glared back. "Don't think I haven't considered it only, knowing my luck, I'd make a mess of that too and end up a gherkin on a gurney."

Her reflection looked pissed. "Okay, okay. So you've fallen off your bicycle. What's the big deal? Just pick yourself up, dust yourself down and start all over again."

Jenny groaned. "Look, it's not that black and white. There are myriad shades of grey in between. Millions of people saw my fall from grace today. I'm a pariah! An outcast from society. Unclean! Unclean! Got a bell I could borrow?" Jenny attempted what she hoped was a brave, little smile which only resulted in her alter ego looking as though it had suffered a sudden and vicious stroke.

"Aw, what are you like? In Kamera is just a Mickey Mouse outfit. If more than half a dozen people saw you make a show of yourself, then I'll eat the frame around this mirror. I mean, cop on to yourself. When the viewing public heard Martyna Michaels was going to be a no-show, Channel 5 ratings suddenly hit the roof. So much so that the station bigwigs have ordered a stay of execution."

Hope lit up Jenny's face, flickered and was replaced by doubt. "You think?"

"Definitely."

"I must admit I hadn't thought of it like that."

The mirror sniffed. "Of course you hadn't. Too full of your own importance, that's your trouble. Personally I blame your underwear drawer. All those g-strings and Wonderbras, powder and paint, make Jenny think she is what she ain't."

"That's not fair."

"No? Well, neither is life. So get over it!"

Jenny pulled herself to her feet.

"Listen, I can't spend all day trading insults with you especially as I can feel a severe hypoglycemic attack coming on and I know for a fact David put a king-size Mars bar in the fridge last night."

"Yeah? Well, be it on your hips if you go and guzzle your son's choccy supply. What can I tell you? Once a loser, always a loser."

Grabbing a shawl from off the nearby coat-stand, Jenny draped it over her accuser's face. "Aw, gimme a break," she said, toddling off to the fridge. "A diet-Coke break and a Mars bar." Funny, she could feel her spirits lift already. And then the phone rang!

Chapter Twenty-five

"Jenny?" It was Marcel. "Get your ass back here tooty sweet!"

"Why?" Masterfully, Jenny struggled to tear off the corner of the Mars bar wrapping with her teeth. "For further pillorying? For death by tabloid?"

A note of excitement entered Marcel's voice. "No, because you're a celeb, Jenny! The switchboard is on overload. There's more bulbs lighting up on it than in Regent Street at Christmas. We're talking syndication here, you know. BBC. ITV. Channel 4, Sky, ABC. Everybody's talkin 'bout the new kid in town. *The Sun* wants you on page three. *Hello* wants a centre spread. Parkinson wants you on his couch. Jesus wants you for a sunbeam. I want you to boost the ratings. Martyna wants you dead! Only joking! She's as chuffed for you as I am."

Reluctantly Jenny put the Mars bar aside, one naked, chocolaty shoulder temptingly revealed, as she sought to make sense of Marcel's enthusiastic tirade.

"Go on. You're having a laugh!"

"No way!" Jenny could almost hear him shaking his head and the bits of dandruff native to it flying off in every direction like confetti at a wedding. "You're hot stuff, Jenny. The new face of chat shows. Directional, that's what they're calling you. I can just see them now, neon titles, fluorescent pink, funky script, graffiti maybe. *'Jenny Jumps In.'*

Absentmindedly, Jenny reached out, pulled the shawl from over the mirror to reveal her reflection looking every bit as gobsmacked as she herself. "Hold your horses, Marcel! Weren't you the one who told me not to get involved? Correct me if I'm wrong but I seem to remember the word 'conduit' tripping from your oh-so-masterful lips?"

"I also asked you, begged you in fact, to kick me senseless at one point but you didn't listen to me then either. And yes, fair enough, I didn't realise it myself till it was pointed out to me by a TV exec from the Beeb waving a fat cheque, but people are fed up to the back teeth of conduit-type chat-show hosts. What they want are moral-high-grounders, hosts and hostesses who, at the first sign of provocation, will jump off the fence and wade in, helter-skelter, all guns blazing, with their own slant on matters be they right or wrong."

Jenny shrugged. "Well. I'm very pleased the scales have fallen from your eyes, Marcel, but if you think for one moment that *I* am putting my butt back in the hot seat, you're sadly mistaken, my man. Once bitten, twice shy! Let Martyna wade in. It was her show I hijacked after all."

"No can do! Martyna's decided on a complete change of career. Going into the restaurant business, if you don't mind, seafood a speciality. Something to do with not even wanting her worst enemy to have to suffer the kind of diarrhoea she herself experienced recently. As a matter of fact she's taking out a franchise in that big chain of seafood restaurants, Sole of Discretion. So you see. It's got to be you. Now what do you say? Shall I send a car for you?"

Jenny prevaricated. "A car? What's wrong with the Tube?"

Marcel snorted. "Tubes are for plebs, Jenny. Limos are for celebs! You'll have to get used to your new status. You're hot property now, kiddo. So whaddya say? Shall we get this show on the road? Remember, she who hesitates is lost. You've got to strike while the iron's hot. A stitch in time saves nine . . ."

Brutally Jenny cut him off at the clichés. "Oh, okay! But I warn you, Marcel, I'd be doing this against my better judgement. *Jenny Jumps In* is right; right out of the frying pan and into the flippin fire."

Calculatedly and quite unashamedly, Marcel dangled a carrot. "Adam will be so proud. I mean, let's face it, everyone wants to boast of bedding a celebrity and when that celebrity happens to be your wife, that ambition becomes reality a whole lot faster. So you see you can scrap your plan to seduce *him*. Your celebrity status will do that for you and Farina will be relegated to the eternal scrap heap of young, used and abused mistresses till another bored, married man happens along at some point and gives her a leg up." Jenny could hear the sudden grin that entered his voice. "In return for which, of course, and at a price, she will allow *him* to get his leg over!"

Jenny swallowed the carrot whole. Marcel had a point. Adam *was* impressed by status, endearingly so, or so she used to think. Once, he'd happened upon Bette Midler in Harrods and trailed her all round the shop hoping, no doubt, that a duly impressed Joe Public would mistake him for part of her retinue. Either that, or that the great diva would herself discover *him* and, at one and the same time, the missing link in her life, causing her to break into an impromptu and rousing rendition of 'The Wind Beneath My Wings'. Like a flaw in a diamond, it was a trait in his character which Jenny had never cared to examine too closely. Actually, there were a lot of traits in Adam's character Jenny had never cared to examine too closely mainly because, whenever they reared up, loyalty forced her to lock them away in her very own Pandora's Box and, if not exactly lose the key, then at least forget where she'd put it. Well, who could blame her? Love is the antidote to commonsense, isn't it? Besides, nobody's perfect! Nothing for it then but to surrender.

"All right then, if it'll help me to get Adam back but I warn you, Marcel, I'm not a happy bunny. I'm also shit-scared, have a bump on my head like Mount Everest and snot on the sleeve of my Chanel."

Marcel was blasé. "Nothing to worry about. You're a natural. The camera loves you. As for the suit, chuck it out. There's plenty more where that came from. In another couple of weeks every designer in town will be hot-footing it to the studios desperate for you to wear their outfits on air. Lend them cachet, as it were!"

Jenny's voice was steely. "I will *not* chuck it out. Not whilst there are people starving in the Third World."

"So what you gonna do? Send it to them to eat?"

"Ha! Ha! Very funny. If wit was shit we'd all be constipated!"

Exasperated, Marcel sighed. "Look, Jenny. Do what you sodding like with the suit. Give it to Oxfam. Rip it up and polish your windows. Casserole, bake or boil it. Only get yourself over here. Like yesterday!"

Jenny echoed the sigh. "All right, keep your hood on! I'm on my way." Banging down the receiver, she cast a last longing look at the Mars bar before returning it to the fridge. "I'll be back," she promised, patting her tummy. "Watch this space."

* * *

"Well, just as long as you don't go believing your own publicity."

"No fear of that, Mother dearest." Wryly, Jenny linked arms with her mother. "Not with you around to whip the rug out from under me."

"Don't be sarcastic. I'm only thinking of you. After all, it's a well-known fact that the great British Press love nothing better than to build someone up to Titan proportions then, at the first sign of feet of clay, knock them flying off their pedestal."

"Not me. I don't warrant that kind of media interest."

Covertly Jenny's mother checked her passing reflection in a plate-glass window. The shark-skin boots were a mistake, she decided, made her look as if *Jaws* had locked on to her legs and any moment now she would be down to just her stumps.

"I don't know so much about that. According to Marcel you're 'what's in', flavour of the month, the cat's pyjamas, not to mention the 'hostess who roasteth'. And what about *Loaded* magazine? I hear *they* want to do a centre-spread on you."

Jenny chuckled. "Want will be their master then! I'm damned if anyone's putting a staple through my midriff. Neither do I fancy putting my cellulite on general release."

Gloria sniffed. "Cellulite? Do me a favour! If you turned sideways these days, you'd be marked absent. You're not suffering from anorexia, are you?"

"My foot!" Jenny scoffed. 'I can't even spell it, let alone suffer from it."

"Yes, well sneer if you must but fame brings its own pressures. Look at all those lollipop-headed women in the States, Nancy Regan, Celine Dion, that Ally McBeal actress woman etc. etc. Stick bodies, massive heads. You can bet your life if they weren't in the glare of the spotlight so often, they'd be pigging out on the carbos like the rest of us."

Grabbing her mother's elbow, Jenny steered her in the direction of a nearby cafe. "Look, you're worrying unnecessarily. There's nothing wrong with my constitution and nothing, not even the Jesus diet, will ever turn me into a waif."

"What's that, some new fad from Rosemary Conley?"

"No! Some old fad from the Bible. Starvation for forty days and forty nights, out in the desert preferably and with the devil to pay at the end of it."

Her mother grinned. "I don't much like the sound of that but I very much like the sound of this."

"Hmm, smoked salmon bagel with tarragon mayonnaise." Jenny stopped to read the menu over which her mother was drooling. "Yep, I could do that! Shall we go in?"

"Just try and stop me. I'm that hungry I could eat a jockey and run after the horse."

"Yes, well try to settle for the bagel, will you?" Cheerfully, Jenny followed her into the cafe stopping en route to sign a couple of autographs and drop a kiss on the red and malignant face of a squalling baby some misguided woman held up for her inspection.

"Jesus!" Her mother's eyebrows rose a couple of stories. "Who does she think you are, the Queen?"

"No. Anthea Turner!" Giggling, Jenny took refuge behind a menu. "I hadn't the heart to disillusion her but I swear I'll never get used to being accosted by perfect strangers. I mean it's just not me! I'm nobody special, for Heaven's sake!"

"You're on the telly. Doesn't matter if you'd ten legs and your face was one big pus-filled open sore, that's enough for some people!" Dryly her mother ran her eye down the menu before reverting back to her first choice. "The salmon it is. What about you?"

"Same!"

"Two salmon bagels, one Earl Grey and one café latte, please," she told the waitress, having to repeat herself twice before her words finally connected with the woman's brain and galvanised her into action. Warily, Jenny's eyes followed the waitress's retreating back.

"God, how embarrassing! I feel like I'm living in a fishbowl! I thought her eyes were going to bore holes in me. Maybe I should invest in a hood like Marcel's."

"Mm. And what about Adam? How's *he* coping with your newfound fame?" Glancing about her innocuously, her mother attempted to slip the question past Jenny's guard, almost as if she weren't really interested in hearing the answer, almost as if it was a throwaway thought that had just occurred to her and not a burning curiosity that had kept her from her sleep for nights on end.

Deliberately, Jenny played into her hands, every bit

as eager to talk about matters as her mother was to hear. "He bought me flowers, actually. Long-stemmed, damask roses punctuated by fronds of baby's breath in fact. You should have seen the girls at work. They were pea-green."

"He sent them to the studios? Why?"

Jenny shrugged, trying hard to look blasé but only succeeding in looking like the cat who got the cream. "Wanted to make a public statement, I suppose. Declare his adoration for all the world to see."

"Wanted to stake a public claim of ownership, more like. Hands off! This woman's taken. Branded by a wedding ring! Talk about saying shit with flowers."

Jenny paused, her bagel halfway to her lips. "Well, thanks for bursting my bubble, Mother! You just can't give him the benefit of the doubt, can you? You just can't imagine that it might simply be that he's come to his senses and realised how much he loves me, after all?"

Appetite suddenly deserting her, Gloria laid down her own roll. "No! What I can imagine though is that, like a phoenix from the ashes, he's seen you rise from obscurity and decided that he might as well hop on the bandwagon." Her voice rose. "And what about Farina? Are you just going to brush that little episode under the carpet; pretend it was all a bad dream, go back to playing happy families?"

Jenny shifted uncomfortably. "There *is* such a thing as forgiveness, you know, and if a thing is worth fighting for . . ."

"But it's *not* worth fighting for.' Imploring, her mother held her hands out. "Your marriage is tarnished, Jenny. Fool's gold. Not worth the marriage certificate it's printed on. What will it take to make you realise that Adam is about as much use as a knitted condom?"

"Oh, why can't you just be happy for me? You know how much I love him and he *is* David's father. We're a family unit! What God has put together . . ."

"Adam's already pulled asunder. Cop yourself on, Jenny, and stop talking like a Catholic periodical. Adam's back for no other reason than that your desire factor has suddenly risen. I'd like to see how long he'd stick around if you suddenly put on ten stone and got a job in Tesco's."

"Oh, come on, he's not *that* shallow!"

Her mother picked up her roll again, turning it this way and that, divining the best strategy for attack. "He *is* that shallow, so shallow in fact, you could paddle your feet in his soul."

Jenny set her lips. "People learn from their mistakes."

"Only if they admit they made a mistake in the first place. I'll bet anything Adam can justify everything he ever did, be it breaking the head off his best friend's Action Man to persuading Farina to divest herself of her kit! Face it. The man thinks his piss is perfume."

Like one of the three wise monkeys, Jenny covered her ears. "I'm not listening to this. I mean it's not as if

Seducing Adam

you've got it sussed. You're going out with a man who thinks he's a dog for God's sake!"

Unfazed, Gloria took a sip from her cup of Earl Grey. "That's right and, like all canines, Rover is a loyal and faithful companion. A one-woman dog, as it were. No fear of him biting the hand that leads him."

Jenny groaned. "You're hopeless. There's just no arguing with you, is there? You've got a logic all your own and an answer for everything."

"If by that you mean I'm quick on the uptake, well, yes I am. I'm also a lot older than you and –"

"I know, I know. Longevity qualifies you to know more than me. I've heard it all before."

Mildly, Gloria picked up a paper napkin, dabbed at the corner of her lips. "Well, why don't you take it on board then? Remember, I was right about Adam. That Hell's Angel would have been a much better bet. I was also right about that so-called friend of yours, Diana Mountford. You can bet your sweet life she won't be sending in to In Kamera for an autographed picture of you. Poison-pen letters would be more her style, I should imagine."

Jenny uncovered her ears. "Well, then you'd imagine wrong! I admit I'm hurt by her attitude but Mounty and I go back a long way and I expect she's got good reason for lying low just now."

'Ain't that the truth!' Lighting up a cigarette, her mother savagely inhaled the words before, like an atom bomb, they could escape into the open and wreak havoc upon the life of the woman sitting in blissful ignorance opposite.

"When Mounty's ready to build some bridges she'll find me waiting with the bricks and mortar."

"Yes? Well, don't hold your breath, that's all." Casually, her eyes strayed over Jenny's shoulder, clashing for a moment with those of the glamorous, red-haired woman who had just come in, rotated some three hundred and sixty degrees and gone back out again. "Don't ask me how I know but I have a feeling the Mounty is not for turning."

Picking up the bill and pushing her chair back from table, Jenny signalled that that particular conversation was now at an end. "Time will tell," she said as, shrugging herself into her jacket, her mother followed suit.

"Indeed it will. I haven't a doubt about it."

Behind the till the waitress jiggled uncomfortably about, seemed to come to a sudden and momentous decision and shoved a piece of paper under Jenny's nose.

"I know I shouldn't ask but, please can I have your autograph?"

"Oh sure." Self-consciously but obligingly, Jenny wrote her name in her best handwriting, a hangover from her school days when bad handwriting was considered indicative of a bad character.

"Jennifer L. Treigh," the waitress read, her face falling a mile. "I thought you were Anthea Turner!"

Chapter Twenty-six

"It simply won't do, my deah. You've got an image to project. You owe it to your public."

"My public? You make me sound like the Queen Mother."

With a dramatic shudder the hairdresser brought a camp hand to his fevered brow. "Oh don't! It's simply too awful! The things I could do for that poor woman. The nation's favourite grandmother and they turn her out in platform shoes and a Paddington Bear hat. Talk about a royal show! Ten minutes with me and I promise you wouldn't recognise her."

Jenny yawned roundly. It had been a hard, if exciting, week and the relaxing shampoo and set (boring but safe) she'd promised herself was turning out to be more like a marathon trek, barefoot up the Andes.

"Yes. Well, I dare say a purple tonsure *would* make most people unrecognisable. But I don't intend being one of them. So scrap any elaborate schemes you may be scheming, my man, and break out the trusty blow-drier."

Far from happy at having his artistic licence if not exactly revoked, then suspended, Salvio – Saliva to his staff – grabbed up the blow-drier and vented hairbrush and faffed sulkily about at the back of her head.

"Look," Jenny applied balm. "the public are fickle. Take Kilroy, for example. His little sortie into the 1990s almost cost him his loyal and faithful following. No, Salvio. Live and learn from Kilroy is what I say. The public are used to my bob. Let's not confuse them with highlights, lowlights, streaks and stripes. When they tune in to *Jenny Jumps In* they have a preconceived idea of me wearing a bob, and why on earth should I shatter their illusions? And therefore, a bob's *exactly* what they'll see me wearing."

With a disparaging sniff, Salvio worked his way round the side of her head deliberately, it seemed to Jenny, scalding the ear off her with the blow-drier. "The customer is always right!"

"Then why do you make it sound like I've asked you to commit murder most foul?"

"Well, you have, in a way. I mean . . . a bob. So *passé!*"

"So?" Jenny snapped, fed up with pandering. "Don't try turning me into a fashion victim. A bob it is! Now get over it and concentrate your mind on life's greater issues such as global warming and the price of tampons!" From somewhere close by a sudden agonized shriek indicated that All Tressed Up's beauty therapist had successfully located/despatched the moustache lately adorning Poppy's upper lip.

"Easy. Don't laugh," Salvio cautioned, reaching for a can of hairspray and lightly spritzing her eyeball. "You're booked in for the works, I understand. Full leg-wax *and* bikini line!"

Jenny shook her head. "Uh huh! Not me, mate! You've obviously mixed me up with someone else. Personally, I'd sooner have legs like a shag-pile carpet than subject myself to that kind of torture."

"But what about your husband?"

"Adam? Don't worry about him. He already *has* legs like a shag-pile carpet."

Salvio spritzed again, sadistically aiming for the other eyeball. "No. I meant doesn't he like you smooth?"

"Nah. He likes his whisky smooth. He just likes me ready!" Actually that was a lie. She'd always been ready. Ready, willing and waiting! But whilst she was showing willing, he was showing willy, only to someone else. Hopefully though, the winds of change were about to blow as Adam was taking her to dine, *dîner à deux*, at La Gavroche tonight and who knew what might turn up on the menu? Mind you, she'd nearly blown the whole thing before ever it had a chance to get off the ground. Well, it *was* kind of unexpected, like winning the lottery when you haven't bought a ticket or finding your heart suddenly starting up again after it's been removed for transplant and stuffed in a picnic box.

"La Gavroche? But what's wrong with Spend A Penne?" she'd said. Not 'Oh, what a splendid idea, darling' or 'First roses, now dinner. Aren't I the lucky girl?' No wonder Adam had looked narked.

"You're a big fish now, Jenny," is what he'd said, "and big fishes swim in big pools where other big fish can see them. Get my drift?"

And she'd nodded, sure that she did. "It's a fish restaurant then, is it? Good, I like fish. Martyna's gone into fish. Full of something or other, fish. Safer than beef too. I mean you never hear of anyone getting mad cod disease, do you?"

Exasperated, Adam had shaken her by the shoulders, his touch equally unexpected, considering he'd spent yonks doing everything he could to avoid her and, on the odd occasion when he had invaded her personal space, she'd had the distinct impression that he'd mentally, if not physically, donned the rubber gloves. "Jenny! Will you stop blathering on. It's not a fish restaurant! It's a *posh* restaurant. High-class, haunt of the rich and famous. Right up your street, I'd say."

"Spend A Penne *is* right up my street, literally. I mean we only had to walk as far as the precinct." Despite herself, her voice grew dreamy. "Remember Adam . . . remember how we shared a single strand of bolognese, the strand getting shorter and shorter till our lips met in the middle and we ended up sharing bolognese kisses?

270

Remember walking home in the moonlight you and I, hand in hand, three sheets to the wind, high on each other and cheap Chianti? Remember Gianni, Adam? *Mamma mia*, he used to say, *Mamma mia*. And one time you asked him when the twins were due."

Adam hrrmphed! "History, Jenny! We've moved on now; move in different circles. The past is irrelevant, over and gone. It's the future that counts. Forget Spend a Penne. Forget Gianni. It's onwards and upwards and you, my girl, are going right to the very pinnacle."

And Farina? Jenny had wanted to ask. What about her? Did she fall off *your* pinnacle? Is she past tense too, a mere grease-spot on your boy scout's badge of fidelity? Will you forget her, just like that? And do you expect me to forget her too? Because I don't know if I can, Adam. I just don't know if I can.

"I'll need to get my hair done," she'd said.

"Good idea. The paparazzi will be hanging about outside, no doubt hoping to snap a celebrity or two and we can't have you looking like something the cat dragged in. Can we?"

"No. I suppose we can't," Jenny'd agreed but in her heart she couldn't help wishing they *were* going to the little Italian bistro on the precinct instead, where nobody was a celebrity and, what's more, nobody gave a toss.

* * *

"There, all done!" With a flourish Salvio held the handmirror up for her to inspect the back of her head.

"I still think some copper lowlights would have added pzazz, though."

"Lovely." Jenny gave the obligatory pat to her hair, turning her head this way and that as if to admire it from all angles. "And who knows, if you live long enough, I might just come in here one day looking for an electric-blue Mohican."

Salvio sniffed. "I won't hold my breath. Now if you'd just like to settle up, I believe your friend has just bolted out the doorway. Honestly, the ingratitude of some people! Don't they know that in order to be beautiful, it is sometimes necessary to suffer a little pain, no?"

Jenny shrugged herself into her jacket. "As a matter of interest, Salvio. Have you ever been to Chaynes?"

"Chaynes?"

"Ah, never mind. It was just a thought. That's all."

Outside All Tressed Up, Poppy, the picture of fury, was stalking up and down with an upper lip like a slab of raw steak.

"Never again!" she vowed, racing up and catching hold of Jenny as she emerged from the salon. "Not in a million years. Not even if I end up looking like Moses with full-on beard will I ever subject myself to that kind of sadism, ever again! Beauty therapist, my foot! The woman's a reincarnation from the Spanish Inquisition, I'd say. Chief Inquisitor, if the truth be known! For tweezers read red-hot pokers!"

Determinedly, Jenny grabbed her elbow and steered

her across the street and into the nearest pub. "Oh come on, Poppy. It couldn't be that bad. Otherwise millions of women would be walking round like the great, hairy apes of China."

Poppy's eyebrows, bushy and mercifully free from plucking for at least ten years, rose cynically. "I didn't know there was such a thing but, in any event, millions of women *are*. Take you, for example. When was the last time *you* had *your* legs waxed or your bikini line?"

"Oh, when I was about sixteen and didn't know any better. Now, when the vegetation gets out of hand, I'm happy simply to whip out my trusty razor and, like one man and his dog, go and mow the meadow." With some difficulty Jenny propped herself up on one of the high stools ranged alongside the bar. "I mean, what is all this waxing and depilatory business about anyway? It's not as if anyone can see your roots, is it? If they ain't visible, they ain't there, as far as I'm concerned."

Poppy shrugged. "Slows the growth apparently. At least that's the fable."

"Yes, well like Santa Claus and happy endings, fables are for children. Now what's your poison?"

"G&T please, with lots of ice. I feel like my lip is on fire. Anyway you *do* believe in happy endings or else what's tonight all about?"

"G&T, ice and a slice, twice please." Jenny told the barman and waited till their drinks were served before turning her attention back to her friend. "Actually, I feel really confused over the whole thing. I mean, I feel like

I should be turning cartwheels, jumping up and down, rushing round and whooping like a mad thing . . . '

"Only?"

"Only, I don't feel like that at all. Instead I feel kind of flat like a glass of champagne left standing too long after a party. No fizz. That's it! I feel like there's no fizz in me, no pep, no sparkle!"

"Jenny, correct me if I'm wrong but we are talking Adam here and not antacids? I mean, for a moment there you sounded just like that advert for Andrews Liver Salts."

"Oh shut up, Poppy!" Playfully Jenny slapped her wrist. "Okay, maybe I am waxing a bit lyrical."

"Aagh! Don't mention that word." Tenderly Poppy patted her upper lip before immersing it beneath the mountain of ice floating at the top of her glass.

Jenny grinned. "Sorry. I didn't mean to be insensitive. I wouldn't hurt you for the world. In fact, as far as I'm concerned, no one can hold a candle to you."

Poppy sent her a killer look. "Ha, ha! Big joke. Now can we get back to the subject in hand or are you deliberately avoiding the issue?"

Suddenly serious again, Jenny shrugged. "Oh hell! I don't know. Maybe I am. It's just that . . . ' She held her hands out in appeal. "Oh, Poppy, help! Am I doing the right thing?"

"Only you can decide that, Jen."

"But what would you do. I mean, if you were in my shoes?"

"If I were in your shoes I don't doubt I'd do the exactly the same thing as you. But, from the standpoint of my own Doc Martens, I wouldn't give the bastard house-room much less go trotting off to La Gavroche with him like some sort of female Rolex to hang on his arm."

Jenny looked interested."And that's what you think he sees me as? An ornament, some kind of status symbol? A trophy wife?" She grinned. "Actually, Pops, that's kind of flattering especially when you consider that, not all that long ago, he saw me as a cross between the Michelin Man and Mama Cass. In fact, I'd go so far as to say that makes me feel rather good."

Poppy flinched as a sliver of ice broke free and stabbed her in the upper lip. "Look, I'm sorry to knock down your sandcastle, but what about the Farina episode? Does that make you feel good too? I mean, do you really think you can just blithely pick up the reins and carry on as before? Personally, I'd have gone for his jugular with a steak knife a long time ago. I'm talking pistols at dawn here, Jenny. You know, shoot to kill!'

Idly, Jenny picked up a swizzle-stick and dunked her slice of lemon. "So, basically, you think I'm weak. Because I haven't gone in there with all guns blazing and put him on the spot, you think I'm weak. A pushover! A bit of a clown! And maybe you're right and maybe I'm crazy but you see, although I *know* he's been unfaithful, so long as I don't actually hear *him* admit it, a tiny, admittedly illogical part of me, can pretend it never really happened – that it was all just a Dallas dream and Bobby's not really dead, just taking a long shower! And you can take that look off your face, Miss. I'm just telling you how I feel. I'm not looking for the Royal Seal of Approval, you know."

Poppy drained her glass and signalled for a refill. "Just as well because, even if it were in my remit, I wouldn't give it to you. It's beyond me though how you think you can go through life without confronting him, if not now, then at some stage. I mean you'd have to be superhuman not to blurt it out in the heat of an argument or something. Surely it's better to get it all out in the open now and then, if you've the stomach for it, pick up the pieces rather than let it fester inside till like a boil coming to a head, it bursts out and spreads infection?"

Jenny set her lips. "Back off, Poppy. Do you not think I've had that self-same argument with myself time and time again till I'm blue in the face? Of course I have. I'm not a total imbecile, you know but Farina or not, I *love* Adam. I've always loved Adam, virtually from the first night I saw him. Honest, Poppy. Talk about explosive! There were bells ringing. Fireworks going off. The works! A real *coup de foudre* as the French would say." Rebellion in every movement, she drained her glass and slammed it on the counter. "And that's the bottom line!"

Poppy sighed. "Farina or not, you say, and

supposing it's *not* Farina what would you say then? Supposing it was, say, a friend of yours your husband was sleeping with. What would you say then or wouldn't that make a difference? Or is love so all-conquering that you could find a way to reconcile that too?"

"What do you mean? Of course it's Farina!"

Poppy pressed her. "But theoretically, say. Supposing you actually knew the woman involved. Supposing she was a friend of yours, a good friend, would that or would that not make a difference?"

Fishing out her slice of lemon, as a kind of afterthought from the empty glass, Jenny nibbled the flesh away from the rind, wincing as its tartness attacked her taste buds.

"I don't know why we're having this pointless conversation but if it makes you happy, well, yes, I suppose it would make a difference. It's like being murdered, isn't it? If you're murdered by a stranger, that's bad enough. But if you're murdered by someone you know, a close member of your own family, that kind of adds insult to injury, don't you think? And I suppose I *would* feel doubly betrayed if Adam's fancy *had* lit upon one of my friends. Especially if I liked and trusted the woman! Which, of course I would, or she wouldn't be my friend!"

Now that she had successfully steered Jenny in this particular direction, Poppy mused, this was, of course, the perfect opportunity to tell her what she suspected but just like Denzil, when push came to shove, Poppy found she didn't have the heart/courage, to puncture her friend's balloon.

Listen, Jenny, I hate to be the one to break it to you but there's no such person as Farina. Farina is a figment of your imagination. Will the real Farina aka Diana Mountford, or Mounty to her friends, please stand up?

It *should* have been that simple. It *should* have been but it wasn't!

Unaware of her friend's moral dilemma, Jenny slid off the barstool. "Anyway, that's enough soul-searching for today. I still haven't a thing to wear for tonight and Monsoon are having a sale. Fancy a browse?"

Poppy shook her head. "No. Count me out. You know me, if it's not ethnic or Oxfam, it's not me. The truth is I wouldn't know a Balenciaga from an Aga and care even less. No, You'll be much better off shopping on your own."

"Oh, okay! I'll catch you later, fill you in on all the gory details about tonight. Wish me luck!"

"Yeah, good luck! Knock him dead, kiddo! Literally!" Poppy muttered the last under her breath as they split up and went their separate ways. "And if you need a hand, you can count on me!"

Chapter Twenty-seven

"Someone's going to have to tell her."

"Well, who better than her own mother?"

"Uh huh! No way, Denzil. She's already convinced my mission in life is to destroy her. Besides, she wouldn't believe me. She'd think it was just another of my many scams to put Adam to rout! No, it'll have to be someone with no axe to grind. What about you, Poppy?"

"Nah. No balls, I'm afraid. I wouldn't mind only I had the perfect opportunity earlier on today but, I hold my hands up, I chickened out."

Grimly, Gloria glanced round the small group of people, all Jenny's friends, assembled in her living-room. Poppy, Denzil from the gym, Marcel and Martyna, herself and Rover, of course, who unmindful of present company was intent on making improper advances to a cushion on the settee!

"Desist, Rover! Go and stand in the corner." Almost

279

absent-mindedly, she clipped him sharply round the ear before turning her attention once more to the matter in hand. "Marcel? Martyna? Don't employers have an obligation towards the welfare of their employees?"

"Well, strictly speaking, Jenny's not really an employee any more." Marcel, as quickly as he was handed it, passed the buck back again like a time bomb, primed and heading towards the countdown. "More like a partner, really. Besides, although I knew Jenny's husband was having an affair I'd never heard of this Mounty woman until Percival over there told me. Isn't that right, Percy? Percy?"

"He'll only answer if you call him Rover," Jenny's mother reminded him. "Well, what about you, Martyna? You must have come across similar situations plenty of times on your show. Any tips on how we might break it to her?"

"Other than come right out with it and say, 'Hey Jen, your husband is screwing your best friend'? Not a clue!" Viciously, Martyna kneed Rover in the face who, cushion abandoned, was intent on nosing up along her left thigh in search of the Promised Land. "I was just a human conduit through which other people aired their grievances. Nothing more! Isn't that right, Marcel?"

"Yeah, no point in asking her. When it comes to tact, Martyna thinks it's something people do sideways in little yachts."

To Rover's disappointment, Martyna widened her eyes but not her thighs. "Well, isn't it?"

"I rest my case."

Awash with rare maternal instincts, Gloria turned her attention to the gym instructor. "Well, what about you, Denzil? I mean, you're probably more intimate with Jenny than any of us. Like, you know her fat composition, for God's sake, the ratio of cellulite per pound of buttock, her propensity for water retention, the depth to which it pools and where, not to mention the amount of blubber she needs to lose in order to reach that perfect size ten."

"She's already a perfect ten. In fact she's perfect in every way. Too perfect for that bastard husband of hers."

"So?" Gloria prompted. feeling her hopes rise at this display of manly passion.

Denzil shrugged. "Sorry but I bottled out myself already."

"When?"

"That day in the gym when Mounty savaged her. I could have told her then. I could have told her how I'd seen them exchanging spit-balls and sweet nothings in Stringfellows, only I didn't. I bottled out, didn't I? Yellow-bellied it! White-feathered it!"

"Yes, well at least you found the courage to look up my number and phone me. Until then Poppy and I only had our suspicions to go on."

"Which brings us round full circle," Poppy interrupted. "Now that we have proof positive, who's going to do the dirty deed and tell Jenny?"

Giving up all attempts at breaching Martyna's

suspenders, Rover surprised them all by turning back into a human being. "I vote we all do. After all, there's safety in numbers and she can't swing for us all. I vote we go en masse to La Gavroche tonight and confront Adam over his plate of moules marinière. That way, not only will Jenny be getting an education, but we'll also be nailing Adam's ass to the mast, as well."

"Lucky Adam," Marcel muttered, his lustful imagination earning him dark and damning looks from the rest of the party.

"All those in favour say aye." Poppy held up her own meaty fist as the ayes came thick and fast. "Right, motion carried. All troops to assemble outside La Gavroche at, say, 22.00 hours. That'll give the quarry just enough time to settle comfortably before we move in for the kill. Okay folks, let's synchronise our watches."

Eyes shining, Marcel rose suddenly and went to lie down by her feet. "Poppy," he gushed, "you're so forceful. I think I love you."

"Piss off, Marcel." In vain, Poppy tried to step over him, but the man had a cling like a limpet and it was only a matter of time before, in order to secure her own release, she had no option but to give in to his baser instincts and kick him senseless.

* * *

"So, what do you think? Sexy or what?"

"Well, I wouldn't throw you out of bed for eating

biscuits though I'm not too pushed on the lippy. A bit too purplish, I think. Makes you look like something that's been found floating face-down in the Thames for two weeks."

"Hmm." Jenny studied her reflection. "Maybe you're right. The carmine is probably a better choice."

"Much better," the mirror reassured her when, lipstick freshly applied, she consulted it once more. "But the pearls need to go. Too much like your Victorian aunt's."

"I don't have a Victorian aunt," Jenny told it, but took them off anyway. "So what then?"

"The black velvet choker."

"Not too 70s? I want to look perfect."

"Not at all. Chokers are back in vogue. You'll be right up there at the forefront of fashion."

"And the hair. Tell me it's not too Anthea Turner."

"Well, if you want me to lie, fair enough. It's not too Anthea Turner."

Jenny knitted her brow. "Oh balls! That means it is. What if I put it up like this?" Grabbing a bull-dog clip in a nice shade of plastic tortoise she skewered her hair up into a loose pile.

"Much better. Just pull a few strands down over your ears and lose those earrings. Hoops went out with the circus. If it were me I'd go for the small, gold peridots."

"But you *are* me," Jenny pointed out, taking its advice nonetheless and rummaging about in her jewellery box.

Her reflection came closer as she put the studs

through her ears, securing them at the back with the miniature butterfly-clips.

"That's the business. Chic. Definitely chic."

"But what about the dress?" Jenny wailed, smoothing it down over her hips. "You don't think it's too much of a frock, do you?"

The mirror shook its head. "Nah. Frocks are what the County set wear. Serious items of couture, acres of shantung, hunting-pink blankets designed with horses in mind. No! What you've got on is definitely a *dress*. And what a dress!"

"Well yes, it is rather nice, isn't it? I picked it up in Harvey Nicks at their end-of-season sale. Nicole Farhi, would you believe?" Turning this way and that Jenny admired the little black-chiffon number seized on with gratitude that afternoon after fruitless hours of trailing round what seemed like every department store and boutique in London. Three-quarter length and cut in the simplest of sheath styles it clung to breasts and hips and showed off her tiny waist to perfection. And though Jenny had balked at the price of the high, strappy Jimmy Choo sandals that completed her outfit, in the heel of the hunt she had to admit they were worth every penny.

"So. What you waiting for? An invite from the Queen! Splash on the Estée, sister, and go git that mother!"

Obediently spritzing her pulse points with Estée Private Collection, Jenny confronted her reflection one last time. "As a matter of interest, why have you suddenly started talking like an escapee from Motown?"

The mirror pulled no punches. "Nerves!" It told her.

Jenny nodded sympathetically. "You and me both, sister! You and me both!"

* * *

"Well, how do I look?"

"Very suave." Jenny waited for a return of the compliment but Adam was already ushering her through the door.

"Limo's here. At a hundred quid an hour we don't want to keep it waiting."

"Limo? What limo? Aren't you taking the Merc?"

"Of course not! People might mistake me for your chauffeur."

Jenny frowned. "I don't get you. I mean, what people? We're only going to a restaurant, for God's sake. Not the Oscars!"

Bundling her into the back of the cream stretch limousine parked in the driveway, Adam took a seat opposite. "Not just any restaurant. La Gavroche is where anyone who's anyone goes. To see and be seen! Members of the glitterati, the jet-set, even a Royal or two."

"But *we're* not anyone! So why are *we* pushing the boat out?"

Adam sighed. "Lord, Jenny. You're so parochial. You've got to think big. You're on TV now. You're a personality. Perhaps it's time we thought about new management for you. Clearly, this Marcel freak doesn't know his ass from his elbow."

His remarks rankling, Jenny leaned forward. "Now listen here, Adam. I was *always* a personality. Okay, okay, so maybe it *was* hidden for a long time under layers of fat and apathy but, make no mistake, it was *always* there. And yes, I may, as you say, be on TV now but I am still *me* i.e. Jennifer Lorelei Treigh and it's far from limousines I was reared! As for Marcel. Number one, he's not a freak, just different and, number two, don't forget it was Marcel who gave me my big break in the first place and I will *not* desert the sinking ship that feeds me. As far as I was aware tonight was simply supposed to be nothing more than you and I, husband and wife, going out for a nice, intimate dinner together. Something we haven't done since Michael Jackson was still black. I wasn't aware hidden agendas were on the menu."

"Neither are they but *carpe diem*. Seize the day! We've been presented with a God-given opportunity and we'd be fools not to milk it for all it's worth. Think of all the networking I could do amongst the rich and famous. I could end up as personal, financial adviser to some of the world's top names. Who knows into what exclusive enclave I might gain entrée. The world of high finance. Can't you just smell the prospects?"

I – I – I! Jenny thought feeling depression run through her bowels like a dose of Epsom salts. Had he always been so self-centred and she just hadn't noticed? Even back in his disco days? But no, the spotty youth in the lime-green frilly shirt and ill-fitting flares had been as far removed from the man sitting opposite, all dickied up in Armani and with a satin cummerbund holding in his paunch, as she was from having Tina Turner's legs. Paunch! In the 70s he'd been so slim you could have used him to cork a bottle. Not, mind you, that she held his middle-age spread against him. People in glass houses, after all . . . Nonetheless, the evening was well and truly off to a bad start and a far cry from the fantasies so blithely woven over the last few days. Sighing, she closed her eyes and lay back against the plush leather interior as the lights of London slipped past like pearls on a neon necklace.

There'd been a long, sweeping staircase, of course. That was obligatory, as was the chandelier casting a mellow pool of light high above the baronial hallway. Invisible violins were softly playing. Something classical. Chopin maybe, or Ravel. She'd always had a soft spot for Bolero, Torville and Dean, B.C. what's more. Adam in quilted Clark Gable smoking jacket was leaning casually against the newel post at the foot of the stairs, eyes hard and soft, all at the same time, alight with love and passion, a slightly cruel twist to his mouth. (NB: Nearly all the romances Jenny had read had described the hero as having a slightly cruel twist to his mouth. And she didn't see why her daydream should lack any of the key ingredients.)

Then, as in all the best MGM musicals, she would appear

at the top of the staircase, head thrown back, proud as a queen in her sexy little black number and high, strappy Jimmy Choo shoes, Estée wafting before her like a benediction!

"Darling," Adam would growl. (No, scrap that one. Growling belonged in her mother's fantasies, not hers.) *"Darling, Adam would murmur throatily. "You look . . ."*

"That choker is a big mistake. Too retro. Didn't you used to have one of those back in the 70s?"

Jenny's eyes shot open, her fantasies once again destroyed by the reality of the man who was her husband.

"Yes. I did have one back in the 70s. So? What's your point?'

Deliberately Adam produced a monogrammed cigar-case from his breast pocket, extracted a slim Panatella and sniffed the bouquet. "Actually, you've just illustrated my point perfectly. You're stuck in the past, Jenny. It's time to get in vogue. Trade in your 70s carpet slippers and slip on the roller-blades of the new millennium. You'll find them just as comfortable *and* you'll go places ten times quicker." Lighting the tip, he inhaled, exhaling a moment later a cloud of noxious smoke that wreathed about Jenny's head before settling on her cleavage. "That's progress, Jenny. Don't be afraid of it!"

Jenny coughed. "And that's cancer!" Contemptuously, Jenny pointed to the cigar. "Be afraid, Adam. Be very afraid!"

Chapter Twenty-eight

"Pâté? You can't have the pâté. Pâté is for plebs."

"Right then, I'll have the prawn cocktail."

"Prawn cocktail! Behave, Jenny! People don't go to La Gavroche and order pâté or prawn cocktail. No! The cognoscenti order delicacies like quails' eggs in aspic or oysters in Pernod."

There! Jenny thought with morbid satisfaction. She'd been right. That Farina cow *had* had a discriminating palate. Look how she'd got her teeth into Adam. Nonetheless, neither quails' eggs nor oysters held any appeal for her and, if only to make a point, Jenny stood her ground. Beckoning over a waiter who was hovering at a discreet distance, she quirked an eyebrow, patently ignoring Adam who, scarlet-faced, dived suddenly behind his menu like a soldier taking cover in a trench.

"You do *do* pâté, I take it?"

"Pâté de fois gras? But of course, madam."

"Uh huh." Jenny shook her head. "Isn't that the stuff they force-feed ducks or geese or something until their livers burst? No, ta very much! Bring me a prawn cocktail instead but go easy on the lettuce."

Without batting an eyelid the waiter, in the time-honoured fashion of waiters everywhere, licked the point of his pencil before obligingly scribbling down her order.

"Certainly, madam. And for monsieur?"

From behind his menu, Adam's voice, when it finally emerged, was riven with a mixture of emotion and pure humiliation. "Er . . . eh. I'll have the quails' eggs, please. And," he continued in a rush before Jenny could shove the oar of ignorance in any further, "for the main course, we'll both have the poussin with seasonal vegetables together with a bottle of your best Chablis. Well chilled."

"And that completes the voting of the English jury," Jenny joked, surrendering her menu and content, having made her point with the starter, to let him have his own way on the main course. Leaning back her glance briefly swept the restaurant, lingering for a moment on an aged gentleman who appeared to have drowned in his consommé. The top of his head was familiar. She was sure she recognized it as having hosted some TV show or other back in the eighties but, other than that, celebrities were about as thin on the ground as snow at the equator. Not that that bothered *her* or anything, but Adam's nose had most definitely been put severely out of joint when, upon emerging from the limo, he'd found himself confronted with no more than a lone, amateur photographer who'd rounded vociferously on Jenny for being a home-wrecker.

"Not me, mate," Jenny'd corrected him mildly. "You've probably mixed me up with that Anthea Turner woman. You know the one? Younger, blonder, richer than me? I'm Jennifer L. Treigh from *Jenny Jumps In*. Ring any bells with you, does it? No? Well, maybe not! Still don't lose any sleep over it. I know I wouldn't!"

Now, safely ensconced in the restaurant and determined to inject a bit of enthusiasm into what so far had been a disastrous evening, Jenny sent a flirtatious look across the table.

"So, how the hell are you anyway, Adam? Long time, no see!"

Immune to her wiles and like a sulky child, Adam glared back before turning his attention to the absorbing process of pleating his napkin. "Believe me, if I'd known you were going to show me up like this, it would have been a whole lot longer! It's true what they say about leopards. You can take the girl from Essex but you can't take Essex from the girl."

Stretching across the table, Jenny knocked soundly on his head. "Hello? Hello? Anyone home? Number one, I'm not from Essex. Number two, if anyone's showing anyone up, it's you. I mean look at that tux, for God's sake. There's so much glitter on it I thought for a moment you'd changed your name to Gary."

"Armani!" Adam snapped.

"Nicole Farhi!" Jenny shot back, holding up her arms and jiggling her bosoms at him like a Greek belly-dancer. "Not that you noticed or anything despite me spending an arm and several limbs kitting myself out in an attempt to look soignée. For you, Adam! So that I *wouldn't* make a show of you." Her voice rose, causing the elderly, drowned gentleman to stage a miraculous recovery and rap loudly for a schooner of port. "But it's not really me you're interested in, is it, Adam? More like what I can do for you, or rather, what my career can do for you. What was that you said? Smell the prospects?" To Jenny's surprise and not a little shame, a hurt look draped itself across her husband's face. The kind of look you saw in the eyes of small, abandoned puppy dogs at Battersea, the kind of look you saw on the faces of the losers on *Blind Date* who despite dressing up like lemons and making complete morons of themselves, don't get picked. The kind of look that said, how could you? How *could* you?

"Is that what you think? Is that what you *really* think? That I'm only interested in you because you've *arrived*, so to speak?" He spread his hands in appeal. "So, if that's the case how come I married you when you were Miss Anonymous? How come I stuck by you through thick and thin? Through fat and slim? I could have had anyone, you know. Oh yes! Make no mistake, there was plenty of scope. Opportunities knocked many times and many's the g-string I could have plucked and made sweet music. But I didn't! I was faithful to you and your belly-warmers. You and David always came first but now, because I'm trying to resurrect something of our married life, to bring back the communication, the romance, *you* accuse me of cashing in! Of attempting to bathe in reflected glory! Of being a user! A hanger-on!"

Jenny had to hand it to him. If he was acting, he was turning in an Oscar performance. She hadn't heard quite such an impassioned speech since Jeffrey Archer'd said "What hooker?"

Adam cleared his throat, took a sip of wine and impaled her with the innocence of his gaze. "You wanted to go to Spend a Penne for old times' sake. *I* wanted to take you to La Gavroche for the sake of new times, new memories, new beginnings. Don't you see, Jenny, I wanted to take you somewhere a bit special, somewhere with éclat. I wanted to show you to the world, to say 'Hey world, this is Jenny. This is my wife'."

Suitably chastened, Jenny hung her head. "God, I'm sorry, Adam." Sorrier than he'd ever know! A huge weight lifted off her shoulders as the realisation slowly trickled through that, plainly, Farina *was* just a figment of her imagination. No more than the blonde and youthful personification of all her insecurities and the man sitting opposite spoke not with forked tongue but straight from the heart. Jenny wanted to shriek for joy. Farina didn't exist! Adam had no more had an affair than she'd had Mel Gibson naked in the bed and gagging for it! Never mind that David had seen him getting into his car with a red-haired woman. *She* could have been anyone. An associate! The wife of a colleague! Anyone! Never mind that he stopped out all night and displayed all the tendencies of a dog on heat. You could always read what you wanted into any situation, add two and three and bully them into making four, knock the corners off square pegs and force them into round holes but that didn't mean you had interpreted the situation correctly. What was worse, not only had she donned the black handkerchief but she'd positively encouraged family and friends to condemn him too. Poor Adam! She'd been such a bitch! What must he have thought all these months when she was cold-shouldering him and doling out little digs left, right and centre about a woman who existed only in her fevered and jealous imagination? Lord! She went cold all over just thinking how her totally incomprehensible behaviour could have forced him straight into the arms of another woman. But he hadn't left, he'd stayed. He'd stayed despite her neurotic behaviour which could only mean one thing. He loved her! *He loved her! Her!* The realisation was a like a shower of cold water, the relief akin to waking up from a nightmare and finding you were not a steerage passenger on the *Titanic* after all. He *loved* her! Jenny felt an overwhelming compulsion to abandon all dignity, leap up on the table and burst into a rendition of Queen's 'We are the Champions'. Either that or start ripping the petals off the vase of roses decorating the table. *He loves me. He loves me not. He loves me. He loves me. HE BLOODY LOVES ME!* Anxious to embark at once upon the delicious process of making amends, Jenny leered across her glass.

"Let's go home," she gasped in what she hoped was a breathy, full-of-promise voice.

"Home? But what about the poussins?"

"Stuff the poussins!"

"Yes, madam. At once, madam!" Coming up behind her and happening to hone in on the tail end of the conversation, the waiter did a full about turn and bore the birds back to the kitchen and to a temperamental chef.

"Zey vant zem stuvved!"

"Oh do they now? They want their arses stuffed the pair of them. That's what they want!"

The waiter, whose repertoire of the English language did not stretch to include the finer points such as sarcasm and irony, nodded in agreement. "Zat's right, zey want zem stuvved!"

Reaching simultaneously for a carving knife and a large box of Paxo and sending a glare through the wall into the restaurant, where Adam and Jenny were heading for the door, the chef made a stabbing motion in the direction of the hapless waiter's genitals.

"Do one, sunshine!" he snarled. "That is unless you want your bollocks to end up in a casserole."

Out in the limo, Jenny waited till Adam had settled himself beside her, then tapped imperiously on the window dividing the chauffeur from his passengers.

"Home, James," she grinned, "and make it snappy!"

Adam grinned back, running his hand up along the length of her thigh. "Patience is a virtue."

"Oh yeah? Well, virtue is not exactly what I had in mind."

Mock-puzzled, Adam's eyebrows hit the roof. "It isn't?"

"Uh huh! Not at all!

"Well, now you've got me stumped and no mistake!" Pushing the boundaries of daring, Adam's hand climbed a little higher, made contact with and pinged her suspender.

Calmly, Jenny removed it, smacked his wrist and dropped it back in his lap."What was that you were saying about patience?"

"Touché," he murmured throatily, *eyes hard and soft, all at the same time, alight with love and passion, a slightly cruel twist to his mouth.*

Flippin' heck! Jenny thought, delighted at the turn things were taking. All she needed now was Ravel and her fantasy would be near enough completed. What she got, as Adam lifted *her* hand and pressed it into his lap, was not *Bolero* but the Hallelujah Chorus with Adam supplying his own Handel.

* * *

"Wow! Get a load of that!" Jenny's mother pressed her face to the window of the black cab as outside a white stretch limo whizzed by in the opposite direction. "Who do you think is in that?"

Denzil sniffed. "Some flash geezer, no doubt. With too much money and not enough sense!"

"Never mind all that." Impatiently, Poppy tapped her watch. "You do realise we're running late, don't you? But then if *some* people will insist on taking animals in cabs."

Gloria took umbrage. "It's not Rover's fault if he was sick. It's a known fact that dogs don't travel very well."

"Whatever!" Poppy rolled her eyes. "But be prepared for the fact that we might be too late!"

"I doubt it," Marcel nodded astutely. "La Gavroche is not like your common-or-garden fast-food outlet, you know. You can grow a beard between courses in those kind of places."

"He's right." Martyna lent her support. "Now, at Sole of Discretion you could wait for the tide to turn between entrée and main course. Like La Gavroche, we offer a 'dining experience' as opposed to a quick nip in and tuck in. People are paying not only for the food but for the décor and ambience. And given the prices, they want to get their money's worth and stay till the waiters are chucking chairs on top of the tables and making cutting asides about deserted wives and orphaned children and 'Have you no homes to go to?'"

Denzil sighed. "Yes. Well, let's hope you're right. I just can't bear to think of that rat sliming his way back into Jenny's affections."

"Yes, but she's going to be so hurt! I'm really not looking forward to this at all. Not a bit!"

Jenny's mother shrugged. "None of us are, Martyna, although I'd be a liar if I didn't admit that the prospect of grinding Adam's face into the mud doesn't have a certain appeal about it."

"Yes, there is that," Denzil admitted. "And let's face it, Jenny would be a darned sight more hurt if later down the line she found out we'd known what he was up to and never told her."

Gloria, edged between Poppy and Marcel, shifted uncomfortably. "I hope Rover's all right. I feel bad that I didn't stay with him." Awkwardly, Marcel extracted his arm from where it had been crushed behind her vertebrae and patted her shoulder with dead fingers.

"Oh, he'll be fine. Anyway, he said he'll follow on as soon as he feels a bit better."

"I hope you're right but his nose was so hot and dry, I'm worried he might be coming down with something more serious."

"What, like rabies you mean?" Marcel gave a comical roll of his eyes.

"Don't mock." The older woman dug him sharply in the ribs. "Mocking is catching!"

"So is rabies," Marcel quipped only to be silenced by a glare from Poppy.

"Stow it, buster!" she snarled. "Can't you see we're almost there? Save your energy for the mud-slinging ahead."

Marcel licked his lips. "Ooh! I do love it when you talk dirty!" Jerking his thumb back in the direction from which they'd come, he shot her what he very much hoped was a come-to-bed look. "Hey, baby. How's about you and me later, back at the studios? Have I got a chair for you!"

Screwing up her face Poppy glanced out the window, angling her head so that she was looking up at the sky. "Oh, look," she said, sweetly venomous, "a flying pig. And guess what, Marcel? It's got your name on it!"

Chapter Twenty-nine

As with so many longed-for things in life now that the wish in the form of Adam had become reality, Jenny didn't quite know where to start. She supposed it was a bit like being one of those lotto winners you saw pictured in the papers, a fat cheque in one hand, a mop in the other. *'Win won't change my life,' vows Mrs. Bilgewater, 94. 'I've been cleanin' them here toilets for the last fifty year and I'll go on cleanin' till the Good Lord says Mavis, put down yer mop and lift up yer wings!'* Why, Jenny asked herself time and time again, if they hadn't wanted their lives to change had they bothered buying a ticket in the first place? *She'd* wanted her life to change. Too bloody right! She'd wanted it to change back – right back to the way it was pre-Farina when any TV scout would have been proud to sign them up, her, Adam and David, as the perfect example of family togetherness. And now it looked like she'd hit the jackpot, gotten all six numbers right and Adam's balls were hers for the taking. But, how to take him? To dive on him or not to dive on him, that was the question. Shamelessly, right then and there on the doorstep with the limo only just pulling away from the door? Or go for the subtle approach? Wait till the limo was out of sight and then dive on him! Option three – encourage him to dive on her? Mentally she tore her hair. God, somebody, somewhere must have written a book on the correct etiquette of getting back in the sack with your ex! After all, they wrote them on everything else, didn't they? Weddings! Being gay! Attending the Queen's garden party! Seduction – perish the thought! Why not a book, something like *Ex-Fax* or *Ex-It?* Though, strictly speaking, at this very moment in time, Ex-Lax might be more appropriate as her stomach went into a series of loops and knots such that any Boy Scout would be proud to put his name to.

"I-er-I'm having a bit of trouble getting the key in the lock." Jabbing futilely in the general area of the keyhole Adam stammered his own nervousness, which should have made her feel a whole lot better. Only it didn't. It made her feel worse, so bad in fact that she quivered and shook like a transvestite in Burton's Menswear. According to her fantasies, Adam was supposed to be in charge, wasn't he? Masterful! Primeval! Fully conversant with what buttons to press, their location and, most important of all, when to engage finger! God she wished he'd hurry up as the nervousness transferred itself to her bladder and she was forced to adopt that standing-up, cross-kneed, cross-ankled, jigging-up-and-down position seen most commonly in schoolgirls in imminent danger of wetting their knickers. Great! Not only were her bowels doing a good impression of the South Circular Road but her bladder was getting in on the act and going into its old Indian rain-dance routine. Thankfully though, before Noah sent his Ark, key met lock and a moment later the door swung open.

"Shall I carry you over the threshold?" Thank Heaven, Neanderthal man was back, peeping out from behind Adam's eyelids and giving rise to the fleeting but enjoyable thought that maybe, just maybe, in true caveman fashion there might be a club secreted down the front of his bearskin. In braver mode she might have investigated, might have given him one of those 'is that a gun in your pocket' quips but, time being of the essence, she callously ignored his offer, barged past and fled to the loo.

"Better?" His eyes were amused, tender, as a short time later she emerged, relief written all over her face.

"Much." Keenly aware of the suddenly charged atmosphere, Jenny sent him what she hoped was an I'll-show-you-my-hormones-if-you-show-me-yours look, at the same time scarcely daring to breathe for fear everything might vaporise into just another one of her lonely daydreams. Whoosh! All gone in a puff of smoke! But, so far, so good! He was still there large as life and every bit as gorgeous.

"C'mere," his voice was low, loving, with just the merest hint of throatiness. "I want to hold you."

Her own voice caught. "Do you, Adam? Do you really?"

His answer was to cross the few steps that separated them, sweep her into his arms and tilt her chin upwards so that her lips were only millimetres away from his own. (Somewhere, in a detached part of her mind she couldn't help making comparisons with that famous *Gone with the Wind* movie-poster where Scarlett O'Hara, her neck forced back at an impossible vertebrae-crushing angle waits for Rhett to come and plunder her mouth.) "Of course, I do. You've no idea how I've longed for this moment. I love you, Jenny."

"And I love you," Jenny slanted a look at him from beneath demurely lowered eyelids. "It's funny, well not funny really, but I never thought I'd hear you say that again." She brushed an imaginary speck off his lapel. "Look, don't laugh but I thought you were having an affair. I even had a name for her. Farina! That's what I called her." Covering her eyes with her hands, she groaned. "Lord, I can't tell you just how stupid I feel. Or how miserable I felt for so long. And to think it could all have been avoided if only I'd had the guts to come right out and ask you."

Prising her hands away Adam silenced her with a kiss, his lips alternately soft, then hard and demanding, rousing long dormant responses that brought her panting to a place she hadn't visited for what seemed like an eternity and where she wanted to stay forever.

304

Drawing a deep ragged breath, when at last he released her, she cuddled into the protective circle of his arms, her legs slightly shaky as if the very bones had dissolved. "You know, Adam, it's true what they say. What a difference a day makes! I mean, if anyone had told me yesterday that within twenty-four hours I'd be standing here with you – like this – I'd have said they were mad."

Anxiously, Adam, scanned her face. "But it feels right, doesn't it?"

Jenny smiled, reached up and with her finger-tip ever so gently traced a loving line from his brow, down along his nose and all around his lips. "It feels more than right, sweetheart. It feels perfect!"

"Good. I want it to be perfect because you're perfect." Gently his hand reached round and slowly unzipped her dress, easing it off bit by bit, revealing first one softly rounded shoulder then the other, tugging it gently over her breasts then down, down over her hips till it puddled in a careless pool around her ankles leaving her simply but sexily attired in black Wonderbra, stockings, suspenders and g-string. Eyes never leaving hers, Adam slipped out of his own jacket, unbuckled his belt and reached for her once more.

"No," gently Jenny extricated herself. "Not here. Let's go upstairs.' Slipping her hand into his she led the way up to the bedroom pleasantly aware of his eyes glued to the undulations of her buttocks with every step she took.

305

"Now, where were we?" Still slightly goggle-eyed, Adam manoeuvred her towards the bed.

"Oh, round about here," she said, amazed by her sudden slightly shocking transition into siren-mode, reaching up and pulling him down onto crisp cotton sheets just begging to be rumpled. *"Rrrr!"* For good measure, she tried an Eartha Kitt growl. "Just round about here . . ."

* * *

"Bloody hell! Just what do you think you're doing?" Five minutes later, Jenny shot out of bed and stood naked and quaking at the side of it. "Never mind S & M – whatever happened to P & O?"

"P & O?" Passions aroused, Adam made a grab for her leg in the vain hopes that having gained purchase on her knee the rest of her would follow.

"You know, as in car-ferries? Roll-on, roll-off, just like you used to do before you discovered all those peculiar ways of contorting your tongue, amongst other things!"

Aroused, Adam lunged again for her leg succeeding only in sliding halfway out of the bed. "So what's wrong with a bit of creativity? I thought you might enjoy it."

Snaking a hand forward, Jenny liberated a sheet from the bed and wound it quickly about her shoulders. "Creativity is Michaelangelo in the Sistine, Adam. Creativity is Tony Blair, pre-election. Creativity is – I don't know what creativity is but what you've just tried to do is just sad. As in Marquis de Sade!"

Ruefully, Adam glanced down beneath the duvet.

"Sod it! You've just managed to dampen my ardour. Now come on, get back into bed and stop playing hard to get."

Rage beginning to build, Jenny widened her eyes. "Is that what you think I'm doing, playing hard to get?"

Adam sighed, wanting with simple male logic merely to get on and get at it without having to embark on a whole raft of negotiation and plea-bargaining. "Well, isn't it? But hey hon, it's not on a spring you know. There's only so many times a man can sit up and beg in one evening." Oblivious to the glacial breath issuing from between his wife's suddenly frozen lips, Adam, eyes half-closed, attempted to slip her what he fondly imagined was a seductive leer. "Now what say you give the Big Dipper here his just rewards? Eh?"

Despite herself Jenny felt her lips begin to curve upwards. "The Big Dipper? That figures! Big Dippers always make me sick." Fastidiously picking up the duvet between finger and thumb, Jenny slanted a look downwards. "Although, realistically speaking, it's not so much a Big Dipper as a little nipper, is it?"

Passion well and truly extinguished, Adam, struggling out of bed, sought frantically for his boxers, retrieved them and immediately set about putting both feet through one leg. "Shit!" He tried again, this time with more success. "Look, I don't know what you think you're playing at, Jenny, but I don't like being made a fool of."

Jenny pounced. "Ah ha! And there was I thinking

we had no common ground left. Funny that though, because *I* don't like being made a fool of either. And that's just what you've been doing, isn't it, Adam, making a fool of me?" Angrily, Jenny grabbed a pillow from the bed and chucked it at his ear, looking wildly about for further, more effective ammunition.

Adam ducked. First the pillow, then a shoe, then the bedside lamp, the china base of which smashed into a million accusations against the bedroom wall. Like a sinner undergoing the undignified process of being stoned, Adam tried desperately to make a shield from his hands and, as in the case of the sinner, it was no go Joe!

"For Christ's sake, Jenny. Get a grip would you? I haven't a clue what you're wittering on about."

Jenny located the companion to the shoe and, practice making perfect, scored a bull's-eye against her cowering husband's nose. "Tell it to the bees, Adam. Better still, tell it to Farina. Because there *was* a Farina, wasn't there? Even if her name was really Jemima, or Portia or Hollandaise or something else equally outlandish!" Wielding aloft a large tome of the *Encyclopaedia Britannica*, Jenny advanced warningly on her errant spouse, totally heedless of the blood that had begun spurting from his nose and which he was endeavouring to staunch by dint of ramming his index finger up his nostril. "Ah! Don't deny it! Your tongue gave you away even if it wasn't so much in words as in deed. You see, you didn't learn that kind of thing in my bed. No way! Whatever it was, I bet I can't even pronounce it! Neither did you learn it from the *Kama Sutra* or an under-the-shelf video. Uh huh! Too practised by half. Real hands-on experience, I'd say. So come on, Adam. Give! What's the low-down? You know the procedure! Name? Number? Rank? Who the blue blazes is she?" Advancing even closer, Jenny held a bunched fist under his chin. "What's the matter? Cat got your tongue?"

Shuffling backwards, he fell on his bottom. "You're mad." His voice was a whine or perhaps that was just the effect of his finger jammed up his nose.

"I *am* mad! Madder than hell if you want to know. So mad, in fact, I could take this encyclopaedia and ram it right up your –"

"Don't do it, Jenny!"

"Jesus!" Breaking off in mid-threat, Jenny did a quick reconnoitre about the bedroom. "Did you hear something? I could have sworn I heard my mother, just now."

"Don't do it, Jenny!"

Puzzled, Jenny glared at her husband suspecting him of having suddenly acquired ventriloquistic abilities. "And Marcel!"

White as a ghost, Adam jerked his head in the direction of the window. "You did! By the sounds of it, they're out on the front lawn."

"Bloody hell, you're right!" Dropping the encyclopaedia like a ton of bricks, Jenny strode over to the bedroom window, roughly pushing the drapes aside. "There's a whole posse on the lawn." Distracted, Jenny knitted her brows. "I suppose I'd better go down and see what they want. In the meantime thank your lucky stars you've been saved by the bell. At least this time!" Grabbing up her dressinggown, she tied it tightly at the waist, sending one last glare in the direction of her husband. "And for Heaven's sake, man, go clean yourself up. You look like the left-over scrapings from an abattoir."

"Bitch!" Adam snarled but only when the door had closed behind her and her footsteps receded further and further as she quickly descended the stairs and flung open the front door.

"Too late!" Poppy elbowed her way to the front of the group, her eyes taking in Jenny's rumpled appearance and the dressinggown clearly donned in a hurry as evidenced by the fact that it was inside out. "Your fault!" Her eyes veered to Jenny's mother. "I told you, you shouldn't have taken Rover in the taxi!"

"Yep!" Marcel, nodded. "Too late! She's already done it. You've already done it, haven't you? Now don't deny it, Jenny. You've got that unmistakable post-prandial look about you."

Gloria elbowed him aside. "Idiot! You mean, post-natal!"

"You're both idiots." Pulling no punches, Poppy took over again. "They mean post-coital, of course."

Bridling, Jenny wrapped her dressinggown closer about her. "I don't know what you mean!"

Reaching out, Marcel laid a kind hand on her arm. "It means –"

Jenny shrugged him off. "Don't be stupid, Marcel! I know full well what *it* means. What I don't know is what the hell you're all doing standing on my lawn at . . ." briefly she consulted her watch, "eleven o'clock at night!"

Coming to the fore, Martyna shrugged, half-apologetic. "We came to rescue you, Jenny. From a fate worse than death! Looks like we came on a fool's errand, though. Because you've already done it, haven't you? The eagle has already landed!"

Jenny stepped back a bit. "Jesus! This is getting farcical. What are you all on, is it illegal and did you buy it on a street corner in Brixton?"

"Sex!" her mother announced baldly. "You've had sex, haven't you?"

Jenny did a cynical eye-bounce from from one to the other. "Well, it may have escaped your collective notice but I do have a twelve-, going on thirteen-, year-old son and as I have neither a halo, a sainthood nor am I called Mary, yes you might safely deduce that I have had sex! And before you start, Mother, I am over sixteen and have been for some years now."

"Don't be obtuse, Jenny. We're talking about tonight. You have had sex tonight, haven't you?"

Grateful for the dark and the light over the front door with its dim forty-watt bulb that hid her blushes, Jenny stammered a little. "Er . . . yes! I mean, no! I mean, it's none of your goddamn business what I do in the privacy of my own home."

"You see!" Poppy wagged her head. "She admits it. I told you we were too late. And it's all that bloody Rover's fault. Just wait till I catch up with him I'll have him in the dog-pound so quick he'll wish he was a human being!"

Gloria was defensive. "Well, most likely you won't have too long to wait. He said he'd catch us up and I daresay once he sees we're not at the restaurant he'll use his canine instincts and follow us here."

"Sez you!" Unimpressed, Poppy turned back to the matter in hand. "Well, Jen, I hope the earth moved for you tonight because by the time we get through with filling you in on what we know, it won't so much move as crumble around your ears."

"W-what do you mean?" Jenny stepped back from the door, dread awareness seeping through that this was no social visit, no Tupperware party congregation. No one was here to convince her of the merits of plastic lunch boxes over your common or garden tinfoil. No one was here to flog her a lettuce-spinner! Mentally she did a quick head count to see if anyone was missing presumed dead but apart from Rover, who didn't count in her book anyway, everyone appeared hale if not exactly hearty. So what then? She took a deep well-you'd-better-hit-me-with-it-whatever-it-may-be breath, vaguely conscious that her limbs had engaged themselves in some grotesque sort of Hokey Cokey.

"Right," her voice was shaky, taking its rhythm from her legs, "you'd better all come in. I don't want all the neighbours earwigging. That nasty old bitch at number twenty-three would just love to get one over on me just because she seems to have found all the weight I've lost." Holding the door ajar, Jenny squashed herself up against the wall as, like Noah's animals, they filed past two by two, her mother and Poppy, Marcel and Martyna, with only Denzil partnerless and looking strangely shamefaced bringing up the rear. "And if you need a drink, just help yourselves," she called, glancing out into the darkness where a set of headlights could be seen slowly wending its way down the drive. The tardy Rover presumably, and driving – what else – a Rover! "And make mine a double. I'm obviously going to need it." Her eyes still fixed on the car, Jenny watched in surprise as it ground suddenly to a halt and a figure leapt from the passenger side and started running back in the direction from which it had come. Seconds later, Rover catapulted from the driver's doorway, immediately bounding off in hot pursuit of the first figure, the identity of whom despite squinting her eyes and craning her neck, Jenny could not discern.

"Sod it!" Shivering as a cold wind caressed her ankles and wound slowly up beneath her dressinggown, Jenny, closed the door. Rover could always bark when he and his mystery companion, no doubt also a party to Poppy's earth-crumbling announcement, wanted admittance. Attempting unsuccessfully to switch into never-trouble-trouble-till-trouble-troubles-you mode, Jenny, like a condemned man, and without the benefit of a hearty meal, headed for the metaphorical gallows she simply knew was under construction in her living-room at that very moment. "Coming, Mother," she called in answer to a querulous query concerning her whereabouts. "Just coming!" But, somehow, her voice never made it quite past her lips!

Chapter Thirty

"Well, you see, we had no real proof. It was all surmise and conjecture."

"Surmise and conjecture? Who are they, a comedy duo? A Morecambe and Wise?"

"Oh shut it, Jenny!" Not backwards at coming forward, Gloria strode over albeit a little unsteadily on account of having imbibed more than her fair share of Jenny's whisky and glowered at her daughter who, perched upon the arm of Poppy's chair was showing about as much reaction as a somnambulist. "Haven't you taken in anything we've said?"

Jenny shrugged although it was an act of bravado rather than unconcern. "Yep. You've told me Adam's been putting himself about. But I already knew that, although for a short time earlier on this evening I almost managed to convince myself it was all just a figment of my imagination."

Poppy patted her arm sympathetically. "Which is when you did it, I suppose."

"Did what?" Thumping the arm of the chair with frustration Jenny glared about the room. "What exactly *is* it that I'm supposed to have done?"

"Why, seduced Adam, of course." Patting his mouth, Marcel mimed a yawn. "Oh, come on, Jenny, you've all but sent us stir-crazy over the last few months banging on about how you were going to seduce him." Casually indicating her state of undress he sent a please-who-do-you-think-you're-fooling look around the room. "I mean, are you trying to tell us now that you didn't? That you didn't let him have his wicked way?"

Relieving Poppy of her glass, Jenny drained it. "Oh blow it out your ass, Marcel! And Mother, don't you dare drink all that whisky!"

"It's my fault." Denzil, who up till now had remained silent, cast the words into the small pool of people gathered in the room, guiltily aware that in the saying the ripples would spread out and engulf at least one of the occupants. "You see, Jenny, I *had* the proof. Long ago. I just bottled out! Will you ever be able to forgive me, do you suppose?"

Jenny shook her head. "It's all right, Denz. I had as much proof as I needed. The truth is I just didn't want to face it. It was easier to play Blind Man's Buff and hope that if I didn't face the bogey full on it would simply disappear."

With a sigh, Denzil decided he'd better make a clean breast of it all. "But there's more to it than that. It's not just that I knew he was being unfaithful. I knew who he

was being unfaithful with and because they threatened
to get me the sack if I exposed their sordid little secret –
although to be fair, Adam did apologise later – I turned
my back on a mate," miserably, Denzil ducked his head,
"to save my own skin! And believe me, Jenny, nothing
you can do or say will make me feel any worse than I
do already."

"I'm sure she could think of something."

"Shut up, Marcel!" Poppy glared, only to merit a
look of dogged devotion from the object of her censure.
"Besides, Denzil phoned your mother, Jenny, and we all
joined forces but –"

"But, it looks like we were too late." Putting her
hand across Marcel's mouth, Martyna successfully
muzzled him for fear of his adding further fuel to the
fire.

"Listen." Mock-patient, Jenny bent a look that took
them all in, one by one. "I *didn't* do it! Okay? Okay, so
we got naked and assumed the horizontal and the
intention was there . . ."

"But?" The prompt was in chorus.

"But he started trying to do things . . ."

Marcel nipped Martyna's fingers away. "But surely
that's the whole idea, darling?"

"Things," Jenny gritted as if the interruption had never
taken place, "that he never attempted before. Things,
which I can only assume, he learned from someone else.
And whatever else she is, she sure ain't shy!"

"Never was!" Gloria nodded judiciously. "Always

gave the impression that butter wouldn't melt. Still, I always recognised her for the harlot she was!"

"Harlot?" Jenny's eyebrows peaked.

"Harlot, tramp, slapper! A tart by any other name is still a tart!"

"Okay, Mother. Have it your own way but could you stop beating about the bush now and name that tune!" Jenny sighed as a tremendous barking and whining suddenly broke out from the vicinity of the front door. "Only hang on for a moment while I go let Rover in."

"See." Jenny's mother shot Poppy a look of triumph. "I told you he'd follow on." And to her daughter. "Stir your stumps, Jenny, before he scratches all the paint off your doorframe."

Grim-lipped, Jenny hurried to do her bidding. "He'd better not. Not if he values his nuts! Put a sock in it, you stupid mutt!" she called, opening the door. "I'm dancing as fast as I can!"

"Call him off, Jenny. I beg you. I'll tell you anything you want, confess everything, only call him off!"

"Mounty?" Incredulous, Jenny blinked, hardly able to believe the little tableau playing out on her front doorstep. "Is that really you, and why on earth are you wearing Rover round your ankle?"

Mounty held out a beseeching hand. "Yes! Yes! It's me! Rounded up against my will by your mother's Rottweiler. Now will you for Christ's sake call him off while I can still stand." Bewildered, Jenny shook her head from side to side as Mounty grew more and more hysterical. "Call him off, dammit! I know what I did was wrong, Jenny, but this . . . this is inhumane! Murderers are shown more mercy!"

"You *know* what you did was wrong," Jenny repeated slowly, wondering if Mounty too, like the crowd assembled in her living-room, was a sandwich short of a picnic. "Well, you know more than I do. Still, I suppose you'd better come in." Baring her teeth and snarling, Jenny aimed an amiable kick at Rover's head. "Cease and desist, Rover. Is that any way to treat a guest?" Reluctantly relinquishing his nylon-clad prey, Rover made the transition from four to two legs.

"Ask me again in five minutes," he snarled. "Then you might just want to bite her yourself!"

"Ah ha!" Gloria's eyes flew to the door at the sound of Mounty's voice outside. "How appropriate, the villain of the piece has arrived. Or, should I say villainess? Everbody in the house come on and let me hear ye say boo now!"

"Boo! Boo! Hiss! Hiss!" Taking her lead from Jenny's mother, Poppy booed, hissed and rapped with gusto. "Watch out, Jenny! She's behind you!" Jenny, Mounty trailing miserably at her heels with Rover in turn snapping at hers, hesitated a moment before entering the room proper.

"Bloody hell! I've only been gone all of two minutes and already you lot have been at the waccy baccy!"

"Boo! Boo! Hiss! Hiss!" Marcel jabbed an accusing finger at Mounty. "Double *boo!* Double *hiss!*"

Martyna slapped him sharply round the head. "Quit it, dick-head! Everyone deserves a fair hearing. Even trollops!"

"Oh, you reckon, do you?" Denzil snapped. "Only, it might surprise you to learn that not everyone is quite as philanthropic as you, Martyna, and that there are still *some* in this world for whom minorities are considered fair game for blackmail and coercion. Isn't that so, Miss Mountford?"

"Oi! Oi! Oi!" Jenny interrupted. "What the hell's got into you all? What is this? Open season on Mounty?"

Poppy curled her lip, her voice venomous. "It's open season on vermin, all year round! Why do you think I've got shares in Rentokil?"

"Okay." Jenny made calming motions with her hands. "Simmer down, everybody. Okay, everybody calm? Good! Now, who'd like to fill me in on what exactly is going on here?"

"Delighted!" Taking centre stage, though with somewhat of a stagger, Jenny's mother indicated Mounty who, with every moment that elapsed, turned a whiter shade of pale. "Jenny. Meet Farina!"

"What?" Like a heroine in a Jane Austen novel, Jenny's hand flew to her throat, fluttering anxiously in the region of her jugular. Her voice, when she found it, was reedy, a thread tautly pulled and ready to snap and had she but known about the efficacy of burnt feathers she would have called for them at once. "What are you saying – that Mounty . . .?"

"That's exactly what she's saying." Mounty's own voice was a mere shadow of its usual more confident self. "But it wasn't how you think. I never meant it to happen . . ." With a little shrug, Mounty, attempted to absolve herself of her wrongdoings. "It was just . . . well you know how it is. One thing led to another! We couldn't help ourselves!"

"One thing led to another! You couldn't help yourselves!" Still reeling from shock Jenny, nonetheless, managed to exude sarcasm from every pore. "The meat and drink of the *Jerry Springer Show.* A studio floor littered with broken hearts and dreams and all because *one thing led to another* and adults, who should know better, *couldn't help themselves!* Because the passion was too strong, eh Mounty? The passion took over, made you forget yourself, your principles, your morals, your best friend!" Like a butterfly on a mounting-board, Jenny pinioned her with her eyes, eyes in which the little party of onlookers could see a whole spectrum of emotions playing out, not the least of which were grief, hurt, despair and betrayal.

"What can I say?" Mounty made a little moue. "I wanted to tell you so many times but –"

"You listened to me!" Like a dagger, Jenny's voice cut her off. "You let me spill my guts to you, positively encouraged me, let me pour out my anxieties about Adam, pretended you were trying to help me."

"And I did try to help you. Honestly I did, at least in the beginning. But then, one night, Adam called round and –"

321

"I know. You've already told me. One thing led to another!" Falteringly, Jenny allowed herself to be pushed down into a chair. By whom, she didn't know, neither did she care. "You went to Italy with him too, didn't you? All that palaver in the gym – all that 'me-crowding-you business'– that's what it was about, wasn't it? You couldn't just come clean with me. Oh no! You let me go on making a fool of myself. I can't believe I didn't make the connection. Christ, if it wasn't so damn sad I could almost laugh at my stupidity." Running an incredulous hand over her eyes, her gaze dropped to the floor, almost as if she would find answers there, spelled out in the long strands of shag pile tripping haphazardly over one another. "Begging your forgiveness!" she continued bitterly. "Blaming myself! Begging my husband's *mistress* for forgiveness when I hadn't done anything wrong." Her gaze lifted, sought that of her friend again. "But you made me believe I had, Mounty, or should I call you Farina! You made me believe that I *had!* How could you have done such a thing? God, you must have laughed your socks off at me! Poor stupid Jenny, so far off the mark she made Mark Thatcher look like a navigational genius!"

Mounty's chin came up in her own defence. "Look, you can't blame me if you were a bit slow, Jenny. For goodness sake, all you had to do was add two and two together. The ingredients were all in the mixing bowl. All you had to do was give it a stir."

"But I *trusted* you. It never even occurred to me that

you, my best friend, would betray me. And with my own husband, at that!" Striding over to her mother, Jenny relieved her of the whisky bottle, put it to her lips and took a long, slow draught, coughing a little as it hit the back of her throat.

Mounty decided to brazen it out. "Well, you know what they say, Jenny. All's fair in love and war, a philosophy I seem to remember you yourself subscribing to in the past. So isn't all this 'little woman scorned' act a bit hypocritical?"

"No way!" Jenny's eyes shot fire. "I never subscribed to being a home-wrecker and as for all being fair, would you say taking an innocent child's father away is fair too?"

Mounty bristled. "Let's get one thing straight here. I didn't *take* Adam away. He went willingly. More than willingly, if the truth be told. And let's face it, given the choice between a cumbersome Lada and a sleek Corvette, which would you plump for? If you'll excuse the expression." Unbelievably, Mounty tittered though, to be fair, it was probably more from nerves than bravado.

Jenny waved a reassuring hand, as a growling Rover began menacingly to circle Mounty's calves. "Shh! Rover! It's okay." And, to the other woman, "You're right, Mounty. I was fat. Fat, lazy and a mess. And yes, I hold my hand up, you *did* give me the impetus to sort myself out. And for that I thank you. But to my dying day I'll never forgive you for what you did later."

"It takes two to tango," Mounty reminded her.

"Much and all as I hate to agree with anything that Jezebel has to say, she's right!" Putting her spoke in, Jenny's mother jerked her head towards the ceiling above. "Bring on the dancing girls, is what I say."

Jenny nodded. "Yes, you're right! If Adam could lie right alongside of her in the bed, there's absolutely no reason why he can't lie right alongside of her in the dock. So go on, Rover. Fetch! You'll find him either in the bedroom or the bathroom and don't come back without him."

"Rrruff!" Pausing only long enough to snarl one last threat at Mounty's leg, Rover bounded out of the room and after a noisy, clearly audible scuffle upstairs, reappeared a few minutes later, Adam in tow, still dressed only in boxer shorts and with half a roll of toilet tissue shoved up his nostrils.

"You! Over there!" With a sharp push, Jenny sent Adam staggering over to stand beside Mounty where, dabbing frantically at his nose, he tried to enlist sympathy from Jenny's supporters – a foolish tactic to say the least – a bit like expecting Arsenal supporters to cheer every time Man U scored a goal.

"She's mad! Look, I'm bleeding."

"If it was me, mate," Poppy interrupted callously, 'you'd be bleeding too. Bleeding dead!"

"I second that!" Jenny's mother waved a victory fist.

"Motion carried!" Marcel got in on the act. "The ayes have it!"

A bloody bubble escaped Adam's nostril, only to

retract immediately as he breathed back in. "Who are all these people anyway? And what the hell are they doing in my living-room?"

"Friends of mine!" Jenny sent a daggers-look in Mounty's direction. *"Real friends!* My mother and Rover you already know and correct me if I'm wrong but you have more than a passing acquaintance with Denzil here. In actual fact, I believe you and he are intimately acquainted enough for you to get in a spot of blackmail." Turning up her eyes, Jenny pretended to search the wide, blue yonder for something that was escaping her. "Ah, yes! Something about you telling his bosses he made a pass at you, I believe, if he had the temerity to tell me about your press-ups with Mounty here."

"I apologised for that, that night in . . ." Adam's voice trailed away as he realised that any mention of Stringfellows could be construed as a confession and might later on be used in evidence against him.

"And over here," Jenny studiously ignored him, "in the blue corner, we have Poppy, Marcel and Martyna, all of whom you've heard me speak of highly as, indeed, I once spoke highly of your playmate, Mounty. And they're all here like a pile-up on the M3 because they came to try and stop me from making a terrible mistake. *And* they were almost too late! Strange that it should be you, yourself, Adam, who stopped me in my tracks!" Turning back to Mounty, Jenny nodded grimly. "You taught him well, Mounty. Presumably he was a quick learner."

"Quick, certainly." Mounty, still the woman scorned, wrinkled her nose. "A little too quick at times, if you get my drift."

Adam's skin tone changed to match that of his blood, which had slowed to a steady trickle. "There's no call for that, Mounty. I told you, I'm sorry, now what do you want me to do?"

"Do?" Mounty almost spat. "It's too late to *do* anything now, Adam. What I wanted you to *do* was to come clean with Jenny, tell her how much you loved me, how we were meant to be together. But, oh no, you couldn't do that, could you, and now look at us!"

Apologetically, Adam's eyes moved from her to Jenny and back again. "No, you're right. I couldn't do that. I couldn't do that because it wouldn't have been true. What you and I had wasn't love, Mounty. Oh, I know you think it was but one day you'll find a man who'll love you as you deserve and you'll see that what you had with me was just a very poor imitation." He shuffled about, examined his feet. "The truth is you and I were looking for different things – you, for true love – me, for something I already had with Jenny but was too stupid to realise." Taking his life in his hands, he took a step forward, engaged his wife in eye contact. "Look, Jen, do you think you could find it in your heart to give me another chance? We can recover from this. I know we can! Lots of marriages have blips." There was desperation in his voice. "We can be stronger, better than ever. I know it won't be easy but we can put all this behind us. One day, even forget! What do you say?"

"I say, screw you, Adam!" Jenny's face was a mask of fury, her eyes black flints, sparking off her anger. "Forget? Not in a million years, Buster! How *can* I forget that when I was breaking my heart *she* was giving you the full Mounty."

"You're not exactly blameless yourself, you know." An extremely shaken Mounty climbed back in the saddle. "If you'd been taking care of business in the first place, he wouldn't have had to come running to me."

Not wanting her to come to his defence, Adam rolled his eyes. "I *didn't* come running to you, Mounty. You *seduced* me!"

Jenny attempted a little grin though it fell at the first hurdle and turned into a grimace. "Seducing Adam! How many hours did we clock up discussing that very topic, Mounty? Me desperate to. Unaware that you already had! No wonder you were so free with your tips. They were already tried and tested, weren't they?" Wearily she ran a hand across her eyes. "Now go away, all of you. In the words of Greta Garbo: 'I just want to be alone!'"

Chapter Thirty-one

"Mum. Dad's gone!"

"I know, David. He left last night when you were over at Simon's house."

"Is he coming back?"

Jenny shook her head, unwilling to lie to him. "No. No, he won't be coming back. Your Dad and I are getting a divorce."

David sank down on the bottom step of the stairs. "But you said . . ."

Gently, Jenny cut him off. "I know what I said but I wasn't in possession of all the facts then."

"So he *was* seeing another woman. Who?"

Jenny struggled a little with her conscience. David had always got on well with Mounty. When he was younger, she had taken him to the zoo, to funfairs and theme parks and, at least once a week, to feed the ducks on the pond on the nearby common. It was, she realised, a double betrayal for David as well as herself.

Still, on balance, it was better if the news came from her rather than from somebody else.

"Mounty."

"Mounty? Your friend, Mounty?"

"The same!"

"I can't believe it, Mum! Are you sure you haven't made a mistake?"

"No mistake, David. They've admitted it."

David shook his head. Wonderingly. "But Dad never liked Mounty. He called her an –"

"East End slapper with tripe for brains. I know. But presumably he developed a taste for tripe."

"That's it!" David clapped his hands. "I'm back to being vegetarian again."

Jenny gave a watery grin. "Oh, dear! What am I going to do with that lovely cooked breakfast on the kitchen table, then?"

David's nose came up. Echoes of Adam! "What have you made exactly?"

"Well, now, let's see. Sausages, bacon, egg, beans and toast. Your favourite! Well, until about two minutes ago, anyway."

David looked considering. "Hmm. It's a sin to waste good food, isn't it?"

"The worst!"

"Right, in that case I'll wait till after breakfast to go vegetarian. Okay?"

"Deal!" Grabbing him by the hand, Jenny drew him into the kitchen. "And I don't want you to think what

330

happened between me and your Dad was your fault in any way. It wasn't. It's just that Daddy and Mummy don't love each other any more. That doesn't mean that –"

"That you don't love me. I know. I know. We've had this little pep talk before, Mum. Remember? Besides, as I've told you a hundred and one times, plenty of my friends' parents are divorced. It's no big deal, you know. It just means that I've become a divorce statistic!"

Distraught, Jenny ran a maternal hand through his hair. "But I never wanted you to become a divorce statistic, David."

Driving the prongs of his fork into the soft, runny centre of his fried egg, David nodded with certainty. "Hey, shit happens, Mum! I'll get over it."

Admiringly, Jenny patted his shoulder. "I expect you will. Resilience is your second name, isn't it?"

"No, it's not. Adam is!" And boy, was that a mistake! Jenny thought, reaching over to pour him a fresh cup of tea and hoping fervently his second name would be all he inherited from his father!

David speared a sausage and dipped it in his egg. "Are Dad and Mounty going to get married?"

"I don't think so. Why? Would you mind?"

David nodded, dipped again. "Yep. Too much like shitting on your own doorstep."

Jenny was shocked. "David!"

"Well it is, Mum! Why did he have to pick on your friend? Why couldn't he have gone off with a stranger?"

He squinted up at her. "Somehow it wouldn't seem quite so bad."

"No, it wouldn't," Jenny admitted. "But as you said yourself, hey, shit happens!"

"Mum!"

Jenny widened her eyes innocently. "What?"

"Language!"

* * *

"Strange! I never thought you and I would be sharing a coffee again. I mean, in a civilised fashion." Jenny leaned back and regarded the woman sitting opposite her. "I could easily imagine pitching one over you, but civilised – strange!"

Mounty slowly stirred her coffee although, as she didn't take sugar, the whole exercise seemed a bit pointless.

"Cut the bullshit, Jenny. You called this little get-together, so cut to the chase. What do you want?"

"Closure! That's what I want. Okay, okay, so it's a very Americanised concept but that's what I want." Candidly, Jenny engaged her former best friend in eye contact. "You see, there are still a few things I need to get sorted in my head and, as Adam's unlikely to enlighten me, who else can I turn to but you?"

"And what makes you think *I'll* be any more forthcoming?"

"Because you *owe* me, Mounty. You *owe* me. Big-time!"

Mounty nodded. Slowly. "Okay, I take that on board. Fire away! What do you want to know?"

Jenny took a deep breath. "Right! Firstly I need to know if you two were together when first I suspected him of playing around. I mean, were you two already involved that night I came round to your house bra-less and bawling all over the place and you told me off for letting myself go? Being past my sell-by-date, I think you said. And we had that big row. Remember?"

"I remember and no, we weren't! Next question."

"So, when *did* you get together?"

Defiant, Mounty's chin came up. "Like I told you before, he came to my house."

"But I don't understand. *Why* did he go to your house?"

Mounty looked sheepish. "He was worried about you, if you want to know. Wanted to enlist my help in sorting you out, getting you back on track."

"And?"

"And I agreed." Mounty shifted uncomfortably, her eyes sliding away to some point in the distance only she could see. "I was worried about you too, you know. No matter what you think of me now."

Jenny frowned. "But if *you* weren't having an affair with him then. Who was? I mean, all those late nights, the change of aftershave, the whispered conversations on the telephone. What was that all about?"

"Tactics! Tactics dreamed up by me to make you think he was seeing someone! Tactics to motivate you into getting a grip. And they worked too. Take a look at yourself. Proof positive!"

"But when . . . exactly?"

"Did we do the dirty deed? Oh, not all that long after. I don't meant to be crass but if he'd been an apple, he would have been ready for plucking."

With an effort Jenny controlled her voice. "A windfall! Was that all he was to you, a windfall? But he was *my* husband, Mounty. David's father! I don't understand. Why, when you could have had any man, did you pick on him? Why, when you knew all the devastation and hurt it would cause? *Why* did you pick on Adam?"

Mounty's eyes came back from their wandering, fixed fully and frankly on Jenny's face. "I don't know. Because he was out of bounds, perhaps! Because I'm a selfish cow? Thrill of the chase? Who knows?" Her voice dropped, all but trailed away. "Or maybe, simply because I was in love with him. I was *always* in love with him."

Jenny sat up straighter. "Oh, my God! I can't believe it. I never *knew*. I mean you were always so scathing about him. *You* said I should have married that Hell's Angel from Wapping."

"I said a lot of things, most of which were just a antidote to my own hurt. That and sour grapes." Leaning a little closer, Mounty sighed. "Look, while I'm doing the penitent and breast-beating bit, I'd better come totally clean with you. Adam *never* loved me! Not even for a minute! Oh sure, when I was teetering up and down on his spine in my six-inch heels, I managed to persuade myself that he did. When I was dreaming up new, exciting and naughty games for us to play, I managed to persuade myself that he did. But in the cold light of day, when the bed was empty and Adam had gone home to you, I couldn't hide the truth from myself. I was nothing more than a diversion, a sop to assuage an ego severely dented by your neglect – just a willing body. But, make no mistake, Jenny, that's all I was and admittedly there were times when I hated you for it." She held up a hand as Jenny made to interrupt. "No, hold on a minute! If you think what you've already heard is damning, wait till you've heard this."

"Go on. It can't be any worse, surely?"

"Oh, but it can. You remember the episode with the food? When you turned yourself into a Japanese smorgasbord? Well, *I* was responsible for encouraging Adam to bring his colleague home for dinner that evening."

Jenny slammed her fist down on the table, uncaring that the other diners in the cafe forsook their own boring conversations to eavesdrop with interest on hers. "You bitch! Have you any idea how much that cost me, not only financially but also in terms of lost dignity? The memory will haunt me to my dying day if only in the shape of the sake-stains all over the living-room carpet, not to mention the fact that to this very day I can't walk past an oriental restaurant without shuddering. Even my dreams, once the nocturnal hangout of Richard Gere, Antonio Banderas and Mr Darcy from *Pride and Prejudice*, are haunted by visions of black beans, noodles and olives with pimiento stuffing!"

Mounty shrugged. "Well, I couldn't take the risk, could I? I knew that if he happened upon you alone like that, he was a lost cause. His eyes always were bigger than your belly."

Jenny ignored the dig. "So all along when I was telling you my plans, you were using them to sabotage me?"

Mounty struck her breast. *"Mea culpa. Mea culpa. Mea maxima culpa!"*

"Jeez, Mounty! You really take the biscuit. You know that?"

"It's been said before. But, whether you believe me or not, Jenny, I'm genuinely sorry for having hurt you and David and I hope, now that you know everything there is to know, you can salvage something of your marriage."

"As easy put a Ming vase together that's been shattered into a million pieces!"

"Worth a try, all the same."

Jenny half rose from the table, thought better of it and sat back down again. "Is it? Is it really? How dare you patronise me, you cow! How *dare* you try to apply a Band-aid to a surgical wound! And all so that you can salve your own conscience!"

Mounty rose, flung a five-pound note into the

middle of the table. "Have it your own way, Jenny. You and I are history. I accept that. But just you remember that every horse is entitled to one stumble at the fence and if you can't see that, then you deserve to lose Adam. For good!" Sweetly venomous, Mounty fluttered her fingers, turned her back and walked away from the wreckage of her best friend's life.

"Six-inch heels teetering up along his spine," Jenny called after her. "No wonder he kept coming back for more. You must have saved him a fortune on chiropractors!"

"Don't knock it till you've tried it. Catch you next millennium, yeah?"

"Bitch!" Ringing up the bill, the waitress spat after Mounty's departing back. "Mine was called Stella. Stella Maris, if you don't mind. Fancied herself as a singer but fancied my Stanley even more. Fifty years we was wed. Then she shows up with her French knickers and phoney French accent and it was curtains for me and my Stan!"

"I'm sorry." Jenny left an extra-generous tip to compensate for the waitress' broken heart.

"Don't be. He was crap between the sheets anyway. Now I got me a man with a salami and a half! Just think what I might have missed!"

"Quite!" Pocketing what remained of her change, Jenny hurried out the door, her resolution already wavering, just a little. "What if Mounty was right? What if Adam deserved one more chance? For David's sake, say? Wouldn't it be wrong not, at least, to consider

it? But first, there was one last thing she'd forgotten to
address. Rummaging in her handbag she pulled out her
mobile phone, called up Mounty's name and dialled the
number.

"Did he take you to Spend A Penne?" The question
was without preamble. "You know that little Italian
restaurant on the precinct?"

"Yes." Mounty's voice was tinny, disembodied. "But
only because I nagged him into it! He wanted to go to
Dolce Vita but I'd heard you banging on about the other
place so often that I didn't want to feel I was missing
out on anything. Childish, I know, but what the heck,
we're all kids at heart aren't we?"

"Where did you sit. Quick! What table?"

"What table? Does it matter?"

"Yes, it matters. Goddammit! I wouldn't ask if it
didn't!"

"Oh, I don't know. Near the door. That's it! Near the
front door beside the umbrella rack. I wasn't all that
impressed I can tell you. It was so cold, I thought we
were dining alfresco."

Jenny felt herself begin to breathe again. Slow, deep
breaths of relief. Near the front door! So they hadn't sat
at the little corner table, *their* table, hers and Adam's,
with the red and white gingham tablecloth, and the
green Chianti bottle, a monument to the drippings of a
hundred wax candles.

Mounty's disembodied voice continued to squawk
indignantly in the vicinity of her ear. "Honestly, Jenny!

And as if the table wasn't bad enough, then some fat git of a waiter only goes and throws espresso over my new white Stella McCartney. Didn't even apologise if you can believe it. Just stood there going *Mamma mia, Mamma mia* like a broken-down record."

For the first time in days a very real smile spread across Jenny's face. Bless you, Gianni! The Deptford waiter's knowledge of Italian was obviously good enough to recognise a *putana* when he saw one. Pressing call ended, Jenny disconnected from a still babbling Mounty. Then slowly, deliberately, and with great enjoyment she pressed the delete button. Childish, she knew, but as Mounty said, what the heck, they were all kids at heart. Weren't they? Besides, that was one number she wouldn't be needing again. Ever!

Chapter Thirty-two

"Right, it's time to date and mate, again." Poppy grinned. "Okay, well maybe not mate. Let's just start with date. Take it one step at a time."

"No!"

"No?"

"No!"

"No?"

"Bloody hell!" Jenny felt her patience begin to wear a bit thin. "What are you, a rapist or something? No means no! In any language! So exactly what part of it do *you* have difficulty with?"

Poppy hummphed. "Oh calm down and take your Valium! I'm only trying to help, you know. No need to blast my head off."

Idly chipping at a cigarette burn on the varnished bar counter with the edge of a fingernail, Jenny heaved a sigh that curled itself all the way from her toes up along the length of her entire body before finally exiting through her mouth.

"God, I'm sorry, Pops. It's just that all this 'second-time around' business is really getting to me. I'm not even *sure* if I want a man in my life, although I must admit the thoughts of living entirely alone for the rest of my life doesn't exactly appeal either. I mean I could turn into one of those eccentric old women you see shuffling along the street muttering to themselves, living off tins of cat food and ending up dead for three months before anyone decides to check out where the stink is coming from."

"Nonsense!" Full of camaraderie, Poppy thumped her on the back. "You'll never be entirely alone as long as you've got David."

Jenny shook her head. "No, David is growing up fast. In a few more years he'll be off doing his own thing. Then it'll be marriage to a woman who can't stand my guts and before you know it he'll have a mortgage, kids and problems enough of his own to preclude him having any time left over for his aged and decrepit mother." A bit of the stain, a tiny fraction of burnt splinter, came loose. Blowing it away, Jenny immediately started picking at a fresh spot. "Besides, I never want to be a burden to him. Kids should never be an insurance policy against their parents' old age."

Poppy made a sawing motion across the crook of her arm. "Jesus Christ! Bring on the Stradivarius. What a lot of old crap! Anyone would think you were ninety with a death rattle instead of a youthful, single-again, glamorous forty-year-old with the world at her feet."

"Aaagh!" Jenny made a cross of her fingers. "Not so much of the forty, eh! Okay, so I'm knock, knock, knockin' on forty's door. But it hasn't opened yet! Allow me to stay on the right side of it for just one more day, please."

"Look, it's not terminal. I survived it, didn't I? Forty is just another number."

"Yeah, number up!" Glumly, Jenny signalled to the barman to refill their glasses. She was on the Jack Daniels tonight, a serious drink as befitted the sombreness of her mood.

"It's like every other age, Jen. It's got its compensations."

"Like?"

Poppy searched the room for inspiration, finding it in the bald and beer-bellied form of a nearby hardened drinker. "Like knowing your own mind. Knowing what you want and what you don't want. Like not being prepared to short-change yourself or lower your standards. Like not being prepared simply to settle for something. Like having the confidence to stand up for yourself, look the world in the eye and spit in it, if necessary."

"Ho hum! You make it sound so attractive. Almost as attractive as wrinkles, sagging buttocks, grey hair and ovaries like dried-up prunes."

"Well, it's up to you, of course, if you want to make a big issue out of it but personally I'd be inclined to treat it as the threshold to something new and wonderful rather than as a landmark commemorating the past. I mean, come on, it's not as if your past was all that rosy.

Your recent past anyway. Anyone in their right mind would be delighted to move onward and upward."

Jenny issued a duplicate of her earlier sigh, finger still diligently chipping away at the counter. "But I'm not in my right mind, am I? Adam saw to that! And Mounty!"

"Well, you know what they say, the best revenge is to be happy. And if you stopped wallowing in self-pity for five minutes or so, you'd soon realise that you've loads to be happy about."

"Such as?"

"Well, David for a start. I mean he's a great kid. Plus, you're the top-rated chat-show hostess in Britain with more fans than a major electrical outlet. You're a stunning size ten, with razor cheekbones and ankles to die for *and* you're only halfway through your life. I'd say that's pretty amazing. Wouldn't you? Reasons to be cheerful!"

Jenny looked doubtful. "I suppose."

"No suppose about it. We're talking facts here. All you need now is a soul mate and life will be pretty much perfect."

"Adam was my soul mate. Or at least I thought he was."

"Yes. Well, you know what thought did?"

"Wet in his Levis and thought he was sweating?"

"No. Thought he was a woman, but he was another man!"

Despite herself, Jenny grinned. "Don't be daft. That was JoJo in the Beatles' song."

"Made you laugh, though. Which proves my point. You've a lot to laugh about and a lot to be happy about."

Reaching out, Jenny put her arms around the other woman's shoulders, gave her a quick squeeze. "You're a good friend, Poppy. I'm sorry for being such a miserable cow."

"Ah, you're all right! Now, as the night is still young and David is staying over with Adam, what do you say we hit a club or two?"

"Must we, Poppy? I mean, couldn't we just stay here and get out of our heads on good old JD?"

"B-o-r-ing!" Poppy gave a quick shufty round the pub. "Besides there's nothing worth looking at in here, much less worth chatting up."

"Yikes!" Jenny almost screeched. "It's years since I chatted anyone up. I've forgotten the art, if ever I knew it in the first place. As far as I can recall, it was Adam who did all the chatting up. I simply made the right noises and tried hard to look sexy."

"Ah, nothing to it." Poppy slid off the barstool. "Just laugh at all their jokes, say the odd "gosh, you're sooo clever" and "silly me, I don't understand these things, cos I'm just a ikka bikka woman" and that's it. Bingo! They're eating out of your hand."

Jenny looked dubious. "I'm not sure I like the sound of that. Rover eats out of my mother's hand and he's definitely not my type."

Sticking out her hand, Poppy hailed a passing taxi.

"Men are all dogs in one form or another. My ex was a real mongrel. In fact with the benefit of hindsight I can truly say that that Sasha bitch did me a big favour when she took him off my hands. Who knows, further down the line, you might feel exactly the same way about Adam."

Jenny followed her into the cab. "God, I hope so, Poppy. Because right now, all I feel is empty. Like half of me is missing. And I can't bear the thoughts of going through life as only half a person. An empty shell."

Poppy bent forward, gripped her kneecaps and, even in the dark interior of the cab, Jenny could see the anger smouldering in her eyes.

"Now you just listen to me, Jen. Adam is the past and the past is dead. And when something is dead, it's traditional to take a big spade, a pine box and bury it. What you've got to do now is to look to the future. For both your own sake *and* for David's! How do you think it feels to him to have a mother going round with a face as long as Jacob's ladder? You're doing exactly what you said you wouldn't do i.e. making him suffer."

"Oh, God! You're right." Distraught, Jenny ran a hand through the black Cleopatra-style wig she had taken to wearing out in public which, when teamed with a pair of dark Jackie O glasses, made her virtually unrecognisable to all but the most eagle-eyed, well-versed-in-spotting-celebs-in disguise fan. "Right that's it! From now on you're going to see a new side to me, a more upbeat me, a much more positive kind of me, a thankful-for-her-blessings-of-which-there-are-many kind of me."

Poppy laughed. "Okay, okay. I get the message. Don't drown me in good intentions. Just pack up your troubles in your old kitbag as Vera Lynn sang, and let's go get laid!"

A note ranging somewhere between scared and absolutely terrified entered Jenny's voice. "One step at a time, Poppy. That's what you said. Don't push me into doing anything I might regret, will you?"

"Of course not. It'll be enough for me to see you tripping the light fantastic and actually enjoying yourself."

Satisfied, Jenny lay back against the upholstery. "What's this place like anyway? Not full of teenyboppers, I hope, cream of the crop-tops, and raw-boned, pimpled youths fond of a fondle?"

"No, it's a singles' club."

"Oh God, not one of those places where the women sit around with desperate tattooed across their foreheads and elderly bachelors in cable-knit beige cardigans try frantically to offload their virginity before death comes a-calling."

"As if," Poppy pooh-poohed the idea. "Credit me with some kind of taste, would you? No, *On The Loose* is a 'professionals only' club, haunt of barristers, stockbrokers and tycoons. None of your flat-cap and mine's-a-pint-of-ale mob."

"But tycoons? Surely they just go out and buy a woman."

"Okay. Well, maybe not tycoons, but a better class of single, nonetheless."

"I hope you're right." Fearfully, Jenny followed Poppy out of the taxi, which had pulled up in front of a rather smart Georgian building, with nothing at all, other than the discreet brass plaque on the door to suggest it was anything other than a private residence.

Leaning in the driver's window, Poppy pulled out her purse. "What's the damage?"

"Nothing, love, providing your mate there gives me her autograph. Beryl, that's the wife, will be made up. Loves her, she does."

Sighing Jenny took the proffered pen and receipt book. *"To Beryl, all my love, Anthea."*

"Anthea?" The taxi driver scratched his head. "Bleedin hell. I thought you was that other bird. You know that chat-show hostess. Jenny something or other."

Rolling her eyes, Jenny followed her companion up the short flight of steps and into the Regency-decorated corridor of *On The Loose*. "You know what, Pops? There's just no winning."

"Hmm. If you're not in, you can't win," Poppy quipped, her eyes straying towards a diffident Hugh Grant type, who had plastered his back flat against a wall in a desperate attempt to merge with it, a ruse that might have worked better had his jacket boasted the same broad gold and burgundy stripes as the wallpaper. "And I think it could be meee! Hi, there, beastman! Waitin for me?"

"Bloody hell!" Jenny muttered *sotto voce,* watching in amazement as Poppy not so much sashayed as bosomed over to the poor chap and pinned him with her nipples. "Way to go, Poppy!"

"Hey, Cleo. Nice asp!"

"Ouch! Do you mind!" Jenny jumped as a large, male hand came out of nowhere, clamped itself on her right buttock and dug in for the evening.

"Not at all. Delighted in fact!" The owner, not at all put off by the icebergs floating in her eyes, grinned cheerfully. "By the way, I'm Mark. Mark Antony."

Bugger! She'd known the Cleopatra wig was a big mistake! Now, every creep from here to Kingdom Come would feel it incumbent upon himself to blind her with his limited knowledge of Egyptology. Blast! She would have opted for the long, black, curly Cher number, if the old bag Nature had seen fit to inflict upon her for a mother hadn't pounced on it first and insisted on buying it as a present for Rover. His very own toy poodle!

"Okay." With a wink, Creep Number One shot her his interpretation of cheeky charm. "You've rumbled me. I'm not *really* Mark Antony."

"Well now, you *do* surprise me." Even the wig dripped sarcasm as she made to pull away.

"Real name's Caesar. Julius Caesar. Licensed to fiddle!"

"That was Nero."

"What was?"

"Nero! Fiddled while, all around him, Rome burned."

"Oh. Well, here's one for you. What *did* Caesar say when a bear ate his mother-in-law?"

Jenny sighed but decided to humour him in the hopes that he might then be persuaded to piss off and annoy someone else. "I don't know," she deadpanned. "What did Caesar say when a bear ate his mother-in-law?"

"I'm gladiator! Glad-he-ate-her! Geddit?"

Jenny bent a surly but quizzical look upon him. "Jesus, my sides are splitting. Tell me? What are you on and does it come in resin or powder form?"

The creep decided to take umbrage. "Now listen. There's no need for sarcasm. We're all in the same boat here, you know. All desperate for a shag! Okay, so I might not have the best chat-up lines in the country but, hey, at least I'm trying."

"Oh, you *are* that. *Very* trying," Jenny agreed, and then, "What? Not laughing? Dear, oh dear. It's a joke, Julius. A little word-play. You said you were trying and I agreed that yes, you *are* trying. Very trying. Like, gladiator and glad-he-ate-her, see?"

The creep, obviously not one to relish being the butt of someone else's wit, turned nasty. "I see you're a bitch. That's what I see. I dare say your old man pissed off with someone else and that's why you've landed up here. Hardly surprising, I'd say." Well into his flow, he paused for a moment before firing a last parting and knowledgeable shot across her bows. "The face that launched a thousand ships. Do me a favour! More like the gob that sank a thousand chips!"

"That was Helen of Troy!" Jenny called after him. "Not Cleopatra! It's pretty obvious what you did during history lessons. Fiddled with yourself while, all around you, others learned!"

"Wow! You're a tough one. I wouldn't like to meet you up a dark alley on a dark night. Actually, I tell a lie. I *would!*"

Blushing furiously, Jenny turned to where a collarbone, well kitted out in immaculate white shirt and understated silk-tie, had materialized beside her. Craning her head upwards she realised that it came complete with a neck, a chin and a face only ever seen in women's fantasies.

"Hi. I'm Matt. Matt Fitzpatrick. And you are . . ."

"Jenny . . . I mean Chloe," Jenny stammered shaking his hand and belatedly remembering the alter ego Poppy had dreamed up to enable her to go out in public without being hassled by autograph hunters and members of the press hungry for a newsworthy photograph. Preferably, a compromising photograph."

"Because, how would it look to see your picture on every newspaper around the country falling out of a singles club in the early hours, pissed as a fart and hanging on the arm of somebody you'd just picked up that evening. Imagine the headlines!"

"Well . . ." The male fantasy looked amused. "Which is it to be? Jenny or Chloe?"

Chapter Thirty-three

"Jenny!" Jenny confessed knowing she'd never be able to keep up the pretence and strangely, considering she had only just met this man, not at all sure that she wanted to. There was something about him, something masterful, compelling and utterly sexy that had her wanting to rip off not only her Cleopatra wig, but also her dress and underwear and hurl herself onto the nearest, flat surface going "Take me now! *Now*, I tell you! *Now!*"

"Well. I must say this is a turn-up for the books, considering how I had to be virtually dragged in here this evening."

Jenny shivered, an orgasmic shiver that fluttered down the length of her spinal column, before fanning out somewhere around her pelvic region. Even his voice, deep, (but not one of those foghorns that blasted babies and small animals out of their sleep), and lightly tinged with the music of Ireland, was perfection.

"Me too," she confessed. "I only came for Poppy's sake, really."

"Poppy?"

Jenny jerked her head. "My friend. The one over there busy reducing the Hugh Grant clone to a nervous wreck. She said there was a better class of single to be found here but, after Mark Antony, I was seriously beginning to have my doubts."

"And now?"

Jenny smiled. "Let's just say, I'm reconsidering."

"I'm very glad to hear it." Taking her arm, the gorgeous Matt led her through to the club proper where those who had 'pulled' were smooching on the floor, and those still on the lookout were regarding every new entrant with a mixture of hope and trepidation. "Dance with me?"

Nodding shyly, Jenny stepped into the protective circle of his arms, body melding deliciously with his to the romantic, breathy sound of 'Three Times A Lady', and then to the even breathier sound of 'Je t'Aime', till her gusset was wringing and she found out the true meaning of water music.

"So, do you suffer from cranial depilation or what?"

"Pardon?" The question took her by surprise as a short time later, he led her across to an empty table on which had appeared, as if by magic, two champagne flutes and a bottle of Bollinger.

"You know, hair loss? Baldness?"

"I most certainly do not!"

"Then, why are you wearing that ridiculous wig?"

Jenny wondered if she should be insulted, decided it was a perfectly valid question, and giggled instead. "It's a disguise!"

Her escort raised his eyebrows, again perfection, twin crescents of black with no danger of them meeting in the middle, which as any old wife would tell you was a sign of deceit and untrustworthiness.

"I'm intrigued. Are you married?"

Jenny stuttered a little."No . . . that is . . . I'm separated with a divorce petition winging its way through the courts."

"Then why the disguise?"

Bowing her head, Jenny, ran her fingers up and down the narrow stem of her champagne glass, totally unaware of the suggestiveness of her movements. "It's to do with my job, you see." Where possible, Jenny, still quite unable to get to grips with her massive public popularity, and not wanting to appear boastful or big-headed, did her best to downplay that side of her life.

Matt grinned. "Don't tell me. Let me guess. You're an agent with MI5! No? Well, a traffic warden then and you're terrified someone you ticketed will seek revenge if they happen to spot you alone and unprotected. No?" Musingly he tapped his chin, his forefinger and middle finger alternating in a kind of digital tattoo. "I know. You're a chat-show hostess on the telly and every time you put your nose out your front door you're mobbed by fans and nutters in quest of someone to stalk."

Feeling a bit foolish, Jenny groaned. "How long have you known?"

"More or less right from the off. It would take more than a wig to disguise your pretty face. Added to which, my ex-wife used to watch you every morning and it was more than my life was worth to switch over to the news."

"I'm sorry."

"Don't be. I didn't *really* want to turn over. I just didn't want her to twig just how much physical stimulation I was getting from watching you."

"Oh God. There's really no answer to that, is there? Anyway, shouldn't you have been at work?"

"I'm a writer. I work from home."

"Ah, brains as well as beauty!"

Matt smiled, refilled her glass. "Admit it. You've always wanted to say that to a guy."

"Predictability! My second name."

"No it's not, it's Lorelei, siren of the Nile, which makes your Cleo wig not all that inappropriate."

Jenny pretended annoyance. "Hmmph! For someone who, half an hour ago, was a perfect stranger you seem to know an awful lot about me. I don't know whether to be flattered or scared witless."

Reaching across, he placed one hand on top of hers. Perfect! Well-shaped and manly with not too much hair on the back and fingers that were long and sensitive but which stopped well short of being map-pointers.

"Research! I always research those topics which interest me."

356

"By which I'm supposed to take it that . . ."

"You interest me? Count on it. So much so that there's nothing I'd like to do more than a little further research. Of the hands-*on* variety."

"Back off, Einstein." Jenny smiled to take the sting out of her words. "You're dealing with the walking wounded here. The once-bitten-twice-shy-school of woman!"

His eyes twinkled. "Ah, but I have a wonderful bedside manner."

Discreetly, Jenny cast about for Poppy who, together with the Hugh Grant clone, was nowhere to be seen and who, at a guess, was most likely busy renewing her long-standing membership of the WC club. Look! She wanted to tell her. Look, Poppy! I'm doing it! I'm actually flirting! You were right. It *is* like eating a bar of chocolate. You never forget the taste.

"So who's been kissing the Blarney stone?" she asked.

"Is that your way of telling me I'm being too smarmy?"

"Not at all. Smarm away. It's only smarmless fun." Making retching motions over her shoulder, Jenny turned penitent. "God, I'm sorry. I can't believe I said that."

Matt shrugged. "Not at all. No smarm in it!" Grinning, he turned her palm over, brought her fingers up to his lips, kissed them. "You see, awful puns! Something else we've got in common."

Her face a little wistful, Jenny shyly extricated her

fingers. "Adam hated when I made puns. He said it was the lowest form of wit."

"Your husband?"

Jenny nodded.

"Well, he was wrong. Generally it's sarcasm that's acknowledged to be the lowest form of wit. But then again, it looks like the man gets quite a lot of things wrong. Take you, for instance. How on earth could he get it so wrong as to let such a beautiful creature as you go?"

Oh Lord! He'd pressed her self-pity button. To her mortification Jenny felt a tear gather in the corner of her eye and trickle slowly down her face, taking half her mascara with it.

"I'm sorry,"she sniffed, rummaging in her handbag for a tissue and finding only a fluff-covered Polo-mint.

Diving into his pocket, Matt produced a spotless white handkerchief and dabbed futilely at her eyes. (I mean, get this! The man actually carried linen handkerchiefs. None of your Kleenex man-size for him!)

"No. *I'm* sorry. I didn't mean to upset you."

Jenny sniffed and gulped in rapid succession. "It's all right. I told you I was the walking-wounded although people keep assuring me time is a great healer and that, one day, I'll mend."

"And you will. Believe me!" And there was something in his voice that made Jenny believe he knew exactly what he was talking about. "I'll tell you what. Let's dance again. Nobody can be sad whilst dancing to the 'Boogie Woogie Bugle Boy from Company B'."

"Okay." Bravely shrugging off her broken heart, Jenny allowed him to lead her onto the floor and another minute found her breathless and laughing and joining in with Bette Midler. After that it was a smooth if noisy transition straight into 'In The Mood' and almost before she knew it Poppy was tugging at her elbow and making 'It's time to go home, Cinderella' noises.

* * *

"So, are you seeing him again?"

Jenny shrugged. "Maybe."

Satisfied, Poppy squinted up at the first tentative signs of dawn breaking outside the taxi window. "Which means you are."

Mischievously, Jenny poked her in the ribs. "And you? Will you be seeing Hugh again? Which reminds me, I noticed a rather long queue outside the toilet at one point in the evening. Tell me it hadn't got anything to do with you?"

"Perish the thought!" Delving into her handbag, the other produced a small, silver hip-flask, offered it to Jenny who refused, and quickly downed a hair of the dog. "Oh all right. I confess. It *was* me. Me and . . . God, I can't for the life of me remember what his name was, only it wasn't Hugh and that's for certain."

"And, did the earth move?"

Poppy frowned, took another gulp. "No. No, it didn't. Actually it was the strangest thing. I mean the guy had it going on, knew all the right moves and even panted on cue but, you know what, midway through I found myself wanting to shout 'Gerroff, would ya, I need to have a pee'."

Deliciously appalled, Jenny sat up straighter. "You didn't though, did you?"

"Nah. But I'll tell you what, Jen, I don't know why but men just don't seem to have the same appeal these days."

Jenny nodded shrewdly. "Probably this Inner-Child business. It's got you all screwed up."

Gloomily examining the back of the taxi driver's neck, which bulged like a goitre over the back of his collar, Poppy nodded violently. "Ain't that the truth though." Determinedly she shrugged off her black mood. "Anyway, tell me about the delicious Matt."

"What's to tell? He's gorgeous. He's sexy. And I think I'm in love."

"No!"

Jenny came clean. "Well, okay. No, but I think I could be, always presuming I can get Adam out of my head."

"Sod Adam! The man's a menace. Maybe you should try aversion therapy."

Jenny looked interested. "Hmm. I seem to have missed that one although I could have sworn between Oprah and Sally they'd covered them all. What is it exactly?"

"Well, take compulsive eaters for example. A touch of the old hypnosis and, hey presto, before their very eyes, the king-size Fruit & Nut clutched in their sweaty little hand starts oozing maggots all over the place. Hence, maggots equal revulsion, equals stomach turning, equals dropping said bar like hot cake, equals calorie overload averted. Aversion therapy!"

"And you think that might work for me?"

"Can't hurt, can it?"

"Not sure really. I mean he already makes me puke but I still –"

"Stop right there!" Poppy commanded. "Don't you dare mention Adam and love in the same sentence. The two are not compatible. Never were! Never will be!"

Idly, Jenny gazed out the window, dimly aware that they were driving over Tower Bridge and starting on the home-run south of the river. "He isn't all bad, Poppy. I mean, until the hoo-ha with Mounty, he was pretty damn-near perfect. There were loads of good times too."

"I know, and you have the stretch marks to prove it." Poppy held up her hand to ward off impending argument. "But that was then, Jenny, and time doesn't stand still. Adam reversed the fairy story. He turned from a prince into a Treigh-frog. Now, if you've any sense at all, you'll see Matt is where it's at. Hey, why don't you invite him to your Christmas do?"

"I can't. I've already asked Denzil. He's having his pink lurex tux specially dry-cleaned for the occasion."

"Balls! Denzil will understand. He's a good mate, Jenny, even if he is adenoidal and a sufferer of heterosexual delusions. At least where you're concerned."

"Maybe." Jenny was noncommittal. "Anyway, I'll jump that particular fence when I come to it." Leaning back she closed her eyes, Poppy following suit, both women content to lapse into a companionable silence that lasted till the taxi pulled up in front of Jenny's house. "Are you sure you won't come in for a nightcap?"

Poppy shook her head."No, I'd better get off home. Thanks for the offer though, and remember what I said."

"I will." Climbing out, Jenny suppressed a yawn. "Now y'all take cahir. D'ye hear me?"

"Sure thing, lil Missy." Totally, unfazed, and not too tired to join in with Jenny's sudden transitions into Annie Oakley or whatever, Poppy responded in kind. "Yeehaw! Catch you later."

"Yeehaw!" Jenny returned the salute, wearily let herself into the house and, without bothering to remove her make-up, summoned what remained of her energy, hurled herself into bed and, despite recent improvements, snored like a Black & Decker for what remained of the night.

* * *

"Are you sure you don't mind, Denz?" Guiltily, Jenny stepped off the fat-monitor which had bleeped in record time. "After all, I did ask you first."

Keeping his head down, Denzil scribbled something on her personal health chart. "No. No, I don't mind.

This Matt bloke sounds like a real, regular guy. You go ahead, have yourself a good time. Besides, somebody pinched my tux."

"What? From the dry-cleaners."

Denzil shuffled a little. "No, from my bedroom."

Jenny grinned. "Ah. I hope he was worth it."

Denzil made a 'so-so' motion with his hand. "I've had better but then again maybe it was me. You see, I wasn't really in the mood. To tell you the truth I'm having a a bit of a crisis at the moment." Confidentially, he grabbed her arm and whispered in her ear. "I think I might be straight."

"No!" Jenny's lips formed an 'o' of disbelief. "Definitely not! No way! You, my son, are as gay as a coot. Not a straight bone in your body."

"Oh yeah, and how do you work that out?"

"Your bum," Jenny responded instantly. "Bums like yours are only ever found on gay guys. And your voice! I mean it's never really broken as such, has it? So there you have it. Guys with high, round, firm bums and high-pitched voices are gay. Everyone knows that! Guys with oblong, deflated, whoopee-cushion buttocks and gravel-pit voices are straight. Everyone, ditto!"

Denzil looked considering. "You don't think you're guilty of stereotyping, do you?"

"Maybe. Maybe not! But, to get back to you. See that guy over there? Yeah, the one with the bulging biceps and natty line in cycling shorts. Don't tell me the sight of so much naked, male torso doesn't undulate your unitard?" She twanged his shoulder strap. "Not even a little, eh?"

Denzil capitulated. "Well, all right, maybe just a flutter."

"So your flag is at half-mast, then?"

A twinkle came into Denzil's eye as the object of their discussion stepped off the treadmill and, having mopped vigorously at his forehead with a paper towel, strode smilingly in their direction. "And rising by the moment."

"Here, Denz. Sorry about the other night but I packed your pink tux in with my things by mistake. I'll drop it by later if you like."

Jenny grinned. "He likes. Catch you later, Denzil. I won't say stay on the straight and narrow but, keep the faith and the flag flying high."

"I will." Denzil was fervent and his voice, as Jenny walked away, was at least two octaves higher.

Chapter Thirty-four

"Don't look at me like that, Poppy! I'm not crazy, you know."

"Oh, yes you are. You should be locked up and the key thrown away."

"Why? Because I didn't fall into his arms on the first date?"

"Or on the second, or on the third . . ."

Jenny's chin came up, a little defiant. "I'm out of practice. Sleeping around doesn't come easy to me. It *never* came easy to me. What can I tell you? Underneath this designer shirt beats an old-fashioned heart with a simple yearning for roses round the door and a white picket fence."

"Garbage! Admit it, you're still carrying a big, fiery torch for Adam."

"I'm not!"

"Oh, yes you are. I mean, what other explanation can there be? Nobody, I don't care who they are, nobody in their right mind would turn down a night in the sack with the delectable Matt Fitzpatrick."

Jenny looked down her nose. "Look, Poppy, I'm not into playing tit-for-tat games. Just because Adam cheated on me doesn't mean I should do the same."

"But you *wouldn't* be cheating on him." Poppy squinted her eyes. "You're divorced, remember?"

"Not quite. Decree absolute hasn't been pronounced yet. Technically we're still man and wife."

Poppy snorted. "And you'd like to keep it that way as long as possible, I suppose!"

"Well, you can't blame me for wishing things were different. But I'm not a complete idiot, Poppy. I know he should carry a government health warning and I *am* getting over him, bit by bit. Still Rome wasn't built in a day, as they say, and neither was our marriage. Okay, so it's in ruins now but amongst all the rubble and debris, there are also broken dreams and sometimes that can be the hardest thing of all to accept."

Poppy gave a long, slow-handed clap. "Bravo! Spoken like a true drama queen."

Jenny ignored her. "And then there's David, of course. I mean, Adam is really giving it welly with him at the moment. You know, doing the big, repentant sinner number. All sweetness, light and reason!" Childishly, Jenny screwed up her mouth in what she hoped was a fair parody of Adam turning on the charm. *'What Daddy did was wrong, son. You mustn't be angry with Mummy. She was right to throw me out. I only wish I could turn the clock back.'*

"Hmm." Poppy nodded. "I see and David carries it all back to you, pressure by proxy. Just as your ex intended."

"That's about the size of it. And, of course, David's just turned thirteen and the hormonal teenager lurking just beneath his, so far mercifully free from spotty, epidermis is ready to erupt at any time, and accuse me of ruining his life." Bestowing a look of horror upon her friend, she gripped her arm. Tightly! "And then you know what would happen. Further down the line he'll turn into the Ripper or Charles Manson and run amok writing victims' names on the wall in blood." Jenny's voice became a wail. "And it'll be all my fault for messing with his head at an impressionable age."

Glancing briefly at her watch, Poppy checked that they were still in good time for the flotation-tank session she'd booked them both in for as a treat, or so she'd assured a sceptical Jenny. "Standard behaviour for a teenager, I would have thought. I seem to remember writing someone's name in blood in my maths book." She snapped her fingers. "That's right! It was Donny Osmond's."

Jenny looked horrified. "What, in blood? Real, live haemoglobin?"

"Mmm! Only it was *my* blood, extracted by dint of a paper-cut. I also seem to remember muttering some kind of invocation, the end result of which was supposed to be him falling madly in love with me and whisking me away on one of those crazy horses he was always singing about."

"And what happened?"

"Well, obviously not that! Mr. Purcell, the maths teacher, caught me and kept me behind for detention as well as for some devilment of his own."

Jenny gave a little shriek. "No! You never did it with your maths teacher."

Bright-eyed with old memories, Poppy grinned. "Well, not exactly, but well, put it like this, I never viewed algebra in the quite the same light after that."

Jenny chuckled. "You know you really cheer me up, Pops."

"Good, but to get back to David, I thought he was cool about the divorce."

"He is, at least to all intents and purposes he is, but remember what it was like when *you* were a teenager. All those mood swings and insecurities, the terrible angst that beset every moment, the desperate craving both to belong and to rebel. A true rebel without a clue, in other words."

"I'm *still* clueless," Poppy confessed. "But look, I'm sorry for harping on about Adam. I can see you're between a rock and a hard place. I hope you know it's only because I care about you."

"I know." Jenny threaded her arm through her friend's. "And I know, Mum and Rover, Marcel and everybody else are only nagging me for my own good. But the truth is, I feel like I'm in a kind of limbo at the moment, eternally running on the spot, unable to go backwards or forwards." She sighed. "Maybe it would be easier if Adam had gone off and set up home with Mounty or someone else even. I'd be forced to get on with my life then, wouldn't I?"

"Maybe. If you didn't go chucking yourself off Beachy Head."

"No. I'd never do that, if only for David's sake. He needs me." Frustrated, she slapped her forehead. "But here we go, you see, back on the hamster's wheel again. He needs Adam too, you see. Oh shit, Poppy. Maybe I should take him back if only for David's sake. What do you think?"

Exerting pressure to the left, Poppy steered her through a gateway and up a short flight of steps. "Look, Jen. You know my feelings on the subject but, having said that, it's your life. What I think, what your mother thinks, what everybody thinks is of no real consequence. You must do whatever *you* think is the right thing. I'll always be here for you whatever you decide."

Agonised, Jenny rolled her eyes. "But that's just the point, I don't bloody know *what* I think. I'm all at sixes and sevens."

Stepping through the automatic doors at the top of the steps, Poppy hauled her through. "All the more reason to go for a float. Very therapeutic, a float! The trick is to empty your mind, which personally takes me all of about two seconds and just float there in your own individual tank in the dark. Ah, bliss!"

"Poppy." Jenny came to a full stop. "Did you say individual, tank and dark?"

Beaming, Poppy urged her on. "Yes. So relaxing! It's like regressing to the womb, lying there in your own little amniotic fluid-filled world with only the thump, thump of your heartbeat for company."

Suddenly digging her heels in like a mule and refusing to budge an inch further, Jenny turned a face that was awful in its panic towards her. "Poppy." If her voice had been mercury in a thermometer, the patient would have died. "You do know I'm claustrophobic, don't you?"

Chapter Thirty-five

"You cannot be serious!"

"Look, I haven't decided anything yet, Marcel. I simply said I was considering things."

"What's to consider? The man's a rat. He cheated on you with your best friend for goodness sake."

"Goodness had nothing to do with it!" Attila the Hun, aka Jenny's make-up lady, quipped mixing up a mixture of what looked like putty and poster paint and trowelling it on Jenny's face.

"Shut it, Mae West!" Marcel snarled. "I don't pay you for your wit, you know. Actually, remind me what I *am* paying you for. I mean what do you think you're doing, mixing up a death mask?"

"Foundation!" The Hun snapped. "The basis of any good make-up. Maybe you should try some, eh? Make your face look less like an arsehole."

Marcel glared but declined to engage in further verbal sparring knowing, from experience, that there

371

would be only one victor and it was unlikely to be him. Instead, he contented himself with a killer glare and went back to haranguing Jenny.

"Post-traumatic stress! That's what it'll be. You've had a severe shock to the system and now you're not capable of rational thought."

"I am perfectly rational and *compos mentis*, thank you, Marcel. Although, maybe not, considering I'm even bothering to discuss my private affairs with you."

Marcel sniffed, then picked up and methodically began pulling the strands of hair out of a blusher brush. "I know! I'll phone your mother."

"You'll do no such thing." Jenny sat bolt upright, almost chinning Attila in the process. "I'm not a child, you know, and I certainly don't need my mother's intervention in my private life."

"No? Well, maybe not. Martyna, then? Poppy?"

"Nobody!" Jenny was emphatic. "Now piss off, Marcel, I'm on air in about two minutes and I need to calm my nerves before I go on."

"Ookay!" Marcel backed slowly away but not before The Hun wrenched what remained of the blusher brush from him and threatened, with graphic gestures, to do unimaginable harm to a particular area of his anatomy. "I only hope you learn something from today's topic because let's face it, it's nothing if not apt."

Exactly two minutes later, Jenny took a deep breath, checked her skirt for VPL and strode out into the middle of Studio Number One.

"Good morning, everybody! Welcome to *Jenny Jumps In!* My name is Jenny Treigh and today we want to find out what happens when *Trust is Bust!* Donna! What happens when trust is bust?" Honing in on a pre-selected 'gob' Jenny crouched down to a woman in the front row and rammed the mike beneath her nose.

"Well, when it's gone, it's gone, innit? It don't come back. I mean, take my old man. Off he goes on a shagging spree and when I finds out what does the bleeder say? It won't 'appen again. Too bleedin right, mate, I says. Sling yer 'ook!"

"Language, Donna," Jenny cautioned. "For all we know, children and young people might be watching this show."

"Well, they bleedin' shouldn't oughter! Oops!" Donna covered her mouth with guilty fingers. "Sorry! Oughter be at bleedin' school. Little sods!"

Thanking Donna for her eloquent contribution, Jenny moved swiftly on, honing in, in a matter of seconds, on 'gob' Number Two, a woman with a face so lined you could map out the roads from Land's End to John O'Groats and still have room for the ferry routes.

"Well, Christine? Do you agree with Donna or do you, like some people, believe that every horse should be allowed one stumble at the fence?"

Shaking her head adamantly, the road-map, a life-long sufferer of catarrh and sundry other respiratory illnesses, hawked into a piece of tissue, wielding it aloft to give emphasis to her viewpoint.

"No! I don't agree with 'er and I don't know about any flamin' 'orses but, tell yer the truth, my old man fell often enough." She cackled like a drain. "Usually comin' home from the pub, mind. But I forgive him, didn't I? I didn't chuck 'im out even though he'd only gone and spent all 'is bleedin' wages on booze and on the gee-gees."

Rolling her eyes, Gob Number One, aka Donna from Balham, glared at the nearest camera as if it were personally responsible for inflicting a savage injury upon her person. "Nah! That ain't the same fing at all! Booze and gee-gees? You're 'avin' a laugh, ain't ya? I'm talking tarts 'ere. Yer know. Other wimmin! Not bleedin' booze and gee-gees! I mean, what would yer do if 'e started puttin it abaht?"

Gob Number Two hawked and spat into her tissue as a prelude to answering. "'E did put it abaht but it were just the once, so I give 'im another chance, didn't I?"

"Ow can yer be sure it were just the once? Mebbe 'e just got clever. Waited till you was at yer Mum's or somethin'? Bleedin' leopards don't bleedin' change their bleedin' spots, yer know."

"Language!" Jenny sighed.

"Nah, it were just the once!"

"But 'ow do yer know?" Gob Number one insisted.

"Because I bleedin' castrated 'im after the first time. That's 'ow I bleedin' know!"

Jenny sighed once more as the audience erupted into

hysterics and the programme, as was customary, disintegrated into chaos around her ears. Still that's what brought the punters back morning after morning and made *Jenny Jumps In* the most widely syndicated chat show throughout Europe and the States. When at last she was able to get a word in edgeways, Jenny appealed for calm.

"Okay! Okay! Let's have a bit of hush because I want you all to meet Monica here who has kindly agreed to tell us her story."

"Yo! Monica!" A wag called from amongst the audience, causing civilisation to break down once more in a rowdy chorus of guffaws. "Smoked any good cigars lately or 'ave yer been too busy down on yer knees!"

"Mon-i-ca." Jenny raised her voice, adding heavy emphasis to each syallable of the woman's name. "Monica from Hampstead!"

To, Jenny's relief, Monica from Hampstead proved to be a cut above. In speech closely approximating that of the Queen's English she calmly aired her sullied, but best-quality, Irish linen before the studio audience and viewing public.

"Well, my husband cheated on me. With his secretary! Terribly tacky, don't you know? Doing it with one's secretary! I mean, it's not as if the gal was even out of the top drawer." Wafting perfectly manicured fingernails beneath her nose as if detecting a bad smell, Monica bent the length of her aristocratic disdain on the rest of the audience, Jenny included. "Terribly bad form, what?"

"But you took him back?" Jenny prompted.

"Yah, I took him back, silly chappy! Well, it was out of his system, don't you know and *she* – Wendy or Tania or whatever the common little tramp's name was – got the sack!"

"And is there a happy ending? Have you managed to reconcile his past mistakes, salvage your marriage and carry on like nothing ever happened?" The woman's answer was important to her personally, Jenny realised, considering the parallels between their situations.

"Oh good God, yes! As long as I've got Matthews, all is well with the world!"

"Matthews?" Jenny queried. "Your husband?"

"No! My gardener! Whenever I remember Harold's little dalliance, off I go down to the rhubarb patch and get it all out of my system."

Jenny was all admiration. "How cathartic! By weeding, planting and sowing?"

"No! By getting my leg over!"

"Roll the commercials," Marcel ordered, almost wetting himself at Monica from Hampstead's transition into Lady Chatterley and the look of dismay still on Jenny's face as she brought the first half of the show to a close a short time later and stumbled towards him like a zombie on Mogadon.

"Well? Learn any salutary lessons, did we?" Quirking a sardonic eyebrow, he pushed a paper cup of coffee into her hand.

"Sadly no! Only that the art of forgiveness is a dying one." She glanced down at her prompt cards. "But let's not be too hasty. We've yet to meet Tricia from Acton and Carol from Walthamstow. Let's see what gems of wisdom they come up with, shall we? Besides, where there's life, there's hope!"

"Even if we *are* talking low life!" Disparaging, Marcel sniffed. "Anyway, it appears you haven't changed your mind – you're still considering giving Adam a second bite at the cherry?"

Jenny sipped the coffee, and made a face. "Certainly, I haven't changed my mind. I think he, at least, deserves a chance to put his side of the case, if only for David's sake, don't you?"

"Frankly no! I think he deserves to be boiled in oil then dismembered slowly whilst having his toenails eased from their cuticles by dint of electrified pliers."

"A case of 'do unto others'," Jenny scoffed, breaking off prematurely as a sudden scuffle at the door heralded the advent of a red-faced and very excited Poppy who had promised to meet up with her at the studios. Something to do with a fantastic new seaweed therapy in non-claustrophobic surroundings.

"Jen! Jen! Come quickly. You'll never guess what but – I've found her! Imagine! She was here all along and I *didn't* know. I didn't know. Can you believe that?"

Puzzled, Jenny looked around. "What . . . who's here? Who did you find? Calm down, Poppy! You're not making sense."

Poppy reached out, enveloped her in a bear hug. "Oh, but I am making sense. I'm making more sense that I ever have before because, *before* there *was* no sense in my life."

"I'm afraid you've lost me, Poppy!"

Poppy widened her eyes, at the same time beckoning towards the open doorway behind her. "No! I haven't lost you! I lost my Inner Child, remember? But now – now I've found her." Grabbing Jenny again, she quickstepped her up and down the studio floor. "I've found her! I've found her! Right here, Jenny! Can you believe it? Right here at In Kamera!"

Slow, slow, quick, quick, slow. Helpless as a leaf in the wind, Jenny spun about in Poppy's wake.

"But who? Where? Where is she?"

"Right there!" Grinding to a halt and with a flourish, Poppy pointed to where Attila stood framed in the open doorway, somehow managing to look incredibly coy for a woman whose complexion could best be described as hirsute.

"What?" Jenny felt her eyeballs spring from her sockets, bounce on the floor, then return as oversized, concentric-circling orbs to her head. "You mean The Hun?"

"Yes! And what a hon she is!"

Lord, Jenny thought, if ever there was an old adage borne out, it was the one about beauty being in the eye of the beholder!

"I . . . er . . . I don't quite know what to say." Jenny

dragged her heels, as determinedly Poppy hauled her towards *she that was lost but now is found*. "I mean I've only ever known her as Attil-er-as my make-up artist."

"Marigold! That's her name." Poppy shook her head from side to side. Wondrous! Reverent, almost. "A beautiful name for a beautiful Inner Child."

"Quite." Hoping her voice would not desert her and grinning inanely, Jenny allowed herself to be led the last few yards. "Hi-er-um Mari-Marigold. I-er-I had no idea you and Poppy meant so much to each other."

Leaning forward, the make-up artist ignored Jenny's outstretched hand, in favour of examining her cheekbones.

"That blusher's crap!" she said. "Wait till I catch up with that little toe-rag, Marcel, and I'll jam that blusher-brush right up his jacksey."

Well there was really no answer to that Jenny thought, so didn't attempt to make one. "Listen," she turned to Poppy. "I'm due back on air in about two seconds when Jane Seymour finishes bleating on about her 'little boxa hair-colour', so, what's the story about the new-fangled seaweed therapy thingummyjig? Are you still up for it?"

Poppy wrinkled her nose, tried for contrite but only succeeded in looking elated. "Do you mind if we don't. It's just that now I've come out of the closet without ever realising that I was in there in the first place, I'm kind of anxious to get stuck in. Would you be really disappointed?"

Jenny shook her head. "Nah, relieved to tell you the truth. The only therapy I'm interested in the moment is going home, having a long aromatic soak and a nice glass of wine, then going into the bedroom to find Brad Pitt already in residence and wearing nowt but a smile."

"Jenny!" Marcel called, pointedly tapping his watch. "Stop gassing and get back to your post. The count-down's about to start."

"Sieg heil!" Sketching a Nazi salute, Jenny clicked her heels. "Sorry, Pops, gotta go – the Führer is on the warpath."

"No problemo, catch you later? Come on, hon."

With a last venomous glance at Marcel, the make-up artist allowed herself to be led away but not before she'd given Marcel the 'finger'. "I'll show him warpath!" she hissed. "I'll show him bloody warpath!"

Giggling, Jenny scurried back across the studio, located her camera and, as the *Jenny Jumps In* signature tune died away, seamlessly introduced the second half of the show.

"Wotcha, Jenny!" Dispensing with the formality of an introduction, Tricia from Acton extended her arm, grabbed the mike and launched into her long-considered opinion on the opposite sex. "Men is all bastards. Men is a big waste of space. Men is shite!"

Retrieving the microphone, Jenny found it difficult to keep a straight face. "I take it you don't like men, Tricia."

Tricia nodded vigorously. "Too bleedin' right, Jenny, love. Men is wankers!"

"Where there's a willy, there's a wanker!" This astute observation came from Carol from Walthamstow who, like a bad case of thrush, had been itching to put in her two-ha'penny worth. "And my old man is the biggest bleedin' wanker of the lot."

"Because . . .?" Jenny encouraged.

"Because bleedin' nothin, he just bleedin is. That's all!"

"Was he unfaithful to you?" Hopefully, Jenny tried to steer the show back on track.

"No." Carol glared at her as if she were as thick as a bottled turd. "But, he pinched me bingo money, the bastard. Out of the tea caddy on top of the cupboard. 'Listen you,' I sez. 'I were savin' that ter to go on the razzle with me mates in Spain and now yer've gone and pissed it all up against the wall.'" Tears of rage in her eyes, she nodded earnestly at the camera. "I worked 'ard fer that, yer know. Double shifts dahn the laundrette, washing other folks' crappy Y-fronts and pissy sheets. Only thing that kept me goin' was the thoughts of me and me mates livin' it up fer two weeks in Ibeetha." Aggrieved, she looked around the audience. "I even went on the cabbage diet ter fit inter me bikini. Christ, I were fartin' that much it were like bleedin' Chernobyl all over again, only in Walthamstow."

A trooper to the last, Jenny, once more, tried to give the show direction. "So trust is definitely bust as far as you're concerned, Carol."

"Trust me arse! I never trusted 'im. How can yer trust a man who gets yer in the club when yer only fifteen, then steals yer friggin' bingo money?"

"See?" Vindicated, Tricia from Acton, grabbed back the camera's attention. "Isn't that what I'm telling yer. Men is all bastards. Men is a big waste of space. Men is shite!"

* * *

"So. I said I was going to phone you."

"Why?"

"Why?" Marcel almost shrieked down the handset. "Because Jenny's your daughter and a child is for life, not just for Christmas."

"Jenny is an adult, Marcel."

"Well, she's not acting like one. She's considering taking Adam back, you know. I mean it's ludicrous. The man's a shit! Someone should have flushed him down the bog years ago."

"Agreed. But let's face it, we did our best, pulled out all the stops. Now she's got to paddle her own canoe and make her own decisions." On the other end of the receiver, Jenny's mother gnawed at the remains of golden nail-polish applied in honour of an orgy the previous night and all but licked off by a fetishist with a love of all things varnish-based. "All we can do is hope that common sense prevails although, if it does, it'll be a first in Jenny's case. I mean, take when she was only six, for instance . . ."

Marcel interrupted. "Sorry! No time for reminiscences, time being of the essence. Oh! I wish Martyna were around to talk some sense into her but *she's* over in Dublin opening up a new Sole of Discretion and hoping to take advantage of the Celtic Tiger."

Jenny's mother's ears pricked up. "Oh? How original of Martyna! A dog is good enough for most of us."

"Don't be daft. That just the name they've given to the booming Irish economy. Nothing whatsoever to do with tigers really."

"Oh well, I wouldn't part with my Rover, anyway. Not for all the tigers in Ireland, though admittedly I might consider a trade-in for a big hairy husky. Only don't tell him I said that."

"Yes.Well, Huskies have pulling power! Everyone knows that! But, to get back to Jenny –"

"What about Poppy? Perhaps she could help."

Marcel sighed. "No, unfortunately. Poppy's discovered her lost Inner Child together with a potent dose of latent lesbian tendencies which she's nothing if not anxious to indulge. Uh huh. It's more than my life's worth to disturb Poppy at play."

Suitably impressed, Jenny's mother dislodged a bit of loose nail-varnish from between her front teeth, examined it speculatively then flicked it away into the atmosphere. "How gratifying. Perhaps she'd like to come along to Chaynes one evening and share her Inner Child with us."

Jesus, Marcel couldn't think of anything guaranteed more likely to empty the club. "Yeah, maybe. When eventually she comes up for air."

"So that leaves you with who? Just Denzil?"

"Yes. Denzil. Queen of the Treadmill, and I can't tell him. It would break his poor little homosexual heart.

He's got the hots for Jenny, you know, and lives in hopes, bless him, of waking up one morning and finding the sight of a naked Tom Cruise leaves him cold."

Gloria chuckled. "And what are the chances of that happening?"

"Oh, somewhere between zilch and zero."

"As high as that. Really!"

"Really! So, all things considered, it looks like Jenny is on her tod on this one."

"She'll be fine, Marcel. She's not the same hapless lump of female helplessness as several months ago, you know. Jenny's grown and matured. She's got self-esteem now. She's a big player in the cut-throat world of television. You don't survive amongst sharks unless you've *got* big teeth and Jenny's got big teeth." She sniffed loudly. "Although, God knows I spent a fortune on orthodontists when she was young. Still, in the end, the viciousness of her overbite defeated us!"

Taking heart from her fervour, Marcel inclined his head. "I suppose you're right. I should have more faith really. I mean, Jenny's got balls. She'll do the right thing, won't she?"

"I haven't a doubt about it. But good things are subjective, aren't they? What's good for one might kill another."

Optimism deserting him like a rat off a sinking ship, Marcel snorted down the phone, "Gee, thanks a lot. That's gone and made me feel a whole lot better!"

Chapter Thirty-six

Her breasts were neither big nor were they pendulous, Jenny noted, surveying her naked figure in front of the full-length bedroom mirror. They still had a slight droop, mind you, and despite light years spent on the pec-dec they'd never see pert again but, at least, they were portable. With the click of a clasp they could be easily secreted inside Wonderbras and Balconettes, bodies and bodices and in her more daring moods, left free to jiggle beneath her FCUK-You tee shirt.

The rest of her, as it happened, was A-okay too. Her stomach was toned and, were it not for the crisscross of stretchmarks traversing her creamy skin, reminiscent of something out of *Baywatch*. Her inner thighs, when her knees were together, formed a perfect oval for which read thin with space between them and, other than a certain crêpiness about the shoulders, her upper arms were a miracle of tautness and could have passed for those of a teenager. Oh all right! Be picky then! A thirty-year-old! In the space of a few short months Jenny's desirability factor had rocketed from bargain basement straight into the higher echelons of this year's most desirable *must haves*. So much so that she found herself fielding off the amorous approaches of an abundance of eligible and handsome men. And, let's be honest about this, some not so eligible. Nor handsome! Downright ugly in fact! Still, since her brief and short-lived dalliance with the learned and most definitely handsome Matt, and notwithstanding persistent badgering, most especially from her mother and Poppy, Jenny had taken herself firmly off the singles market.

"Because I need to sort my head out and concentrate on my career," she'd told them, which sounded pretty kosher. Career! Boy, that was a turn-up for the books. To the old fat 'before' Jenny, career was something people did, all over the stage, on *Springer*. And, generally, the more careering the better the show!

Nonetheless, her career *did* go from strength to strength, which strengthening process involved being interviewed by the press in general, all the women's mags and guesting on sundry TV shows including *Good Morning with Richard and Judy* and to her mother's rapture, *Kilroy*. The pinnacle of her daughter's career, as far as that good woman was concerned! And, far from feeling neglected as Jenny had feared, David found the whole process immensely exciting, displaying an enterprising and entrepreneurial streak by flogging signed photos of her to his schoolmates' parents. More echoes of Adam!

Luckily though, he'd balked at a suggestion made by one of the less scrupulous members of the tabloid press that he try and 'snap her in the nude' or even better 'making out' with somebody, and this despite being offered massive and ever-increasing cash incentives. More than enough for a brand-new, multi media computer with intel pentium processor, CD Rom and DVD drive. *And* a web-cam! *And* a CD writer. *And* a six-bedroom house in St John's Wood with security gates and a Rottweiler for added insurance. *And* at that point he had stopped dreaming of what might have been, and got on with the less profitable, but morally superior business of shifting the signed photographs of his mother. To his credit he'd even managed to offload one on his father who promptly hung it on the wall of the swish warehouse-conversion he was renting, following up the exercise with much regretful shakings of the head and an expression that said 'if only'. *'If only!'*

"In Docklands, of course," Jenny had told Poppy with heavy emphasis. "Trendy, up-and-coming, exactly the right spot for an aging, single-again philanderer to make his lair. All zebra-skin settees, no doubt, recessed lights and a waterbed!"

And to David, trying hard to sound unconcerned. "I expect he goes out on the trowel all weekend leaving you in the care of a baby-sitter?"

David had snorted at that one. "Mum, I'm too old for a baby-sitter. Besides, Dad never goes any place without me and if what you're really trying to find out is whether he's got another woman, then the answer is no. No, he hasn't! All he ever does is talk about you and what a dickhead he's been and how he wishes things could be different and I don't mind telling you that it's all becoming a bit boring."

Sniffing, Jenny continued signing the large pile of photographs piled up on one side of her for despatching to various fan clubs around the country and abroad. On the other side rested an equally large pile of fan mail, which, in one of her more philanthropic moods, admittedly fuelled by a Breezer too many, Jenny had vowed to answer in person. As her fingers showed definite signs of developing RSI, it was a promise she was rapidly coming to regret.

"I'm not in the least bit bothered. Your father could have ten women on the go all at one time and it wouldn't take a feather out of me. He's a free agent now, you know. Well, more or less, anyway. What he does or doesn't do is absolutely one hundred per cent none of my business."

"So why are you always asking then?" David looked miffed. "And he's the same, always asking what you're doing and if you're seeing anybody and if you're happy. I don't know why you just don't get back together and then you can ask each other."

Jenny started guiltily. "Is that what you want, David? Your father and me to get back together? For us to be a family again?"

David shrugged. "Well, isn't that what *you* want? And Dad! At least that's what it sounds like to me. I don't know what's stopping you. I mean it doesn't take a genius to figure out that neither one of you is Mr Happy."

Jenny's head rocked. "Excuse *me!* Just what makes you think I'm not happy? I'm perfectly happy, thank you very much. For your information, Smart Alec, I can't remember a time when I felt more blissful, tranquil and content. Mellow, even!"

Ducking away in anticipation of getting his ear clipped, her son grinned. "So why have you taken to scoffing my Mars bars, then? You only ever do that if you have PMT or are feeling miserable. And even I know you don't get PMT all month long."

Not a little rattled, and grateful for the excuse to stretch her weary limbs, Jenny rose and shooed him out the door. "All right, Sherlock, do one! In my day, kids didn't know about things like that, much less discuss them."

"Well, kids today are more advanced." Completely unfazed, David halted at a safe distance. "And right now I'm boning up on the menopause so I can be prepared for next year, when it happens to you."

"Next year?" In one fluid moment, Jenny stooped down, removed her shoe and brandished it threateningly. "Listen, squirt, there's a good ten years between me and the menopause. Hopefully anyway! Now clear off to Simon's before I really lose my temper and murder you."

Jokingly, David made placatory movements with his hands. "Okay, okay. Calm down, woman. Only I can't help wondering why, if there's ten years between you and the menopause, you're having a hot flush. Like now!"

Not bothering to stick around for the reply, he skittered off up the garden path, leaving his mother to blaspheme at the cat who, until she'd come out and upset the equilibrium, had been quite innocently stalking a bird. With a narrowing of amber eyes, it hissed displeasure, shooting out a sharpened claw and threatening her ankle in much the same way as she'd threatened David with her shoe. Big mistake! Had its intellect not been severely damaged as a result of having been locked in the washing machine at one point in its miserable life, it would, presumably, have remembered to engage brain before setting claw in motion. As things stood, however, it ended up wearing the footprint of Jenny's shoe on its backside and perilously damn close to losing the last of its nine lives. Retrieving her shoe and with a last, for good measure, oath at the cat, Jenny retreated back to the mound of photos and letters on the table inside.

David was right about one thing. She *was* back on the Mars bars again. Exactly what the significance of that was, though, she couldn't be sure, except that it had nothing whatsoever to do with Adam. At least, she didn't think it did! With a sigh, Jenny finished off the pile of photographs, turning immediately to the letters. Picking up the first one she slit the envelope with the tip of her ballpoint pen.

"*Dear, Jenny,' she read, "I would be grateful if you could please send me a pair of your used panties . . .*"

* * *

With an effort Jenny heaved her mind back to the present and continued titivating herself before the mirror.

"So, what do you think? Not bad for forty, eh?"

Curling its lip, her reflection looked her up and down, much as a butcher would size up a prime carcass, before delivering its considered opinion. "Put it to you like this, if I was drunk and it was dark, you might just pass, although you still need to work on the cellulite. If you ask me your bum looks like cottage cheese, all lumps and bumps and a most unattractive shade of white."

"I didn't ask you. Well, all right, I did, but there's no need to be so brutally honest."

"Honesty is the best policy." Her reflection curled its lip. "You might try it yourself some time."

"And what's that supposed to mean?" With a last admiring hoist of her breasts, Jenny rummaged amongst the mound of scanties on the bed behind her and extracted a black satin Wonderbra.

"You know precisely what it's supposed to mean. It's this Adam business. You're not being honest about it. All this crap about it being for *David's* sake. What a pile of shite! David isn't the least bit bothered. Why should he be? After all, he's got two homes, two mountain bikes, two Playstations, parents prepared to indulge his every whim in order to prove that *they're* the good guy. In other words, pants! *You* want him back because you're too much of a wuss to imagine life without him."

Turning the bra back to front, Jenny slotted the hooks

and eyes into place, before sliding it round front again and slipping her arms through the straps. She reached for a pair of panties, black satin to match the bra.

"Not true! What do *I* need *him* for? I'm a woman of substance now, financially independent, with a glittering career and any number of men wanting to wine and dine me. No, my intentions are purely altruistic. I want what's best for my son and if that means giving his bastard of a father a second chance, then the least I can do is consider it."

Her reflection reached down, scratched its crotch, tucked a stray pubic hair beneath her knicker-line. "Tell it to my fanny! You've already made up your mind, haven't you. Else why all the seduction gear? I mean, black satin? So obvious! So Linda Lovelace! I expect there's a suspender belt lurking somewhere in the midst of that pile on the bed."

"And what if there is? It's a myth that women only wear sexy underwear to titillate men. Not at all! They wear it to make themselves feel good and to make other women jealous in communal changing-rooms."

"So how come white cotton Sloggis are good enough for you every other day?"

"Because tonight I feel like dressing up. Okay? It's called fancying a change."

"It's called fooling yourself!" Her alter ego pulled no punches. "And the real reason is because tonight you're meeting *him* and, even if you won't admit it, subconsciously you're hoping all paths will eventually lead to nookie and from thence to reconciliation and Happy Ever After Land."

"Rubbish! I'm meeting Adam purely to give him the chance to put his side of the story. It's as much as I gave Mounty, after all."

"Then why are you meeting him in Spend a Penne? Your old stomping ground? Filled with the heady smells of cooking pasta, garlic and old memories." Truculent, it leaned a little closer. "I mean, why not Victoria Station or The Hawk & Spit, somewhere neutral. Somewhere where the past can't influence your decision?"

Jenny shrugged. "Because it's convenient and we both like the food."

"So who booked it, anyway? Adam?"

"And what if he did?"

"It's a psychology thing! He knows you'll be more vulnerable there, more susceptible to his smarm and charm."

"Get thee behind me, Freud!" Grabbing a black dress from the wardrobe, Jenny held it up against herself, thought better and replaced it with a red.

"The Lady in Red," her reflection scoffed. "Of course *he* was having it away too. That singer bloke!"

"Oh, mind your own business. Anyway, I'm wearing my blue Donatella Versace."

"You *are* my business," the mirror reminded her, "and yeah, I won't quibble with the blue. The blue's good, matches your eyes. But, to get back to Adam. You know things could never be the same again."

"Okay," Jenny conceded that particular point. "Maybe not the same but that doesn't mean they couldn't be better."

"Or worse! Imagine every time things started to get a bit heated in the old passion department, you'd constantly be wondering if he did the same thing with her. I mean you've already had experience of that. Remember the tongue thing? It's human nature, isn't it? It seems to me that the only way to avoid that particular bugbear is to spend the rest of your lives as missionaries. B-o-r-ing!"

Jenny snorted, stepping into the blue silk designer sheath and almost dislocating her shoulder in an effort to reach behind and do up the zip. "Ouch! Well, you're jumping the gun a bit, aren't you? I haven't even seen him yet and already you've got us ripping the clothes off each other and rutting like stallions."

"Just don't say I didn't warn you. That's all."

Jenny quirked a sarcastic eyebrow. "Oh well, I won't be able to say that, will I? Talk about the voice of doom." Bending down, she slipped on a pair of navy patent court shoes, put the finishing touches to her make-up, sprayed a cloud of Chanel No. 5 into the air and walked through the mist, which the beauty consultant at Harvey Nicks had assured her was the correct way to apply perfume. A final check in her evening bag for lipstick, Gold Spot, credit cards and keys and she was ready to face her nemesis.

"*Hasta la vista*, baby!" she called, switching off the

light, taking the stairs two at a time and wondering what her fan club would have to say if they knew about the marathon conversations she had with her reflection. Probably think she was mad but so what? Obviously, judging from the kind of letters she got in her mailbag, it was six of one and half a dozen of the other. Besides, there was method in her particular brand of madness. With her reflection playing devil's advocate she could as near as dammit get two different perspectives on any situation. A way of covering all the angles, if you liked. And surprisingly often it worked and she would find herself more confident about making a certain decision or going down a certain path. But tonight was different! When it came to Adam, she had to admit, she still didn't know her ass from her elbow!

As it was a clear night, with a full moon, the kind of moon romantic writers often prefaced with the word 'gallows', Jenny decided to leave the car behind and walk. A slight frost in the air turned her breath to a twenty-a-day smoker's, and experimentally pursing her lips in a way she'd seen Mounty do, she attempted to blow a smoke-ring. It didn't work. Behind her, the illuminated clock on the spire of St Nicholas lied that it was eight-thirty pm. It was a lie it had told every day for the past five years and which it would continue to tell until such time as the vicar managed to raise enough funds to have the hands unjammed. Until then, those who did not run to wristwatches and clocks relied on the verger or somebody trotting out and tolling the bells every hour, on the hour.

Glancing at her own wristwatch, Jenny saw that it was actually nine o'clock, only half an hour to go before she met Adam. Ridiculously, there were butterflies in her tummy. Ridiculous because forty-year-old women don't get butterflies! But they were there all right, fluttering and diving by turns, till like a teenage girl after a designer lager too many, she felt like opening her mouth and puking her guts up all over the pavement. Taking a steadying breath, Jenny focussed on the lights of the piazza ahead, immediately wishing she hadn't, as strung out from lamppost to lamppost, they conjured up visions of other identical, frosty nights, when hand in hand and cocooned in togetherness, she and Adam had strolled home unaware of the storm clouds gathering on the not-so-distant horizon. Drawing abreast of the Hawk & Spit, it was the work of a moment to make a sharp left, push through the doors and, almost sprinting to the bar, order a double G & T. Sod the ice and a slice!

Chapter Thirty-seven

"Senora! Senora Treigh! Bella Senora Treigh! How 'appy I am to see you!" Smiling at the waiter's effusiveness, and reeking of gin and tonic, Jenny, having managed to tear herself away from the bar with only ten minutes to spare, followed his corpulent body to the corner table where Adam was already seated. Damn! That was a bit of a bummer considering how she'd hoped to upgrade the Dutch levels a little further before having to face him. Added to that, she always felt that the person already in possession of the table had more of an advantage. Actually, she didn't feel any such thing. In fact, that was a phrase she'd read somewhere, probably in an M& B book. Still there was no denying it sounded good and, as Adam measuredly eyed her up and down, as, like a gauche schoolgirl, she stood waiting for Gianni to pull her chair out, she couldn't help feeling that there might be more than just a grain of truth in it.

"Thank you, Gianni. It's good to see you too." With a nod to Adam, and hoping he didn't detect the shake in her voice, she promptly sat down, painfully scraping the skin off her knee on the edge of the table as she did so.

"You will have your usual, senora. No?"

"Yes, yes. The usual will be fine." The usual! How normal that sounded. Pâté, spaghetti bolognese, ordinary, un-extraordinary dishes! As if nothing had changed! As if there had been no interlude where her husband had committed adultery with her best friend. As if everything was still the same. But it *wasn't* the same. The man sitting across from her had changed everything. Waiting till Gianni had taken himself off in a waft of garlic and unwashed apron, Jenny picked up the glass of Chianti already awaiting her and raised it to her lips.

"Salute!"

Pulled up short, Jenny regarded her soon-to-be-ex husband with surprise. "*Salute*? What do you mean '*Salute*'? What have you got to be so *Salute* about?" Oh, dear, she hadn't meant to go on the attack so soon, hadn't meant to go on the attack at all. No, the plan had been to stay cool, sophisticated, devil-may-care, to be indifferent and as different from the Jenny of old as was humanly possible. To show him the polished diamond, hewn from the uncut stone. The finished product! To fill him with regrets, in other words. For disrespecting her! For cheating on her! With her best friend! The bastard!

"Christ!" Adam rolled his eyes. "It just means 'cheers' in Italian, Jenny. Nothing to get your knickers in a twist over."

Jenny's eyes shot sparks. "What do you think I am?

Ignorant? I know full well what it means. I just don't think it's appropriate that's all. I mean, under the circumstances. I mean what's to cheer about?"

Adam quirked an eyebrow. Strange, it seemed to be connected via invisible wire to the butterflies in her stomach, which immediately went into overdrive.

"Look, I thought this was going to be a civilised meeting and that you'd brought me here to discuss finalising the divorce and contact arrangements for David."

"I brought *you* here?" Jenny's head shot forward, her chin belligerently invading his personal space. "I didn't bring *you* here! *You* wanted to come *here*. It's a psychology thing. My mirror told me."

Completely ignoring the reference to her mirror, with which fixation Adam was very familiar, he nodded reasonably. "Okay. You're right. I wanted to come here and you didn't object. Now, do you think we can start again?"

"Why not?" Jenny could be reasonable too. Raising her glass, she pushed the boat out. *"Salute!"*

"Salute!" Touching his glass to hers, Adam smiled and, like a bolt from the blue, it happened again; that old sinking feeling, that sudden lurch in the pit of her stomach that made her feel like her uterus had prolapsed straight onto the floor. Any moment now and she'd start trying to absorb him through her pores. Fortunately, before she could embark upon such process, Gianni returned with the starters – pâté and toast for her, king prawns in coriander and lime for him.

"I made a bet with myself," Adam said, with a half-smile bordering on satisfaction, as she sliced a corner off the pâté and spread it on her bread. "That you'd choose either the pâté or the prawn cocktail."

"Really?" Jenny's voice was dry. "Well, congratulations! You've just won your bet, although by a process of hedging." Cynically she took a bite, heedless of the crumbs collecting on the bosom of her blue Donatella Versace. "Because it was bound to be one or the other, wasn't it Adam? I mean, good old predictable Jenny. Or, should I say boring old predictable Jenny!"

Biting into a prawn, Adam refused to rise to her bait. "You know very well that's not what I meant." His tongue darted out, licked a drop of lime and coriander juice from the side of his mouth, the same tongue that did *things* with other women. Reminded, Jenny knew her pores were safe for the moment. "There's a comfort in familiar things, a feeling of well-being, rather like slipping one's feet into a tatty old pair of carpet slippers."

Jesus, she sincerely hoped that wasn't supposed to be a compliment because, if it was, the man was losing his touch. Much more of those and he'd never get another woman, no matter what he did with his tongue.

"Right! Now that we've established that I'm both predictable and reminiscent of a pair of holey slippers, do you think we can get on with the business in hand?" Oh no! Jenny gave an internal grimace. He'd got that hangdog look on his face again, the hurt puppy look. It made her feel bad, but heck, in the grand scheme of things, him sleeping with Mounty, made her feel a whole lot worse.

"Okay." He met her rebuff with a least the semblance of dignity. "Only don't let's fight over stupid things, like who gets to keep the cat."

"Wouldn't dream of it." Jenny laid her knife across her plate and pushed it away from her. "*You* can have the cat!"

"Pass!" Adam leaned back as Gianni removed the starter dishes and replaced them with a large dish of spaghetti with a separate serving of bolognese sauce. No danger of them sharing a single strand tonight, with the strand getting shorter and shorter till their lips met in the middle and . . . Determinedly she tore her thoughts away.

"Fine! I'll keep the cat if it's so repugnant to you. What *do* you want? Did you make a list?"

Adam shook his head. "No! No list. You can have everything except . . ."

"Except?" Here it came, the textbook unreasonable demand. All the self-help divorce books had warned her of the likelihood of receiving at least one.

Looking a little shamefaced, Adam buried his face behind a large forkful of spaghetti, lending more than a little weight to her suspicion. "Except my 70s gear."

His 70s gear! No! No! He couldn't have that. Panic-stricken, Jenny drained her wine glass. "No way!" she said, her lips both sulky and wine-stained. "It's communal property."

"No, it's not." Torn between amusement and

bewilderment, Adam refilled her glass. "How could my flares and kipper ties be communal property, for Heaven's sakes. It's not as though *you* ever wore them." True! She hadn't worn them, but *he* had! When he was young Adam, Deep Purple-loving Adam, Jenny-obsessed Adam. There were precious memories invested in those trousers. Precious hopes and psychedelic dreams! Young, acned dreams, raw, unformed but passionate, the precursors to the happiest time of her life. Beady-eyed, Jenny regarded him steadily over the rim of her wine glass.

"Communal property!" she said again in her best we-will-not-be-moved voice.

Adam shrugged, still reasonable. "Okay. Well, just my lime-green, frilly shirt then! Surely there can be no objection to that?" No! No! No! Not the lime-green frilly shirt! He'd been wearing that the first time he'd kissed her. She remembered it clearly, the slightly scratchy texture of the bri-nylon material as she rested her hands on his shoulders, a loose thread on the fall of frills that caught against her nostril and made her sneeze, the overpowering shout of the Brut aftershave he'd all but bathed in, in an effort to impress her. And then, like a benediction, that first kiss! The unforgettable tang of his lips, a mixture of Colgate, lager and inexperience!

"No!"

"No?"

"No! Anything but the 70s gear."

"Why?" There was no anger in his voice, only puzzlement.

"Because."

Adam waited patiently for her explanation. "Because?" he prompted gently some minutes later when it became apparent that she had no intention of giving one.

"Because, if you have to ask that question you don't deserve them! That's why!" Pettishly, Jenny dug her fork into the mound of pasta on her plate, twisting it round and round, loading and reloading till she couldn't possibly fit it all in her mouth. "I'll tell you what, you can have the cat!"

"I don't *want* the sodding cat! I want my shirt! Still, if you're determined to be unreasonable, perhaps we can move on to discussing David."

"What about him?" Deliberately obtuse, which was the only way she could stop herself from bursting into tears, Jenny abandoned all pretence at eating her food and pushed it away. "You see him regularly, don't you? I mean I haven't denied you contact, have I?"

Adam shook his head. "No. But these things really ought to be formalised – leaves less room for misunderstandings to occur."

"And perish the thought that there might be misunderstandings." Despite herself, all the bitterness and hurt of the past few months welled up like a canker inside her, forcing its way out into the open, taking form and hanging like steam over the pair of them. "Why did you do it, Adam?" There! The question was out. Stark and unadorned! The real reason she had agreed to meet him even if she hadn't dared to admit it.

Worthy of an honest answer! "Of all the women in all the world, why, Mounty? Why my best friend?"

Taken by surprise, Adam tried for flippant. "Would you believe me if I told you it was because I had a bad back and *she* had very high shoes and a knack for balancing?"

Incredulous, Jenny leaned across and searched his eyes, for some sign, any sign of repentance. So far, there wasn't any, just her own image staring back like a rabbit paralyzed in the glare of an oncoming HGV. She had to try though, if only for her own peace of mind, to try and understand – for closure, as she had already told Mounty.

"Please, Adam. I think, at least, you owe me some sort of an explanation. I mean, I really don't feel I can go through life not knowing." Candidly, she went for broke. "Was I so very unattractive? Is that what it was? And you found me repulsive, a complete turn-off, a big waste of space with the emphasis on the big! Oh, come on, Adam! It's not as though anything you say can hurt me any more than I've already been hurt. Help me understand, please! I need to know!" There was a struggle going on behind his eyes, two combatants, the Good Angel and the Bad Angel. The Good Angel won. Frankly, he held her gaze.

"Look, it would be easy for me to pass the buck, to put all the onus on you, to blame your size, your snoring, your obsession with *Jerry Springer*, but quite simply, it wouldn't be true. Neither would it be true to put all the blame on Mounty, the scarlet woman of the piece. You've heard the saying, a standing prick has no conscience." Wryly curling his lip, he nodded towards his lap. "May I refer you to exhibit number one, the deadly weapon in question!"

Jenny's lip trembled. "But it wasn't just the once, Adam. It wasn't just one mad act of uncontrollable passion. I might have understood that but you – you went back to the trough again and again." Picking up her napkin, Jenny worried the linen, scrunching it between her fingers in a way that would have brought tears to many a grown man's eyes. "Was the sex so very much better with her?"

Adam shook his head. "Not better. Just different. A novelty, really. I never stopped loving you, not even for a minute. Not even when your bottom was size twenty and your ankles boiled over the sides of your shoes." Reaching inside his pocket he drew out a half-Corona, clipped off the end and lit it. There was a slight tremble in his fingers. "Besides, I thought you were indifferent to me."

"How? How did you think I was indifferent to you?" The words, despite the fact that she knew he was right, were a spray of bullets fired from between murderous lips. But, hey, get real, in some situations you were allowed to be unreasonable, and finding yourself being berated by an adulterous husband was one of them! "What possible reason could you have to think I was indifferent to you?"

A dangerous glint entered Adam's own eyes. "Maybe the fact that you never went anywhere with me any more. The fact that you always had your head stuck in the TV gawking at some chat show or other which, in all fairness, seems to have paid off for you now. The fact that between you and Mounty, then you and Poppy, not to mention your old bat of a mother and that thing she drags around on a leash, *I* rarely got so much as a look in. Neither did David, come to that. It wouldn't surprise me if one day he turns into an axe murderer of something of the kind. And it'll be all your fault!"

So much for not attributing blame! Jenny hung her head, then flung it back up again, a blazing look in her eye, as another thought suddenly struck her. "And what about Denzil, you homophobic bastard? What about your little blackmail scam, eh?" A harder note entered her voice. That was a good thing. It kept the tears at bay a little longer. "I mean what did he ever do to you apart from teaching you how to fence. Mind you, you learned to duck and dive all by your little lonesome, didn't you?"

Adam held his hands up, cigar smoke scrawling his confession in the air. "I'm not proud of that although, strictly speaking, it was Mounty who put the frighteners on him. The best I can do is to tell you I went along with it out of fear, and credit where it's due, I did apologise as soon as the chance arose."

"Please do not ask for credit, as a smack in the mouth often offends," Jenny quipped dryly, quoting from a sign pasted to the cash register in her local corner shop. "And as for fear? Fear, my Aunt Fanny's bloomers!"

Adam strove for dignity. "Yes, Jenny, fear! Fear of you finding out. Fear of losing you!"

406

"Fear that I'd put an end to your little shenanigans, you mean."

"No, not that. Actually, I'd put an end to that before ever you found out."

"But you took her to Italy, bought her Cerutti, no doubt, and Italian underwear."

To her surprise, the man had the grace if not exactly to blush, at least to flush rosily in the region of his Adam's apple. "I bought *you* a pepper-grinder."

"Yes, you did." Reminded, Jenny found herself eyeing her discarded knife with more than just culinary interest. "In fact, I was going to have one of those tee shirts made up. You know the ones. Big, black writing across the chest! My Husband Went to Italy and All I Got was this Lousy Pepper-grinder!"

"Actually, I didn't invite her. She wangled it. It was a complete shock, if you must know, to find her on the same plane."

Taking time out, on Gianni's tentative approach, to order a cappuccino, whilst her husband opted for a brandy, Jenny returned fresh to the fray.

"Poor you! And I suppose you consoled yourself by shagging her every chance you got."

"It wasn't like that."

"Oh really? You do surprise me! What was it like then?"

Swilling his brandy around in its glass, Adam gazed into the amber liquid like Mystic Meg into her crystal ball, leaving a cynical Jenny to wonder if maybe she shouldn't call for a suspension of hostilities whilst she got him to call out the winning lottery numbers,

"Look, Jenny. This isn't getting us anywhere. What's the good of opening old wounds! You want a divorce and I respect your wishes. I've given you grounds, I know, but I also want you to know this." Stubbing out his half-smoked cigar, he bent forward, earnestly imprisoned her fingers in his own. "I love you. Size ten or size twenty, TV junkie or successful chat-show hostess, I love you in all your guises. I've always loved you, right from the very first moment I saw you, bopping away in the nightclub, ABBA's very own Dancing Queen. Appalling Farrah Fawcett hairdo notwithstanding!" He cleared his throat and, as she gently disengaged her fingers, picked up and studied, without really seeing, his reflection in the back of a dessert spoon. "Would you believe me if I told you that one night I even sneaked into your bedroom and stood there watching you while you slept. You were so beautiful, like a modern-day Sleeping Beauty." His eyes lifted, frank, truthful. "I simply had to kiss you."

"Don't!" Jenny felt a very big lump build in her throat, threaten to choke her. "Oh, don't!" Knocking over her chair, she leapt up and bolted for the loo, much to the consternation of a number of diners who couldn't help wondering what on earth had happened to reduce the famous chat-show hostess to floods of tears and which sent at least one of them scurrying off in search of a telephone and a tabloid newspaper. Luckily the Ladies was empty. Staggering over to the washbasin, Jenny turned on the cold tap, dashed the water against her face, uncaring that her flawless make-up by Elizabeth Arden was disappearing down the plug-hole faster than a robotic hare on a greyhound track. In the fly-speckled mirror above the sink, her reflection waited patiently, head bent in sympathy with hers, mascara staining its cheeks.

"Was it worth it then?" it asked as eventually she resurfaced. "All the black satin? The suspenders cutting into your backside? The fifty quid's worth of Chanel misting your bedroom carpet. Tell me, was it all worth it?" Spreading her hands, she appealed to herself. "Sleeping Beauty, my foot! I mean, do I look like I came over on the last banana boat? Despite his fine talk, there isn't really an ounce of remorse in the whole of his handsome, lithe (paunch excepted), heavenly example of a masculine body! The truth is he doesn't *really* think he's done anything wrong. He's paying lip-service, that's all. It's just as well your divorce is going through because he'd never make you happy, you know. You'd never be able to trust him again. Any time he was late home from work, you'd always be wondering where he was. Who he was with! *And* you don't need me to tell you that if he wants you back, it's only because you're *someone* now! You can *do* things for him. Introduce him to bigwigs. Advance his career!" Taking a deep breath, her reflection gave a watery smile. "Now, on with some fresh slap and go back out there with your head held high because you're not just Jenny Treigh any more, Adam's overweight failure of a wife, are you? No!

You're *Jenny Jumps In*, rich, popular, desirable and successful, with the world at your feet."

Much to her surprise, Jenny managed a feeble grin. "I don't know so much about the world being at my feet but I've only got to say the word and Marcel will be there in a flash."

"That's the Dunkirk spirit!" her reflection approved. "Down with the Nazis!"

"Are you all right!" Eyeing her with concern upon her return, Adam half-rose from the table.

Jenny waved him back down. "Never better! It was just the cappuccino. Don't you remember, Adam, cappuccino depresses me? Does something to my temporal lobe. One cappuccino and I'm morose, two and I'm tying the noose, three – I'm swinging from it." She was bullshitting. He knew she was bullshitting.

"Whatever you say." His face was pale she noticed, and there were little spots of perspiration beading each side of his nose. Clearing his throat, he absent-mindedly pushed a stray squashed-ant lump of bolognese about on the tablecloth in a kind of culinary version of Subbuteo. "So where do we go from here? I mean do you *really* want to carry on with this divorce business?" He scored an own-goal against the salt cellar. "I know I don't and I know there's nothing David would like better than to have his parents back together again."

"Did *he* tell you that?"

Adam shook his head. "He's a *teenager*, Jenny! Teenagers don't tell you anything. I just know how I felt, at fourteen, when my own parents split up. Honestly! I thought my world had ended."

"Is that right?" Jenny snapped. "Well, perhaps you should have thought of the effect it might have had on your own son, before *you* started playing fast and loose with Mounty!" Running a finger around the inside of her cup, she collected what remained of the froth from her cappuccino, angrily popping it into her mouth, daring him to mention nooses. "Besides, David's quite happy. He's got two homes, two Playstations, two bicycles, two of everything –"

Adam cut her off. "Yes, but he can only live in one home at a time, play on one Playstation at a time, ride one bike at a time. What I'm saying is, he doesn't need *two* of everything. What he does need though is *two* parents, living together under *one* roof."

Jenny shook her head so hard from side to side that her brain rattled. "No! You're not going to blackmail me with David, tug at my maternal heartstrings. Try another technique, Adam, because that one won't work!" But despite the fury of her actions there was an uncertainty in her voice, the merest tremble, enough for the man sitting opposite to immediately hone in on.

"Look, Jen. I'm truly sorry for cheating on you. I'd do anything to turn the clock back." He reached for her hand and, as she flinched backwards, hesitated a moment before withdrawing his own. "Besides, surely every horse is entitled to just one stumble at the fence?" And with that last sentence, Adam, who quite unbeknownst to himself had started to make good inroads, demolished them all in one fell swoop.

He was quoting Mounty! The bastard! Not content with screwing her, he was now quoting her. To her! Jenny, his wife! Oh she remembered that phrase all right! Mounty, sweetly venomous, in yet another restaurant, surrounded by the wreckage of her best friend's life, daring to give her advice.

'. . . *just you remember that every horse is entitled to one stumble at the fence and if you can't see that, then you deserve to lose Adam. For good!*'

Heck, she'd even borrowed it herself – used it on her show one morning. Biting her lip, Jenny rose to her feet, but not before flinging a handful of bills into the middle of the table. She wouldn't give him the satisfaction of taking *anything* from him! Not even a half-eaten plate of spaghetti bolognese!

"I don't think there's any more to be said, Adam." Thrusting her arms into the sleeves of her coat which, courtesy of Gianni, had appeared as if by magic, she turned and strode towards the door, not daring to look back, knowing that if she did, she was as good as lost.

"*Mamma mia!*" Opening the door for her, Gianni, slowly shook his head from side to side. "*Mamma mia*". But tonight, imbued as they were with sadness, there was nothing funny about the words, nothing to laugh at. And stepping out into the frosty night, Jenny found it hard to see the stars studding the clear sky, for the tears clouding her eyes.

Chapter Thirty-eight

"It's only a piece of paper. Stop looking at it like it's going to explode and blow your head off."

Shakily, Jenny folded the document she'd been holding back into its envelope and turned tear-filled eyes to her mother. "It's *not* just a piece of paper though, is it. It's the tangible proof that my marriage has ended. It's official. In the eyes of the world Adam and I are no longer a couple."

"Old news!" Gloria sniffed. "It's not as if you just split up yesterday. Most people have probably forgotten you were ever a couple in the first place. Your decree absolute is not a death certificate, Jenny, more like the passport to freedom. You are now officially young, free and single. So cast off the mourning, shove on your red shoes and get partying."

"Not so young and I don't feel like partying. I feel like crying. And before you tell me what a bastard Adam is and how much better off I am without him, I *know* all that but I just can't help wishing things were different. I saw us growing old together, you see. Me, with a blue rinse, him with an irritable prostate, but together, drinking Horlicks and searching our grandchildren's faces for family resemblances and signs of delinquency and drug abuse."

"Yeah, yeah, Darby and Joan swinging on the front porch at night like *The Waltons*. Get a grip, Jenny. What's done is done. The writing is on the divorce settlement and now you've got to write a new script which, when you think about it, is pretty marvellous. I mean you get to reinvent yourself, cast yourself as anything. Have a new, starring role in your life. Honestly, it makes me feel quite envious."

A tear rolling down her nose, Jenny looked sceptical. "Oh yeah, like *you're* in a real hurry to off-load Rover and strike out into the sunset all on your lonesome?"

"It's different for me. I'm already in God's waiting-room, on the countdown to my own little six by four allotment as it were but you're still in the prime of life. You can move mountains, if only you put your mind to it."

Seeing that her nose had begun to run, Jenny wiped it on the back of her sleeve, gulping the residue deep into the back of her throat with a sound that turned her mother's stomach inside out. "Easier said than done. Besides, I don't want to move mountains, I want to turn the clock back."

Unsympathetically, Gloria shoved a mug of tea across the table towards her. "Well, you can't. All you can do is make better use of your time from now on, and if I were you, I'd make a start by spending an hour or two with that gorgeous Matt Fitzpatrick writer bloke you were dating not all that long ago."

Stirring the hot brown liquid in her cup, Jenny whipped up a tiny froth in the middle that spun hypnotically round and round before breaking up and dispersing in a myriad of tiny, beige bubbles. "I can't. I told him I didn't want to see him any more."

"So?" Her mother looked amazed that anyone might let a tiny little consideration like that stop them. "Ring him up and say you've changed your mind. It is the twenty-first century, you know. You *are* allowed to make the first move in this day and age."

Jenny looked depressed. "I can't, even if I wanted to. I threw away his number and I've no idea where he lives."

"Pity!" Her mother took a thoughtful sip of her own tea. "Still, there's plenty more fish in the sea, though not many that'll give you a whale of a time, I grant you."

Jenny shrugged. "It doesn't matter anyway. I'm off men for life. From now on it's just me, David and the cat."

"And what happens when David flies the nest and the cat uses up its last life in the washing machine?"

"Then it'll just be me, I guess. Me and my shadow! Me, myself and I!"

"That's a pretty dismal prospect, unless you happen to love your own company. Maybe Rover and I should move in with you."

"No!" Horrified at the thought, Jenny spluttered and choked on a mouthful of tea. "No need for that. I'll just get a new cat."

A little put out by this lack of filial enthusiasm, her mother emptied her own cup and carried it over to the sink. "Suit yourself. It was just a suggestion. No need to soil yourself."

"I'm sorry, Mum. It's good of you to offer. It's just that I wouldn't like to put you to so much trouble."

"A likely story! Look it's okay. It was a crap idea anyway. It's not as if you and Rover ever got on together."

A wicked glint entered Jenny's eye. "Of course, there's always the risk that we could learn to get on too well together, if you get my drift, and where would that leave you?"

"You wouldn't! You couldn't! Not after what Mounty did to you."

Reminded, the depression which had just begun to lift came down around Jenny's shoulders again like a dark and dismal shroud. "You're right. I could never do that to anyone I cared about. Cow! May her cellulite calcify and her boobs drop off!"

Desperate to avert the dirge before her daughter really got into her stride, the older woman hoisted a listen-to-this-for-a-bright-idea kind of smile on her face. "Look, how's about you and me hitting the West End for a bit of shopping therapy. It's Rover's birthday soon and I want to get him something really special. Your input would be gratefully received, honest."

Curling a derisive lip, Jenny hit on the irritating idea of clanging the spoon against the side of the cup, the milk jug and the sugar bowl in sequential unmusical succession. "My input?" Clang! Clang! "What do I know about dogs apart from the fact that they're dirty, smelly, four-legged transport for fleas and, without exception, crotch-sniffers *extraordinaire*?"

Completely unfazed by this unflattering description, her mother forcibly relieved her of the teaspoon and chucked it into the sink. "Well, that's enough to be going on with. So, you'll come?"

"Oh, okay. I suppose I do need to get some new outfits for the show, anyway. Might as well kill two birds with the one stone."

"Good, give me five minutes for a quick top-and-tail and we'll be off." As her mother disappeared upstairs to the bathroom, Jenny delved once more into the envelope containing the stark, surprisingly brief document that gave the seal of officialdom to the end of her marriage. The decree absolute, the final decree in divorce proceedings. Should she so desire, she was now free to remarry. So, of course, was Adam, the thoughts of which were enough to send her spiralling downwards again so that when her mother reappeared she found herself faced with a gibbering wreck who drooled out the side of her mouth and made unintelligible grunting noises.

"Enough!" Grabbing her by the shoulders she slapped her daughter's face and shook her soundly. "Put that damn envelope away before I set light to it. It's not as if you weren't expecting it, for Heaven's sake, so I don't see why you should go all hysterical like it's a bolt from the blue."

"I know," Jenny gulped. "It's just that it makes it all seem so final, kind of like a death."

"Which, I suppose it is, in a way but then again some things shouldn't be allowed to go on living." Picking up the jacket which Jenny had slung across the back of her chair, her mother thrust it into her arms. "Having said that, *you're* not dead, Jenny. You're very much alive. So do you think you could possibly get your butt in gear, like before the end of the year?"

With a very bad grace, Jenny struggled to her feet. "Okay! Okay! But I never remember you being so keen on getting *me* a birthday present. Old Rover must be doing something right."

Making like a cat, Gloria arched her hands into claws and made spitting noises. "*Miaow! Miaow! Hiss. Hiss.* And, as for old, let me remind you, he's younger than you. Now come on, Miss Catty, before my repressed psychopathic tendencies come hurtling to the fore."

"Not so repressed!" Jenny muttered, scuttling ahead nonetheless as her mother threw speculative looks at the cutlery drawer. "What do you want to get him anyway, a muzzle?"

"No, a book. *My Life as a Dog* by somebody or other.

It's been in the bestseller list at Waterstones for the last six weeks despite crap reviews in *The Times*."

"Yes, well dogs and crap do rather go together. Anyway, come on if we're going but, please, if you see me heading in the direction of any psycho-babble books on seduction or otherwise, kill me, okay? And drive a stake through my heart just to be sure you've done the job properly."

Pushing her through the door, the older woman leered wickedly. "Don't tempt me. Now put a spurt on, will you, before we miss our train."

* * *

"Admit it! It's a set-up." Horrified, Jenny took a step back from the giant poster in the bookshop window. "You old Judas goat. You led me straight to the slaughter. How could you!"

Unrepentant, her mother followed her gaze. "Well, someone had to stop you from throwing away the best opportunity you've had in years. I mean, come on, he *is* rather gorgeous. Manly! Unlike Adam who, if he hadn't fathered David, could well have a large question mark hanging over his head. I mean, I've often wondered if maybe he didn't bat for both sides. There's something effeminate about him, don't you think? A weakness about the chin! A peculiarity about his gait as if he'd a red-hot poker stuck up –"

"Mother!" Outraged, Jenny stopped her in her tracks. "That's enough! Adam may not be whiter than

419

the driven but I won't have you slandering him either. As you so rightly pointed out, he *is* David's father and that fact alone makes him worthy of respect."

"Ah, but is he? I mean David's nothing like him. I've often wondered, took consolation if the truth be told, in the thoughts that you might have had an affair and that David was the product of a passionate one-night stand. In fact my money's on the Hell's Angel from Wapping."

Dumbfounded, Jenny shook her head from side to side "Words fail me. Just when I think there's nothing you can say or do any more that will surprise me, just when I think it's safe to go back in the water, you open your mouth and there I am stuck to the floor. Just like when I was ten and you flashed your boobs at the head-mistress on parents' evening."

Her mother chuckled. "I'd forgotten about that. Besides, you were twelve, too old to be shocked."

"No, I was twelve when you went one better and mooned at her."

"Well, served her right, the old bag! Talk about the Harper Valley PTA! Now are we going in or what? Let's face it, it's not exactly as if you're averse to him and you *did* say you'd lost his telephone number."

"Yes, but –" Jenny stuttered, shooting out a panic-stricken arm and latching onto the nearest lamppost as her mother struggled to manoeuvre her into the shop. 'That was ages ago. I'm sure he's found somebody else by now. Just look at that poster, what does it say? Matt Fitzgerald, winner of this year's Booker Prize, that's

what it says. One free autograph with every copy of
Looking for Mrs Right! He's not going to be bothered with
me. I daresay he's lined up a pneumatic, pert-breasted
twenty-five-year-old by now. One with a permanent lisp
and a breathy voice that has nothing to do with asthma,
with another half-dozen panting in the wings!"

"Oh pooh! Not every man is Adam in disguise.
Besides, you're pretty famous yourself *and* you've won
a Golden Gob award."

"A Golden Globe award," Jenny corrected through
gritted teeth.

"Added to which he's expecting you."

"What!" Caught off guard, Jenny released her hold
on the lamppost, big mistake, as she found herself
immediately hustled through the automatic doors.

"Well, if you must know I saw him early this
morning when I popped in to get Rover's present and
of course he recognised me as being your mother. I
mean you *did* introduce us on a previous occasion, you
know, and let's face it, I *am* rather unforgettable."

"What do you mean?" Jenny panted desperately
trying to dig her heels into the floor. "Are you seriously
telling me the whole purpose of this outing was just to
inveigle me into getting back with Matt?"

"Yep. Just a ruse!" Oblivious to dirty looks and
caustic asides, Gloria gave her daughter an intensive
lesson in queue-jumping, as using her elbows to good
effect she dragged and pulled her to the top where,
with an agility remarkable in a woman of her age, she

quickly interposed herself between a fawning reader and the delectable Matt Fitzgerald who was busy signing the woman's book.

"Do you mind?" The woman's nose went up in the air.

"No." Jenny's mother's tone of voice was reasonable. "And, you'd better not if you know what's good for you. Now beat it before I lose my temper." Never before having encountered a psychotic, leopard-skin-clad OAP, the woman decided this was probably wise advice and with an indignant though muted sniff grabbed the book and stalked off.

"Jenny!" Pushing aside a pile of books, Matt Fitzgerald rose and came round the table, both hands held out in greeting. "How have you been? It's good to see you."

Shyly Jenny placed her hands in his as, with an apologetic nod to the waiting queue, he drew her behind a nearby pillar.

"Hi, Matt. It's good to see you too though I have to tell you I was kind of tricked into it." This last with a filthy look for her mother who was looking remarkably like the cat that got the cream.

"Oh." His face fell. "Do I take it that you'd rather not see me, then?"

Jenny blushed. "No. Of course not! It's just that well –" Freeing a hand, she indicated the scene all round them, the queues of people, the piles of books on the desk, the posters adorning every window and spare inch of the store. "I'm sure you've got better things on your mind."

He shook his head. "No. That's where you're wrong, Jenny. There's always room in my life for my friends and we are friends still aren't we, despite your blowing me out as a lover?"

"Her decree absolute came through this morning," her mother interrupted helpfully, receiving a sharp kick on the shins for her efforts.

"Shut up, Mother. I'm sure Matt has no interest in my private affairs."

"Oh but I have." The words were so soft, Jenny wasn't quite sure if she'd heard correctly but judging from the soft and searching look in his eye, no other interpretation was possible. "Look, if you can hang on for fifteen minutes or so I'm due a lunch break and I'd love to treat you both to lunch. What do you say?"

"I'd really love to Matt but I'm committed elsewhere." With a huge conspiratorial wink, Gloria made it plain that she was not in the running to spoil love's middle-aged dream by playing gooseberry. "But there's no reason whatsoever why Jenny can't join you. Anyway, got to see a dog about a dog. Catch you later, yeah?"

Half-turning away so that Matt couldn't see her face, Jenny narrowed her eyes and mouthed the word 'bitch' at her rapidly retreating parent.

"She's a miracle of balance really, isn't she?" With an admiring glance Matt Fitzgerald followed the older woman's progress as she teetered down the length of the store, her six-inch heels impediment to neither speed nor determination.

"A miracle of unbalance more like. I'm telling you there's saner people in Broadmoor. If I had my way I'd lock her up and throw the key into the middle of the North Sea. She's been nothing but a plague to me since the day I was born."

Matt grinned. "Look, I've got to get back to signing these things but there's a little Italian place in the precinct round the corner. Let's meet there, say, in twenty minutes?"

Suddenly panic-stricken, Jenny felt as though her heart might burst. Spend A Penne! He meant Spend A Penne, of course. Their restaurant, hers and Adam's, with the little corner table, red and white gingham table cloth and wax-covered Chianti bottle. It had to be. There *was* no other Italian restaurant in the precinct. Her first reaction was to blurt out no. No! She couldn't stand Italian. No! She was allergic to bolognese. No! Being within twenty paces of an Italian, apron-wearing waiter made her come over all unnecessary and brought her out in scurvy. But then the irony of it struck her, the irony of dining with another man in the very self-same restaurant where she and Adam had indulged in many a happy, marital meal, eyes meeting across the candle-flame, promising without need for words afters not listed on the menu. Yes, very ironic, especially considering the day that was in it. The day she had received her decree absolute.

"All right," her voice, after what seem like an age

yet in reality was probably no more than a few seconds, came out soft yet with a steely core of determination running through it. "I'll see you there, then." With a slight flutter of her fingers and much to the relief of the waiting queue who were beginning to look as though each and every one of them was capable of committing murder, she turned and marched off, determined all of a sudden to go lay some ghosts.

* * *

"*Senora! Bella senora!* "Ow 'appy I am to see you. Such an 'appy day. I donta know eef I am feeling like a laughing or crying or maybe even a seenging."

Jenny found herself stepping back a pace, stunned by the Italian waiter's even more than usually effusive welcome.

"Jesus, Gianni! Is this how you greet all your customers?"

Wiping his hands on his apron, he thrust the umbilical hernia that doubled as his stomach forwards, grinned genially and shook his head, all in one fluid moment. "No. Only de special ones. Only de ones who are een love. Ah, but my 'eart is soft and beeg. Beeg like a Roman amphitheatre."

"Oh? Got many of those in Deptford, have you?" Jenny smiled to take the sting out of her words. "Now if you could stop soliloquising for a moment, how about a table?" Then going for broke. "If possible my usual one in the corner?"

Gianni shrugged grandiloquently. "Eef possible, she say? Good a God, don't a she know, een love, everytheeng is possible. Come!" Grabbing her by the elbow he steered her through the restaurant, round a recessed alcove, and over to the little corner table where, shock, horror, Adam was already in residence.

"You!" Jenny's eyebrows hit the roof, passed through it, passed Concorde, passed out of the earth's atmosphere and went straight into orbit. "Just what the hell are you doing here? Waiting for some bimbo, I suppose. In *our* restaurant! At *our* table! And on the day our decree absolute came through, what's more." The fact that she herself was guilty of exactly the same crime didn't seem to occur to her as, with a voice like a whiplash, she flayed him with a succession of hysterical accusations that had him practically ducking for cover under the table."Bastard!" Picking up a folded napkin, she ran round the table and beat him round the head with it. "So what is it then?" *Whack!* "A case of the wife is dead?" *Whack! Whack!* "Long live the bimbo?" *Whack! Whack!* "You couldn't wait, could you? You just couldn't wait till my corpse was cold before you came in here to lay the ghost. Or should I say lay the bimbo." *Whack! A flurry of whacks!*

Taking her by surprise, Adam leapt suddenly to his feet grabbing her wrist in a vice-like grip. Wrestling the napkin from her, he threw it the length of the restaurant where, landing upon the head of an innocent diner, it had the not uncomical effect of turning him from Surrey stockbroker-belt respectability into Yasser Arafat. "Shut up! Just, shut up! We're divorced, remember? It's a free country. I can go where I like with whomever I want. And that includes here!"

"So, I was right." Dispiritedly, Jenny freed her wrist and sank down into a chair. "You *are* waiting for someone. Who is it? Is it Mounty?" Her voice shook a little.

"No."

"Who then? Someone from work, your secretary? Someone you met at a party? Godot?"

Adam looked a little embarrassed. "None of the above. Clearing his throat, he decided to come clean. "Actually, I wasn't waiting for anybody. The truth, stupid and all as it sounds, is I see this place as a kind of shrine. Some people swear we leave behind emotions in the very fabric of buildings and I suppose I wanted to see if there was any truth in that and if I could feel some of them again, yours and mine, the happier ones, the ones where we shared a single strand of spaghetti with the strand becoming shorter and shorter till . . ."

Our lips met in the middle and we ended up sharing bolognese kisses. Jenny finished the thought in her mind.

Bending his head, Adam hid his face from her. "Silly of me, I suppose, especially now that the decree absolute has come through. I mean I know it's over and I've got to move on in life, just like you've managed to do. Because you're the one who's *really* waiting for someone, aren't you? *You* came here to lay *my* ghost, didn't you?"

"Yes." Jenny lowered her own head, her hand going out to fiddle uneasily with the edge of the tablecloth. "Yes, you're right. I *did* come here to lay your ghost though poor old Gianni at least, seems to have gotten hold of the wrong end of the stick. And yes, I *am* waiting for someone. His name is Matt Fitzgerald and he's a writer. Maybe you've heard of him. He's just won the Booker prize with *Waiting for Mrs Right.*" Now what on earth had possessed her to tell him all that? It smacked of trying to put one over on him which, let's face it, was nothing, if not childish. And she didn't want to appear childish. No way! She wanted to play the cool sophisticate, the mature woman of the world, Mrs Robinson from *The Graduate* although, admittedly, the napkin business had let her down a bit.

"And *has* he found Mrs Right?"

"Don't be ridiculous, Adam. I hardly know him. Besides, I doubt if I'll ever marry again. I mean, what's the point. It's just giving someone *carte blanche* to hurt you."

"Like me, you mean."

"If the cap fits . . ."

"Yeah, you're right. I hurt you. I'm sorry I hurt you. God, if only you knew how sorry I am but . . . well, we've been all over that old ground before."

"Tell me again, anyway," Jenny encouraged. "I like hearing you grovel. You've no idea how good it makes me feel."

Resigned, Adam shrugged. "Revenge is sweet, is it? You're enjoying getting your own back, watching me clutch for comfort at old memories whilst you wait for your lover to come and feed you grissini."

Jenny bit her lip, her assumed cloak of sophistication suddenly crumbling, suddenly all burned out, dissolving like embers into ashes. "Revenge, like ice cream, is a dish best served cold. And yes, whilst there's nothing I'd rather do than be blasé, than pretend I'm on the up and up, the truth is I'm still stumbling from day to day, hoping that tomorrow I'll be over you, hoping that tomorrow Time, the great healer, will get his finger out and come a knocking on my door."

Adam's voice was dry. "Well, wait no longer. Here he comes now or could it be that Matt bloke you were banging on about?" Shrugging his shoulders, he attempted a smile. "You've got to feel sorry for poor old Gianni though. Just look at him, helpless as a babe in arms, desperately trying to figure out how to fit a *ménage à trois* round a table built for two." Pushing his chair back, he got to his feet. "Anyway, I'll go, shall I? Put him out of his misery and leave the field clear for you and Matt the Pratt."

Ignoring the slight on her lunch date, Jenny, a little hesitant, stretched out a detaining hand. "No. *We'll* go. You were here first."

"Indeed, I was. In every sense of the word!"

Shaking her off, and with the dreaded, hurt puppy-dog look in his eyes again, Adam headed for the door, roughly shouldering his way past Gianni and squaring up to the puzzled-looking man accompanying him. "Don't hurt her, mate," he warned as they drew abreast. "You hear me? Just don't hurt her or you'll have me to deal with."

Taking the seat which Gianni, with a bad grace, pulled out for him, Matt sent her an interrogatory glance. "Your husband, I take it?"

"Ex-husband." Jenny tried for hard but only managed to sound distraught. "What did he say to you, anyway?"

"He threatened me, warned me not to hurt you. The man obviously has feelings for you still."

Jenny sniffed. "Yes, well unfortunately, not only had he feelings for, but he was also *feeling* my best friend. Hence, the reason he's now my *ex*-husband."

"Yes, I know. You told me before. Several times, in fact."

Stricken, Jenny blushed. "I'm sorry. You must think I'm a right bore."

"People with broken hearts generally are. I know *I* was when my own marriage broke up."

"But you're over her now?" Jenny asked, knowing from something he'd told her before that his wife had run off with her gynaecologist – obviously a man who liked to take his work home!

"Yes. I'm over her now although I must admit I still have the most horrendous aversion to men who wear stethoscopes and work in hospitals." Waving away

Gianni who had made at least three tentative attempts to take their order, he leaned a little forward. "But here's the thing, *you're* not over Adam and judging by the look on your face as he left the restaurant, I don't think you ever will be. You still love him, Jenny. It's plain as day and if the threats he made to me are anything to go by, he still loves you." Resignedly, he scanned her face. "So why on earth am I sitting here when it ought to be Adam? Go after him, why don't you? Don't throw it all away for the sake of pride. Give him a second bite at the cherry because you can be sure of one thing, Mounty's apple has given him the most awful indigestion."

"Serves him right, the snake," Jenny snapped, but there was a marked lack of venom in the remark, an uncertainty in her voice and a longing in her eyes that practically begged him to convince her.

He took the hint. "Do the right thing. Swallow your pride and go after him. Forgive and maybe one day you'll even manage to forget." A little self-conscious, he picked up and dismantled the last remaining napkin, which some creative soul had fashioned into a pink linen rose. "You know, I've often thought love is a bit like a bus. If you don't catch the right one you could find yourself on a one-way ticket to nowhere." A sudden urgency entered his voice. "Catch that bus, Jenny. Go on, jump on board before it leaves without you and you find yourself standing at the terminus marked 'rest of your life' wondering what might have been if only you'd had the courage to follow your heart."

"Wow!" Jenny sat back in admiration. "I'm not surprised you're a writer. Mind you, if ever you decide to give it up, you could always apply for the position of Minister of Transport."

Abashed, Matt grinned. "Sorry. Was I waxing too lyrical?"

"A bit," Jenny admitted. "But there's a lot of sense in what you've just said. The problem is I've never *been* sensible. It's an alien concept to me like faithful men, the World Cup and caviare. I mean, if I were sensible, I'd never have married Adam in the first place although a lot of the blame for that must rest firmly on my mother's shoulders."

"What, she pushed you into it, do you mean?"

"Good Lord, no, quite the opposite! She loathed him. Detested him, in fact, did everything she possibly could to split us up including telling him I was a lesbian who hadn't yet come out of the closet."

Matt wrinkled his forehead. "I'm sorry. I don't follow. How could she have pushed you into it if, by all accounts, she was dead set against the match."

Jenny grinned. "Easy! I always do the exact opposite of what she wants me to do."

"Ah! Houston, we have lift-off!" Matt's brow cleared then furrowed again. "So I take it there's no way on earth she'd want you two to get back together."

"None!" Jenny confirmed.

"But, I thought you said you always do the opposite of what she wants or is this the exception that proves the rule?"

"No. No exceptions." Jenny said positively, a sudden light bulb coming on over her head and pulsating brightly. "Bloody hell, Matt. You're absolutely right! The woman must think she's got it made. Forty years I've spent resisting her and here I am playing right into her arms. Well, it's time to bawl the baby!" Pushing back her chair, she leapt to her feet, came round and dropped a kiss on his brow. "You know it's an awful shame I met Adam first, because I really think I could have fallen for you."

"My loss." Reaching up, Matt pulled her head down and kissed her soundly on the lips. "It's a shame I'm such a nice guy, otherwise Adam wouldn't have the ghost of a chance. Now, I'm sure I heard a bus drawing up outside. Better run if you don't want to miss it."

"Outta here!" Bright-eyed, Jenny grinned, truly happy for the first time in months. "And thanks, Matt. Thanks for . . . well . . . everything."

With a declamatory wave, Matt almost pushed her away. "Quick! Go, before I change my mind, drag you back to my cave and club you into submission."

"Another time, maybe," Jenny beamed, hurtling towards the exit and almost cannoning into poor Gianni who, grabbing her by the arm, brought her screeching to a halt.

"He say sometheeng to upset you, eh? *Bastardo!*"

Baring his teeth he made a snipping motion with his fingers. "I speet in his minestrone! I cut off his moules and make gnocchi, eh?"

Shrugging him off, Jenny backed towards the doorway. "No. He didn't upset me, Gianni. Far from it! It's all thanks to him that I'm going after Adam." Excited, her voice rose. "Do you hear me, Gianni. I'm going after Adam! We're going to be a family again. Me, David and Adam!"

A smile lit up Gianni's face. "Bueno. I give 'im beeg drink. On de 'ouse and next time you come to Spend a Penne I give you and Adam beeg drink also. *Una bottiglia di Chianti.* Is deal?"

Jenny winked. "You bet it's a deal but right now I've places to go, people to see, buses to catch. So, so long, Gianni. See you later, alligator!"

"Si," Gianni grinned, kissing his fingers to the air. "In a while, eh bambina?"

Chapter Thirty-nine

"Jenny! Jenny! Guess who that was on the phone?" Marcel, his face a mixture of incredulity and delight, bounded into make-up where Marigold was busy trowelling foundation onto Jenny's face with all the skill of a seasoned bricklayer.

"I don't know. Go on, surprise me!"

"Harpo Productions." And, as Jenny looked blank. "You know Oprah's production company. Harpo being Oprah spelt backwards. I would have thought you, of all people, would know that! Anyway, she wants you to appear on her show, the ultimate accolade. There's nothing left for you to wish for now except maybe the red-book treatment from Michael Aspel."

"You're joking!" Rocketing upward, Jenny collapsed again like an empty balloon as Marigold aka Poppy's Inner Child whacked her sharply across the head with the back of a hairbrush.

Marcel directed a quelling look at the make-up artist.

"How many times must I tell you not to damage the merchandise! Oprah's not going to want her with a face like a bag of spanners, is she?" Then, turning once more to Jenny. "No joke, Jen! Can't you just smell the bright lights, the eggs, sunny-side-up, the bagels, the hot-dogs, the crack-cocaine! The Walk Don't Walk signs! The Big Apple, hot dogs and Bing Crosby roasting on an open fire!"

Torn between panic and amazement, Jenny risked life and limb by daring to sit up again. "But you're sure it's legit and not just someone pulling your leg?"

"It's legit, all right. You, my girl are going Stateside, all expenses paid and as your manager I, of course, am going with you."

"And what about me?" Attila poked him with the sharpened end of a pair of nail scissors. "She needs *my* foundation. Only I know the secret of covering all those little, red worms squiggling all over her cheeks."

Jenny narrowed her eyes. "Thread veins, if you don't mind *and* there's only a few. Sun damage! But she's right, Marcel. Much and all as I hate to admit it, when it comes to make-up, she really does know her oats from her onions."

Never having heard of magnanimity in defeat, Marigold gloated. "Which means, of course, that Poppy must come too because without Poppy I cannot be happy and if *I* am not happy, I will make a big mess of somebody's face." Punctuating each word with a stab of the nail scissors she glowered at Marcel. "And I'm not talking powder blusher in cherry pink!"

Knowing when he was beaten, Marcel sighed. "And I suppose Martyna will want to come too especially as she's been making noises about giving up fish and moving to CNN."

"*And* Denzil," Jenny reminded him. "He *is* my personal trainer after all and there's no way I can appear on *Oprah* looking like a sack of spuds especially now that she's fast approaching svelte." Obediently, Jenny blotted her lips with the tissue Attila held out to her. "Although she does have a distinct advantage in that she has her own personal chef whilst *I* have to make do with my own cooking."

Marcel nodded. "True. True."

"*And,* naturally, I'll need Adam to come along for moral support *and* David because there's no way I'm leaving the country and leaving my son in the care of strangers."

Marcel frowned. "Surely he can stay with your mother and Rover?"

Jenny tried not to blink as the make-up woman turned her attentions to attacking her with a curved mascara-wand that doubled as a miniature cutlass.

"I *said* there's no way I'm leaving him with strangers and believe me, Marcel, there's none stranger than my mother and Rover." Starting as the mascara-wand missed her lashes and stabbed her eye, Jenny blinked furiously causing the make-up artist to swear blue murder as a trail of black ran down her freshly powdered cheek and dripped off her chin. "Nonetheless, he *is* very attached to them both, so I suppose they'd better come along too."

Marcel sighed. "Fair enough. I suppose the Yanks will expect someone of your calibre to have an entire retinue in any case. They'd probably be disappointed if you didn't. Pomp and circumstance! They swallow it hook, line and sinker, don't they? I mean look at the throngs of gum-chewing geriatrics hanging about outside Buckingham Palace every day hoping to catch a glimpse of the Queen's credentials."

"Assuming she wears any!" Jenny joked.

"Boom! Boom!"

"She'd better have a bodyguard too." With a final wield of the mascara-wand that almost had Jenny's eye out, the make-up artist demonstrated that she was not just a pretty face. "Everybody who is anybody has a bodyguard. Even hookers have a bodyguard. And now, you stupid cow, I'll have to do your foundation all over again."

Marcel shook his head. "No! Hookers don't have bodyguards. Hookers have pimps! But you're right, she *does* need a bodyguard if only for effect, but who?"

Jenny clicked her fingers. "I have it! Gianni can be my bodyguard."

"Gianni?"

"Waiter from Spend A Penne, real Italian job from Deptford with an umbilical hernia the size of the Colosseum and a nice line in Godfather-speak."

Marcel rubbed his hands together. "Right, he'll do nicely. Now, have we left anyone out?"

"Don't think so." Jenny racked her brains but could come up with only one more name. Mounty. Strange, how she still missed her even though, from time to time, she could still feel the pain of the knife-wound in her back. It was a bit like having a phantom limb, she supposed. You had it amputated for your own good, but somehow it still hung around if only in spirit, aching, reminding you of what you had once, of what you'd lost. As, with a heavy hand, Marigold turned her attention to repairing the mess on her face, Jenny realised she didn't hate Mounty any more. She only hated what she'd done and, let's face it, there was too much history between them, most of it good, for her to harbour resentment forever. Besides, who was it who said that the best revenge is to be happy? And she was happy Jenny realised suddenly. There were birds singing in her heart, thrushes warbling, robins chirruping and with that realisation came a peace of mind, and a knowledge that what was past was past and better forgotten for everyone's sake. Adam and David, on the other hand were the here, the now and the future. Adam, David and *Oprah* not to mention the loyal but motley group of friends and okay, her mother too, who had pushed and pulled her, bullied and coerced her all through the valley of darkness till, like a mole, she'd emerged, blinking, confused but safe on the other side.

"Marcel?" Her voice was soft. "Do you know how much I love you?" Quick to take advantage, he dropped to his knees.

"If you really love me, you'd kick me."

Jenny sighed. "Marigold. Would *you* do the honours?"

Moving back several feet so that she could get in a good run, the make-up artist pawed at the ground like a stallion.

THE END